Dangerous Ally

A Novel by

Michelle Grey

For my husband, Jim

The love of my life

And

believer in my dreams

Prologue

"You said he could handle the second dose."

Panic laced the man's words. He followed the instructions he was given and latched the handcuffs, staring at the figure lying across the bed. "I can't tell if he's even breathing."

"He's breathing. He'll be fine," the other man growled as he pushed him out of the room. "If you'd dosed him right the first time, he wouldn't have started to wake up before you got him here."

"What if he doesn't wake up at all? If we can't get the codes, this was all for nothing." He could hear the whine in his voice and wondered again how the hell he'd gotten into this mess.

The smaller man snarled. "There shouldn't have been any damn encryption. He must've suspected you. Why else would he have scrubbed the data?"

Cowering from the venom in his boss's voice, his words tumbled out. "I was cool, I swear. I don't know what spooked him." A bead of sweat trickled down his spine. "At least we got the laptop."

They locked the front door and stepped out into the cold chill of early morning. His boss's lips curled into a ghost of a smile, his eyes gleaming. "Exactly. Nothing else matters. He's playing my game now. And I'm holding all the cards."

Chapter 1

Lacey Jordan had figured today would be the day from hell. She flipped the sign in the front window and locked the door. Sometimes, it was good to be wrong.

Folding her long legs into her vintage Firebird, she shifted gears from the busyness of the day to the relaxing evening ahead. She switched on her headlights in the rapidly encroaching dusk, then after a quick stop to drop off the bank deposit, headed to the farm.

Friday night dinners with her dad had become a favorite tradition, but she had a feeling tonight would be extra special. Her hunch told her he was finally going to ask Mona Nicholson to marry him and, as far as she was concerned, it was about time. Mona's fun personality was a perfect foil for her dad's more serious side.

Lacey smiled as she rolled in and parked behind the house next to her dad's Buick. Her first foray into match-making and she was batting a thousand. Grabbing the bottle of wine from the front seat, she climbed out of her car. The bright orange and yellow mums she'd brought from the shop adorned the walking paths between the house, the barn, and her dad's office.

She twisted the handle on the back door and stepped inside the comfortable old farmhouse. In all her years growing up here, no one except strangers and salespeople ever used the front door. Lacey strolled into the shadowed kitchen, her tennis shoes squeaking with each step. Squinting, she noticed the table had been set for three instead of four, a sure sign that Spencer was still being a jerk about letting his mom get on with her life. Which meant no announcement.

She set the wine on the counter and sighed. That was a battle for her dad and Mona to fight.

"Dad? Where are you?" Silence greeted her, broken only by the steady tick-tock of the grandfather clock.

She moved through the kitchen and living room, turning on lights as she went. Her pace slowed as she approached the stairs that led to the bedrooms.

"Hello? Dad?" More silence drifted back down the stairs, raising goose flesh on her arms. He'd sounded fine when he called this morning, but since his last doctor's appointment had revealed an uptick in his blood pressure and cholesterol, she had to admit that his health crossed her mind more frequently than it used to.

Fighting her trepidation, Lacey mounted the steps. After scanning the empty rooms, she released the breath she'd been holding. Her dad was her rock, the one constant in her life since cancer had stolen her mom away when she was eight. Just thinking about something happening to him caused a pit in her stomach.

Sounds from below interrupted her thoughts. Smiling, she bounded down the stairs and rounded the corner into the kitchen. "Dad, you had me worried. I didn't know where you went." She stopped short as Mona turned from the fridge, a head of lettuce in hand.

"Hey, honey. I'm surprised you beat me here. Was the shop crazy today without Paige? I thought about coming down to help out but I figured you'd rather I stay home and work on the Christmas quilts."

Lacey shrugged, smiling. "A little bit, but not bad. Paige'll be back from her honeymoon before the holiday season gets moving. And you know we'll sell out of those quilts as fast as you can make them." She grabbed her jacket. "I'll be back in a minute to help with dinner. Dad must be out in the office."

Mona winked then reached for the colander. "He's probably lost track of the time. Call me if you need reinforcements. If he's knee-deep in a file, it'll take both of us to pry him out of there."

With the sun long gone, a brisk chill rode on the autumn breeze. Lacey jogged down the path, her way illuminated by the stark yellow yard light.

She opened the door to the metal outbuilding that served as her father's private research retreat, the fluorescent light spilling out into the yard. A quick glance at the two computer workstations yielded no information, and no dad, so she strode past them to the supply room.

Certain she was about to solve her mystery, Lacey turned the handle. "You're going to be in the doghouse if –" The words died on her lips as she yanked open the door and was greeted by darkness. She switched on the lights, but a quick walk-through revealed that this room, too, was empty.

Retracing her steps to the house, she closed the back door against the cool night air. *Where on earth could he have gone?*

"Mona, did Dad mention any errands he had to run?"

Wiping her hands, Mona looked up. "He's not in his office?"

"No. He's not here anywhere."

"That's odd. His car's here." Mona paused. "Do you think one of the neighbors came by and needed some help?"

"I guess it's possible. I'll make a couple of calls." Tugging a hair tie from her wrist, Lacey pulled her tawny hair off her face into a short pony tail before sitting down at the table. She dialed the neighbors on either side of their property but neither one had seen her father. Lacey gnawed on her lip, her brow furrowed.

"Did you try his cell?"

Lacey blinked. What the hell was wrong with her? She hadn't even thought about calling his cell. Shaking her head, she laughed. "I'm still not used to him carrying it. I tried for years to bring him into the twenty-first century, but all it took from you was a look."

Grinning, Mona shrugged her petite shoulders. "What can I say? It was a very stern look."

Lacey punched in the number and waited through two rings before a ringtone pierced the silence. They turned in unison toward the corner hutch. Dashing to the cabinet, Lacey dropped to her knees, her fingers reaching toward the sound.

The anxiety Lacey had tried to ignore came roaring to life. She looked at Mona, her fear reflected in Mona's eyes. This wasn't right. Not right at all.

Lacey hopped to her feet and tossed the phone to Mona. "I'm going outside. I need to see if maybe the four-wheeler's out of the barn. He's got to be somewhere around here."

"Good idea. I'll call the school. Maybe someone there has spoken to him," Mona said, digging her own phone out of her purse.

Lacey spent an hour combing the property, industrial strength flashlight in hand, before she called it quits. Bone cold and shivering, she prayed Mona had news. But a quick glance at the older woman's face told Lacey that she wasn't the only one who'd struck out.

"No luck on the calls?"

Mona shook her head. "I couldn't get anyone at the school. I was hoping someone would be working late, but no one answered his office line or the phone in the lab."

Lacey checked her watch. Not quite nine. She took a deep breath then blew it out slowly, rubbing her frozen hands together. "Okay. We need to slow down a minute. He's not here, but there are a million places he could be." She couldn't think of a single one, but that was beside the point. "Let's not let our imaginations run away with us. We should go ahead and eat. He'll probably be here before we're even finished."

Looking relieved to have a task, Mona nodded. "I'll toss the salad if that works for you. I'm not up for a steak and it's too dark to grill anyway."

Lacey's appetite was gone, but she pasted a smile on her face. "Sounds good."

Mona brought the large bowl of salad to the table. "So," she said a little too brightly, "everything went smoothly today at the shop?"

The question didn't fool either of them, but Lacey played along. Filling their plates, she nodded. "Very well, actually. Sam's a huge help."

Mona smiled. "I think she's the sweetest young lady. Seems to have a lot of potential."

Lacey agreed. In the few months since they'd hired her on as their first employee, she'd developed a real knack with the floral arrangements and she was a natural with the customers. After two years of pinching pennies and running the shop on their own, Lacey and her best friend turned business partner, Paige, agreed that Sam was just about perfect.

As Lacey shared the details of her day, she looked at her watch. Again. Time dragged. By ten, the dishes had been dried and put away, the entire pot of coffee finished off, and still her dad hadn't come home.

Mona ran a hand through her short spiky hair, her normally bright eyes smudged with worry. "Is it okay to say I'm more than a little concerned?"

Lacey rose and gave Mona's shoulders a quick, reassuring squeeze. "Yes. And I'll even give you first dibs on dressing him down when he gets here."

Minutes ticked by as Lacey paced the kitchen. She replayed the conversation she'd had with her dad that morning. Had she missed something?

Mona stepped in front of her, her words chilling Lacey's blood. "Should we call nine-one-one?"

Their worried gazes locked. Nine-one-one meant emergency. And Lacey didn't want this to be an emergency. She turned and started digging through the stack of industry magazines on the hutch until she located an old phone book in the back. "I'll just call the station. Somebody there should be able to help."

"Riley County Police."

The monotone voice jolted Lacey. *Do not freak out.* With a deep breath, she explained her situation first to the operator and then again to the officer on duty.

Leaning against the wall, she answered several questions then, with shaking fingers, punched the end key on her phone before turning to face Mona. "He said twenty-four hours was pretty standard before they start getting concerned."

"Twenty-four hours is an awfully long time."

My thoughts exactly. Lacey stretched to loosen the knots in her shoulders. "I know. I'll call them first thing in the morning. If I need to." She blew out a deep breath and said a quick, silent prayer that she wouldn't. "You might as well head home. I'm going to stick around here tonight. I'll call you with any news."

7

Mona looked poised to object, but didn't. She heaved a sigh of her own. "I probably should. Spencer may call the house and wonder why I'm not there."

Lacey refrained from commenting. Spencer's issues were the least of her concerns right now.

Mona pulled her jacket around her shoulders. "Will you be okay out here by yourself?"

"I'll be fine." Lacey pushed the door closed, the night air causing her to shiver. As she twisted the lock and heard it click into place, a thought came unbidden to her mind.

Maybe this was the day from hell after all.

Chapter 2

Caleb Mansfield pulled up his collar as the jagged north wind whipped straight through his insulated trench coat. He dodged the first icy raindrops, dashing for the heavy doors of Twenty Michigan Avenue, national headquarters of BioTech Corporation.

He glanced around the atrium. Not much had changed since he left ten months ago. And now he was back for good, just in time for winter in Chicago. Timing could've been better, but it was good to be back.

BioTech Corporation occupied the bottom two floors of the eight-story building. The first floor was dedicated to office space while the second floor housed the labs and research library. Caleb made his way past the public elevators on his left to a reception area where two women sat behind a waist-high circular counter.

Gretchen, the one he recognized, was on the phone. He guessed her age as mid-thirties, a couple of years older than himself, but she'd manned the front desk, keeping them all organized, for as long as he could remember. She was as predictable as clockwork and Caleb believed the company would fall apart without her.

He didn't recognize the other woman, but the nameplate on the white granite countertop identified her as Susie Blakely.

"May I help you?" The words were innocent enough, but the woman's blatant perusal made her question feel like a pickup line.

Caleb ignored the suggestion. He shrugged out of his overcoat and was about to introduce himself when Gretchen finished her phone call. "Good morning, Mr. Mansfield," she smiled. "Welcome back. Mr. Cantwell sent an email that you'd be in today."

Susie looked from Gretchen to Caleb, her eyes widening. She stood up and leaned toward Caleb, extending her manicured hand and displaying a healthy dose of cleavage in the process. "Let me start over," she purred. Caleb accepted her hand then she covered his hand with her free one. "Mr. Mansfield, it's a pleasure to meet you. If Gretchen had bothered to give me your description, I can assure you I wouldn't have forgotten it."

Caleb extricated his hand from her grip. "Don't worry about it," he said with a distracted smile. "I've been gone so long half the people here have probably forgotten what I look like by now." He turned to Gretchen. "Did Roger happen to give you the meeting agenda for today?"

Susie scrambled around Gretchen. "Oh, let me get that for you." She looked at Gretchen for help. "Which file is it?"

Caleb caught Gretchen's look of irritation as she reached for a manila folder and handed it to Caleb. "The meeting agenda and pertinent notes on everything other than the European expansion are in here. Oh, and I placed a FedEx envelope on your desk that arrived a couple of days ago. I was going to forward it to you in Paris, but Mr. Cantwell said you were on your way back."

Caleb nodded his thanks then opened the folder, his mind already on the meeting to come.

"What on earth was that all about?" Gretchen frowned at Susie. "I don't think you'd have moved that fast if a bear was chasing you."

Susie sat down and grabbed her purse from beneath the counter. Gretchen tapped her fingers as she watched the other woman rummage through her bag until she found her lipstick. After Susie applied it and snapped the compact closed, she turned to Gretchen.

"Forget what he looks like? Seriously? Like that's even possible. I mean did you see those baby blues? And he sure looks like a guy who knows his way around a gym. Damn." Susie fanned herself with her hand.

Gretchen read the calculating glint in Susie's eyes. "Looking is all you'll do if you intend to remain employed here," she warned, perching her glasses on her nose. "Mr. Mansfield doesn't mix business with pleasure." She watched Susie's face fall and almost laughed. "You'll get over it."

10

Susie threw her purse back under the counter and tossed her platinum curls over her shoulder. "Maybe I'll be the one to make him change his mind."

***

Caleb looked around his office, his eyes landing on the potted plant sitting on the corner of his broad oak desk. He picked up the card propped against it.

Thanks for the hard work. Glad you're back. Maybe it's time for you to put down some roots of your own. Roger.

He ignored the edge of restlessness that whispered through him and pulled the computer out of his bag. Roots had never been part of the plan. His effort this time meant the final contracts were in place with all three distribution channels in Europe. He'd now completed everything Roger Cantwell, BioTech's CEO, had brought him in to do.

Roger had encouraged him to come in on Monday, giving him time to recover from jet lag, but Caleb wanted to get them all up to speed as soon as possible. He noticed the FedEx envelope Gretchen had mentioned, intrigued to see that it had come from Bill Jordan. He smiled. It had been months since he'd talked to his former mentor.

He had just enough time to read the name before Meg Richards, BioTech's Chief Operating Officer, blew into the room. Caleb wondered what had taken her so long.

Meg marched to his desk, her ever-present stiletto heels clicking across the hardwood floor. Sharp brown eyes connected with Caleb's, her color high beneath her mahogany skin.

"Thank God you're back. I know you've probably read the meeting agenda, but I'm going to give you a little heads up on an item that's not on it. You need to help me rein Ian in, Caleb. He's determined to divert a portion of R&D funding to research for human applications." She waved her hand in the air. "Roger's been tabling the issue, but I know Ian's going to hit it hard today. I just wanted you to be prepared."

Caleb was pretty sure she hadn't taken a breath during her diatribe. "Good to see you too, Meg," he said wryly.

11

"I think Roger's just tired of fighting him," she continued. "Sometimes I think the only reason Ian's still here is because he's Roger's old college buddy and he feels sorry for him." She paced in front of his desk. "We need to present a united front today and let Ian know the direction of the company in no uncertain terms."

Caleb nodded. Roger had kept him up to speed on Ian's increasingly erratic behavior. "I'm aware of some of what he's been talking about. Today's meeting should help Ian refocus." *Or motivate Roger to start looking for Ian's replacement.*

"Okay. See you at nine." She got to the door before she turned around. "Oh, and Caleb." He looked up and caught her grin. "Welcome back."

"It's good to be back. I think."

***

Caleb leafed through his documents, ready to get the meeting underway. He was already seated with Meg and Roger at the long oak conference table when Ian Cox rushed into the room. Caleb had always respected Ian's work as a scientist but that was about as far as it went. His passive aggressive behavior toward Roger, Meg, and himself to a lesser degree, had taught Caleb to keep his distance.

But Caleb was taken aback by Ian's haggard appearance. He looked thinner than Caleb had ever seen him, almost gaunt. His sunken eyes, bloodshot and red-rimmed, said he hadn't slept in days.

Ian's lips thinned into an almost non-existent line as he turned his focus first to Meg, then to Caleb. He hurried to the empty chair across from Caleb, his files clutched to his lab coat.

Roger stood when Ian took his seat. Even though Roger wasn't much taller than Meg, his presence filled the room. "Anyone care for a cup of coffee before we get started?" he asked as he walked over to the credenza. "Ian?"

The wrinkles on Ian's forehead deepened in a frown. "I'm fine."

Roger returned to the table with his cup, but remained standing. His usual quick smile wasn't in evidence as he watched Ian for another

12

moment. He shook his head and folded his stocky arms over the high back of the leather chair.

"We have a lot to celebrate today. And a lot of work to do. As you all know, Caleb has laid the ground work to put us in a position to be a major player in the European animal nutrition and bioscience market." Pride tinged his voice. "We have two major concerns about moving forward that we'll need to address immediately. First, Ian," Roger leaned forward, his eyes penetrating, "there are a few product modifications that need to be implemented on a broad scale to accommodate European regulations. I'll let Caleb get into the specifics in a minute.

"Secondly, Meg," his gaze shifted to the other side of the table, "based on the data Caleb has, we're going to need at least four operating centers and personnel to handle the logistics and supply chain. While that's no small undertaking, I'm confident we can be on the ground and operational within six months."

Caleb and Meg nodded. Ian sat back in his chair and folded his arms. "That's way too aggressive," he said. "We have several high-level projects on our plate in research as it is. Plus, we also have the issues of re-branding and marketing the modified products."

The marketing fell under Meg's umbrella of responsibilities and she immediately spoke up. "We can handle the re-branding and we'll introduce a marketing campaign in alignment with our new distributorship as soon as the product modifications allow. So, really Ian, your department is the only thing that can slow down our launch."

Caleb watched Ian bristle at Meg's obvious challenge. Before things could escalate, he stood. "It's going to be impossible to build a timeline until Ian's team is aware of what the modifications are, so let me get to that." Caleb handed out prepared packets to each of them. Roger sat down and grabbed his coffee, his relief obvious.

Twenty minutes later, Caleb concluded. "So, while there's quite a laundry list of things to finish to make the products compliant, I don't think any of it is insurmountable in the time line that Roger's laid out."

Caleb absorbed the animosity radiating from Ian.

"That's because you have no idea what's been going on here, what we're already working on," he rasped, his face turning red all the way to his receding hairline. "I love the way you people want to bend R&D to your every beck and call. I've built a brilliant team of scientists with vision." His voice began to shake. "Look at Brandon Thomas. He's brilliant and we're wasting him! BioTech is capable of so much more than animal feed and supplements. If we weren't so pigeon-holed, we'd already be branching out to other products and other applications for current products." He looked at Roger. "When will you see the potential –" his voice cracked.

"Enough, Ian," Caleb warned.

Roger sat up straighter in his chair, his voice tired but firm. "Ian, this is not a new conversation. The direction of this company isn't going to change as long as I'm in charge. Your options are the same as they've always been. You can stay with me and with this company, which is the option I'd naturally prefer. Or you can pursue your other areas of interest outside this organization."

Ian's bluster faded, but Caleb still sensed his anger.

"Fine. We'll do it your way," Ian grumbled as he stuffed papers into his folder. "Just like always. If you'll excuse me, I have work to do."

Caleb thought the tourists across the street might've heard the door slam behind Ian.

"Meg," Roger rubbed his forehead and sighed as he sat back in his chair. "Can you get a list to me by end of day with possible warehousing locations? We'll start on a personnel search next week."

"Of course." Meg's red-tipped fingers flew across her page as she made notes. "There are a couple domestic issues I'd like to go over with you as well."

"We'll do that later this afternoon," Roger agreed. "I need a few minutes with Caleb now, if you don't mind."

"No problem."

Caleb's eyes pegged Roger as Meg shut the door behind her. The silence stretched between them. "You want to tell me what the hell that was all about? When we talked, you mentioned Ian was struggling, but Roger, the guy's on the edge."

Caleb had never seen Roger look quite so tired, but at least he didn't pretend to misunderstand. Roger tossed his glasses on the table and rubbed the back of his neck. "I know," he muttered. "He seems to be less and less in control. Ten years ago…hell, two years ago, he would've never talked or acted the way he did just now. He's a great researcher and we've been friends for so long that I just can't bring myself to –" He paused.

"Create an exit strategy for him?" Caleb interjected.

Roger winced. "I guess that's the nice way to put it." He sent Caleb a crooked smile. "Back in our college days, we had such grand plans - Ian, Bill and I. We were going to make our mark on the world. Bill's enjoying his teaching and his research, and now I think he's truly happy with Mona in his life. For my part, the business has grown well, especially in the last several years. And Rosalee and the family are my whole world. But for Ian, I just don't think his life has turned out quite the way he'd hoped."

Caleb bit back words that were better left unsaid. His thoughts strayed to his own father and a familiar bitterness settled on his shoulders. He had little patience for those who chose to be victims of their circumstances.

His mind flicked to the package he'd received from Bill. He hoped to have a few minutes to get to it this afternoon. Realizing his mind was drifting, he got up and poured a cup of coffee. He had too much to do today to lose focus. Turning, he caught Roger watching him with narrowed eyes.

"You look damn tired."

Caleb cocked his brow, and forced a thin smile. "Yeah, I am tired. I'll probably be on Paris time for another couple days but I'll be good after that."

Roger continued to watch him. Caleb knew he looked like hell and he braced himself for Roger's next words.

"I want you to take some time off, at least a few days."

It wasn't the first time Roger had brought up this particular subject. Caleb rolled his eyes, his voice bordering on sarcasm. "I'm tired, Roger. Not incapacitated."

"Bullshit. Your work ethic even makes me feel guilty, Caleb. As much as I love this company, there's more to life than this place."

Caleb gathered up his papers. After Roger's heart attack a few years back, he'd cut down his hours at the office and was rarely there past five. While Caleb knew he was still intent on building the business, their conversations were increasingly about personal things – his wife, dates with his grandkids.

"It wasn't a request," Roger stated, his voice taking on an edge as he stood. "You're close to burning out and I can't let that happen. Especially now. Six years is too long to go without a break." He sighed. "If I wasn't so selfish, I would've forced the issue a long time ago."

"I had my own motivations for –"

"I know, but I still should've insisted." Roger walked to the window and watched the sleet harass the pedestrians below before turning back to Caleb. "If I could afford to let you be gone for a few weeks, I would. But come hell or high water, you're out of here for no less than a week. Understand?"

Caleb felt his temperature rising as he confronted Roger. "That's ridiculous. Timing isn't good right now for me to be gone. We've got the logistics of the expansion to deal with –"

"Meg is perfectly capable," Roger interrupted.

"Not to mention the issues with Ian –"

"I'll handle him. Brandon can take the lead. Ian's right about him, you know. He's got a lot of vision for the future. I'm actually surprised we haven't lost him to a competitor."

Caleb frowned. "He'd be crazy to leave. We're the best in the business."

Roger smiled. "Agreed, but he's not really the type to play second fiddle."

"Maybe he shouldn't be second fiddle." Caleb waited to see if Roger would bite.

16

The older man sighed. "We can discuss it when you get back." Caleb didn't respond. "Relax, Caleb. We're talking about a few days of deserved downtime. Use it to recharge and think about our next conquest."

Caleb rolled his shoulders and stared out the window, the leaden clouds mirroring his mood. A full minute passed in silence. "I'd need time to make sure Meg's up to speed on the details," he hedged.

"Of course," Roger concurred, a smile tugging at the corners of his mouth. "I'll clear her calendar for the rest of the afternoon and you can download your brain to her."

Caleb tried to lighten up, but God, he hated being forced into anything.

Roger clapped him on the back. "Looks pretty cold out there. How about someplace warm? Or maybe a trip home to see your family?"

Caleb thought about his younger brothers and sisters. Rachel, who kept the world on its axis, already had a Christmas thing planned that should fall right around the birth of his youngest sister Sarah's first baby. He was looking forward to it and was anxious to check in with the boys too, but as restless as he felt right now, he knew he wouldn't be very good company.

"I'll figure it out later." Caleb turned on his heel and headed out of the conference room. "I'm going to find Meg."

**

Exhaustion threatened to overwhelm Caleb. He gathered his laptop, shoved Bill's FedEx envelope in his bag, and somehow made it from the office to his apartment building. By rote, he exited the elevator at the right floor, found his door, and slid his key in the lock. He tossed his bag on the bar and headed straight for the shower.

The water's near-scalding temperature revived him enough to get through what was left of the evening. As he scoured the kitchen cabinets, he was thankful for the building's shopping service, but couldn't find anything that didn't require preparation. He just wasn't up to cooking a meal. Settling on a handful of dry cereal and a beer, he plopped down on the leather sofa and clicked on the massive flat screen TV mounted on the far wall.

Half-listening to the sports recap, he thought about the mandate Roger had given him and tried to be objective. Was he burning out? He was restless, but he'd always pictured burnout as something bigger and darker.

Caleb booted up his laptop and stared at the Google homepage, trying to think of a destination for his forced vacation. When he realized he hadn't made a single keystroke in several minutes, he shoved the computer aside. Tomorrow was soon enough to make plans.

Glancing at his bag, he noticed the corner of the envelope he'd intended to open several times already today. Curiosity overcame lethargy, and he reached for it.

Funny that Roger had just talked about Bill earlier in the day. Bill's relationship with Roger had opened the door years ago for Caleb at BioTech, but Caleb's affection for him ran much deeper than that. Bill was the only real father figure he'd ever had.

He ripped open the envelope to find a thumb drive and a single sheet of paper with four six-digit codes and a note scribbled at the bottom.

For your eyes only, Caleb. We always believed it was possible. Call me after review. Bill

Anticipation began to buzz through his veins. He plugged in the drive and, at the prompt, entered in the numbers on the paper. To his utter shock, the cumulative total of all Bill's research on BR-714 scrolled on Caleb's screen, including the clinical trial data.

Caleb lurched forward on the sofa, his exhaustion disappearing as he studied the information. *Holy shit. He was right. He'd done it!* The project they'd worked on together in its infancy had finally come to fruition.

He picked up his phone to call Bill and noticed the time. Damn. Almost eleven. He hesitated then slowly returned the phone to the table.

Caleb tucked the drive back into the envelope, his thoughts racing. How long would it take to get to market? And would Bill continue to teach? He certainly wouldn't have to. When this was all said and done, his former mentor was going to be a very wealthy man.

Chapter 3

Caleb groaned as he rolled toward the windows. He forced his eyes open, squinting at the thin line of sunlight edging the blinds. Yawning, he glanced at the clock on the side table. His eyes widened. Noon? Shit! Jet lag had killed him.

Adrenaline kicked in as Caleb remembered the file Bill had sent. He couldn't wait to get him on the phone. Caleb threw off the covers and, within minutes, was drumming his fingers on the kitchen countertop, waiting for the call to connect. When did Gretchen say the envelope had arrived? *He's probably wondering what the hell took me so long.*

***

Lacey jumped as her dad's phone vibrated in her pocket. She hopped out of the back of the delivery van and yanked out the unit, stopping short when she saw the caller ID.

CALEB MANSFIELD

A quick ripple of faded heartache tumbled through her. Just seeing his name brought back memories of that long-ago summer. The summer he'd interned with her dad. The summer she'd given her heart to him, and he'd walked away. *Did she really need this right now?*

Ditching her initial reaction to ignore the call and let it go to voicemail, she hit the talk button. "Bill Jordan's phone."

A brief hesitation. "Lacey?"

"Yes."

"It's Caleb."

19

In the silence, Lacey wondered if he'd ask if she remembered him. Thank God he didn't. "I know. Caller ID."

He laughed, a strained sound. "So, how've you been?"

"Fine. Good." The utter absurdity of her answer almost choked her.

Caleb cleared his throat in the thick silence. "I won't keep you. I was really hoping to catch your dad for a couple of minutes. I haven't had a chance to talk to him in months. When would be a good time to call him back?"

Her vision blurred as she fought to speak around the tightness in her throat. "I don't know," she whispered. "I don't know where he is." Looking around the bustling parking lot, she willed the tears away then forced the words past her lips. "He's missing, Caleb."

His voice turned hard in an instant. "Define missing."

Before she could answer, he launched into a stream of rapid-fire questions, many of them similar to the ones she'd addressed with the police earlier in the day.

"Detective Abrams said they would 'attempt to locate'. Whatever that means. Several of Dad's neighbors are helping me post flyers around town and Mona is up on campus spreading the word. The police said there's nothing else we can do at this point."

Lacey bit her lip as her voice wavered. "I feel so useless. I combed every inch of the farm this morning and called everyone I can think of. The police told me not to overreact, but something is wrong. He just wouldn't disappear like this."

"I agree. I'll make some calls too. You obviously have my number. Call me if you hear anything."

Yeah, right. Hitting the end button, she cringed with regret. Why did she even share her situation? She'd just broken her personal vow to never speak to him again.

She shook her head, embarrassed by her petty thoughts. *Ancient history, Lacey.* She had to find her dad. Nothing else mattered, especially not Caleb Mansfield. Maybe he could help spread the word. The bio-feed industry was small. Everyone knew everyone.

***

Lacey forced her protesting body out of the van, her lack of sleep catching up with her. After running the deliveries and posting signs, she was drained. Big time. As she opened the back door, the raised voice of an irate customer reached her ears.

Dear Lord, this too? Glancing in the mirror, she ignored the puffiness under her bloodshot eyes and pasted a smile to her face. "I love this business," she muttered.

She repeated the mantra as she approached the sales floor, but it only took about three seconds for Lacey to realize the rail-thin man wasn't a customer. He had Sam backed against the wall, hemmed in by displays on either side, his right hand squeezing her upper arm.

He gave the young girl a hard shake then thrust his face within inches of hers. His voice had dropped to a menacing whisper. "You're going to do what I say, understand?"

Who was this jerk?

She rushed forward. "What's going on here?" she demanded.

The man whipped around, his hot anger quickly masked. His tongue shoved a dangling toothpick to the side of his mouth as he gave Lacey a once-over before offering a slow grin. He held up his hands. "There's no problem here. My girl and I were just havin' us a little discussion. Right, Sam?" He turned slightly and Lacey got a good look at Sam's pale face and wide eyes, along with the deep red imprints on her arm.

Lacey seared the man with her gaze. "You need to leave my shop. Now."

Recognizing the man's latent anger, Lacey briefly wondered if she'd remember any of her self-defense moves if it became necessary. He wasn't much taller than her five-foot-eight frame and even though she was thin, she probably had a good ten pounds on him. Her stomach knotted, but her eyes never wavered.

He smirked. "Sure thing, ma'am." Touching the brim of his dirty John Deere ball cap, he sidled by her before shooting a hard look at Sam. "We'll be talkin' later, darlin'. Count on it."

21

Moments later, he was gone. Sam slid down the wall, visibly shaking. "Oh, my God, Lacey, I'm so sorry. I'm so sorry," she sobbed, her face buried in her hands.

Lacey crouched down and pulled the girl into her arms, thinking that Sam looked closer to fourteen than nineteen. "Are you okay?"

"I didn't think he knew I was working here."

"Who is he?"

Tears slipped down her cheeks. "His name is Gary. Gary Finley. He's my ex-boyfriend. We broke up a couple of months ago."

Lacey plucked a tissue from her apron and handed it to Sam.

"Please don't fire me. I like it here and I really need this job."

Sitting back on her heels, Lacey waited for Sam to look at her again. "Firing you is the farthest thing from my mind." She waited another second then plowed on, hoping for a level of trust she wasn't sure existed yet in their young relationship. "I get the impression this has happened before. You want to tell me the story with this guy?"

Lacey stood and pulled Sam to her feet, both of them a little shaky, still riding the adrenaline wave.

Sam blanched, folding her arms. "Not much of a story. He hit me a couple of times and I knew I needed to get out."

Lacey heard a thread of defiance behind the fear. *Thank God.*

"I can't believe this happened. I'm so sorry, Lacey. You've got enough to worry about today without me adding anything else to it. Have you heard from your dad yet?"

Lacey sighed. "Not yet." She straightened her shoulders. "We've covered the town in flyers and filed a missing persons report. That's about all we can do right now." Lacey caught Sam's gaze. "Speaking of police filings, this Gary guy's not somebody to mess around with. Sounds like he should be in jail. Have you filed a restraining order against him?"

Sam shrugged. "I've been hoping he'll find somebody else and forget about me."

22

Lacey grabbed a couple of bottles of water out of the fridge. She tossed one to Sam. "Why don't you go hang out in the cooler for a little bit? Take some time to relax and work on a few of Monday's arrangements. I'll take over out front."

Dropping onto a stool at the sales counter, Lacey rested her chin in her hand, thinking about what Sam had shared with her. How had she gotten mixed up with someone like Gary? He wasn't just persistent, he was frightening.

Lacey's phone rang, jarring her from her thoughts. "Mona. Please tell me you found out something on campus."

Mona's voice sounded strained. "I talked to several people but no one's seen Bill since Friday morning." She hesitated. "But there's something else I need to tell you."

A slick panic twisted through Lacey. She hated those words. "What?"

"I think Spencer is missing, too."

Chapter 4

Lacey threw her car into park, a sense of déjà vu stealing over her. As dusk gathered at the farm, long shadows formed causing Lacey to quicken her steps to the house. A full twenty-four hours had passed.

Her dad was now officially considered a missing person.

She scanned the quiet empty rooms, praying and hoping. When she couldn't stand thinking for another single minute about where he might be, she switched gears, allowing her thoughts to travel to Mona's concerns about Spencer.

Lacey didn't voice it, but her gut reaction was altogether different. With no job and no plan for college, it wasn't a secret that Spencer was heading down a destructive path. And he had real issues with her father.

She wandered upstairs, unable to resist searching the bedrooms again. Just how big were Spencer's issues with her dad? Surely not enough to cause him to do something crazy. Guilt crawled down her spine. What if she'd arrived sooner yesterday? Would her dad have still been here? A fresh surge of anger overrode her guilt as she jogged back down to the kitchen. She racked her brain. *There had to be something else she could do.*

Intending to make a list of action items, she threw a pencil and pad of paper on the table then poured a glass of orange juice. Standing at the sink, she stared out the window at the barn, trying to make sense of her jumbled thoughts. It took her a minute to recognize the crunch of tires in the gravel driveway.

She dropped the glass on the countertop and ran through the living room to the front door. *Oh, Dear God. Dad!* She skidded to a stop on the porch, her heart slamming against her ribs as her breath left her lungs.

Caleb Mansfield stepped out of a black Ford Taurus. Her eyes worked to adjust to the waning early evening light, but even though she hadn't seen him in years, there was no mistaking his tall, muscular frame. She watched him in silence, her mouth dropping open. *What the hell was he doing here?*

Caleb took in everything at once – her anxious eyes, her tense body, her stunned expression. He climbed the steps and stopped, waiting.

During the flight, he imagined what she'd look like now, but he wasn't prepared for the stunning woman in front of him. So much was the same – those full lips that used to respond to his kiss, the small cleft in her chin. And that body. His eyes traveled her length, taking in the sweet curves he thought he'd never see again. There were differences, of course. Her honey blond hair had darkened a little over the years and was shorter than he remembered, her deep amber eyes more guarded now.

Lacey's sharp words slapped him back from his thoughts. "What are you doing here?" Her brow furrowed. "I thought you told me you were in Chicago? You said you'd just returned from Europe."

He ignored the shock of electricity that ran through him as he took her elbow and guided her back inside. "Yeah, I did. I caught the first flight I could get then drove over from Kansas City."

Lacey left Caleb standing in the living room. She'd had just about all the surprises she could handle for one day. She looked around the kitchen, overwhelmed. Could his timing be any worse?

Her eyes landed on a sponge near the sink. She wetted it then began haphazardly swiping at the juice she'd spilled. Caleb's footsteps followed her into the room, but she didn't turn.

Lacey corralled her rioting thoughts, although his presence wasn't helping her state of mind. "Listen, Caleb. I hate to be rude, but I've had a long day and I've still got things to do tonight. I really don't have time to play hostess."

Caleb came up quietly behind her and took the sponge from her, tossing it into the sink. "I'll make coffee. You sit down at the table," he insisted.

She bristled for a moment before accepting the fact that she didn't have the strength to challenge him. The energy that had driven her just minutes before drained out of her. She looked up into the handsome face that was familiar but not.

Falling into the chair, she watched him fill the pot with water. Numb and scared, she folded her hands together to stop their shaking.

He took the chair opposite her, pulled his phone from his pocket and leaned forward, elbows resting on the table. "There's no easy way to start this conversation," he said, his tone calm and even. "Your dad's in trouble. I want to help."

Her eyes met his. When she didn't speak, he continued.

"You and I agree that your dad wouldn't just leave. It's obvious to me that we're dealing with an outside force. The question is – who would do this, and why?"

Lacey closed her eyes. She couldn't quite catch a breath. The nightmare was real. She jumped up from the chair and paced the kitchen. "I've been racking my brain since last night trying to think of anyone who would have a grudge against Dad." She wiped her hands on her jeans. "And there's only one person who keeps coming back into my mind."

Caleb stood. "Who?"

"It's ridiculous."

"Who?" He advanced toward her.

Lacey stepped back, surprised at the dark anger sparking in his eyes. She blew out her breath. "Spencer Nicholson."

"Spencer? Mona's kid?" Caleb said quickly. "Why?"

It disturbed her that Caleb knew about Mona. It shouldn't have, but it did. The fact that her dad still had a relationship with Caleb was none of her business.

She shook her head, coming back to his question. "He's angry. Dad's the first person Mona's dated since Spencer's father passed and they're pretty serious. He's nineteen now and I thought it would get better with time, but it seems to have gotten worse."

"What do you mean *gotten worse?*"

"I don't know. I thought by now he'd be more accepting of their relationship. But he's making it hard on them. I know there's nothing he'd like more than to break them up." Lacey poured the coffee, absently adding a spoon of sugar to Caleb's mug. She passed it to him then grabbed her own mug and returned to the table.

"And you think he's angry enough to do something?" he asked skeptically as he followed her back to the scarred oak table.

"I have no idea," she exclaimed. "It seems far-fetched. I'm just concerned because Mona thinks —"

"What?"

She bit her lip. Thinking something and saying it out loud were two different things. "I don't know what to think. Spencer's not home. Mona said he hasn't been there since she came home yesterday."

"Did you happen to mention your theory to the police?"

Lacey frowned. "Of course not. It's not really a theory. Spencer's just a kid. I haven't been thinking very clearly."

Caleb took a quick gulp of coffee as he watched Lacey. "I think it'd be foolish to rule anything out."

He thought about the envelope he'd received from Bill as a chill of apprehension slithered over him. He hoped like hell Spencer was involved, that he was throwing some kind of post-adolescent temper tantrum.

Bill's discovery was going to revolutionize treatment for aggressive cancers in the digestive tract. It would be a huge payday for whoever brought it to market. He had to find out who else knew about the data.

"What about his research? How many people know what he's working on?"

"I don't know." She paused, staring at him. "Why?"

Caleb matched her gaze. "Just thinking out loud. Did he discuss his projects with you?" He waited for Lacy to answer, wondering what was going through her mind.

"No. Not really. I knew he was finishing up his project, and that he was excited about some possible human applications, but I don't know any of the details."

Was it possible she really didn't know? Caleb pressed on. "Who *would* know?"

She placed her mug on the table with a little too much force. "I don't have time to sit around and play twenty questions with you. I've already gone through everything I know with the police." Grabbing the mugs, Lacey rose from the table and rinsed them in the sink. "I need to get over to Mona's, see if I can figure out what's happening with Spencer."

She shoved her phone into her bag. "Thank you for coming, Caleb." She hesitated. "I've got your cell number. I'll call you as soon as I know anything." She started around him but he stepped into her path, his eyes coolly challenging.

"I didn't come here to sit around and wait for you to call me with updates. I could've done that in Chicago." His voice lowered. He reached for her arm but she stepped out of his reach. "Lacey, I came to help. Let me go with you to see Mona." It sounded more like a demand than a request.

Lacey fumed. She wanted to tell him to go to hell. What gave him the right to walk back into her life now? She looked into his eyes, ready for a fight until she glimpsed the fear lurking behind his cool façade. With a jolt, she realized that Caleb was just as worried as she was.

She sighed, certain she'd regret her decision. "Fine. Follow me to Mona's house."

Chapter 5

Caleb stood next to Lacey as she rapped on the door, a fine mist falling around them.

"Mona, it's Lacey."

He heard the chain slide just before the door opened, but he wasn't able to see the petite woman as she drew Lacey into a fierce hug.

"I'm so glad you're here. I was just thinking about you." Mona paused. "Any news?"

Whatever mental image Caleb had painted of mid-western quilt makers was promptly erased as Mona pulled back from Lacey's embrace. Bill had talked to him about Mona several times, but somehow, this stylish put-together woman with short-cropped spiky salt-and-pepper hair wasn't at all what he'd expected.

Lacey shook her head. "Nothing. The police said I shouldn't expect to hear from them for a day or two unless they need more information." She tilted her head in Caleb's direction. "We wanted to talk to you for a few minutes. Can we come in?"

Caleb watched Mona's sharp eyes bounce from Lacey to him then back to Lacey, brows raised. "Of course. Excuse me." She reached around Lacey and shook Caleb's hand before ushering them into the foyer. "Mona Nicholson. Come on inside. It's awfully chilly out tonight."

Lacey shrugged out of her jacket. "This is Caleb Mansfield. Dad might have mentioned him —"

Mona's features shifted from curiosity to recognition in an instant. "Absolutely. Oh my goodness! Welcome, Caleb. I'm so glad to meet you." Her eyes clouded. "I would've preferred different circumstances, though. Bill has told me so much about you. Why, you know he considers you the son he never had, don't you?"

Caleb's throat tightened. "Thank you, ma'am. That's probably the nicest compliment I've ever received."

Mona turned from placing their jackets in the closet. "Please. No 'ma'am' for me. You'll only make me feel older than I already do tonight." She waved them down the hall. "Come into the kitchen. How about some coffee to warm you up? And I've got some crumb cake, too."

He sniffed appreciatively as the rich aromas of cinnamon and sugar wafted toward them, reminding him that he hadn't eaten all day. "That sounds great."

"Have a seat," she offered, pointing to the small glass-top dinette in the center of the room. "I've been baking all evening since I got back from campus. Nervous energy, I guess."

Lacey's earlier impatience fled as she watched Mona bustle around the tidy kitchen, filling their mugs and setting plates in front of them. In the lingering silence, Lacey's mind swirled around her fears about Spencer's possible involvement in her dad's disappearance.

She finally laid down the fork she'd been using to toy with the cake. Opting for the direct route, Lacey dove in. "Has Spencer come home yet?"

Mona's hand trembled slightly as she picked up her coffee then, without drinking, slowly placed it back on the table. She met Lacey's gaze. "No. He hasn't."

"Where do you think he might be?"

"I really have no idea." Mona sighed, a deep weary sound. She appeared to have aged ten years in the last couple minutes.

"I know what he told me, but I can't tell you if he was telling the truth." Mona broke eye contact. "It's getting really difficult to trust him. I wanted to believe he'd straighten up, but he's not even pretending to look for jobs anymore, and I've started hiding my wallet when he's home." Her voice quieted. "He's getting violent, too."

Lacey's head snapped up and she grabbed Mona's hand, searching her face. "Has he hurt you?"

"He hasn't touched me," she assured her. "I don't think he would. He's just more…aggressive I guess is the word, more threatening. Everything makes him angry. I know this is horrible to say about my own son, but there've been a couple times that I've actually been afraid of him."

"Who does he spend his time with?" Caleb asked.

Mona cringed. "He has a group of young men he hangs out with, but I don't allow them to come here. I use the term 'young men' very loosely. They're trouble. I can feel it. I try to discourage Spencer from spending time with them but I may as well be talking to a wall."

"Was he here Friday? Do you remember?"

Mona's brow wrinkled. "He was. Until about noon. He told me he was going to spend the night with a couple friends and he had an overnight bag, so I wasn't surprised when I got home last night and he was gone. But I expected him home sometime today and he's still not here. I've called his cell phone several times but it goes straight to voicemail."

Lacey feared her next words could drive a wedge between them that might never heal. Her stomach clenched as she prayed for the right words. "I know this is difficult for you, but do you have any reason to believe he might have something to do with Dad's disappearance?"

After a moment, Mona straightened her shoulders, her eyes locking with Lacey's. There was fear in their depths, but no anger. "I've asked myself the same question over the past several hours. The short answer is, I just don't know. I'm not sure I even know my own son anymore." She lifted her mug again and, this time, managed to take a small sip. "To be completely honest, I should've stepped in a long time ago when I first started noticing the changes in his behavior, but I didn't. I bought him a nice car, a new wardrobe. Somehow, I thought that those things would help him take pride in himself, but he's continued down the wrong path. I'm prepared now to do whatever it takes to straighten him out."

Mona stood and walked to the kitchen window, her back to them. "This is humbling for a parent to admit, but I searched his room today and found empty alcohol bottles under his bed and some evidence of drug use."

Lacey watched Mona shiver as if the cold breeze outside had swept through the room, and her heart broke.

Mona's voice wavered. "I love my son, but I won't protect him when what he's doing is harmful to himself and possibly others."

Coming to stand behind her, Lacey placed her hands on Mona's shoulders. "Does Dad know?"

Mona's shoulders sagged. "We've talked some, but he doesn't know everything. Spencer had already been so horrible to him, I didn't want him to look even worse in Bill's eyes."

Lacey turned Mona until she could look at her face-to-face and gave her shoulders a tiny shake. "We're family. Dad would want to know. Everything. And so would I. We'll do whatever we can to help him."

She hadn't heard Caleb rise from the table, but she immediately felt his presence behind her.

"I know I'm not family, but I'd like to meet him. It wasn't too long ago I dealt with a similar situation with my youngest brother. It sounds like Spencer's walking on the edge, but if he hasn't gone over, there's time to help him."

Lacey stiffened. *Damn straight you're not family. Who did he think he was?*

Biting back the words, Lacey watched Mona fight for control of her emotions as relief and hope flared behind the gleam of moisture in her eyes. "Do you want to have a seat in the living room? Might be more comfortable."

At Mona's nod, Lacey turned to Caleb. She opened her mouth to ask him to take her, but he'd already stepped around her and, taking Mona's elbow, led her out of the room. Chivalrous or not, Caleb's very presence annoyed Lacey. By the time she made quick work of the clean up and joined Mona and Caleb in the living room, they were sitting on the sofa sharing about her dad as if they were old friends.

It felt too much like funeral talk. *He's not dead!* She wanted to scream it, but instead she took a deep breath and sat down on the edge of one of the two overstuffed chairs facing the sofa. Watching Caleb, she was unable to deny the fresh twinge of annoyance tweaking her at his insinuation into their lives. He didn't belong here.

When there was a pause in the conversation, she turned to look at Mona directly. "You were up on campus today, and you know Dad's co-workers way better than I do. Can you think of anybody at the school who might have a problem with him?"

"We don't socialize with too many of them, but Bill is so well-liked and respected I certainly can't imagine anyone taking issue with him. Everyone I talked to today was shocked and very worried."

Caleb leaned forward. "Do you happen to know the names of his research assistants?"

"Of course. You know how Bill is. He's very close to them. Mason James and Zach Coughlin were working with him throughout most of his current project. Zach still is. If I remember correctly, Mason's wife got transferred with her job up to Washington."

"Who took his place?"

"Stan Jacobson. Nice young man. I've met him a couple times when I went to see Bill at school. I remember him because he showed me pictures of his two-year-old twins. Cute little guys." She smiled. "They look just like their daddy, too."

Lacey caught Caleb's expression. "What? You know him?"

Caleb shrugged. "Name sounds familiar. Not sure why." He drummed his fingers on his knee. "Maybe he's written some journal article I've read recently."

Lacey glanced at her watch and realized it was almost ten.

As if on cue, Caleb rose from the sofa and turned to Mona. "It was so nice to finally meet you. Thanks for your hospitality. I hope I get the chance to meet your son, too."

After throwing on her jacket, Lacey leaned over and gave Mona a quick hug. "If you need anything at all, you call me, okay?"

Mona nodded and Lacey again caught a glimmer of tears in the older woman's eyes. "I'm so sorry Lacey," she said. "God, I pray Spencer's not involved in any of this, but I just don't know."

Lacey slogged to her car, completely drained. The slick mist was gone but the temperature had to be below freezing. She shivered, reaching for the door handle as Caleb joined her.

He put his hand on her arm. "I'll be at the Ramada if you hear anything."

She glanced up at him, nodding. "Okay." As Caleb continued to regard her, she pointed to his car parked behind hers. "You'll need to move so I can get out."

Caleb's turned toward his car then pivoted back. "You didn't eat Mona's cake and I doubt you've eaten much of anything today. Do you want to grab a quick bite?"

She didn't want to eat. Or sit with Caleb. Or talk. She wanted to go home and cry her brains out and pray like crazy that when she woke up tomorrow, her dad would be home and Caleb would be gone.

Her shoulders tight, she opened her car door. "I don't think so."

Caleb shoved a hand through his hair. "Lacey, we need to talk."

"Not tonight. Good night, Caleb." Lacey sank into her seat and closed the door.

He stood outside her door until she rolled down the window.

"I've got to go." She started the engine and snapped her seat belt. Moments later, she caught his retreating figure in her rear-view mirror, relieved as his headlights disappeared down the street.

***

Dumping her purse and jacket on the floor next to her front door, Lacey fell onto the sofa with her head in her hands, finally allowing the scalding tears she'd held off all day to course down her cheeks unchecked. Wrenching sobs convulsed her body until she was completely spent.

Unable to muster enough energy to make it to her bedroom, Lacey lay back on the cushions, flinging her arms over the side of the couch. She didn't expect to sleep, but she must've dozed because when she tried to lift her arms from above her head, they'd gone numb.

With a grimace, she forced her arms to her chest and checked her watch. Two-thirty. She lay still, hoping to slip back into her dreamless sleep, but by the time the tingling subsided in her arms, she was wide awake.

Pushing off the couch, Lacey stumbled to the galley kitchen and started a pot of coffee, throwing in an extra scoop for good measure. She toasted a bagel while she waited, her thoughts churning.

When the coffee was ready, she planted herself at the small dining room table. Thinking about her dad made her head hurt. Even though she was grown and hadn't lived at home for several years, for her whole life, he'd been her champion. She couldn't envision a scenario where he wasn't front and center in her world.

Her eyes misted as memories tumbled through her mind. She thought about how he'd run into the school when she broke her arm in sixth grade gym class. And how, when she didn't get asked to the sophomore dance, he'd taken her dancing instead.

She took a deep shuddering breath, praying the tears didn't get the upper hand again. She'd cried so much, she wondered if she would run out of tears. She sniffed and swiped at her eyes. Apparently, the answer was no.

Nibbling on her bagel, her thoughts wandered to the only real time she and her dad had ever deeply disagreed – the summer Caleb had lived with them.

She'd wanted to leave with Caleb at the end of that summer, go off to Chicago with him, start a life with him. Her dad forbade it. He insisted that she stay in Manhattan and go to college. Convinced that Caleb would stand by her side and defend their love to her father, she was devastated when he agreed with her dad and insisted that she stay.

The two most important men in her life had, within moments, broken her heart. In time, she'd forgiven her dad. He never knew how deeply she'd fallen in love with Caleb. But Caleb had known. She'd trusted him then, and he'd broken that trust.

She climbed out of her reverie and took a sip of strong coffee. It had been years since she'd thought of that summer. No sense reliving her stupidity.

Her thoughts turned to the man today. He was still drop-dead gorgeous, maybe even more so now. He wore his confidence like a second skin. And she had to admit she'd been impressed by how he'd handled Mona. But what else did she know about him?

She listened to the whisper of unease that had been with her since she left Mona's house. Even though she was convinced Caleb's concern was genuine, something wasn't right. If it had been months since he'd spoken to her dad, why call now? And why was Caleb so curious about her dad's work?

Dark thoughts invaded as a wave of nausea coursed through her. She dropped the bagel on her plate, unable to finish. She'd believed without question that Caleb was here to help her. But was he? There was no sign of forced entry at the house and her dad's car was there. Which implied that if her dad was taken, it was by someone he trusted. Was she being naïve about Caleb again? Could he be involved?

Chapter 6

Caleb ran the razor around the day's worth of dark growth, frowning into the mirror in the tiny hotel bathroom.

His original goal for today had been to locate Zach and Stan and find out what they knew. But after last night, it was obvious he had a more urgent priority. He needed Lacey to realize he was on her side. If she didn't let him in, there'd be no way for him to be able to stay up on what was going on with the investigation.

He ran a comb through his hair then slapped it down on the counter, giving up the fight that had warred within him all night long. Yesterday, he would've said that finding Bill was the only reason to get close to her. But that was before he'd seen her again.

All the years that had gone by should've insulated him from the punch in the gut he felt when he saw her, but they didn't. He urgently wanted to help her find Bill. But to his surprise, he couldn't ignore his desire to discover if, underneath her aloof exterior, she was still the same girl from his past.

He dressed quickly then dialed Lacey's number.

"Hello?"

"Lacey, Caleb. Have breakfast with me. We need to talk."

"You're exactly right. I'll meet you in twenty minutes at Charlie's. Fifth and Main." Her clipped tone disturbed him. Man, did he have his work cut out for him.

"I remember the place. Best pancakes in Manhattan." Cold silence filled the line. "Okay. See you in a few."

Caleb disconnected the call then grabbed his jacket. He wasn't about to be late.

***

He found the old diner with no trouble. Just like it had in college, the place still felt like he was stepping into an episode of Happy Days. Caleb found a table to the right of the door and was waiting there when Lacey walked in.

She removed her sunglasses when she saw him, her eyes shadowed above the dark smudges that told him she hadn't slept much better than he had. Caleb stood, pulling out her chair.

Frowning, she hung her bag over the chair and sat. "I don't have much time. I'm –"

A waitress appeared at the table with small glasses of water. "Coffee?" she asked as she placed cups down in front of them.

Caleb nodded.

The woman poured then laid two menus on the table. "Let me know when you're ready to order."

As she ambled away, Caleb looked at Lacey. "I know you're in a hurry. I take it you haven't heard anything?"

She looked like she wanted to get up and leave but she took a deep breath instead. She placed her hands on the table, palms down, and leaned forward, her eyes flashing fire. "Why are you here?"

Caleb stared at her for a second. He'd been waiting for the salvo since she walked in. Calmly, he answered. "You know why I'm here. I want to help find your dad."

Her hands shook as they tightened into fists. "Really?" she spat. "You expect me to believe that you just happened to call my dad for the first time in months the day after he goes missing? That's an awfully big coincidence. Call me crazy, but I'm not a big fan of coincidence. And you're sniffing around his work like a freaking bloodhound. It's not adding up, Caleb, at least not in your favor."

Caleb's eyes bored into Lacey's. "You need to trust me. I'm here for the right reasons."

Lacey snorted. "Trust you? You're kidding, right? I trusted you when I knew you and that was a huge mistake. I don't even know you now. Why the hell would I trust you?"

Caleb ignored the barb. He had a ridiculous urge to come around the table and yank her into his arms. The pain and fear radiating from her were living breathing things. She needed an ally. She needed him. She just didn't know it yet.

By the rapid rise and fall of her chest as she challenged him, he figured she was seconds away from walking out the door. He only had one weapon in his arsenal. He hoped it was enough.

He captured her cold hands is his warm ones. "You need to trust me because your dad did," he said quietly.

Lacey jerked her hands away. "What are you talking about?"

Caleb leaned into the table, hoping she could sense his sincerity. "A couple of days ago, your dad sent a package to me."

The frown was back in force as she crossed her arms. "What? What kind of package?"

"You know the project he was working on? It's called BR-714. He sent me the entire research file. Everything."

Lacey continued to watch him. "And?"

He had to make her understand. "Lacey, this wasn't some little project he wanted to share with me. This project started six years ago at the farm. As far as I know, outside of his researchers and the trial group, who would've all been required to sign non-disclosures, there are very few people who know what he's been working on."

She paused, seeming to weigh her words. "What's so important about it? And why would he send it to you?"

His concern about discussing it in public was eclipsed by his desire to make her understand. As he filled her in briefly on the details of the research and the potential benefits, he could almost see the gears turning in her head.

She still looked skeptical until he produced the file from his briefcase and laid it, along with the note, on the table. She grabbed the piece of paper, her eyes roving over Bill's distinctive scrawl. Finally, she raised wide frightened eyes.

"Do you think he knew something was going to happen?" she whispered.

Caleb frowned. He wasn't going to lie. "From his words I wouldn't think so, but something or someone prompted him to send me the finished research when he did. I've got to talk to the people here who are involved. And I need to know what the police uncover. I can't do that without you."

Lacey blinked away the moisture in her eyes as she listened to Caleb place their orders. Somewhere in her mind, she'd allowed herself to believe that there was a simple explanation for why her dad was gone. That he'd show up any minute and wrap his arms around her and laugh at her silly worries about him.

That wasn't going to happen. Not only was he missing, he was in danger. The proof was staring her in the face. Fear strangled her as tears welled up in her eyes. "Caleb, what if –"

He cut her off. "Let's not play 'what if', okay?" He covered her hands again to stop their trembling and his eyes connected with hers. "We're going to find him. And he's going to be all right."

This time, Lacey let the heat from Caleb's hands warm her while his words calmed her racing heart. She wouldn't be any help at all if she didn't pull herself together. "We need to get this information to the police. And the media."

Caleb shook his head. "Not happening. If we tell the police this file exists, they'll want it. There's no way this file is going to them. We'll point them toward his work, but this file's staying with me."

"Won't they wonder why we think his abduction was work-related?"

"We'll suggest that he was working on an important project. I'm sure they're pursuing that angle anyway. But we need to know who they talk to and what they find out. I'm going to try and track down Zach and Stan today. See if they can get me into the lab on campus."

"What about Spencer?" She studied Caleb's face.

"I don't know. I thought about it last night. It's still feasible that someone recruited his involvement. I'm not willing to rule that out at this point."

Lacey rubbed her hands over her face. "*Shit.*"

"My thoughts exactly."

The waitress brought two steaming short stacks with bacon, and Lacey was surprised to find that she was hungry. The older woman placed the syrup dispensers on the table and topped off their coffee. "Anything else I can get you?"

"I think we're all set. Thanks." Lacey grimaced as Caleb grabbed the strawberry syrup and doused his pancakes in the rich red liquid. "Want a little pancake with your syrup?" she joked.

Caleb looked up from his plate with a half-grin before diving back into his breakfast, and Lacey's heart did a little somersault. In that moment, he reminded her so much of the man she remembered. She looked down, and clearing her throat, unrolled her silverware from the paper napkin. She didn't have time for such ridiculous thoughts.

"I'll call Detective Abrams. And I'm going to the newspaper office and television station." She held up her hand at his frown. "Obviously, not to share this information. I just need as many people as possible to know that he's missing. I've got to increase my chances of finding him."

"What are you doing after that?"

She took a sip of coffee and shook her head. "Don't know. The shop's closed on Sundays so I've got time on my hands. Which sucks."

Caleb tossed his napkin on the table. "Does your dad still have his office at the farm?" At Lacey's nod, he continued. "I'd sure love to check his hard drives. Any chance you'd let me take a look at his equipment?"

Lacey studied him, considering his request. Could he have contrived this whole story just to get access to her dad's computers? Her eyes were drawn again to her dad's hand-written codes then back to Caleb. His gaze was open, his crystal blue eyes locking onto hers.

She sighed. Maybe he'd be able to find something that could help. "Okay. I'll head out there as soon as I'm done in town."

41

Lacey cut into her breakfast, taking a bite just as Caleb spoke.

"Speaking of the shop, Mona said you're in the floral business. I envisioned you running your own rescue operation by now. As I recall, you loved fostering horses."

She swallowed, surprised that he remembered something so personal about her. Glancing around the room, she tried to get her bearings. How bizarre it was to be sitting here at breakfast with Caleb talking about their lives.

"I stopped working with rescue horses when I moved into town to finish school. I still stay in touch with the Cleaver's operation, though. It's amazing to see them place the horses with the right families. They rescue something like two hundred animals a year."

She paused to wash down her bite of pancake. Did she want to share any details of her life with him?

Get over it, already. He's a guest. And he's here to help find Dad.

Forgoing her cynicism, she began. "The idea for the floral business was Paige Marshall's. Well, Paige Stewart now. Do you remember her?"

He squinted, his hand rubbing his chin. "The red-head? Bossy?"

She nodded. "That's her. We're in business together. It started out as a business class project for her. But the more we talked about a gift and flower shop, the more feasible it became in our minds. The best part was that we decided early on to feature works by local artists in several different genres."

"And now, you're up and running. And doing well, I presume?"

She glanced at the Rolex on his left wrist. "We are. Probably not by any standards you're used to, but it's been a great experience so far. We're both learning all the time…what works, what doesn't."

"You had quite a gift with the flowers at the farm. I'm sure this is a great fit for you."

Lacey paused. "There are things about it that I enjoy but I miss working with the rescue operation. Sometimes I wonder if I'm doing what I'm really supposed to be doing." She looked over at him, guilt over her disloyal statement bringing a rush of heat to her cheeks. She'd thought it a million times, but had never said the words out loud.

"Believe it or not, I can relate," he said with a shrug.

She cocked an eyebrow. "I have a hard time believing that. You were always so certain about your future." She mentally smacked her forehead. *Could we avoid any personal reference, please?* "So fill me in before we get out of here," she quickly added. "What's kept you busy all these years?"

He downed the last of his coffee, and sat back rubbing his flat stomach. "I've spent the last several years mostly abroad working to make BioTech an international company. I think the groundwork there is finally done."

Lacey was impressed, but not surprised at the simplicity of his statement. There was no arrogance in it, but it was obvious to her that he'd known before he began what the eventual outcome would be.

"I haven't had much chance to sit down with Roger since I've been back to talk about the future and what's next. He insisted that I take some time off. And now, I'm here. Right place, right time, I think."

Lacey looked away from his unnerving gaze. She didn't question why Roger had insisted on the vacation. She already knew. Caleb hadn't changed. He was still the same relentless, driven man he'd always been. Fine with her. She needed relentless and driven to help find her dad.

She gathered her purse and grabbed the ticket the waitress had left behind.

Caleb took it from her hand. "I'll get that."

She didn't argue. She knew it would be pointless. "Thank you." She put on her sunglasses. "I'll call you when I get to the farm. You can meet me out there when you're done on campus."

***

Caleb pulled out his phone and dialed Lacey's number. Hopefully, she'd had better results that he'd had.

He jumped in as soon as she answered. "Anything new from the police?"

"No. Nothing worth mentioning. Abrams said he talked to Zach Coughlin, and he was able to confirm his alibi for Friday. He hasn't reached Stan Jacobson yet."

"Did you make it over to the paper?"

"Yes. And they're going to run an article. There's supposed to be something on the evening news tonight, too. Somebody has to know something." She paused, and Caleb could hear the frustration in her voice. "Please tell me you have good news."

"I was able to track Zach down at the rec center on campus. Obviously, he knew about your dad's disappearance so after I pulled a few strings, he let me in to the lab."

"And?"

Rolling his shoulders, he wished he had something, anything, to encourage her. Instead, he gave her the truth. "There's no record of Bill's research anywhere on the school's computers. If he stored anything there, someone's scrubbed it completely clean."

"What does that mean for us?"

He liked her choice of words. "There are only two possible scenarios. Either he scrubbed them because he knew his data was in danger of being compromised. Or –" He paused.

"Or someone else did to cover their ass."

"Exactly. Which means, to my mind, his disappearance has to be connected to his work. And it's very possibly an inside job." Caleb blew out a breath as he switched gears. "I'm done here. I'll be there in twenty minutes give or take. It won't take long for me to review the files on his computers."

"Don't bother."

Caleb stopped, his hand on the door handle of his rental car. Had she changed her mind about letting him have access? He didn't hear any animosity in her tone. "Why not?"

"His computers are gone. The monitors are still here but the PCs themselves are gone. I didn't even think about looking under the desks when I came out here Friday night. *Damn it,*" she muttered. "Whoever this bastard is stole my dad's equipment. And I never even noticed."

Caleb tightened his grip on the phone. "Lacey, listen. It wouldn't have mattered if they were there Friday night or not. It wouldn't have changed anything. That just continues to validate our hypothesis that Bill's disappearance is related to his work."

"You sound an awful lot like a scientist."

"Yeah, well, you can take the scientist out of the lab…" Caleb started the car, trying to invent an excuse to keep her on the line.

Lacey sighed. "I'm headed home. I've got work in the morning and I'm supposed to do another interview with the paper tomorrow. I'll call you if Abrams calls."

Frustrated that nothing had come to mind, Caleb reluctantly let her go. "Be careful what you say, and don't trust anyone."

Her pause spoke volumes. "I need to remember that."

Chapter 7

Thunder boomed, rousing Bill Jordan out of his drug-induced sleep. He recognized the brisk staccato of pounding rain on the roof. Turning his head from the wan light breaking through the boards on the window, his attention was drawn to the steady drip of water pooling in the corner of the room.

Was it day two or day three? His foggy brain couldn't be sure. His system still wasn't completely free from the effects of the drugs he'd been given. A mouse skittered in the corner near a neat stack of computer equipment. He squinted. His computer equipment.

He sat up and scooted to the edge of the bed, surprised and thankful to see his glasses in one piece lying on the floor. He leaned down and put them on, a wave of nausea catching him by surprise. He didn't have anything in his system to purge, but he lay down on the bed until the feeling passed.

As his senses cleared, he surveyed his surroundings. The room was small. Peeling plaster hung from a couple of holes in the ceiling, and the place hadn't seen the right side of a broom or mop in a long time. A wrecking crew would've been an improvement.

Snatches of conversation floated through his head. He remembered now. They wanted the codes, the data.

The handcuff securing him to the old iron headboard bit into his wrist as he tried to reach the window. Of course, for now, they needed him. And hell would freeze over before he'd give them what they wanted.

He struggled to move the heavy bed frame until his wrist bled and still he couldn't get to the window. Sweat beaded on his brow. Since he was no longer gagged, he leaned as close to the window as he could and yelled for help. His throat was dry and scratchy but his shouts were loud enough to keep him from hearing the key turn in the lock of the door.

"You're a fool. No one can hear you. And even if they could, this isn't exactly a neighborhood watch area."

Bill whipped around and backed up against the bed.

The man tossed a bag of food and a bottle of water on the bed. "You might as well eat. Got to keep your strength up."

Bill grabbed the water bottle and guzzled it. He wiped several drops from his chin with the back of his hand then pulled a still-warm chicken sandwich from the paper bag, devouring it in minutes. *Was there any way to talk himself out of here?* He had to try.

"This doesn't have to go any further. Please, let me go. I can help you."

The atmosphere in the room flipped like a switch. "Help?" he mocked. "*I* need help? Coming from the guy handcuffed to the bed, that's priceless."

He came nose to nose with Bill. The scent of stale alcohol mingled with his sharp aftershave, sending Bill's stomach to his throat. "You really want to help me?" he sneered. Bill stood his ground but said nothing. "All you have to do is hand over the codes. Simple, right?"

"You know I won't do that. I can't."

The man's fist connected with Bill's jaw, snapping his head back as he landed on the bed.

"You can, you bastard. And you will. You want me to believe your research is the most important thing to you? Well, I know better." His eyes glistened. "Is it worth more to you than your little girl?"

Bill lurched forward as far as the handcuff would allow. By luck alone, his punch connected with the man's mouth and sent him sprawling backwards. "You go anywhere near her and I'll kill you myself."

Stan Jacobson ran into the room. "What's going on? I heard —" He stopped at the door, gaping. "What the hell happened?"

"Nothing to worry about." The man stood and dusted his slacks, working his jaw. He skirted around Bill as he walked toward the door. Dabbing the blood from the corner of his mouth, he motioned toward the crumpled bag on the bed. Hatred burned in his eyes, his smile evil. "Hope you enjoyed your food. It's the last you'll get until I get my codes."

As the man walked out of the room, Bill was aware of the suppressed rage fueling his words.

"Drug him. Give him a double dose. And I want him gagged and both hands bound. That son of a bitch won't touch me again."

Bill watched Stan advance toward him. "Stan, this is insane. Please. Don't do this." Sensing indecision, Bill pressed. "Think about it. I'm going to be a loose end. And so are you. He's not going to keep you around."

He looked for fear in Stan's eyes, but found anger instead. "You don't know what you're talking about. This guy's a genius. He's going to make us both rich."

Bill fought with reason and his fist, but in the end, he lay shaking on the bed, his arms duct taped together above his head, a cloth gag in his mouth. As the drugs began to force him back into a dreamless sleep, his thoughts weren't on Stan, or the food, or the beating he'd just endured. They were on Lacey. *Dear God, keep these monsters away from my daughter.*

Chapter 8

Lacey pulled the purple hyacinths and white carnations out of the cooler before going back for the autumn mums. Death couldn't care less about her personal problems.

She'd awakened to a text from Davidson's Funeral home about Mr. Hale's visitation this evening. It had taken months to get them to even take a look at using her shop. Last week, she'd have been thrilled with the message. But not now.

Perched on a stool in front of her work bench, she clipped flower stems. Providing beauty and comfort at a time of sadness was one of the perks of her job, but her focus was way off today. Her stomach rolled as her work took on a different dimension. What if she had to plan her dad's funeral? Could she sit here and create beauty for that? What kind of flowers would he want? They'd certainly never discussed it.

Mentally slapping herself, she forced back the hot sting of tears. *Stop it. You're not helping.*

At a light tap against the glass front door, Lacey glanced up, welcoming the distraction from her morbid thoughts. Mona held up two steaming Starbucks cups in her mittened hands. Lacey hurried over and unlocked the door, the bell tinkling as the cold wind pushed in around Mona.

"Brrrr." Mona's teeth chattered as she handed the cups to Lacey before shedding her coat and gloves. "This is ridiculous. Just a few days ago, it was in the sixties."

Lacey breathed in the rich coffee. "Thanks so much for coming. You're a life saver. The job's too big to take care of around everything else during store hours."

Mona grabbed one of the lattés and put her other hand on her hip. "Oh, please. Your timing was perfect. I'm worrying myself sick over your father at home by myself. Is Sam on her way?"

Shaking her head, Lacey picked up a yellow mum and positioned it in the spray. "I left her a message but she hasn't called me back. I take it Spencer's not home yet? Did you decide to file a report?"

"Not yet. I'm going to give him a couple more days. It's not like this is the first time it's happened. I was jumping to conclusions on Saturday because of Bill." Mona shook her head and forced a smile. "Enough about that. I can't think of anywhere else I'd rather be."

Lacey knew a mindless task was what Mona needed. What they both needed. She hugged Mona then handed her the hand-written orders, listing the required flowers for each corresponding arrangement. "Can you go pull these flowers from the cooler?"

On auto-pilot, Lacey put the finishing touches on the casket spray. By the time she was done, Mona had methodically sorted the flowers for the first three arrangements.

Lacey glanced over at the neat stacks. "Very impressive." She nudged Mona's shoulder. "And efficient. If you ever decide to expand your horizons, I know a quaint little floral and gift shop that could use somebody like you."

Mona sighed. "I wish finding your dad was this easy. I'm still having a hard time believing this is real. I keep expecting him to walk through the door."

Lacey's smile faded. "I know. It's so frustrating and we're not making any progress."

Mona straightened a lace doily on one of the display tables. "I saw the story last night on the news. Hopefully something will come out of that."

"I hope so. I was thinking last night about his email files. I wonder if anyone's scanned them yet. Even if they have, I'd like to see them myself."

"Wasn't Caleb up on campus yesterday? Did he have a chance to see them?"

Lacey hadn't given much thought to Caleb this morning. She was still trying to adjust to the notion of him being part of the conversation. "I don't think so. He was more interested in the lab." Lacey wondered how much Mona knew about her dad's work. Probably not much more than she did.

Mona continued to fidget. "Hmmm." She nodded. "I thought a lot about what Caleb said about dealing with his younger brother." Turning toward Lacey, she folded her arms. "You know him. Do you think there's a chance he could help Spencer?"

Lacey paused. *You know him.* The words rattled around in her head. *Did she? Could she vouch for his character? Hardly.*

She'd accepted that he was here to help find her father. But did that put him in the good guy category? And, how much did Mona know about their history? One thing was certain. There was no way she wanted Mona to get too attached to Caleb, or come to depend on him. Better to nip this in the bud.

Pulling a towel from her apron pocket, Lacey wiped her hands and shrugged. "I'm sure he has the best intentions, but I wouldn't get my hopes up."

Mona's face fell. "I understand. I'm sure he'll have to get back to Chicago soon."

Lacey's gut clenched. She felt like she'd just kicked a dog. Handing scissors to Mona, she scooted around her, anxious to get past the subject. "Will you trim these stems? I'm going to run upstairs and get the display easels."

Lacey wandered around the cramped storage room, moving boxes around until she found the decorative iron pieces. Her conscience began to niggle at her.

Crap. Had she told Mona the truth, or just her truth? She didn't even know Caleb anymore. Was it fair to taint Mona's image of him based on her bad experience?

Lacey lugged the pieces downstairs, guilt weighing on her as she recognized the anxiety etched on Mona's face. With everything going on, she'd just taken away Mona's one ray of hope. *Nice going, Lacey.*

51

She motioned to Mona to join her at the workbench. "Want to help me position these and make sure they look okay?"

Mona rallied. "Sure. Just tell me what I'm looking for."

After explaining, Lacey placed another few flowers to achieve balance. Her conscience refused to leave her alone. Plopping down on the stool, she sighed. "What I said a few minutes ago wasn't fair."

Mona looked up from the white carnation she was about to add. "What?"

"About Caleb. I think he'd love to help with Spencer. I have a bit of a jaded opinion. Water under the bridge."

Mona's wise eyes continued to watch her, and Lacey wondered why she'd opened this particular can of worms.

Reaching for another flower, Mona broke the expanding silence. "Pretty deep water, huh?"

Lacey shrugged. "I thought so at the time." She added a ribbon to the arrangement, a weak smile cracking her face. "First true love and all that."

"Ah," Mona sighed. "That is deep stuff. What happened?"

"Pretty simple really. I thought we were in love. I was wrong. I thought we were going to spend our lives together. Wrong again. He left and that was it." Lacey cocked her head and nodded, satisfied with her arrangement. She removed it from the easel and disappeared into the cooler.

Lacey waited an extra minute after she stored the arrangement, hoping Mona would take the hint and let the conversation about Caleb die. She should've known better. Mona's keen gaze tracked her as she returned and studied the next arrangement.

"My experience tells me that things like that are rarely simple. Why did he leave?"

Lacey wasn't interested in telling the whole story, but Mona would be like a dog with a bone if she tried to dodge her question. She stifled a sigh. "He was, is, the oldest of six kids. I don't know much about his upbringing. He never talked about it, but Dad had mentioned that his parents were out of the picture. All I knew was that he was the primary provider for his siblings. It was up to him to make sure they had financial resources. While he was in college, he worked full time to support them. After college, he interned with my dad for a summer then headed off to Chicago to make his fortune."

Mona leaned forward into Lacey's line of sight. "That seems pretty noble to me."

Lacey rushed to explain. "Oh, it was. I admired him for it. We talked a lot about his plans and dreams that summer. I was foolish enough to make the assumption that I was part of those plans, and when it turned out that I wasn't, I was devastated."

"That would've hurt. Did he stay in touch with you?"

Making quick work of the second arrangement, Lacey added the ribbon and pulled it off the easel. "We were both young, and I was hurt and angry. It was easier to sever ties, so that's what we did. We hadn't spoken until he showed up at the farm on Saturday."

"Huh," Mona said, her brow knitting.

Don't ask.

Lacey stopped and turned around. "Huh, what?"

"I was just thinking that fate's a funny thing."

Frowning, Lacey hoisted the easel and headed to the cooler. The only intervention of fate she cared about was making sure her dad survived and returned home safe and sound.

***

Lacey gave the tissue a final fluffing and handed over the bag as Mrs. Moyer plied her with questions about her father's disappearance. After several similar conversations throughout the morning, Lacey wondered if her decision to keep the shop open had been a mistake. But she couldn't stand the thought of sitting around, waiting for something to happen. She had to stay busy.

The problem was, she was doing all the talking. No one knew anything. They clucked their tongues, and told her how very sorry they were, which didn't help at all.

She handed off the receipt then stepped around the counter to check on another patron when the back door opened and Sam rushed in.

"Lacey, I'm so sorry for being late." Sam's words tumbled out in a hushed whisper. She glanced around. "Has it been super busy?"

"Nothing I couldn't handle. Mona ran out to get some bagels, but she's been here since seven helping me with the Hale funeral flowers." Lacey turned. "Can you take over out here for a few minutes? I've got a couple of calls I need to return."

"About your dad? Has there been any news?"

Lacey shook her head. "Unfortunately, no. The police are still trying to track down leads."

"Oh. Have you talked to Paige?"

"No. I know if I do, she'll be on the next plane back here. If I thought there was anything she could do, I would. But until the police turn up something or we receive some kind of ransom note, we're just treading water." Lacey rubbed her face then shoved her hands through her hair. "It's the waiting I hate the most. I just want something to happen. Something we can act on."

"I'm sorry, Lacey. Go do what you need to do. I'll be fine. I'll come get you if I need help." Sam's eyes didn't meet Lacey's as she turned and quickly busied herself straightening a display of curios.

Lacey, puzzled over Sam's odd behavior, watched her for a moment longer. Had Gary harassed her again? Lacey shelved her curiosity until she emerged from the office minutes later and spotted Sam on her way to the cooler. "Everything okay?"

Sam paused. "Yep. Just took care of the last customer. I thought I'd get the deliveries ready."

Lacey put a hand on Sam's arm. "Got a second?"

Sam stopped, turning anxious eyes to Lacey. "Sure. And before you say anything, I'm really sorry for being late this morning. It won't happen again. And I didn't see the missed call from you on my phone until after I got here."

"It's okay. I was just starting to worry about you."

Sam visibly tightened. "I, uh, had a doctor's appointment this morning that ran a little late."

Lacey was startled by how strained Sam's voice and demeanor became. "Sam," she said, "it's fine if you had a doctor's appointment. I was afraid that maybe Gary had tried to bother you again."

Sam shook her head vehemently. "Not at all. I swear."

Lacey watched her closely. "Okay. Give me a call next time so I won't be worried. Deal?"

Her relief obvious, Sam smiled. "Deal."

Mona came and went with a promise to call Lacey if Spencer surfaced. The steady flow of customers and paperwork drove the episode with Sam from Lacey's mind and by the time she checked the clock, half the day had disappeared.

Lacey pulled up the university's staff directory and dashed off an email to the members of her dad's department, imploring them to contact the police with anything out of the ordinary that they might have seen on Friday. Taking a deep breath, she refocused on finalizing the delivery orders for Sam, then went to check on her progress.

"Nice work," she said, touching Sam on the shoulder.

Sam whipped around as if she'd been branded, her eyes wide.

Lacey took a step back. "I didn't mean to startle you."

Clutching her chest, Sam gave a shaky laugh. "No. It's okay." She sat back down on the stool. "I guess I'm a little jumpy. I didn't hear you come in."

Lacey eyed her with concern. "Sam, I'm not trying to be nosey, but is something wrong? You seem to be a little stressed today."

"Everything's fine," she said, attempting a smile. "I guess I was just off in my own world." Sam pushed her loaded cart around Lacey. "I'll get loaded and be out of here in a few minutes."

Lacey was certain things weren't fine, but she let Sam off the hook. "Okay. I'll be out front. When you're done with the deliveries you can call it a day."

Sam nodded and stepped out of the cooler, looking everywhere but at Lacey as she snatched the van keys off the wall. Within minutes, Sam was gone.

As Lacey stepped into her office, a vile thought stopped her in her tracks. *Could Sam be involved in her dad's disappearance? Was that why she was so nervous?*

Lacey ordered herself to slow down. Sam was dealing with her own issues right now. Not everything was about her dad. Thinking about Sam's initial reaction to her dad's disappearance, Lacey took a step back, embarrassed by her momentary presumption of guilt. She trusted Sam. Plain and simple.

Keep your head on straight.

The morning's hours had ticked by and she'd done her best to ignore the frustrating lack of communication from the police. But why weren't they talking to her? They had to be working on something. Anything. Unwilling to wait any longer, she picked up the phone.

"Riley County Police."

"Detective Abrams, please."

As the receptionist placed her on hold, reality slammed into her. Again. Her hand shook as she clutched the phone. She was on hold, waiting to talk to a police officer because her dad was missing. As many times as she'd processed the situation in her mind, another wave of fear washed over her, threatening to take her under.

"One moment. I'll transfer you."

Lacey took several calming breaths before Abrams' voicemail message filled her ear, turning her fear, once again, into frustration. Biting her tongue, she left a short message before slamming the phone to its cradle. Seriously? Was it too much to ask for them to pick up the freaking phone?

She forced down a few tasteless bites of her microwaved lunch then tossed the remnants. God, she felt old. Rolling her tight shoulders, Lacey walked back her anger, cutting the detective some slack. He couldn't follow up on leads *and* sit at his desk waiting for her to call.

She'd never considered herself short on patience, but she was surely being tested now. With time on her hands, she forced her fears back into their box and started on the Christmas displays. She climbed the stairs to the storage area to grab some of the decorations, but before she even began sifting through the boxes, the insistent buzz of her cell phone vibrated her hip. Her stomach clenched. If Abrams was returning her call that quickly, he must have news.

Lacey snatched the phone out of her pocket and saw Caleb's number illuminating the screen, sending a streak of ambivalence racing through her.

She was thankful for his help. She was. He could probably open doors in her dad's industry that she wouldn't even know existed. But couldn't he do that from Chicago? Did he need to be here? Truth be told, his presence sparked feelings that she didn't have time or desire to analyze.

With a distinct lack of enthusiasm, she answered the call.

"How're you feeling? Any word from the police?" The low timbre of Caleb's voice nudged her emotions off-center, which didn't sit well.

"Nothing. I just left a message. I'm not really feeling the whole 'no news is good news' thing." She rubbed her forehead and blew out a breath. "If anything changes, I'll call you."

She was about to hang up when Caleb spoke again.

"How about this? Why don't we plan on dinner when you get done there? You pick the place."

Lacey paused. If the person on the other end of the line were anyone else, her decision would be simple. She'd go.

Caleb must have sensed her indecision. "You've got to eat, right? I've been kicking a few things around today that I'd like to run by you. How about if I come by your shop and pick you up?"

Her curiosity won out. Any new ideas would be worth the time. God knew she wasn't coming up with anything on her own. "Okay," she said finally. "But don't pick me up here. I'll be here til seven, so how about CoCo Bolos at…. seven-thirty? It's in the parking lot of Cedar Pointe Mall." Brief and in public, she thought. Perfect.

Between trips up and down the stairs hauling out holiday décor, Lacey called the police station three more times before three o'clock. Finally on her fourth call, she got through.

Abrams' update was concise and way too quick. The Jacobson family was still out of town so they hadn't interviewed Stan yet. The forensics team had been out to the farm again, and they were still reviewing email files, but there was nothing profound to report.

Pushing her hair back from her face, Lacey punched the END button on the phone and returned it to the charger. Her reservations about Spencer resurfaced. Was she making a mistake by not talking to the police about him?

The team working on her dad's case was competent, but her patience was wearing thin. He didn't just vanish into thin air, and she was more convinced than ever that his research was the reason behind the abduction.

Someone he'd trusted had taken him. She needed a list of everyone involved with his research. Maybe it was time to take matters into her own hands.

Chapter 9

Lacey walked into the restaurant, her eyes drawn to Caleb's tall form standing with his back to her at the hostess' podium. It was impossible not to notice him. His height and broad shoulders made him one of those guys who stood out in a crowd.

As if sensing her presence, he turned and held his arm out to her, his face set in a polite smile. "Your timing's perfect. They can seat us immediately."

Trying to ignore the warmth that spread from his hand at the small of her back, Lacey followed the hostess to their table.

"I like this place already," he commented in her ear as he pulled out her chair. "Smells good and spicy."

Lacey glanced around at the bright colors and the open exhibit kitchen that usually made for a fun dining experience. It was different though, through the prism of her dad's disappearance. Everything was different.

He seated himself. "So, did you hear from Abrams?"

She nodded. "Still no news." Getting right to her point, she caught and held his gaze. "Listen. I need your help. It'll just be a loan, but I need twenty-five hundred dollars. I've found a private investigator. He'll do all the research and get me information on everyone professionally connected to my dad."

Caleb frowned. "Slow down. What are you talking about?"

A waiter appeared at the table. Caleb glanced at the menu and ordered Coronas and the restaurant's signature wood-fired nachos, as his words twisted through Lacey's head.

What on earth had she been thinking? She wished she could take the words back. Her need to find her dad had obviously overruled her common sense. Caleb was the very last person she wanted to owe. She'd find another solution.

Shaking her head, she reached for her napkin. "Forget it. I'll figure something else out. I shouldn't have asked."

Caleb's hand closed over her icy fingers, his eyes boring into hers. "Lacey, I wasn't saying no. You almost trusted me for a minute. Let's go with that. Tell me what you found."

Lacey hesitated. The warmth from Caleb's gaze radiated through her, challenged her. She dropped her eyes to the table. It was much easier to concentrate that way. After she finished her pitch, she looked at him again. "Do you think he'd be able to uncover anything the police can't?"

He shrugged. "I don't know. To be honest, I have a couple of concerns. I'd be a little nervous that he'd step on the toes of the investigators. That's not as big of a deal to me. But I'm also afraid that if he got wind of the discovery, or somehow got his hands on the data, greed might overrule his ethics."

Lacey considered his words. "I agree that we don't want too many people in on the details of the investigation, but God, I need something to happen."

Caleb's thumb caressed her hand, sending a surprising current of heat to her stomach. What in the hell was wrong with her? This was Love-em-and-leave-em Mansfield. She obviously needed some sleep.

Caleb was talking again and she hurried to catch up. "See what else you can find out about him tomorrow. Then, if you still want to hire him, we'll do it, okay?"

"Okay." Lacey pulled her hand away and threaded her fingers together, anxious to put some distance between them. "Did you find out anything today?"

Caleb paused as the waiter brought the beers and a small dish of lime wedges. "I called Roger to see if he could place Stan Jacobson's name. I couldn't help thinking that I knew him from somewhere. Turns out, Roger has a better memory than me. Right before I went back to Europe, we

60

interviewed Stan for a position on the research team. I don't remember many details about it, only that he wasn't a good fit. Roger's going to look for his résumé to get a cell phone number, an email address, something portable."

"Good." Lacey picked up a slice of the fruit, squeezing the liquid into the bottle. She looked at Caleb just as she popped her finger into her mouth to catch an extra drop of the sweet juice. His eyes tracked her movements, sending heat to her cheeks.

Caleb cleared his throat and took a long pull from his beer. "Roger's worried. About your dad. And you. He wanted to come down, but I told him there was no point in one more person being frustrated here. Work has him stuck in Chicago, but he promised to do everything he can from there. It's a small industry."

Lacey nodded. "Thank him for me when you talk to him again. I'm sure he has a ton of contacts." She smiled at a distant memory. "It's probably been fifteen years since I've seen him. After Mom died, Roger came to visit several times. I think I used to call him Uncle Roger back then. It's been so long, though, I wonder if I'd even recognize him."

Taking a drink, she voiced the question that filled her mind. "Does he need you to go back?" She was surprised by the quick rush of panic that lanced through her. *Wasn't that what she wanted?*

Caleb's voice turned hard. "No. His problems are coming from R&D. Not my area of expertise. Ian Cox heads up that group, and he went on a rant today and told Roger he was taking some time off. They've been butting heads, but timing is terrible and Ian knows it. Personally, I think he's hell bent on punishing Roger, and he thinks this is the best way to do it." He blew out a breath. "I don't know why Roger puts up with Ian's bullshit. If it was up to me, he'd have been out on his ass a long time ago."

Lacey choked out a laugh. "Good friend of yours, huh?"

"Ian?" Caleb mouth twisted in a sardonic smile. "Let's just say that he and I don't see eye to eye on much."

Caleb's attention was diverted by the enormous platter of nachos the waiter placed in the center of the table. Lacey filled one of the serving plates and handed it to Caleb.

61

He tasted the food and groaned in appreciation. "You were right," he said between mouthfuls. "This is great." Winking, he motioned to her plate. "You better dig in quick or you'll end up on the short side of this split."

Lacey loaded her plate then ordered another round of beers. As Caleb distracted her with entertaining stories about his time abroad, the magnetic pull of his deep baritone made her almost forget why he was back in her life. Almost.

When the platter was cleared and removed, Caleb looked into her eyes, his tone and demeanor suddenly serious.

"Lacey, there's something else I wanted to talk to you about."

Her stomach did a little flip and she swallowed hard. What the hell was wrong with her tonight? Everything he said, every look, had her pulse quickening.

"I'm concerned. About you." He paused for a second and downed the rest of his beer.

She frowned. "What about me?" No way could he guess where her mind had wandered.

"I'm not trying to scare you, but there's at least a possibility that you could be in danger, too."

Well, that did the trick. She wasn't thinking about Caleb anymore. Surprised, she focused in on his words. "That's kind of a stretch, don't you think?"

"Maybe. Probably. But if I'm right, this involves your dad's research and I'd rather be safe than sorry."

Lacey squeezed her eyes closed. If Caleb thought she might be in danger, what did that mean for her dad? Her eyes closed against the bloodied and bruised images that flashed through her mind.

Leaning across the table, Caleb touched her hand.

She looked up, refocusing. The worry on his face told her he knew exactly what she was thinking. Lacey swallowed, the food she'd eaten sitting like a rock in her stomach. "I think I need to get out of here."

In a blink, Caleb settled the check and helped her into her jacket. The cold night air blasted them when they walked out, causing Lacey to shiver.

Caleb pulled her into his side as they hurried to her car. He opened the door and helped her inside. "I'll follow you to your place."

Her teeth chattered. "You don't need to —"

He closed the door, cutting off her words.

Lacey huddled into her jacket. She felt vulnerable, her fears exposed. In that state, the last thing she needed was to spend more time with Caleb. Why couldn't he be the man she remembered? The jerk who'd walked away.

Caleb pulled in her driveway a second after she did and Lacey tamped down the urge to run and barricade herself inside. She fumbled with her keys, and by the time she got the front door unlocked, he was standing quietly behind her.

"Let me go in first and have a look around. Stay here."

She rolled her eyes. "I'm sure everything is fine."

Once again, he ignored her. That was becoming a bad habit.

She, who could never be labeled a neat-freak, made a mental list of every cluttered corner of her house as she listened to him move from room to room in her small ranch. Could he hurry up already? Or better yet, just leave?

Caleb returned to the front door, trying to conjure reasons he should walk right past her and leave, but nothing came to mind. During dinner, he'd been tempted more times than he could count by the curve of her full lips. He'd wanted to kiss her then. He was dying to now.

She hooked her jacket on the hall tree and turned toward him. "Are we safe?"

Not even. Caleb's brain told him to move away, but his body wasn't listening. His hands slid up her arms, gently pulling her to him then his lips brushed hers, once, twice. Applying gentle pressure, he urged her to open her lips for him.

After a moment, Lacey stiffened, her eyes clouded and dark. "Stop." Her hands pushed against his chest. "I can't do this."

Caleb's eyes didn't leave hers. "I've wanted to do that since I saw you Saturday."

Backing out of his arms, she ran a shaking hand through her hair then grabbed the handle, opening the door wide. "You should go." Her voice had turned husky, stoking his desire. "Thank you for dinner," she murmured.

Caleb watched her for a moment longer, wishing she'd look at him, before stepping into the frosty night. "I'll call you tomorrow."

The soft click of the door closing was his answer.

Pulling into the dimly lit parking lot of the Ramada, Caleb could still feel the softness of Lacey's lips. She tasted and felt as good as he remembered.

Shit. He climbed out of the car and walked into the quiet hotel lobby, his conscience warring with him. Timing sucked. What kind of jerk was he to come on to her with everything else she was facing?

Sure, he'd thought about her a few times over the years, but he'd put it behind him. He knew he'd hurt her, knew she'd never forgive him. Before he arrived, reconnecting with Lacey hadn't crossed his mind. But right this second, he was having a damn hard time thinking about anything else.

Chapter 10

The shop was deserted. *Thank God.* Between the silence from the police, and her mental rehashing of last night's kiss, the day had been an exercise in frustration, and Lacey was ready to close up early. It was only thirty minutes. Would anyone even notice?

She cleaned out the cash register and took the contents to the office. Glancing at the blinking red light, she picked up her cell phone and listened to Caleb's second message. Again. She had no idea how to respond to his request to join him for dinner.

"Temporary insanity," she whispered. That's what had prompted her to forget everything and let Caleb kiss her last night. She hadn't analyzed his motives, but that was one big fat complication she didn't need. And now, she couldn't even figure out how to be the mature adult and return his phone call.

She turned her attention to the day's receipts and quickly tallied the deposit. Rubbing her hands over her face, she checked her watch. Exhaustion burned her eyes. Twenty-two minutes.

The front door chimed, interrupting her wandering thoughts. She stood up and sighed, trying to get excited about facing a customer. She loaded the bag and shoved in the deposit slip then pasted on a smile and walked out of the office.

At first glance, she didn't see anyone.

"Hello?"

A rush of air blew past her just before the pain exploded through her skull.

Damn it. Why didn't she answer?

Caleb paced his cracker-box hotel room like a caged tiger. He'd spent the day following up with some contacts Roger had given him and he put out a couple of fires for BioTech, but more than once he'd found his thoughts firmly fixated on last night. On Lacey.

The room was getting smaller. Caleb checked his phone again then clicked on the television. Frowning, he watched in disgust as people yelled and plotted behind each others' backs.

Caleb switched to the History Channel when another thought stopped him cold.

What if Lacey had received news about Bill?

Sure as hell she'd call him, wouldn't she? He bolted from his room and made the ten-minute drive to Lacey's house in six flat.

The house was dark and silent. After two perfunctory knocks, he pulled out his phone and dialed Mona. She assured him she hadn't heard anything new regarding the case and suggested that Lacey might be working late.

His shoulders tensed. *Or hiding from him.*

Jotting down the shop address, he thanked Mona then backed his sedan out of the short driveway. On the way over, he thought about the day he'd walked away. He'd had no choice. He believed that then. He'd known that moving to Chicago and building BioTech would take everything he had. And he'd needed to do it right, for himself and his siblings. There hadn't been room for anything, or anyone, else.

With Seth, his youngest brother, graduating from high school earlier in the year, Caleb finally felt like he could breathe a sigh of relief. Of course, the effort he put into raising his siblings paled in comparison to his sister Rachel's. While he'd made sure the family's financial needs were met, she'd managed the rest. He still didn't know how she'd made it through high school, then college, while standing in as full-time parent, counselor, and warden.

He made a mental note to call her. She'd said she'd call with a final date for their Christmas get-together, but he hadn't heard from her.

Caleb pulled into the parking stall closest to the door. He needed to believe that leaving Lacey had been the right decision, but seeing her now made him wonder how different his life could've been.

He opened the front door, curious to see this part of her life. Assuming Lacey was in the back office, Caleb raised his voice. "Hello? Anybody here? Lacey, your sign says you're only supposed to be open until seven. You want me to – oh, my God, Lacey!"

Caleb's heart stopped as his gaze landed on her prone body sprawled out on the floor at the end of the long main aisle. A giant rubber band squeezed his chest as he skidded on his knees to her side. He dialed nine-one-one, raw panic clawing at his throat, then searched for a pulse with shaking hands. Relief flooded his system when he found it, strong under her pale skin.

His hands skimmed her hair, the sticky blood on his fingers from her scalp forcing bile into his throat. He wanted to lift her, to hold her, but he didn't dare. The operator kept him calm as his eyes darted between her face and her chest, confirming every few seconds that she was still breathing.

"Where the hell are they?" he growled into the phone. As the man started to respond, Caleb's ears caught the distant sirens, their volume increasing steadily until he saw the flashing lights out front.

"Back here. Hurry," Caleb barked.

Two police officers forced him to step back as the paramedics knelt to examine her. Fists clenched, he watched them descend on her. The skilled techs worked in tandem as they quickly put on the collar, started the IV line and secured her to the spine board.

His gut churned. "She's going to be okay, right?"

The paramedic closest to him, a young looking kid with freckles, glanced up. "She's got a good bump and a gash on the back of her head. Cut's not that big, but they do tend to bleed quite a bit. We'll know more when we get her to Mercy."

The policeman closest to Caleb pulled out a notepad. "You're Caleb Mansfield, right? You called this in?"

Caleb nodded, his gaze never leaving the technicians as they worked over Lacey.

"Any idea how long she's been unconscious?"

"I don't know. I got here around six-fifty."

Lacey moaned and tried to stretch against the straps securing her as she was lifted onto the gurney. Caleb pushed around the technician and leaned down by Lacey's ear.

"Lacey, can you hear me?" Worry sharpened his voice, but he was rewarded as Lacey opened one eye.

"My…head…hurts," she croaked. She frowned as she again tried to raise her arm.

He laid his palm on her cheek and kept his voice steady. "Shhh. Don't move. They're taking you to the hospital. It's going to be okay, Babe. I promise."

The paramedics loaded Lacey into the waiting ambulance. Caleb climbed in as the medics secured the gurney. He watched the red and blue lights from the two police cruisers flicker across her face through the open doors, as fear and anger warred within him.

Lacey woke again and squinted against the brightness, her eyes a little clearer. "What happened?" she whispered.

He put his hand over hers to keep her from dislodging the oxygen sensor from her finger. "Looks like your head took a blow. And I thought you were hard-headed." His attempt at humor earned him a weak smile. He was about to ask her what she remembered when the paramedic looked over at him.

"Sir, we're taking her now. You can follow us." A police officer climbed in and took a seat on the opposite side of the gurney.

Caleb nodded. He squeezed Lacey's hand. "I'll be right there with you." He looked out the back door at the still bright storefront then turned back to her. "Lacey," he said softly, "can you tell me where you keep the keys? I'll lock up the store then get to the hospital."

Lacey's eyes closed, her forehead puckering in a frown. "My purse," she whispered after a minute. "My purse is in the desk drawer in the office."

Caleb touched her shoulder, encouraged that her thoughts were clear. "Okay, I'll be over before you're even allowed visitors."

The remaining three officers stood near the counter talking in hushed tones. As Caleb approached, a man whose badge identified him as Officer Drummond turned and handed him a card. "Officer Tracy went with Ms. Jordan to get her statement. We'd like to ask you a few more questions."

Caleb nodded. In addition to answering their questions, he filled them in on Bill's disappearance and suggested the possibility that the attack might be related.

"If this incident is connected to her father's disappearance, it's likely that Ms. Jordan's still in danger." The officer rubbed his chin and frowned. "Although, it doesn't make much sense unless the intent was just to scare her."

Caleb had already reached both those conclusions. His frustration peaked as he checked his watch. He hated pieces that didn't fit. "Are you done here? I need to get to the hospital." He found Lacey's purse as the officers finished up and followed them out the door.

Thumping the steering wheel as he waited at a red light, Caleb reminded himself for the hundredth time that Lacey was alive and safe. He tried to take a deep breath, but couldn't pull enough air into his lungs. God, the image of her lying there, still as death, was burned into his brain. He shuddered, then blinked as a sudden thought struck him.

Admit it. You want a second chance.

He shook his head, trying to shove the idea aside. Now wasn't the time to think about it, but it settled deep in his gut like it belonged there.

Caleb broke every speed limit on the way to Mercy Regional. As he parked his car in the nearly deserted lot behind the emergency room entrance, one thing became crystal clear. He wasn't letting her out of his sight again. Period.

He slammed the car door and entered the hospital, marching directly to the admission desk on the right.

69

It took less than two minutes to find out that Lacey was awake and in examination room E, but it felt like twenty. A wan smile lit her clear amber eyes as he approached the bed, and the weight on his chest receded slightly.

Ignoring the police officer, Caleb studied her as he walked to her side. "How you feeling? What did the doctor say?"

"You brought my bag. Thank you," she said softly. "Other than a killer headache, I'm fine. I was awake and aware by the time I got here and the dizziness and blurry vision are gone. The doctor said something about a concussion, but they won't confirm without the imaging results."

He nodded. "Do you remember what happened?"

She shook her head then winced. "Damn. That wasn't a good idea," she whispered. The color in her cheeks faded to match the white of her hospital gown. "They said they can't give me anything for the pain, but it's getting better."

Caleb caressed her arm as she battled the wave of nausea. He kept his touch light, but fury caused his pulse to race.

Releasing a deep breath, Lacey opened her eyes. "I was explaining to Officer Tracy that I'd decided to close a few minutes early. I'd finished the deposit when the front door chimed. When I got out there, I didn't see anyone. Pain shot up the back of my head and then the next thing I remember is being in the ambulance."

Caleb clenched his jaw, and the edges of his vision hazed red. His hands fisted as he envisioned getting his hands on the son of a bitch.

Officer Tracy interrupted Caleb's thoughts. "Did you leave the deposit bag in the office?"

"Yes. I remember laying it down." Lacey paused when she saw the look on his face. "Oh, no. It's gone, isn't it?" She turned her head toward Caleb then sighed. "Of course it is."

"We need to find out if anything, other than the deposit bag, was taken. Who else would be able to help us with that?"

"My partner, Paige, is in Mexico on her honeymoon. She's been gone since last week. And I'd prefer she not be notified of this incident. I'll be able to tell you tomorrow if there's anything else missing."

70

"What about employees?"

"We only have one but she's too new to know much about the inventory."

Caleb noticed the pucker between Lacey's brows and knew she needed a break.

"Officer, if you have any other questions, can they wait until tomorrow? I'm sure Ms. Jordan will feel much more capable of giving you the information you need then."

The officer looked at Lacey then back at Caleb, nodding. "All right." He snapped his notebook closed. "They'll have dusted the place for prints and if we're lucky we'll get one or two to run through the system. What's the best way for us to contact you?"

Lacey gave him all her numbers and thanked him. After he left, Lacey turned to Caleb. "You have a knack for being at the right place at the right time," she whispered. "Thank you."

Resisting the urge to pull her into his arms, he reached up and brushed a tendril of hair from her cheek. "I'd intended to talk you into spending the evening with me again, but this wasn't exactly what I had in mind."

Lacey smiled as a man whipped the curtain aside and walked around to the other side of Lacey's bed. His crisp manner identified him immediately as Lacey's doctor. He looked up from his notes. "Well, it looks like good news. The CT scans don't indicate any cranial bleeding. Without knowing how long you were unconscious, it's difficult to know the severity of the concussion but," he pulled out his pen light and examined her pupils, "you're responding well. I think I'd like to keep you overnight, just as a precaution."

"Doctor, I can't stay here overnight," Lacey pleaded. Hospitals made her nervous, reminded her of her mom. The fear was irrational, but that didn't make it any less real. "I'm feeling so much better." She watched the doctor scan her chart then glance at Caleb.

"Are you responsible for her?"

"Yes."

"No," Lacey said at the same time.

The doctor looked at them in confusion. "Let me rephrase that. Are you responsible for getting her home tonight?" Caleb looked at Lacey, waiting for her to answer.

She paused, avoiding his gaze. "Yes. He's responsible for getting me home tonight."

The doctor finally nodded. "If you're feeling up to going home, I'm not going to order you to be admitted as long as you have someone there with you." He looked at Caleb before turning to her again with a smile. "I will order you, however, to take it easy for the next few days. No contact sports and no overdoing it."

"I promise."

Caleb listened to the doctor's instructions. Words like disorientation and loss of consciousness fired him up all over again. He gathered up Lacey's things, his hands shaking with anger. By God, he'd find out who the hell had done this to her.

Chapter 11

Feeling almost human, Lacey settled into the passenger seat of Caleb's car. Still, finding a nice, quiet place and turning off the world sounded really appealing.

"I'm not sure how you pulled that off, but I was certainly impressed."

Lacey opened one eye and frowned at Caleb's grin. "What?"

"I bet you use that same technique to get out of speeding tickets don't you?"

She closed her eyes again, her lids heavy. "For your information, I hardly ever speed. It's not worth the risk of getting caught."

Lacey dozed, then lifted her head, squinting against the bright lights of the hotel parking lot. "What are we doing here?" she mumbled.

"I'll just be a minute."

Lacey pulled Caleb's jacket from the back seat, his scent reminding her of woods, and spice, and a long ago summer. Nestling into the cocoon of warmth, her eyes slid shut again until she heard the back door open and watched Caleb toss his bag on the back seat.

His bag.

Instantly awake, she sat up in her seat and shot him a look. "What are you doing?"

"Taking you home."

"I know that," she squeaked. "But you don't need your bag to take me home."

"Doctor's orders. Somebody needs to make sure you're okay."

"I just said that so they'd release me," she sputtered. "I don't want or need you –"

His hard gaze cut her off. "You've made that perfectly clear, but here's the deal." His voice was as unyielding as his eyes. "We don't know anything about what's happening – whether this has to do with your dad or not. So, until we find him and your life gets back to normal, I'm your shadow. Got it?"

Lacey stared out the window, clenching her teeth to stop the words threatening to force their way out of her mouth. By the time they pulled up to her house, her head was pounding again.

She dug around in her bag for her keys. Pulling them out, she reached for the door handle, but the second she looked away, Caleb swiped the keys from her hand.

"Stay here," he commanded, "and lock the door."

Lacey closed her eyes, her frustration growing by the minute. Did she have control of any part of her life? She took a deep breath, struggling to hold back tears. Truth be told, tonight's events had shaken her, and she didn't want to be alone. But being alone with Caleb created more problems than it solved.

When he came back for her, she walked past him and avoided eye contact, dropping her bag on the recliner in the living room. She refused to let him see her break down. She didn't want his sympathy. She wanted him to leave.

Lacey didn't speak a word as she started down the hall toward the privacy of the bathroom. She'd only made it a few steps when she felt firm hands on her shoulders, preventing her escape.

"Let go of me," she ground out, tears clogging her throat.

Instead of letting go, he gently forced her to turn around. He stood, unmoving, until she looked up at him, the hot sting of tears pricking her eyes.

"Don't be nice to me," she warned. "I am totally pissed off. I have a headache from hell. My business was robbed. My dad's been missing for four days and no one can find him." She shook his hands off her shoulders then winced from the sharp movement. "And now, you're here. What the hell else can go wrong?"

***

Lacey made the water as hot as she could stand it, then added her favorite bath salts. The soothing aroma mingled with the steam as she climbed into the deep tub. Sighing, she trailed the water across her neck and back, pushing away the stress of the day.

Careful to avoid the bump on her head, she leaned back in the tub, allowing the water to cover her to her neck, and closed her eyes. Why was she so keyed up about Caleb? She wasn't a nineteen-year-old girl anymore who believed in knights in shining armor. So what if there was still a tiny corner of her heart that wished things would've turned out differently between them? Another sigh escaped her lips. That was a lifetime ago and there was no going back.

Calmer and in more control by the time the water cooled, Lacey toweled off then wrapped herself in the old terry robe hanging on the back of the bathroom door. She belted it tight then wiped the steam from the mirror.

Distorted image or not, she looked like hell. No amount of make-up would disguise the dark smudges under her eyes. It was a darn good thing she wasn't out to impress anybody.

Lacey ignored the little lazy flop her heart made as she walked into her bedroom and spotted Caleb. Did he have to look so damn good? As he placed a tray on her bedside table then turned down her comforter, she was mesmerized by the play of muscles under his cotton shirt.

He glanced up then made a sweeping gesture with his hand. "I made you some tea and toast," he said. "Did the bath help?"

Lacey realized she was staring. "Um, yes. Very much." Her gaze moved to the bed, the thought of crawling under her heavy comforter almost irresistible.

Caleb crossed the room in two strides. "Come on. You look like you're about to fall over."

Nodding, Lacey let him lead her to the bed. "Your blankets…"

"I'll figure it out. You get some rest. I'll be back in later to wake you. Doctor's orders." He gave her shoulders a slight squeeze then left the room.

Lacey waited for the click of the door latch, then gingerly slid off her robe, trading it for comfy cotton pajamas. Not exactly Victoria's Secret.

Doesn't matter.

Sighing, she snuggled under the sheets and took a sip of the still-warm tea, shelving that little budding fantasy her contrary heart had conjured. Caleb was here for her safety. Nothing more, nothing less. She could trust him to that point. And, she admitted, she did feel safer with him in the house.

She rolled over onto her side as flashes of the kiss they'd shared skittered through her mind, the familiarity of his lips an aching reminder of the past. She couldn't help but wonder where it might've lead if she hadn't stopped it. Squeezing her eyes closed, she tried to block the thoughts. *Better not go there.*

Oh, she had no doubt that Caleb would protect her. But who would protect her from him?

Caleb lay on his back on the twin-size bed across the hall from Lacey, hands stacked behind his head, staring at the ceiling. He'd originally intended to sleep on the sofa, but he wanted to be closer, to hear her if she needed him.

Stretching out his legs, he allowed his feet to dangle over the end of the too-short mattress and considered Lacey's reaction. She didn't want him here. That much was obvious. But, whether she wanted to admit it or not, she needed him. It wasn't exactly a positive because Lord knew she wasn't happy about it, but he'd take it.

She'd taken one hell of a blow, though. The now familiar tightness in his chest began again, but he let the rush of anger go by this time, his mind trying to put it all together.

Spencer still hadn't shown. Was he somehow a player? Caleb had tried to rule it out, but couldn't. He knew the kid didn't have a job, but would he risk doing something like this for money? Or was his intention to hurt Lacey, or maybe scare her? No way was it a random robbery. Too coincidental.

Caleb didn't have a damned answer to a single question, and it was driving him crazy. He shoved himself off the bed and paced the room, but being confined in such a small space didn't help at all. Grabbing a tee shirt and boxers, he hoped a quick shower would take the edge off his frustration.

Lacey's scent still lingered in the bathroom, which sent his frustration to a whole different level. Damn, she smelled good. It took every bit of willpower he'd had to walk out of her bedroom. She'd looked so innocent, but so hot, in that little robe. He climbed into the shower. If he didn't come up with a different line of thinking, he'd be switching the water to cold in a hurry.

The shower did little to ease his mind, on either front. He passed Lacey's door, then paused as low whimpers reached his ears. He threw his damp towel down the hallway and slipped into her room. He realized the problem as soon as he pulled the chain on the small Tiffany lamp next to the bed. Sometime during her sleep, Lacey had rolled onto her back putting pressure on her injury.

He gently turned her onto her side and nudged her shoulder. She moaned softly but didn't wake up, then sighed into her pillow.

"Lacey," he whispered.

No response.

"Lacey," he tried again, more forcefully.

She frowned then opened her eyes, confusion in their depths. "Caleb?" she whispered.

"I need to wake you up, remember?" He watched her beautiful eyes shift from bewilderment to understanding.

She nodded slowly then scooted to a sitting position. "I'm awake."

He sat next to her. "Good. What's your address?"

She frowned again and rattled off the information. "I'm okay," she said, her voice husky from sleep. She scooted back down onto her pillow, her legs pushing him off the bed. "Can I go back to sleep now?"

Caleb looked at her closed eyes and smiled. She wasn't waiting for his permission. He brushed her hair back from her face then placed a soft kiss on her forehead. He stepped toward the door, but stopped. What if he didn't hear her next time?

He spied the chaise in the corner. Without a second thought, he got a blanket from his room and, shoving a throw pillow behind his head, settled in for the night.

Lacey's peaceful, even breathing lulled him as he thought about the bizarre circumstances that had brought him back into her life. Until now, he'd never considered why none of the other women he'd dated over the years had been long-term. But now, it hit him right between the eyes. *None of those women were Lacey.* The familiar edge of restlessness whispered through him. Is this what was missing?

Caleb looked around the room in the filtered lamp light. The rest of her house shouted functionality, but Lacey must've gotten permission from her landlord to make over the bedroom because it was simply her – all soft colors and soft pillows. Lots of pillows.

Before his mind could go in another direction, he continued his inspection, his eyes drawn to her white dresser where several pictures stood in assorted frames. Caleb perused the images casually until one caught his eye. He leaned forward, squinting.

He recognized the photo Lacey had taken of him and Bill the week before he'd left the farm. He fell back against the chair, a hint of a smile on his lips. Could you really hate someone and still keep his picture in your bedroom? He hoped the answer, for Lacey at least, was no.

Why wouldn't he let her sleep?

Lacey turned away from the tap on her shoulder.

"Lacey," Caleb whispered again. "Do you want to go to work today? We didn't set the alarm."

Lacey growled and rolled away from Caleb's annoyingly chipper voice. A minute later, her eyes snapped open. She struggled to sit up, pulling the covers up to her chin. "What are you doing in my room?"

God, she sounded like an outraged virgin in a Shakespearean melodrama, but she couldn't for the life of her understand what was going on.

Caleb smiled. "What do you remember about last night?"

She looked up at him warily. "What *should* I remember about last night?" Surely, she wouldn't have…no. No way. She would've remembered that.

His hair was tousled and he hadn't seen a razor yet, but the smile on his face warmed his crystal blue eyes, making her toes curl under the covers. Her face heated and she imagined she was red to her hairline.

She needed coffee. Now. Her brain barely functioned before she'd had her first cup.

Caleb had mercy on her. "I came in here last night to wake you. You'd rolled onto your back. I stayed to make sure you didn't do it again." He raised an eyebrow. "But I'd probably be okay with any other explanations you'd like to come up with."

The events of last night snapped into focus. She raised her hand, flinching as she tested the tender bump. Climbing out of bed, she wrapped the robe over her pajamas, then nudged him in the shoulder to get him to move. "I think we'd be better off sticking to the truth."

Lacey rolled her shoulders, working out the kinks. She hadn't expected to wake up so sore. Silence stretched as she felt Caleb's gaze follow her to the closet. What she wouldn't have given for a walk-in so she could duck the sexy energy coming from him. She pulled out a pair of black wool slacks and a black, ivory and green silk shirt then turned to face him.

He stepped toward her as she laid the clothes on the bed. Clasping her wrists, he held them at her sides. All the humor left his face. "No BS," he said. "How's the head today?"

His nearness made it hard to breathe, and the intensity of his gaze mesmerized her. There was something about his rugged look in the mornings that had always appealed to her. She pulled away from him and, glancing around for a distraction, settled on straightening the covers. "I feel a lot better this morning," she assured him. "Very minor headache. The bump's still a little swollen, but even that's not as sore as it was last night."

"Do you want to close the shop today?"

She stood, frowning. "No. People are counting on me and it's too much for Sam to handle on her own. Plus, I want to take a look around. See if anything else is out of place."

"The police will want to interview you again today. I'll hang out at the shop with you and Sam and maybe you can put me to work," he said.

"Maybe," she said, slipping past him. "Coffee first."

***

Lacey sat at the desk in the small office. Caleb stood behind her, leaning casually against the refrigerator, arms crossed over his chest. The quiet of the morning vanished as the police joined them.

Detective Abrams, accompanied by a petite woman who identified herself as Officer Maria Lopez, sat in the two chairs opposite Lacey's at the desk.

Officer Lopez, who'd been on scene the night before, walked Lacey through the events leading up to her attack. "So far, we know that the assailant took the deposit bag. Any idea of how much cash they got?"

Lacey pulled out her copy of the deposit slip and sales receipts from the drawer on her right. "The bulk of what we have are debit and credit transactions." She shook her head, frowning at the receipt. "We had a pretty good day, but there was only about four hundred dollars in cash. I'm sure whoever did this was disappointed. That was a whole lot of risk for not much money."

Officer Lopez stopped writing and looked up at Lacey. "I've seen worse than this for a lot less money. And you're the third small business hit in the past week. Criminals who take this kind of risk are generally either greedy or desperate or both," she said.

"That's assuming this particular criminal was after the money," Caleb interjected, looking at Abrams. "Even with the other crimes, I hope you're not ruling out the possibility that this is connected to her father's case."

Abrams shook his head. "That's why I'm here with Officer Lopez. The timing is a little suspect." He looked at Lacey. "However, until we have some kind of motive to go on in your dad's disappearance, it's hard to connect the dots."

Officer Lopez turned her attention to Lacey again. "Have you noticed anything else missing this morning?"

Lacey shrugged her shoulders. "I looked around when I got here. The only other thing I noticed was an antique verdigris vase. There was a set of three on a table near the far corner of the shop, but there were only two there this morning. The largest of the set was missing."

Abrams glanced at Lopez. "Yeah, we have that one," he confirmed. "We think it was the weapon the assailant used. It was on the floor near you last night when we arrived. There were no fingerprints. It'd been wiped clean."

Lacey put her elbows on the desk and rubbed her temples. No doubt last night had freaked her out, but it was nothing next to the topic that haunted most every moment. She opened her eyes and looked at the Detective. "So I'm assuming there's nothing new regarding my dad?"

His sharp features softened. "I'm sorry. I know this is frustrating, but we're working every angle. There's an email from a Dr. Ian Cox that we're following up on, but other than that we're still looking for a concrete lead."

Lacey ignored the stab of pain in her skull as she swiveled toward Caleb.

He came and stood next to her. "From Ian? What did it say?"

Abrams looked at Caleb. "You know the guy?"

"We work together. What did he say?"

"It wasn't threatening, per se, more of a rant about Bill always winning. How unfair life was. That kind of stuff. There's no reference to anything specific."

Lacey clutched her hands in her lap, her heart constricting. She felt Caleb's hand on her shoulder. "So what does that mean? Is someone talking to him?"

Abrams nodded. "They're interviewing him today. His boss, too." Holding up his hand, he cautioned them. "This may be completely unrelated. We just want to be as thorough as possible."

Caleb filled the detective in on Ian's frequent mood swings. "Maybe I should make a few phone calls myself, find out what the hell's going on."

Lacey studied the hard contours of Caleb's face, his anger simmering through his fingertips.

"Please, don't," Abrams advised. "Let us work through this, find out what we can. We'll keep you in the loop. I promise."

Lacey tried to swallow her fear as she led the officers to the door. Every minute, every hour, that passed she felt her father slipping away from her. Caleb had taken her seat when she returned to the office, his voice loud in the small room as he barked into his cell phone.

"Details, Roger. Give me everything you can remember about his behavior. What's been going on in his life?" He paused.

Lacey sat down across the desk, her eyes trained on him as he listened to the voice in his ear. He made eye contact with her a few times in between scribbling notes.

"Okay, call me after you talk to the police today." Caleb stood, shoving a hand through his hair.

Lacey hurried around the desk. "What? What did Roger say?"

Caleb blew out a breath. "Everything I thought, and worse. Ian's been drinking. A lot. Over the past several months, it's apparently gotten out of control. And his attitude about work, about life in general, has taken a big nose dive."

Lacey's fears were mirrored in the worry lines on Caleb's face. "Why would he be angry with my dad? I don't understand. Did my dad ever come up in conversations you had with him?"

Caleb eyes sharpened to cold blue steel. "I wouldn't have been part of any casual conversations with Ian. Our relationship is strictly business, and barely functional. Something's going on there, though. No doubt about it. He's changed."

"I know it's a small industry, but why would he target my dad?" She paused, fingers of fear crawling down her spine. "Do you think he knew?"

"I don't know. God, I just saw him Friday. What if the bastard —"

Lacey met his gaze. Her heart pounded in her ears, drowning out the end of that thought. Unwilling to think about the things over which she had no control, she took a deep breath then squeezed his hand across the desk. "That's a big if. But, if he's involved, the police are onto him. Let's wait and hear what they have to say."

Caleb's grip softened, but he didn't let go of her hand. Lacey, sensing he'd gotten his anger under control, stood and pulled him up with her. "Come on, we've got work to do." Dragging him out of the office, she led him to the storage room and pointed out the large pieces she needed for the front window display. "Here you go, big guy. Knock yourself out."

Lacey called Mona, the stress from the morning igniting a dull throb in her skull. After giving her a very condensed and sanitized version of last night's events and filling her in on what they'd learned from Abrams, she made it through the morning by keeping her movements to a minimum and letting Sam handle most of the customers.

But by late afternoon, with still no word from the police, her headache was so intense, she felt physically ill. Squinting, she focused on the inventory sheets, but since the columns of numbers wouldn't cooperate, she shoved them back in the folder. She'd try again later.

Sam offered to stay and close up the shop, but even through the haze of her blinding headache, Lacey could see the dark circles under Sam's eyes. And she'd been trying to hide her yawns all day.

"You go on home," Lacey said, forcing a tight smile as she settled onto one of the stools behind the counter. "Caleb's here. He can help me close." Lacey glanced at Caleb, her brow furrowing at his sharp frown.

"If you're sure..." Sam began.

"I'm sure. I'll see you tomorrow morning."

Sam grabbed her jacket and pulled her keys out of her pocket. While Caleb walked her out, Lacey went to the office to close her eyes for a minute. She wasn't at all prepared for the arrival of Hurricane Caleb.

"What the hell was that all about?" he insisted, his voice angry.

Lacey looked up at his imposing form in the doorway, pain blurring her vision. "What?" she asked.

He shook his head. "Why did you let her go? You're in obvious pain, your eyes are bloodshot, and you look like you got run over by a freight train."

Despite feeling just exactly as he'd described her, her lips twisted in a ghost of a grin. "That good, huh?"

She didn't get even a hint of a smile out of him. He folded his arms and continued to stare at her, the muscle in the side of his jaw twitching.

Lacey sighed. "She was so tired she could barely stay on her feet."

Caleb looked at her like her head injury might've caused permanent damage. "*She* was tired?" He sat down on the corner of the desk, his leg just inches from her. "Correct me if I'm wrong, but aren't you the one who took a blow to the head less than twenty-four hours ago?"

"And," she continued as if he hadn't interrupted, "I couldn't leave her here alone. If someone came tonight and hurt her, I could never live with myself." She closed her eyes again. "Give me a couple of minutes. I'll be fine."

Silence reigned and Lacey, proud that she'd won the battle of wills, assumed Caleb had left the office. But when she opened her eyes, he was leaning against the door frame, his gaze tender.

Oh, crap. Please don't look at me that way.

She made an effort to refocus on her ledger, but now it was more than just her headache keeping her from it. Instead of numbers, all she could see was Caleb. He seemed so strong, so safe. Picking up her pencil, she waited for her jaded heart to remind her that he was anything but.

Caleb shoved off the wall and grabbed a bottle of water out of the fridge. "When's the last time you took something for the pain?"

Lacey gathered her wayward thoughts and stored them away. "I don't know. Probably noonish."

Grabbing her bag, Caleb rummaged through it until he came up with the bottle of Tylenol. He handed Lacey the water and the pills then whipped the paperwork around to the other side of the desk.

He shoved the inventory sheets back in her folder. "That can wait until tomorrow." Barely looking up, he gathered the day's receipts and began tallying the numbers. "Let me do the deposit for you. We'll drop it by the bank then grab some take-out Chinese and go home and relax. There's nothing else we can do tonight, anyway. I guarantee you a nice, quiet evening. Sound good?"

And she thought *she'd* won the battle of wills? Sighing, she settled back in her seat. It sounded wonderful, Lacey admitted. And that was exactly the problem.

Chapter 12

Lacey curled up on her couch wrapped in a blanket with containers of lo mein and cashew chicken balanced on her lap. Aside from the call from Roger that had set her nerves on edge, the evening was nice and quiet, just like Caleb had promised.

He handed her a bottle of water then sat down in her recliner. Funny, that chair always seemed so big and inviting when she sat in it, but his tall muscular frame dwarfed it.

"How's the headache? Getting any better?"

"Much," she said, thankful that the Tylenol was winning the fight. She dug her fork into her food but her eyes followed him. Caleb had changed into clean jeans. His gray cotton shirt hugged his biceps and he hadn't bothered with shoes and socks. He seemed so relaxed. And so damn sexy.

Holy cow, Lacey. Focus. It's going to be a long night if you keep fixating on how he fills out his Levis. She cleared her throat. "So, was there anything else to Roger's interview today?"

Caleb had taken the call on the drive home. Her head had cleared enough by the time he'd picked up the food that she was able to listen to Caleb's recap, but she needed to hear more. Maybe some detail had escaped him.

He sighed. "It was pretty cut and dried. They interviewed Roger at the office. Just routine questions about Ian's background and behavior. What disturbed Roger though, was Ian's call to him after his interview, accusing Roger of planting the email. I don't know. I'll be anxious to hear Abrams' take on the whole thing."

Lacey took one more bite of her dinner before shoving the containers aside. Her mind wouldn't let her rest. Should she go to Chicago? Confront Ian herself? "Maybe we should call Abrams tonight." Reaching for her phone, she felt Caleb's hand cover hers.

"Lacey, if anything happens tonight, he'll call you." He pulled her to her feet and she let him wrap his arms around her, his hands rubbing slow circles on her back. "He's doing all he can, Babe."

Lacey pulled back, ignoring the little spike in her pulse from his casual endearment. "I know. You're right." The muscles in her neck tightened and her headache started again. Rolling her shoulders, she closed her eyes.

"Hey," he coaxed. "How about a movie?"

Her gaze was caught by the warmth in his eyes. She doubted that he really cared to watch a movie, but she appreciated what he was doing. Deciding to play along, she nodded. "Okay."

"I'll make the popcorn, you pick the movie."

Her lower back still tingled where his clasped hands had rested. Lord, she needed to stop thinking about him like that. He probably had no idea what kind of havoc he was wreaking. As she perused her limited selection of movies, opting for a light comedy, she resolved again to get her thoughts under control.

Caleb returned from the kitchen, placing a big bowl of popcorn on the coffee table. "Scooch over."

Lacey's eyes widened as he settled in next to her. He turned her so her back faced him, and she held her breath, waiting to see what he'd do next. She didn't want to overreact, but his nearness made it a little difficult to breathe.

"Relax," he whispered. His hands lightly kneaded the bunched muscles in her neck and back.

Sighing, Lacey ignored the distant clang of warning bells in her head and took his advice. Truth be told, she lacked the willpower to move away. It felt so good to let her thoughts go, to let the unanswered questions that defined her life slip away for a few minutes.

The unwelcome thought that she'd spent many evenings like this with Jason flitted through her mind. It had been months since she'd discovered the truth about the lying jerk, and despite Paige's matchmaking attempts, Lacey had thus far avoided getting back on that particular bicycle.

Of course, this was hardly the same situation. She and Caleb weren't in a relationship, and they definitely weren't sleeping together. Oh, and Caleb wasn't married.

Lacey watched the story unfold on the screen, cuddled against Caleb. The rumble in his broad chest when he laughed made her smile, but the warning bells were sounding like a sonic boom as the heat from his body enveloped her. Her brain told her to move. Her body refused to cooperate.

When the movie ended, Lacey sighed and looked up at Caleb, half-expecting him to be asleep.

Big mistake.

Without a word, he sat up, holding her tight against him, their faces inches apart. She couldn't help staring. He really was gorgeous.

And he was waiting for her to make the next move. Her gaze fell to his hard mouth, and her resistance fled. She couldn't come up with a single logical reason not to kiss him. In fact, the only thought she was able to hang on to was how his mouth would feel on hers. She raised her hand and gently traced his eyebrow and the strong line of his jaw, amazed at the strength and power she saw there.

Passion ignited in Caleb's eyes. He pulled her to him, his lips taking possession of hers. His tongue slid across her lips, enticing her to open to him. The moment she did, he plundered her mouth with his tongue. She returned the dueling love play, the heat of the kiss consuming her.

A throaty moan escaped Lacey's lips and she felt Caleb's warm hands under her shirt, hard against her back, pulling her into even closer contact with his powerful body. Her hands skimmed his rock hard arms, reveling in the solid heat of him.

Lacey lost track of time as Caleb overwhelmed her with sweet kisses on her eyes, her nose, the sensitive spot behind her ear, before again capturing her lips.

When Caleb finally ended his assault, Lacey was gasping for breath. She watched him calm his own breathing as he moved shaking hands to either side of her flushed face. He didn't speak, but under the heat of his intense gaze, she could do nothing but stare back at him. Before she realized what was happening, he sat up, separating their bodies.

The air chilled her flushed skin. There were probably several things she could've said, but none came to mind as Lacey struggled to regain her composure. Listening to Caleb's sexy growl wasn't helping.

"Your doctor warned you to limit your physical activity for twenty-four to forty-eight hours. What I have in mind right now would definitely be considered a full contact sport." He leaned toward her, placing feather soft kisses on her lips, as if he couldn't quite get enough.

Lacey jumped as Caleb's phone vibrated in his pocket. Thank God for small favors. He must've known she wasn't winning this battle on her own. She pulled back, her voice trembling. "Maybe you should answer that."

As he stepped away and checked his caller ID, Lacey stood, jerking her shirt straight, anger at her own lack of self control sending heat to her cheeks. So much for her mental pep talk earlier. One look from the guy and she'd gone all mushy. Hoping she didn't look as flustered as she felt, Lacey turned and noticed Caleb's scowl as he ignored the call.

"Work call?"

"No." He shoved the phone back in his pocket. "I'll call them back."

Lacey nodded but didn't make eye contact. All the words she wanted to say eluded her. She crossed her arms and turned away. "Good night, then."

She didn't wait for a response. Behind the closed bedroom door she let out a deep shuddering breath. She had to figure out a plan to avoid temptation in the future. Trusting Caleb wasn't an option, and much to her dismay, she'd just proven she could no longer trust herself.

Alone, Caleb sat back down on the couch, running a hand through his hair. He should probably thank his sister for ruining the moment. Because even though he'd intended to take things slow, his body had come up with at least fifteen reasons to ignore his best intentions.

Yeah, he might remember to thank her later. Right now, he wasn't feeling particularly grateful.

***

Thursday came and went as a bundle of frustrated emotions for Lacey. Her first phone call of the morning came from Detective Abrams. He gave her a brief rundown on the interviews with Roger and Ian, but only time would tell if the surveillance on Ian would yield any results.

If that wasn't enough frustration, Caleb once again insisted on staying with her at the shop. How was she supposed to develop a plan to avoid temptation if she couldn't avoid the tempter? She found her train of thought deserting her almost every time she looked over at him.

She knew she was in trouble when Mrs. Canton caught her staring.

"He's quite a handsome young man."

Lacey jumped a foot. The sweet old woman had to be at least eighty, but she had eyes like a hawk. "Mrs. Canton. I didn't hear you come in. How can I help you today?"

Mr. Canton had passed years ago, and Lacey and Paige considered Mrs. Canton a regular. Although she always arrived with a particular need, Lacey suspected that most times, she was simply lonely.

"I'm looking for a new scent. It's coming up toward Christmas. What's come in?"

Lacey led her to the candle selection which, thankfully, was on the opposite end of the store from where Caleb was unpacking the UPS delivery.

After successfully distracting Mrs. Canton and sending her off with an assortment of gingerbread, pine, and holly berry scents, Lacey intended to finally tackle the inventory list when Mona called and invited her and Caleb to dinner.

Hanging up the phone, Lacey sighed and dug into the paperwork. Mona sounded like she could use the company. Lacey's heart ached for the double dose of stress Mona was under. She looked forward to giving her a big hug and spending the evening with her. It was an added bonus that she could put off being alone with Caleb.

90

Before Lacey and Caleb made it up the front walk, Mona opened the door. Even with the lighting behind her, Lacey could see the weariness around Mona's eyes. Lacey imagined she looked quite the same. The not knowing was taking its toll on all of them.

Mona hugged them and ushered them into the living room, the small gas fireplace twinkling. "Can I get you a glass of wine, or tea? Dinner's almost ready."

When Mona returned with the tea glasses, Lacey filled her in on the interviews conducted in Chicago, but her mind was distracted. How many times had she and her dad come over here for dinner? His essence, even now, filled the room.

Caleb leaned over and squeezed her hand. As Mona eyed the move, Lacey pulled her hand away. The last thing she needed was for Mona to get any ideas about her and Caleb. Ignoring Caleb's questioning look, she jumped into a question about Spencer.

"I called the parents of one of the boys Spencer said he'd be with. Their son's not home either. As crazy as it sounds, it gives me hope that Spencer's really not involved. I just wish he'd come home. Or at least answer his phone."

Lacey listened as Caleb asked several more questions about Spencer. Mona's eyes brightened with every question, and Lacey sent up a silent prayer that he'd either stay and help or just stop leading Mona on.

She checked herself. *What are you thinking? Caleb sticking around to help Mona with Spencer isn't reality. He may not even be around until we find Dad. Quit counting on him.*

Her nerves jangled at the thought of trekking down that slippery slope. She couldn't do it. No way. Jumping up from the sofa, she needed to close this topic of conversation. "Something smells good. Maybe we should eat."

Mona stood, smiling. "You're going to be excited. I had time on my hands today so I baked a lasagna, your favorite."

It wasn't just Lacey's favorite. In her opinion, it was practically legendary. Feeling a little more in control, she looked over at Caleb. "Come on. You're in for a treat."

Mona hurried ahead of them and was pulling the monstrous pan out of the oven when they entered the kitchen. The rich smells of garlic and oregano filled the air. Lacey's mouth watered as the red sauce bubbled under the layer of mozzarella. A loaf of Italian bread, cut into thick slices, waited on the counter.

"I'm in heaven," she whispered reverently. "It feels like it's been forever since you've made this."

Mona pulled plates out of the cabinet. "It has been. Remember I made it the last time you brought Jason over. And he absolutely hated it. Well, he didn't say that exactly, but I could tell."

Further proof that he was a complete moron, Lacey thought. She glanced over at Caleb and found him watching her.

"Who's Jason?"

Lacey saw Mona start to speak and she quickly cut her off. "Nobody important." She turned to Mona. "Can I serve?"

She felt Caleb's eyes on her throughout the meal, but thankfully he didn't bring up the subject again. She couldn't imagine the look on his face if he knew the truth of what she'd done.

Determined not to waste the wonderful home-cooked meal, Lacey put Jason out of her mind and slathered butter onto a piece of the crusty bread. Despite rehashing all of the things they didn't know about her dad's case and the gut-level fears that went undiscussed, she ate almost two pieces of lasagna and when she couldn't stuff one more bite into her mouth, she pushed her plate away. "That was even better than I remember."

"Delicious," Caleb added as he wiped sauce from the corner of his mouth.

Lacey's gaze settled for a moment on his lips, and the temperature in the room must've spiked twenty degrees. She looked away but not before she caught the glint of humor, and hunger, in his eyes.

As she cleaned up and put away the leftovers, Lacey listened to Mona share more stories about Spencer. She could hear the relief in Mona's voice and realized that being able to open up and talk about her worries and fears for her son appeared to be wonderful therapy.

Lacey and Caleb drove home in near silence, the tension between them crackling. She'd spent the day fortifying her defenses against his undeniable sex appeal and had felt pretty good about her chances of survival. Then he'd gone and been sweet to Mona. And nice. And caring.

She had no defense against that at all.

After making a curt comment about being very tired then yawning for good measure, Lacey took a shower and made a beeline for her bedroom. It wasn't until she was in bed, a book nestled on her lap, that she glanced at the clock on the bedside table. Ten o'clock and she wasn't the least bit tired. She slammed the book closed, rolled over, and groaned into her pillow. She had to come up with a better plan.

Caleb headed for the shower. The colder, the better. He couldn't decide what was driving him crazier, the form-fitting jeans that made her legs look a mile long and hugged her perfect backside, or her sincere smiles that seemed to come as naturally as breathing. More than that, though, he knew the hell she was going through and was amazed by her sheer resolve to work through her fears.

He stood under the stream of water, his mind consumed by Lacey. And tonight, she was running from him. He knew it and understood it. She was scared of him. Scared of where this could go.

He thought about the brief moments of passion they shared last night. Despite the deep emotions swirling around them, and maybe because of them, it was too powerful to ignore much longer.

Chapter 13

Bill gagged as the crusty cloth was yanked from his mouth. As he struggled to sit up, the metallic tang of blood seeped into his mouth from his dry cracked lips.

"Care for a drink of water?" his captor asked.

Bill nodded. One eye was swollen shut, but the other locked on the bottle.

"Please," he croaked. "Water. Please."

At the man's nod, Stan uncapped the bottle and put it to Bill's lips.

He gulped half the bottle before looking up. "Thank you," he whispered.

"See how nice I can be? I've even brought you dinner." He nodded again and Stan used his pocket knife to slice the duct tape from Bill's wrists before laying out the fast food meal on the bed in front of Bill.

Bill eyed them both, hoping this wasn't some kind of trick they were playing on him. The aroma of fried chicken filled his nostrils. His stomach growled in response.

The man in charge motioned to the food. "Go ahead. Eat," he said. "You're not much good to me dead, now are you?" He swiveled toward Stan. "Keep an eye on him. I've got a few things to get from the car."

Bill devoured the meal, licking the last of the chicken grease from his fingers before downing another bottle of water. He could feel Stan's glare from across the room.

"You know you're not getting out of here without giving up the freaking codes." Stan wiped his brow. "I've got to get back home, you son of a bitch. Why don't you make it easy on all of us and give him what he wants?"

Bill looked at the man he'd worked so closely with for the past several months. What could've driven Stan to get involved with this whole nightmare? He had his wife, his twins, his whole life in front of him. "What I know is that I'm a dead man if he has the codes."

He stared at Stan, catching a glimpse of the anxiety behind his anger. Recognizing that Stan was in way over his head, Bill found his first glimmer of hope. *Could Stan become an ally?*

"The biggest question I'd be asking if I was you, Stan, is whether or not he'd really need you either," Bill shrugged. "When this is over, one way or another, all you'll be is a complication."

Stan bristled. "That's not true," he hissed. "I already know what's in it for me after this is over." He stood up tall, but Bill could see the doubt behind his eyes. "He told me I'm going to be a silent partner."

Bill had his own idea about what that would likely mean for Stan, but before he could press any further, the other man strode back into the room and wiped his hands on Bill's discarded napkins.

"You smell like gasoline," Stan frowned. "Why?"

Bill watched a quick flash of anger cross the other man's features.

He tossed his head toward the hallway. "Little accident in the kitchen. One of the containers I brought in spilled."

Stan stared, his eyes wide. "Containers of gasoline? For what?"

His boss finished cleaning his fingers before looking up. "I like things to be neat and tidy," he said. "When the time comes, we'll use it to destroy any evidence that we were ever here." His malevolent gaze settled on Bill. "Bill here gets to decide if he's going to be part of the evidence."

Bill picked up the water bottle with a calm he was far from feeling and drank the remainder of its contents. "Listen —" he began.

"Yes, Bill? Shall I get your laptop?"

95

Looking down at his soiled clothing, Bill paused, and considered trying to strike some kind of a deal. He'd gone for days without a bathroom or shower. Hot tears of anger and frustration filled his eyes. His beautiful Lacey flashed into his mind. And Mona. After all these years, he'd finally found love again. God, they must be worried sick. He had to find a way out of this nightmare.

He looked squarely into the eyes of his captor, his resolve firmly back in place. "Go to hell."

A dark smile twisted the man's features. "I actually think I underestimated you, Bill. Yes I did. You're not nearly as malleable as I thought. I must admit though, I'm getting tired of our little game. I think it's time to up the ante, so to speak."

***

He gritted his teeth, snarling. "Shut your mouth. You eat like a damn pig."

Stan picked up his napkin and wiped the mayo from his chin. "Sorry, man." He forced down his bite. "I'm glad you decided to feed him. He scared me when we walked in, lying so still like that. For a second, I wasn't sure he was alive."

Tightening his fingers on the steering wheel, he wished he could open the door and push the bastard out. That would solve one of his problems, at least. But not his biggest one. How the hell was he going to get those damn codes?

He took a deep breath, willing himself to calm down. He had to think logically. And he needed a drink. Because tonight hadn't turned out at all like he'd planned.

It had been an empty threat before, but not anymore. Getting the girl meant getting the codes. He slammed his fist on the steering wheel. He *had* to get his hands on that girl.

"How do we get her?" He voiced his thought out loud, hardly expecting an answer from the imbecile next to him.

Stan flinched. "I don't know. I can't go back. They'll be looking for me for sure." He paused. "Do you think it was a good idea to skip the drugs tonight? What if he tries to escape?"

Stifling a sigh, and the urge to beat his head into the window, he glanced at Stan. "How? He's cuffed to the bed and he's not exactly at full strength. No. He needs to be able to think clearly about what it means to his family if he continues to refuse me." He paused. "But I need a plan to get her."

Silence filled the car as it headed north. Suddenly, Stan sat up in his seat and turned toward him, reminding him of an over-eager puppy. "Patrick Littlejohn," he exclaimed.

He tried not to sneer. "What?"

"Patrick Littlejohn. He's who we can use to get her."

"Details."

"He's an enforcer for…" he cleared his throat. "I met him once or twice when I was in trouble, running a little bit behind."

The man mulled over the possibilities. Not that he had many, he acknowledged. Maybe it was worth a shot. "Do you know how to get in touch with him?"

Stan nodded. "I'll find him. God knows, I'm ready to get this whole fucking mess over with."

"Indeed."

Chapter 14

"Do not leave the shop."

Lacey ignored the scowl on Caleb's face as he opened her car door. In truth, she was looking forward to a few hours away from him. She needed to get her head on straight.

The morning was cold, a heavy mist in the air. She walked around Sam's little Chevy pick-up, its rusted out fenders making her wonder how reliable the old truck might be.

Distracted, Lacey almost stumbled into Caleb when he stopped and turned around in front of her. His hands circled her upper arms, their heat radiating through her down jacket.

His intense gaze took her breath and seemed to look right into her soul. She wasn't at all prepared when he bent his head and captured her lips in a hard demanding kiss. If she had been, maybe she wouldn't have responded so willingly to the onslaught.

The kiss ended as abruptly as it started then Caleb was talking, his tone as hard as his stare. "Sam's already here so the back door needs to stay locked at all times. You're feeling okay?"

If she hadn't been so frustrated by her response to him, she might've smiled at his over-protective attitude. "I'm fine. No headache at all today. Go run your errands. Sam and I will be fine. Nothing's happened out of the ordinary since that night. If you want to be a hero, bring us back lunch when you come."

"I won't be long." He dropped one more quick kiss on her forehead then released her.

Dutifully locking the door behind her, Lacey breathed a heavy sigh. She'd been so close to leaning into him. She'd wanted him to kiss her again. Really kiss her.

Bucking up her resolve, Lacey notched her coat on the peg and rehashed her mental list of reasons why getting involved with Caleb was a really bad idea when Sam exploded around the corner.

"Oh, Lacey, thank God you're here." Sam was on the verge of tears, clutching an army green bank deposit bag to her chest.

Lacey froze, her gaze locked on the bag. "Where did you get that?" she hissed.

Sam's words tumbled out, most of them drowned out by her tears. Lacey led Sam to the office, her mind whirling. Why the hell did she have the shop's deposit bag?

There had to be a logical explanation. She watched Sam drop it onto the desk like a hot potato. Lacey's intuition, and the distress in Sam's eyes, relieved Lacey's biggest fear. There was no way Sam was involved in the robbery.

She sat next to Sam, giving her a minute to compose herself. When Sam finally looked at her, Lacey squeezed her hand. "Everything's going to be okay, but you've got to be completely honest with me."

Sam nodded vigorously.

"Start from the beginning." The sadness Lacey saw in Sam's eyes made her heart ache.

Sam took a deep breath and shuddered. "I'm pregnant, Lacey."

Lacey blinked, her brow furrowing. Whatever she'd expected to hear, that wasn't it.

That news would certainly be traumatizing because Sam was so young, and as far as Lacey knew, single. But what on earth did that have to do with her stolen bank deposit? She waited. There was obviously more to the story.

"Is that why you were at the doctor the other day? Do you have a due date yet?" Lacey put her arm around Sam's shoulders. "We can work through this. You don't have to worry about having a place here – I hope you know how valuable you are to us. But, you've got to tell me about the bag. Where did you get it?"

She stopped talking when she noticed Sam shaking her head.

"Lacey, I didn't just find out I'm pregnant," she whispered. "I'm six months pregnant. I'm due in February." More tears clouded her eyes and slid silently down her cheeks.

Lacey was stunned. It was coming up on Thanksgiving. How could she not have noticed?

In the silence, little pieces came together. Sam's loose fitting wardrobe, her late afternoon fatigue. "What about your family? What about the father?" As soon as the words were out of her mouth, a horrible realization crashed through Lacey's mind. "Oh, Sam. Gary's the father, isn't he?"

Sam's shoulders slumped, the sobs coming in earnest. "I didn't leave Gary just because of the abuse. I left because he was pressuring me to have an abortion. I'd already told him that I wouldn't name him as the father and I'd never ask for a penny in child support but he wouldn't let it drop.

"I could never get an abortion, Lacey. I just couldn't. I tried to hide from him until I was too far along, but he found out where I live now. And where I work. The day he came to the shop, he told me he'd found a doctor in Wichita who would do a late-term abortion for fifteen hundred dollars. The thought made me ill. I said the first thing that popped into my mind – that neither one of us had any way of coming up with that kind of money. He told me he'd take care of it."

And that's where the deposit bag comes in, Lacey thought.

Sam forced the words around her sobbing hiccups. "Last night, he came to my apartment. I could tell he'd been drinking. He was beating on the door and making so much noise, I let him in so my neighbors wouldn't throw a fit. He handed me the money bag along with a hand-drawn map to the doctor's office in Wichita." She rocked back and forth in her seat. "He already has the appointment scheduled for next Wednesday."

Anger twisted Lacey's stomach into knots. "You're not going anywhere you don't want to go."

Sam stood and paced the small office. "I can't even think about that right now. All I can think about is what he did to you. He was so proud of himself – telling me all about how he came to the shop Tuesday night. How he waited until almost closing time. And that he hid in the shadows," her voice broke on a sob, "waiting for you to come out of the office. Lacey, you could've been killed!"

Lacey pulled her into a hug where they stayed, silent, for several minutes.

Finally, Sam pulled away. "I don't know if that's all he took from you or not. If it isn't, I'll figure out a way to pay the rest back to you."

Lacey opened the bag and thumbed the assortment of bills, a sense of calmness settling over her.

"We have a phone call to make," she told Sam, her voice resolute. Lacey rummaged through her purse for Officer Lopez's card. She reached the officer on the second ring, and was instructed not to touch the bag again until she arrived.

While they waited, Lacey learned all about Sam's history with Gary. The more she heard, the angrier she got. Not only was Sam being pressured by Gary to terminate the pregnancy, she had no other guidance. Her parents had been killed in a car accident two months after her high school graduation.

How much was one nineteen-year-old girl supposed to take?

"You're going to be fine," Lacey insisted. "When Officer Lopez comes, you need to file a restraining order against Gary. Not that it's going to matter now, but it still needs to be done."

Lacey threw open the office door. Her indignation over Sam's circumstances energized her. "Come on, let's get our day started."

Sam turned a watery smile on Lacey. "Sounds like a plan." She headed for the small bathroom. "Give me just a minute and I'll be out."

When Sam returned, Lacey looked up from the notepad she was writing on. Lacey thought Sam was already walking a little bit taller.

"Are you working on today's orders?" Sam asked.

Lacey turned the notepad toward Sam with one word at the top of the page: OPTIONS.

"I think we need to face this situation head-on." She smiled and held out the pencil to Sam.

Sam's eyes started to fill with tears all over again. "I'm really scared," she whispered.

Lacey nodded. "I would imagine. But you're not alone anymore." She nudged Sam with her elbow and gave her an encouraging smile. "Now, let's talk it through."

Sam squared her shoulders and took a deep breath. "I've been going around in circles for months. There are so many things to consider." She drew out her three choices and immediately crossed off abortion. "That leaves keeping the baby or giving it up for adoption."

"Good. Now this is going to sound really crazy, but this is what my dad always had me do when I had a big decision to make. I want you to take a couple sheets of paper, divide each into two columns and write down the pros and cons of each decision." Sam eyed her skeptically. "I know, it sounds too simple but it's really very enlightening. You'll be amazed at how easy it'll make your decision."

Lacey sauntered away from the counter and after unlocking the front door, headed to the cooler. "I'm going to work on some arrangements. Let me know when Officer Lopez gets here."

Minutes later, Sam barged into the cooler, the papers clutched to her chest. "I've made a decision," she exclaimed.

Lacey grinned. "Yeah? Well, let's hear it."

"I'm giving they baby up for adoption," she announced, her eyes shining. She slapped down the sheets of paper on the work bench and flattened out the wrinkles. "When you put down all the facts, it's the only decision that makes sense. Oh, Lacey," she cried, "You can't imagine how relieved I feel!"

Caught up in Sam's enthusiasm, Lacey scanned the list, impressed by the depth of Sam's thoughts. She wondered how many sleepless nights Sam must've spent, wrestling with her choices alone.

Lacey wrapped Sam in a bear hug. "Looks like we've got a pretty clear winner, doesn't it?"

Sam pulled back and nodded, smiling. "I don't know the first thing about adoption or how to find an agency," she paused, her brow furrowing. "Do you think they're listed in the phone book? Or would they be online?"

Lacey gathered the papers and handed them back to Sam. "How about this. You take these home. Take the weekend to think over your decision. If it still feels right to you on Monday, we'll jump in together and figure it all out, agreed?"

Sam clasped her hand. "Deal."

Officer Lopez opened the cooler door and poked her head in. "I was wondering where everybody was," she said. "I called out for you but no one answered. Made me nervous for a minute."

Lacey immediately sobered. "We're fine. I'm sorry about that. Thank you for coming over so quickly." She led them back to the office where the evidence waited.

Officer Lopez took turns with Lacey and Sam getting their statements. Thirty minutes later, she walked out the door with a promise to update them as soon as Gary was apprehended.

As Sam finished up with a customer, Lacey joined her at the counter. "Wow, what a morning, huh? Never a dull moment."

Sam smiled as she closed the register drawer. She looked out the store windows and laughed. "You know what's so funny? Even with this horrible relationship and all that's happened, I still believe my real Mr. Right is out there somewhere." She leaned onto the counter and propped her chin in her hand. "Maybe I'm just a hopeless romantic, but I can't help but believe it."

"I'm sure you're right." Lacey shrugged and forced a smile. She hoped Sam would realize she deserved someone who would treat her right, and that she should set her standards a little higher than somebody like Gary Finley.

Sam's eyes held a sparkle Lacey hadn't seen in a while. "I think your Mr. Right is out there, too," she said. "But he's a lot closer than mine."

Lacey stared after Sam, dumbfounded. Where did that come from? She assumed Sam meant Caleb, but he wasn't her Mr. Right. Caleb wasn't her anything. And, in her case anyway, she was pretty sure Mr. Right was nothing more than fantasy.

Sam popped back around the corner. "Oh, hey Lacey?"

Lacey snapped out of her musings. "Yes?"

"Are you going to tell Caleb?"

Lacey looked squarely at Sam. "I have to tell him what happened, but I don't have to tell him about the baby if you don't want me to."

Sam stood quietly. "I'm sure he'll think I'm a complete idiot."

Lacey pondered that for a minute as she shuffled papers at the counter. It didn't even take that long for her heart to acknowledge the truth. He wouldn't judge. He'd be steady. And strong. And willing to help.

Oh, brother. Back up the bus or you're going right over the edge.

"No," Lacey said quietly. "It'll be just fine."

Sam nodded and smiled. "Okay."

Lacey tried to shake the melancholy that settled around her and threw herself into her work for the rest of the morning. Her frustration only mounted, though, as her thoughts circled back around to her dad. It almost would've been easier if Lacey's assailant had been connected to his abduction. At least then they might have a direction to take the investigation. Maybe she should've opted for the private investigator. Could he have found something already?

Lacey was on edge and hungry when Caleb strolled in with a bulging Panera Bread bag. She'd already mentally defended her decision to wait to talk to Caleb about the morning's revelations.

One, she didn't want to lean on him anymore than she already had. In the few days they'd spent together, it had become so easy, too easy, to depend on him. And two, she knew he'd come charging back over to the shop as soon as he heard and she needed more time away from him.

The only problem was that she hadn't resolved a single thing where Caleb was concerned. Her stomach still did that ridiculous little flip at the sight of him, his intense eyes catching hers the moment he walked in.

He looked tired to her, but he smiled when he got to the counter. "Hope you're hungry. I didn't know what you liked, so I got a little bit of everything."

Lacey quickly broke eye contact and hopped off her stool, motioning for him to follow her to the office. "Smells great. Let me grab Sam."

Sam chose a sandwich from the bag then ducked out. "Thanks for lunch, Caleb. I'll eat out front and take care of any walk-ins."

Still unsure of how to start the conversation about the morning's events, and frustrated by her heart's reaction to his arrival, Lacey finally broke the unnerving silence that hung between them. "Did you find out anything today?" she asked, a spoonful of broccoli cheddar soup poised at her lips.

Caleb let it pass that she avoided his gaze while she asked the question. Again. He was frustrated with his lack of progress this morning, and her avid fascination with anything except him was starting to piss him off.

He grabbed his sandwich and sat back in the chair facing her. "I went over to check on Mona this morning, and to see if she'd heard anything from Spencer." Lacey's gazed snapped to him. He held up his hand. "Nothing yet. She's giving him until the weekend before she files a report. I also stopped by the police station. Abrams said they still haven't gotten in touch with Stan Jacobson and they're getting more than a little suspicious of the timing. Until today, no one's been at the home when they stopped by. It was starting to look like the whole family just took off. From what I understand, though, Mrs. Jacobson is back in town so they're headed over to see her this afternoon. Abrams' gut instinct is that there's another woman involved. He said that's the usual scenario."

Lacey put down her spoon. "Wouldn't surprise me," her voice quivered. "It happens all the time."

"I'm going over to the university this afternoon, see if there's anything I can shake loose there." He paused, baffled by Lacey's mood, his own frustration high. He tossed his sandwich on the desk. "Do I have something in my teeth?" he snapped. "You've barely looked at me since I walked in the door."

Her eyebrows shot up. "That's not true. I —"

The office phone rang. Lacey jumped then grabbed the receiver. "Good Graces Floral and Gift. This is Lacey."

Caleb could hear Officer Lopez's short staccato resonating through the line. His eyes snapped to Lacey's before he rounded the corner of her desk. She tried to move away from him but he leaned down, his ear next to the phone, cornering her.

"We found Mr. Finley about an hour ago. We brought him in for questioning and have enough information to obtain a search warrant for his car and apartment."

Caleb frowned at Lacey, his eyes narrowing. She tried to push him away but the harder she pushed the more resolute he became. He wasn't going anywhere. With a glare, she turned her back on him.

"Mr. Finley is being held this afternoon but may be released unless our search turns up something significant. I'll call you later to let you know. If he is released, you need to be prepared to file a restraining order against him also."

After Lacey hung up the phone, Caleb stepped away from her, waiting to speak until he was certain he wouldn't yell. "You want to tell me what the hell that was all about?"

As Lacey explained the events of the morning, Caleb's anger mounted. "Why didn't you call me?"

He hadn't wanted to leave her this morning, but she'd convinced him to go. If she wasn't going to keep him in the loop, by God he'd stick to her like glue. He ran a hand through his hair. How long was it going to take to get her to trust him?

Lacey's spine straightened and defiance flashed in her deep brown eyes. "Call you when? It just happened. I was going to explain it all when you got here," she fired back. "I didn't intentionally keep it from you. I just —"

He came up behind her, his voice low. "We can't afford to keep secrets. I thought we were on the same team here."

She opened her mouth to respond, but whatever words she might've said were drowned out by the doubt in her eyes. Doubts about him. Still.

He strode past her out of the office, his disappointment sharpening his words. "I'll be back to pick you up at seven."

Chapter 15

Detective Mark Abrams knocked again.

He hoped like hell this wasn't another dead end. He'd moved to the middle of nowhere to escape big city crime, and watching Bill Jordan's family go through this ordeal reminded him why he'd left. It had been a week since the abduction and the clock was ticking. Time was no longer on their side.

A curtain in the front room swayed before he heard voices and then an avalanche of footfalls. Moments later, a woman pulled open the door. She blocked one toddler from escape with her knee as she corralled the other in her arms.

"Diedre Jacobson?"

"Yes." Her brow furrowed as her eyes flitted to his gun. "Can I help you?"

Abrams whipped out his badge and introduced himself. "Is your husband home?"

The squirming boy in her arms snagged her hair, trying to get her attention. "He's got a gun, mommy," he whispered loudly.

She patted his curls then set him on the floor next to his twin. "Excuse me. It's like Grand Central Station around here." Still blocking the exit, she continued. "No, I'm sorry. He's away right now. Can I ask what this is about?"

"Maybe we could visit for a moment inside," Abrams said. He didn't think she'd last much longer as a barricade against the two very determined toddlers working their way around her legs.

She acknowledged her losing battle with a rueful smile. "Of course, come in, please." She led him to the living room where she took a moment to settle the twins on mats with some dry cereal. She blew her dark brown hair out of her eyes and wiped the cereal dust off her hands.

"Sorry about that," she said. "It's a little crazy around here right now. My husband is out of town, so it's me and these two little monkeys twenty-four-seven." She sat for a moment before she jumped up from the couch to break up a budding brawl over a stray piece of cereal. She picked up one of the kids and brought him back to the couch with her.

Abrams was getting tired just watching her, but he didn't see any nervousness. "Mrs. Jacobson, I'll get right to the point." He whipped out his note pad. "Your husband works with Bill Jordan, correct?"

"Yes," she replied. "He's been working for him for close to a year." Her eyes widened. "Oh my gosh, is this about Dr. Jordan's disappearance? I read about that in the paper. I'm sure his family is going crazy with worry."

"Yes, I'm the detective in charge of the investigation. We've been by a couple times this week. Have you been out of town?"

"I was at my mother's in Sabetha for a few days. I don't get over there as often as I should so I decided to take advantage of my husband's time away. Do you have any leads?" she asked, her eyes troubled. "I wish Stan was here to help. He'd be shocked by the news."

Abrams looked up from his notepad. "So you haven't talked with your husband about Dr. Jordan?"

"I haven't had a chance to talk to him at all. He's at a retreat in Arizona," she said. "It's one of those fire-in-the-pit purifying intensives." She rolled her eyes. "I'm sure you've heard of them. It's supposed to be a hard-core, challenge your manhood kind of thing. Personally, I can't imagine why you'd want to do that to yourself, but whatever."

Abrams started writing again. "Yeah, I've heard of them," he paused. "Do you know the name of the facility?"

The woman stood again, plugging in a video for the boys. When she turned to face him, the frown was back. "I don't. I'm sorry. As part of their initiation into this event, they had to manage everything in secret. He wasn't allowed to share any of the details of the trip with me or anyone else. I guess it was to help prove their independence and self-sufficiency."

"Does that seem odd to you that you have no way to contact him in case of an emergency?"

"It does. But he was adamant that he follow the rules. To be honest, he'd been working so hard and he's talked about wanting to do this for months, I just didn't have the heart to protest."

With the boys once again settled in front of the TV, she came back and sat down. "Since the project is over, we may end up relocating again, and I'd rather have him get this out of his system before we have to deal with a move."

"You do that frequently? Relocate?"

She nodded. "Unfortunately. I'm really hoping we get to stay here though. This is the first time since we've been married that we're close to my family."

Abrams jotted a note. "Do you work outside the home, Mrs. Jacobson?"

She shook her head. "Not right now. I'm a paralegal but I haven't worked the past couple years. Maybe when the boys go to school, but it's just not feasible now."

Rising from the sofa, Abrams closed his notepad. "Do you have any idea at all when your husband will return? A week, a month?"

"He was fuzzy on the details but I got the impression it wasn't supposed to last more than a week or two. I certainly hope it's soon. I'm ready for a vacation myself." Smiling, she held the door for him. "I'll have him contact you the minute he returns. Hopefully, Dr. Jordan will be home before Stan is."

Abrams shook her hand and gave her his card. "Thank you for your time. We'll be back in touch if we have any other questions."

"That'll be fine. I'm not planning to leave again. Oh, and Detective? If you speak to Dr. Jordan's family, please let them know I'm praying for them. I can only imagine what they're going through."

Chapter 16

Caleb's phone rang, breaking the taut silence in the car. He snapped it open, checked the caller ID and let out a frustrated sigh. "Yeah, what's up?"

Lacey couldn't hear the other end of the conversation but she felt a little sorry for whoever was on the line. They were certainly getting the full force of Caleb's rotten mood. She'd hoped that after he'd had time to calm down his attitude would've improved, but apparently not.

"I can't talk right now." He drummed his fingers on the steering wheel until the other person quit speaking. "No, it's fine." A pause. "Yes, I'm sure I'm not avoiding you. I'll call you later."

He hung up the phone and Lacey glanced at Caleb's brooding profile as they pulled into her driveway. The blustery wind and heavy clouds that had hung around all day mirrored the mood as Lacey pulled her jacket around her and scurried to the front door.

As she slid the key into the lock, she felt his presence directly behind her. He hadn't said five words to her since he picked her up, and she was running out of patience. It wasn't her fault that there were no new stones to turn over, or that Gary had robbed the store.

"You'll need to come in and get your things," she said, her tone tart.

He strode past her into the house. As she closed the door, he turned and with the quickness of a panther, his large body caged her. His eyes were hot and that little muscle in the side of his jaw worked furiously.

She attempted a calm, reasonable tone. "Look, Caleb. I know you're frustrated, but you're making a much bigger deal out of this than it is." He was standing so close to her now, she was having trouble breathing. She swallowed and mustered her courage. "But let's be logical. My attack wasn't related to my dad's disappearance. And, I'm fine now, so there's no need for you to stay here."

Unable to hold his gaze, she stared at the strong column of his throat. Her argument was valid, but his nearness was causing her to lose her train of thought. Pushing against his chest, she tried to put some distance between them.

He didn't move so much as a muscle in the seconds that ticked by before he finally responded. Anger and something else edged his words. "You may be feeling fine, but as far as I'm concerned, you're not out of danger until your dad is found. And Lacey," he said, his voice like silk as her eyes snapped to his, "I'm not going anywhere."

Lacey felt the heat emanating from his long lean body just inches from her. Lord, it was warm in her house. Caleb's eyes tracked her tongue as it darted out to moisten her lips. She sucked in her breath. In that split second, she knew he was going to kiss her. She also knew that deep down she didn't want him to stop with a kiss.

She fisted her hands at his chest, her head falling forward. All the frustration from her mixed-up emotions came out in a tortured whisper. "I don't want to want you."

He forced her chin up and she could see the smoldering desire in his eyes.

"I know."

She barely heard him as their lips met with crushing intensity and her hands teased the hard planes of his chest. Caleb's wide palms splayed against her back, forcing her to acknowledge his body's reaction to her touch. Her breath caught as his tongue delved deeper. Reveling in his power, she was only vaguely aware of Caleb tossing their jackets aside.

He finally broke the kiss. Lacey stood motionless, lost in sensation, as Caleb unbuttoned her shirt. The silky material slid down her arms as Caleb skimmed her collarbone with his fingertips sending a shiver through her. Her lacy white bra fell to the floor seconds later.

Lacey tried to latch on to a coherent thought. Shouldn't she stop this? Could she still stop it? She opened her eyes just as he bent his head to take one straining nipple into his mouth.

"My God," he breathed, seconds before his mouth found its mark. His hands spanned her rib cage, pulling her even closer. Lacey wasn't prepared for the sharp stab of desire deep inside her belly. Her hands clenched fistfuls of his dark brown hair as his mouth moved from one breast to the other, hot lightning coursing through her body. The sensations were too raw, too powerful to deny.

Any fleeting thought of resistance fled.

"Caleb, please," she moaned, barely recognizing her own voice. He trailed hot kisses along her neck until his mouth met hers again in an explosive exchange that left her panting and needing more. A lot more.

Caleb removed his sweater, exposing his chest, every muscle tightly defined. As he pulled her against him, Lacey gasped at the contact of her naked breasts against the coarse hair. Her head fell back, her arguments completely overshadowed by her clamoring need for release. How had she survived six years without this feeling? Without him?

They found their way to her bed, the last of their clothes marking a trail. Caleb pulled back the covers, pillows flying in every direction. He picked her up and placed her gently on the mattress.

She felt his low growl as his body covered her. His lips nipped at hers again and every nerve ending in Lacey's body caught fire. She ran her hands through his hair then down the thick muscles of his upper back and arms, lightly scoring him with her nails.

His hand grazed her breast once, then again, until she pressed against him, encouraging him to take full possession. He cupped her then plucked at her eager nipples until they were straining for him. Lacey's uninhibited passion almost sent him over the edge.

He wedged her legs apart with his knee, poised at the entrance to her body.

Shoving his hands into her hair on either side of her face, he held her captive. For a brief moment, he simply looked at her, his breathing raspy.

"God, you're so beautiful." His hands once more traveled down her body, loving and caressing every contour. "I want to wait, Lacey, but I can't."

"Please, don't wait," she whispered.

That was all the invitation he needed. He drove into her until he was completely embedded. Lacey's hips arched off the bed, her body demanding more as they blended into a once-familiar rhythm. She dug her nails into his shoulders as he opened her even more fully to himself, their bodies moving in powerful harmony.

Lacey sensed the intense heat seconds before it broke over her as wave after wave of high current energy jolted her body. Caleb was lost, her contractions around him forcing him to follow. With a shout, he exploded into her, his body throbbing in the aftershocks of the most intense orgasm he'd ever experienced.

His body came back down on hers, both of them unable to move. Finally, Caleb grunted and rolled over on his side, taking Lacey with him, still deep inside her. When Lacey opened her eyes, Caleb was staring at her, his striking eyes still smoldering with desire. She reached out and brushed away a lock of hair from his forehead. He captured her hand and brushed a teasing kiss on her palm then interlaced his fingers with hers.

She couldn't have turned away if the house was on fire. His fingers moved softly over hers, causing fresh tremors to quake through her body. Unnerved at the sweet intimacy, she started to shift her body away from his, but his hand caught her hip and held her steady.

"I'm a scientist by nature," he murmured, his body already hardening inside her. "I'm thinking we should try this experiment again to see if we can replicate the results." He rolled her onto her back and with one hand grasped her wrists above her head. Lowering his head, he circled her nipple with his tongue.

Lacey's sigh ended in a small moan. "We could be on the verge of a breakthrough."

He choked out a hoarse laugh just before he captured her lips. Caleb forgot all about his intention to take his time. He discovered that patience was evidently not one of her virtues either, and her passion rivaled his own.

Her curves and the sexy sounds she made as she moved beneath him drove him to another mindless explosion. Minutes later, when he could finally move, Caleb pulled the discarded covers over them and settled beside her, holding her to him.

She snuggled into his side as her breathing slowed and evened out. He sighed. She'd shared her body with him, and in sleep, she trusted him. Could she allow her scars to heal?

The conviction that he wanted another chance with Lacey became clearer to him every day they spent together. But where would tonight leave her? Would she have regrets? Would she think he'd taken advantage of the situation? He relaxed the tensed muscles in his neck, exhaling deeply.

One step at a time, Caleb. One step at a time.

***

"Wake up, sleepyhead."

Caleb's gratingly cheerful voice intruded on her sleep from the doorway of her bedroom. Sprawled on the bed, Lacey opened one eye and groaned. If he hadn't had a cup of coffee in his hand, she might've thrown her pillow at him.

Lacey forced herself up, pulling the sheets against her chest. She leaned against the headboard and shoved her rumpled hair out of her eyes. "Oh, God." Her eyes darted to the bedside table where her phone should've been. "What time is it? Has Abrams called?"

Caleb handed her a cup of coffee, then touched her shoulder. "Take it easy, babe. It's only eight and the guy's got to sleep sometime."

She nodded, mostly to give herself time to control her reaction to his husky voice and his touch. She really needed to get a grip. Taking a sip of the dark roast, she let out a sigh. Conscious of her nakedness under the sheets, she spied her robe on the chair and pointed to it. "Could you grab that for me?"

He pivoted and tossed it to her. "You don't have to put that on for me," he said, a hint of laughter in his voice. "I much prefer the unobstructed view."

Lacey scrambled out of bed, quickly cinching the robe's belt. His light banter set her on edge. How could he be so nonchalant when she was floundering with no way to rationalize last night? No way to escape the fact that she'd slept with him, or that she'd enjoyed it. That fact only frustrated her more. Time to get them back on solid ground. "Caleb," she said, her voice firm, "I don't know exactly how or why last night happened, but it probably wasn't a very good idea." His eyes narrowed. "We're in a horrible situation. And it's only natural, I suppose, to find comfort where we can, but –"

He crossed his arms, waiting.

She struggled for words, feeling open and vulnerable for the first time in a long time. It didn't feel good. Her tone sharpened. "I like you. And that's hard to admit because, to be honest, I didn't want to. But, I don't want to get to the end of this road and lose what could've been a decent friendship." She took a breath, her eyes focused on the tips of his Kenneth Coles. "I'm going to shower. While I'm doing that, you'll have time to gather up your things. I think it'd be best if you go back to the Ramada."

She glanced at his hardened face, taking his silence for agreement. Turning on her heel, she headed to the bathroom.

"Come here, Lacey."

His words stopped her, but she didn't turn around. She needed him to leave. Now. Her lame defenses against him were crumbling around her. "I'm right on this, Caleb."

She took a step toward the door, but he was behind her in a second. He touched her arm, turning her to face him. "Look at me and tell me you want me to leave," he challenged.

She stared at the floor. "I want you to leave."

"Look at me," he said tightly, his grip on her shoulders, unrelenting.

Why the hell did it matter to him? Lacey raised her eyes to him, her doubt and confusion surely showing on her face. Caleb growled low in his throat and pulled her to him, his mouth on hers, forcing her to return the kiss. Her lips opened underneath his and she couldn't remember anything anymore. Nothing made sense except the kiss.

116

He ended the kiss abruptly, and shook her slightly. She opened her dazed eyes to his. "Now tell me you want me to leave."

She was lost. And she knew it. She stood for a silent minute, hating her weakness. "I can't," she said quietly.

Caleb's chest heaved a sigh, his arms encircling her shaking body as his hand soothed her rumpled hair. "We'll get through this nightmare together, okay?"

She nodded against his chest, but her heart was heavy. *How long until temporary insanity wasn't considered temporary?*

Chapter 17

Guilt shrouded her. She'd had sex. With Caleb. While her dad was God knows where. She locked the bathroom door at the shop and stared at her drawn face in the mirror.

There were no tears, but a gut-wrenching grief seeped into her bones. Would she ever see her father again? *Oh, God, please. If he's alive, please let us find him. Please let him be okay.*

She squared her shoulders and closed her eyes until she was able to control the fear. She needed to be strong for him. He would never stop looking for her if she was missing. And by God, she wouldn't rest until he was found.

Thankfully, business was brisk for a Saturday, and between the phone calls she made to the police station and to campus hoping for any new scrap of information, Lacey found a certain comfort in the hectic pace. These things – the customers, the business – she could control. Today, they were a welcome distraction from the growing sense that she was failing her dad.

She had the store cordless phone crooked on her shoulder taking an order when her cell phone rang. *Shit.* She couldn't let a call go by without knowing who it was. As Caleb came around the corner, Lacey motioned frantically for him to grab it off the edge of the counter.

Caleb snatched it up. "Caleb Mansfield."

"Caleb. Oh, thank God. It's Mona. Spencer's back. I don't know what to do. I –"

He could hear the borderline hysteria in her voice. "Mona, stop. Take a deep breath then tell me what's going on."

Mona complied, but her words still came out in a rush. "Spencer came home sometime during the night. I was up early today but I didn't notice his bedroom door was ajar until this afternoon. When I looked inside, he was there—passed out on his bed. I called the police. They should be here any minute, but I'm afraid he'll wake up and I'm not sure what to do –"

"Don't do a thing. Let him sleep." Conscious of her distress, he softened his tone. "You did the right thing by calling us and the police. I'll head right over. If the police beat me there, it won't be by much." He filled Lacey in as soon as she was off the phone.

Her face hardened as she marched to the office and pulled her purse out of the desk. "I'm going with you."

Caleb followed her. "Lacey," he said calmly, "you have a shop full of customers and Sam is out on deliveries. The police will question him and I'll be your eyes and ears, okay? Give us a chance to find out how or if he's even connected."

Her eyes mirrored her angst as she shoved her purse back into the drawer. "Damn it," she spat. "Hurry then. Call me as soon as you find out anything."

Caleb touched her elbow as she started to walk past him, his eyes capturing hers. "I will. Trust me." He leaned down and brushed her lips with his then he was gone.

***

Caleb saw the squad car parked in front of Mona's house as he rounded the corner. He pulled into Mona's two-car driveway next to a newer black Ford Mustang angled with its front passenger side tire two feet onto the grass on the far side of the drive.

He jogged around his car and flung open the Mustang's driver's side door. The stench of stale alcohol and cigarettes rolled over him. A cursory glance at the floorboards revealed at least two empty Wild Turkey bottles peeking out around the piles of fast food trash and coke bottles.

Holy crap, the kid's lucky to be alive.

119

Caleb ran up the front walk and knocked on the door. He waited only a moment before Mona opened it and motioned him inside. She led him into the living room where he nodded curtly to Detective Abrams and Officer Lopez.

"The police just arrived and Spencer's still asleep," Mona whispered as if she was afraid her voice would wake him. She looked around the room. "Can I get you all some coffee?" she offered.

They all quickly declined then Abrams spoke up. "Mrs. Nicholson, we need to speak to your son. Would you like to go wake him or would you prefer that I do it?"

Caleb watched alarm flash across Mona's features. He put his arm around her shoulders and nodded to the detective. "Why don't you go?"

Abrams glanced at Lopez and headed off to the room Mona indicated. Minutes later, Spencer stumbled to the sofa, his arm supported by the detective. He looked and smelled like he hadn't seen a shower in days.

As he dropped onto the upholstered seat, his bewildered bloodshot eyes darted to the others in the room before settling on his mother. Caleb squeezed Mona's shoulder as her eyes clouded with tears but she stood firm, waiting for the officers to begin.

As Caleb watched Spencer swallow convulsively, he figured the kid was probably wishing he had a drink right about now. Excusing himself, Caleb headed to the kitchen. He returned in moments carrying a glass of ice water. Although his gesture was met with a frown, Spencer gulped half the contents of the glass in seconds before setting it down on the table with shaking hands.

Lopez spoke first, her voice hard. "We need to know where you were last Friday."

Spencer shook his head, his brow furrowed. "Last Friday?" He sat for a moment, his eyes flitting to Abrams. "I went to Kansas City with some friends. I think Friday night we went to the one of the casinos."

Caleb watched Spencer intensely, looking for any sign that he might be lying.

"Why would you go to a casino?" Abrams demanded. "You're only nineteen. How'd you get in?"

Spencer's adams apple bobbed as a sheen of sweat developed on his forehead. "I-I didn't," he stammered. "There was a concert. We went to see a show there."

Abrams shot back. "What show?"

Spencer sat in silence then dropped his head in his hands. "I don't remember," he mumbled. "Let me think."

Abrams exchanged a glance with Lopez before he spoke. "Bill Jordan is missing. We believe he was taken from his home sometime last Friday. Were you aware of that?"

A sob escaped from Mona. Spencer's head shot up, his gaze flying to his mother's face before he looked again at Abrams. He stood abruptly, fear in his eyes. "No! God, no. I swear it." His voice rose as, again, his eyes went back to Mona. "Mom, you believe me, don't you?"

She nodded as tears ran down her cheeks. "Just answer their questions honestly," she choked out.

Abrams continued the interrogation regarding Spencer's whereabouts during the past week. Finally, apparently satisfied with the answers, he wound down the interview. "Why did you come home now?" he asked.

Spencer's entire body started shaking, his own eyes filling with tears. "I was out of money and out of booze," he whispered, desperation in his voice. "I didn't have anywhere else to go."

Caleb decided Spencer was either being honest or he was a damn fine actor. The kid looked scared to death.

Abrams looked at Lopez. "Anything else?" After she shook her head, he turned to Spencer. "Don't leave town for the next twenty-four hours."

Spencer's head jerked in a nod as he swallowed audibly. "I won't," he promised.

***

Lacey's nerves were stretched to the breaking point. Between customers, she used her nervous energy to straighten and organize every tabletop, nook and cranny in the store. The two texts she'd received from Caleb provided precious little relief from her anxiety.

The first told her that Spencer was willingly answering questions. He sent the second one when they were wrapping up.

Spencer's scared and hung over. Almost done. Nothing on your dad.

When Caleb finally walked back into the shop, Lacey's heart raced. Had there been any revelations? Any clues? It took every ounce of discipline she possessed to stay seated at the table with the young bride-to-be. Lacey's eyes tracked his progress as he walked to the counter. She wanted to read his face, but he barely glanced her way.

Lacey forced herself to finish the meeting and schedule the follow-up before ushering the girl out the front door. Since it was almost five, she didn't hesitate to flip the sign to CLOSED and lock the front door.

Caleb was standing at the back door holding out her jacket. "Let's get out of here," he said.

She grabbed his arm, her eyes searching his. "Talk to me. Is it bad news?"

He looked like he was weighing his words. "I think it's bad news for us."

She shook her head questioningly as he helped her into her coat. He took her elbow as they walked out into the chilly night air, their breath white puffs in front of them.

"What do you mean? And where are we going?"

"I don't know anything for certain yet. The police questioned Spencer for hours. But my gut's telling me he's not involved. He was clueless."

"Then where's he been?" Frustration laced her words as Caleb closed her door.

As Caleb slid into the driver's seat, his hand squeezed her leg gently. "Food first. Then we'll go through everything."

Chapter 18

It was early enough at the Pizza Station that there wasn't much of a crowd. Caleb ordered a pitcher of beer and a large pizza, loaded.

Lacey's gaze didn't leave his face as she waited to hear him out. Her frustration and agony were palpable. Caleb vowed that the bastards behind this nightmare were going to pay.

"From what Spencer told us, he was on a week-long binge in Kansas City with friends. If his car was any indication, I'm inclined to believe him." Caleb recalled as many pertinent details as he could then reached across the table and grabbed her hand as the young waitress came over with the pitcher and glasses.

After the waitress poured, Lacey pulled her hand from his and took a long drink. Setting her glass back on the table, she traced the edge of it with her fingertip before looking at Caleb. "You really believe he's innocent?" she whispered.

Caleb missed the warmth of her hand in his. He wanted the connection, wanted her to know she wasn't alone. God, he wished she'd let him in. He also wished he had better news, but telling her anything less than the truth was unacceptable. "Yes, I do."

Her shoulders slumped. "Another dead end," she mused. "It seems like the more we learn, the less we know." She looked away from him, but not before he saw the gleam of tears in her eyes.

"I didn't want him to be involved, you know." Her whispered words were thick with unshed tears. "But I'm running out of options. I'm losing my dad, Caleb. I can feel it." When she finally returned her gaze to his, the intensity of her grief almost stole his breath. "I can't stand not knowing where he is, or if he's even alive. If the police are doing all they can, then it's not enough. And the newspaper people aren't even calling anymore."

She swiped at a tear trailing down her cheek. "Do you know what the front page story was today?" Her laugh was high and brittle. "The zoo is getting a new giraffe. A new giraffe! My dad is still missing. And they've moved on to a freaking giraffe."

Caleb moved to the chair next to Lacey's and grabbed her shaking hands, his eyes boring into hers. "Every possibility that we check off this list helps us. Helps our focus."

"I know," she cried. "But what if we never find out what happened?"

He squeezed her hands, his voice unyielding. "That's not an option. We're going to find him. Alive."

Lacey stared at him, her eyes swimming in tears, as if judging his conviction. Something inside her must have steadied itself. Taking a deep breath, she gave him a shaky smile. "Thank you. I needed to hear that. I spend a lot of time in my own head with god-awful thoughts that I could never say out loud." She shifted in her seat and cleared her throat. "Sorry for the melt down. I just need to find something concrete, something that will help us figure out where he is."

Caleb looked at the slight blush on her cheeks and knew it had cost her to open up, especially to him. He released Lacey's hands as the waitress arrived carrying a huge pizza.

The woman served the hot thick slices onto plates, catching the cheese as it dripped off the sides. Lacey looked at it, her mantel of self-control firmly back in place, then grabbed her extra plate. "I think I'll start with the salad bar."

As Caleb waited for her to return, an idea formed that he hoped Lacey would buy into. God knew, she needed a break from her nightmare.

Lacey dropped into her seat and took a drink from the beer mug Caleb had topped off. Her eyes, still a bit red-rimmed, must have caught the slight smile on his face.

She quirked an eyebrow. "What?"

He waited a moment then spoke. "What if, just for tonight, we put it all out of our minds?"

Her brow furrowed as she popped a cherry tomato into her mouth.

"I'm serious. Tonight it's you and me. On a date, having fun. No worries, no tomorrow. Eat your salad if you must, then dive into this huge pizza with me. After that, we'll go dancing and work it all back off."

Caught by the sparkle in his eyes, Lacey felt a grin tug at the corners of her mouth. The idea of releasing the constant stress and fear for a few hours sounded wonderful.

She tossed him a saucy smile. "You and me, on a date? Like old times, huh?" Her insides cringed. As soon as the words were out of her mouth, she wished them back. The last thing she needed to do was dig up old memories just when she was starting to like the new Caleb.

"I'm sorry," she looked down and stabbed her salad. "It's probably best if we don't go there." She felt Caleb's stare, but couldn't quite bring herself to meet it.

He put down his fork. "I think *there* is a good place to start." When she didn't respond, he continued. "I've spent quite a bit of time thinking about what happened that summer."

Could she get up and leave without making a scene? She hadn't meant to open this discussion and she certainly wasn't up for a patronizing lecture about how much wiser he'd been or how young and foolish her ideals were.

Lacey shrugged. "Look, I understand. I mistook what was going on for something much bigger than it was. You were looking for an extra pass-time that summer, and I was convenient. There's nothing else that needs to be said. I was young, and very naïve." Anger simmered beneath her words. "But I've learned a lot since then."

Caleb was watching her over the rim of his beer mug, his face a mask of hard lines. "Is that really what you think? That you were just an easy lay for me?" He set the glass down with a little too much force. "I was crazy about you. And it was killing me that I couldn't take you with me."

Lacey froze, her eyes flashing fire. "No rewriting history, Caleb. I don't remember you challenging my dad when he refused to let me go with you. You knew I'd fallen for you. I thought we had something special, something real. He said no and you stood there and watched it happen. You *let* it happen. That's a fact. Lie to me again and I'm out of here."

His gaze held hers. "I didn't challenge him because I'm the one who asked him to do it."

She flinched at the quick sucker punch. "Nice. If that's what you do to people you're crazy about, I feel sorry for your enemies." She took a gulp of her beer, trying desperately to hide the pain his words had inflicted, even after all this time. "Maybe we need to leave. It's been a long day."

She reached for her bag, but Caleb stopped her.

"Listen to me, damn it."

She glanced from the hand around her wrist to his face, certain she would find a glint of self-satisfaction there. What she found instead stunned her. Caleb's eyes were unguarded, almost vulnerable. She didn't pull her hand away.

"I was leaving. And I knew what was going to be required of me. If I'd taken you with me, I'd have deposited you in a city where you didn't know anybody. And left. I wouldn't have been around. Hell, I *wasn't* around for most of the past six years. Maybe not at first, but in time you'd have hated your life. Hated me for it. I talked it over with your dad and he agreed."

"You didn't talk to *me* about it. Never even gave me a chance to –"

"To what? Talk me into taking you with me? I couldn't give you the opportunity. Because you probably could've done it. But you wouldn't have known what was coming."

She searched his face for any sign of deceit, half-hoping she'd find it. "So you, in your infinite wisdom, knew what was best. You couldn't imagine that I'd have paid the price to be with you."

He at least had the grace to look sheepish. After a minute, his face broke into a wry grin. "Well, when you put it that way, maybe my wisdom wasn't quite as infallible as I imagined it was at twenty-four, huh?" His eyes locked on hers. "I'm sorry I hurt you."

Lacey sat still, accepting the moment, as the dam of reserve broke within her. Releasing the sadness she'd buried all those years ago, she shook her head. "We were so young. Probably too young." She grabbed her mug and held it up, mentally closing the book on that painful chapter in her life. "I may never admit you made the right call, but at least we can drink to closure."

He held up his mug and clinked hers with it. "And new beginnings."

Lacey let his comment slide and sat back in her seat. Picking up her fork, she dug into her pizza. She tried to focus on her food, but over and over his eyes drew her, causing heat to pool low in her belly. Maybe it was the beer talking, but she threw caution to the wind. This wasn't a new beginning, but it was now. And for right now, she knew what she wanted. Placing her napkin on the table, she met his gaze. "I appreciate the offer to go out, but if it's all the same to you, I think I'd rather just go home tonight."

***

Lacey didn't speak as they tossed their jackets on her sofa. Words weren't necessary, and she'd rather not talk anyway. Caleb took her hand and led her toward her bedroom. She was already on fire, impatient for his touch. If she was compensating for the nightmare, so be it.

She tried to undo the buttons on her blouse with shaking fingers. Caleb laid his warm hands over hers, stilling them. She met his eyes and could feel the blue fire in their depths.

"Let me," he whispered.

Her breath hitched as his fingers slowly and expertly divested her of her clothes. Everywhere he touched, her skin burned for more.

When she didn't think she could stand one more moment of the sweet torment, she opened her eyes. He'd undressed also, standing before her, watching her. The heat in his eyes and the hard contours of his face told her that he was fighting for control. He gave up the battle, pulling her into his arms.

They tumbled onto the bed, their lips locked in a ferocious kiss that fanned the flames higher. She ran her hands over his back and arms, loving the solid heat of him. There was a sense of newness, of freedom from the past that heightened her desire. "Caleb, please," she moaned.

Caleb's lips caught hers again and his fingers slid into her. She lifted her hips, trying to deepen the contact. Once again, he found himself unable to control the raging desire coursing through him.

Without another thought, he drove himself into her sheath. She arched against him and let out a deep moan as her body rocked in rhythm to his.

He tried to slow the pace but her nails scored his shoulders until they were both so lost that nothing else mattered. He felt her tighten around him and heard her alternately calling out to God and to him. He increased the pace and moments later, exploded into her.

He collapsed on top of her then rolled onto his back and hauled her up against his side. He was drifting back into reality and felt the wetness of her tears on his shoulders. Afraid he'd been too rough, he leaned up and gently lifted her face to his.

"Did I hurt you?" he asked.

She was too overwhelmed to speak. Nothing in her experience, not even what she'd felt for Caleb as a teenager, could've prepared her for the depth of feeling she just experienced and it scared her to death. She looked at him with tears still trailing down her cheeks. Silently, she shook her head.

He held her close, searching her face. "Are you sure?"

Lacey nodded into his shoulder, her voice a whisper. "I'm sure."

This wasn't real. She knew that. Caleb provided a temporary, albeit amazing, escape from reality. Nothing more. She dried her eyes then settled into the crook of his arm as it tightened around her. For tonight, she'd allow herself to indulge in the fantasy.

Tomorrow was soon enough to jump back into chaos.

***

Caleb was glad for the quiet of the early Sunday morning. He knew Lacey would sleep for at least another hour, but it took all his discipline to walk away from her half-covered body.

He made coffee and took the steaming mug to the living room along with his laptop to check email. As he booted up the machine, his mind wandered again to Lacey.

Progress was slow, but she'd begun to open up to him. He was looking forward to learning more. The smile on his lips evaporated as he scanned his email. Rolling his eyes he looked at three messages from Susie Blakely, BioTech's receptionist.

The woman was emailing him from her home account. He was far from politically correct, but her actions and the content of her messages were over the edge of sexual innuendo and into harassment. He'd have to talk to Roger about it when he got back to Chicago.

As he clicked through a couple of messages from Meg, he heard his phone vibrate on the kitchen table. By the time he scrambled off the couch and reached it, the call had gone to voicemail.

He skipped the message from his sister and decided that now was as good a time as any to call her back and get the details about their family Christmas gathering. She answered on the first ring.

Lacey rolled over onto her back and stretched, her body still glowing from last night's lovemaking. She wasn't sure how many times she and Caleb came to each other during the night but she should be tired this morning. Somehow, though, she wasn't.

Self-preservation mode kicked into high gear. Tying her robe, she migrated toward the smell of fresh coffee. She didn't want to open the door with Caleb again, but as she listened to the low rumble of his voice in her kitchen, the butterflies in her stomach made her wonder if maybe she already had.

She frowned. Was he on the phone? Who'd call this early? Fear congealed around her heart, pushing out every other thought. Had something happened with her dad's case and the police hadn't been able to get in touch with her?

Lacey stood at the entrance to the kitchen, trying to make sense of the one-sided conversation. Caleb's broad back was to her, his voice hushed, but clear. So clear, she couldn't possibly mistake the words.

"I know. I'm sorry. I meant to call you back the other day. It's been hectic here." He paused. "I have no idea. I know," he said again, sighing. "That sounds good. That date should work."

Another long pause. "No. I'm sure I'll be there. I told you I wouldn't miss it. The baby will be here by then and we'll have reason to celebrate."

Stunned, Lacey listened in horrid fascination. What the hell was he talking about? What baby? As the damning realization hit, she spun on her heel and propelled herself toward the bathroom where she shut the door, leaning against it. Her mind reeled. This couldn't be happening.

Not again.

Her stomach wretched as guilt smashed down on her. Guilt she thought she'd conquered. Vicki Calloway's face swam into her vision. Jason, her husband, had duped Lacey into a six-month-long relationship until fate intervened and revealed him for the duplicitous asshole he was.

But as awful as that moment of discovery had been, it paled in comparison. She'd never truly given her heart to Jason. But she'd given it to Caleb once, and, despite her chronic denial, had been perilously close to doing it again.

That bastard! How could he be here, acting like he cared when there was another woman. And a baby. A baby! God, she was a fool… again! How could fate be cruel enough to put her in this situation twice?

Palms on the counter, she stared at her horrified eyes in the mirror.

It wasn't fate. You did this to yourself. You trusted him.

The searing pain took her breath. It felt so much more vivid than she remembered. She saw the tears pooling in her eyes, and anger washed over her.

You will not cry over him.

Questions flew through her mind almost faster than she could process them. How the hell had she let this happen? What was wrong with her? She

130

thought she'd learned the signs. Was she so blinded by her physical desire for him that she'd chosen to disregard what was right in front of her?

She searched her own conscience as she replayed the past week in her mind. Suddenly, the phone calls he'd ignored, and even the ones he'd taken flashed through her mind.

"I can't talk to you right now. No, everything's fine." A pause. "Yes, I'm sure I'm not avoiding you. I'll call you later."

She shoved away from the bathroom counter, determined to stop beating herself up. The reality was that he'd played her well. And she'd made too many assumptions.

But he didn't know yet that it wasn't his game to win. She needed time away from him. Time to pick up the pieces of her heart that she'd exposed. Time to make certain her emotions were in check.

She'd use him to help find her father. There was no doubt that his connections in the industry were valuable. She wasn't fool enough to throw them away for the sake of her lacerated pride. But, by God, she'd make it perfectly clear that was all she wanted from him.

Chapter 19

Caleb was in a foul mood. His conversation with his sister was worse than being cross examined in a courtroom. Every time there was a family function, she asked if he was going to bring someone with him. And he always told her no. He should've known better than to open his big mouth, but when the errant thought of bringing Lacey to the Christmas gathering popped into his head, he mentioned it to Rachel. Then she pounced.

Could he have waved a bigger red cape in front of his sister's face? Probably not. And, truth be told, he was jumping the gun. Lacey's life was, understandably, on hold until they found Bill.

He felt the fear and the anger all over again. *They would find him.*

But until then, there wasn't room for anything else. Not yet.

When he finally ended the call, an email from Meg informed him that there was a snag in product licensing that could cause BioTech's European launch to be postponed indefinitely.

To make matters worse, he needed to get cleaned up and ready for the day but Lacey was taking forever in the bathroom. Knuckle extended, he rapped on the bathroom door. Something clattered to the floor then he heard a muffled oath.

"Are you okay in there? Abrams called. He's coming by in twenty minutes."

"Why?"

He heard the wealth of worry in that one word. "No major developments. He said he wants to get us up to speed on the investigation." He stood across the hall from the door, arms crossed. "Are you going to be much longer?"

Caleb sounded surly. Probably a guilty conscience, Lacey fumed. She waited another ten minutes, until she was certain she could maintain her composure, before coming out. She opened the door, surprised by Caleb's tall, muscular form standing in her path.

As she tried to squeeze past, his hands came around her shoulders and pulled her to him. "You okay this morning?"

She breathed into his chest and held herself stiff against his embrace. "I'm fine. You'd better get ready." She felt his lips on her hair, and every nerve ending in her body threatened to recoil.

Breaking out of his embrace, she avoided his gaze. She got dressed and was rinsing her oatmeal bowl in the kitchen sink by the time the bathroom door opened again. She heard Caleb's mumbled complaint about his cold shower as his voice faded down the hall to the guest room. Had she not been so furious with him, she would've found it humorous.

The doorbell rang and Lacey rushed to answer it. Detective Abrams stood on the porch. Though the sunlight was bright behind him, the air carried a bitter chill. Fall was losing the battle to winter.

Lacey took his jacket and offered him a cup of coffee.

He accepted with a nod. "Mr. Mansfield's here, right? I'd like to talk with you both."

Heat infused her cheeks. Afraid the detective assumed they were sleeping together, Lacey felt compelled to explain. "Well, yes, actually. He's been staying in the guest bedroom since the incident at the shop."

Abrams nodded as he glanced around the room. "Makes sense."

Lacey pasted a serene smile on her face. "I'll go get him. Have a seat."

Her shoulder muscles tightened. She didn't want to face Caleb. Didn't want him to suspect that she knew. But she was desperate to hear whatever news Abrams brought, which, she reminded herself, was all that really mattered.

Knocking on the partially opened door, she peeked inside. "The detective is here. He'd like to speak with us." She hoped her voice held just the right amount of indifference.

Caleb looked up from tying his shoe and wondered if Lacey was coming down with a cold. She sounded like she'd swallowed a frog. "I'll be right there."

He arrived at the table the same time Lacey appeared from the kitchen with a mug of coffee for Abrams. She didn't look at him or acknowledge him, and Caleb's blood ran cold.

Something was very wrong. Had Abrams brought bad news after all? Within moments of Abrams first words though, Caleb breathed a sigh of relief. They were still on the hunt.

The detective began by validating what Caleb had assumed from their meeting with Spencer yesterday. "We had an opportunity to confirm Spencer Nicholson's story about his whereabouts during the past week. We interviewed the two people he went to Kansas City with and we also were able to procure video footage from the casino Friday night proving Spencer's claim."

Caleb caught Lacey's nod out of the corner of his eye. Her hands were clasped tight, her white knuckles belying her calm veneer.

Abrams continued. "We've also concluded that Stan Jacobson likely lied to his wife about his activities. After visiting with her yesterday, I'm pretty confident that she's not involved. Her story is bizarre though, so we're monitoring her phone lines. So far, we haven't picked up any contact with him. We've decided it's worth the time to do a little more digging into his background. If anything comes from it we'll let you know."

Again, Lacey nodded.

Caleb glanced at her stricken features. Justice couldn't be swift enough. He swallowed his anger and caught Abrams attention. "What about Gary Finley? Were you able to obtain the warrant?"

Abrams sipped from his mug and shook his head. "It was too late on Friday to get in front of a judge. We'll get it tomorrow."

134

Caleb's scowl deepened and he started to protest, but Abrams held up his hand and cut him off before he could speak.

"We were able to hold him over the weekend on a previous warrant." Abrams took one more drink of his coffee and stood to leave. "We're working on linking him to the other robberies prior to yours. Lopez talked to him and she thinks he'll sing so I doubt he'll be a problem going forward. Stan Jacobson, though, is very much a person of interest for us and becoming more so every day that he doesn't surface. That's where we're going to be focusing our attention until or unless something more promising comes along."

He reminded them again to contact him with any new or relevant information.

Lacey walked him to the front door. "Thank you for everything." As she closed the door, she shivered from the blast of frigid air. "I think I'll head over to Mona's," she said, her head bent.

Caleb watched from the table as she jerked her coat on then flipped her hair from under the collar. He knew she was frustrated over the lack of information Abrams had to share and he understood her need to keep moving, keep doing something. He felt it, too.

"I'll go with you," he said, sliding his chair back from the table.

"No," she said. Her chin came up and anger blazed in her eyes.

Caleb stared. *What the hell was going on with her this morning?*

He wanted to spend some time with Spencer, and he wasn't going to give her the fight she was obviously spoiling for. His hands squeezed her upper arms. "Look, I know it feels like we're going in circles, but I'm on your side, remember?"

Lacey shrugged away from his grip and leaned over the chair to pick up her purse. When she stood and looked at him again the spark of anger he'd seen in her eyes had been replaced by indifference. "Of course. You can ride over there with me. I just don't know how long I'll be staying."

Her rigid politeness was as wrong as her anger, but he didn't have time to question her further. She was already halfway out the front door. Caleb grabbed his coat and followed, closing the door behind him with a solid thud. The ride to Mona's was taut with silence. Caleb tried twice to get her talking, but both times, her monosyllabic answers ended the conversation.

He considered asking her point-blank what was eating at her, but he hoped she'd come around and open up on her own. Patience had never been his strong suit, but she obviously needed some time and space to process. And he needed to give it to her.

If Lacey hadn't been so focused on Caleb's deceit, she'd have thought to call Mona ahead of time instead of showing up unannounced. But as she pulled into the drive, she breathed a quiet sigh of relief because not only was Mona home, Spencer's car was there, too. Hopefully, Caleb was at least being honest about wanting to spend some time with him.

She bounded out of the car and knocked on the front door before Caleb had time to join her. Mona opened the door and enveloped Lacey in a wide hug.

"Oh, honey. I meant to call you last night, but Spencer and I stayed up most of the evening talking. I figured Caleb would fill you in on the details, anyway." She pulled back, her eyes tired, but bright.

Lacey almost lost it in Mona's arms. She wanted to cry, and rant, and scream at every injustice in her life, but as she watched Mona's eyes cloud over with worry, she shook her head and forced a smile.

"Yep. He did." She barely glanced at Caleb as he came up beside her. "I just wanted to stop by and see how you were doing, but if it's a bad time –"

"Don't be silly. Come on in," Mona welcomed them in and took the opportunity to formally introduce Caleb to Spencer.

Lacey was reluctantly impressed by how quickly Caleb was able to get Spencer to connect with him. Within minutes, Caleb asked Spencer if he'd be willing to go for a drive. Spencer agreed after a quick glance at his mom. Lacey guessed that, after the past week of mayhem, he was looking for anything he could do to get back in her good graces.

Sitting over mugs of peppermint mocha at Mona's kitchen table, Lacey listened as Mona shared some of last night's conversation with her son.

"He's been so angry," Mona murmured. "Angry at his dad for leaving him. Then when it looked like I'd moved on, his anger transferred to me, and by extension, Bill."

Lacey cupped her mug, its warmth seeping into her cold hands. "Surely he wants you to find happiness again, doesn't he?"

Mona nodded. "I think it's just a matter of perspective. By accepting, or even acknowledging, my relationship with Bill, it was forcing him to think about his own future. Rather than do that, he just rebelled and got caught up in ways to escape."

"He looks tired."

Smiling, Mona took a sip of her coffee. "He looks great compared to yesterday." She wrinkled her nose. "Smells a lot better, too."

The conversation veered away from Spencer to her dad and the case, but they didn't linger there long. Lacey didn't have the heart to go over all the things they didn't know.

Shaking off the melancholy that talking about her dad evoked, Lacey plucked a sugar cookie off the plate between them. She broke it and took a bite, then shared Sam's situation with Mona. After her initial shock, Mona offered to help in any way she could.

"Speaking of help," the older woman said. "Caleb's been a wonderful one, hasn't he?"

Lacey forced a smile. "Yes."

Mona winked. "I really like him. Wouldn't mind it at all if he ended up sticking around. He's going to make some woman a great husband, don't you think?"

Having just taken a drink of her coffee to wash down the cookie, Lacey almost choked. She was used to Mona saying what was on her mind, but holy crap. That was exactly what she didn't need to hear today.

Refusing to give Mona one more thing to worry about, Lacey decided to keep her thoughts about that subject to herself. She took another sip of coffee and shrugged. "I'm sure that's true for someone."

***

137

Spencer walked into the kitchen in front of Caleb, grabbed two sodas out of the refrigerator and handed one to Caleb. Lacey's eyes went back and forth between them. She could tell Mona was dying of curiosity, too.

Neither man spoke, but Spencer looked like he'd been crying. She assumed that Caleb must have read him the riot act for his behavior. That pissed her off. Not because Spencer didn't deserve it, but because Caleb was continuing to burrow deeper into their lives. He had his own life. *His own family.* Couldn't he leave hers alone?

Spencer turned around and shook Caleb's hand and thanked him.

Lacey and Mona exchanged surprised glances but said nothing.

"We'll talk tomorrow." Caleb pounded Spencer on the shoulder and then looked at Lacey. "Are you just about finished with your visit?"

She nodded and quickly stood. Gathering the mugs, she rinsed them in the sink, taking those few moments to try to reconcile her thoughts, but nothing made sense. How could this two-timing deceiver seem so genuine in his concern for Spencer and Mona? *And me?*

Lacey stared out the window as Caleb drove her home, her thoughts ricocheting between Caleb and her dad. By the time they arrived at her house, her head was pounding like a drum.

She made a beeline for the bathroom medicine cabinet. Downing a couple of extra-strength pills, she heard Caleb call her from the kitchen.

"I think I'll order take-out from Applebee's. What would you like?"

Lacey rubbed her forehead, the pain searing. "I've got a killer headache. You're on your own for dinner." She headed to her room, tossing the words over her shoulder.

Caleb followed her down the hall. His booted foot blocked her from closing the door, his face a granite mask. "You need to eat," he muttered.

"I'm not hungry. I had a snack at Mona's." She looked down at his foot and back up at him.

He didn't move.

She crossed her arms and leaned against the wall, a pucker between her brows. Her voice turned to ice. "You may be helping find my dad, but

you're *not* my dad. I said I'm not hungry. That's all you need to know."
Ignoring his frown, she continued. "I also think you should go back to the
Ramada. It was more than a little awkward this morning when Abrams
assumed you were staying here."

He lifted an eyebrow. "I am staying here."

"Exactly. And you shouldn't be. The worry about Gary is over."

Caleb's sigh was almost a growl. "You want to tell me what the hell is
going on, Lacey?" He shoved his hair back from his forehead. "Last night
was incredible and intense, and today –"

She pushed off the wall, her hand on the door. "Today's a different day.
And last night shouldn't have happened."

The cold certainty in her eyes startled him. He couldn't get a handle on
it. How could she seem so convicted when he didn't feel certain about a
damn thing right now? "That may be your opinion, but it doesn't change
facts. I don't give a shit that Finley's behind bars. Leaving you here
unprotected is not an option. Period."

For a minute, he was sure she'd argue, but she stared him down then
shrugged her shoulders. "Suit yourself. You're welcome to the guest room.
Good night, Caleb."

The quiet click of the door was louder than a slam. He returned to the
kitchen, but the pang he felt had little to do with hunger. Lacey was making
it abundantly clear that a relationship with him was off the table. And she
wasn't a game player. So, what the hell? Had she decided he wasn't worth
the risk?

Caleb laid awake hours later. He tried to reconcile the riddle of Lacey's
attitude shift but he was drawing blanks. Thoughts that he'd tried to
obliterate from his memory seeped into his brain – old specters of not
being worth loving. It'd taken until he was an adult, looking back
objectively at his childhood, to figure out that his dad's lack of love and
respect wasn't about Caleb as much as the alcohol. But Lacey was different.
And he didn't even know where to start.

With a weary sigh, he shoved his frustration aside. *Screw it.* The process of compartmentalizing his brain was second nature. By necessity, he'd learned it as a child. By choice, he'd perfected it as a businessman.

He whipped out his laptop and shot off emails to Meg and Brandon Thomas. According to Meg, Brandon was helping fill in the holes Ian seemed to be intentionally digging. Since Meg wasn't prone to giving lavish praise, Caleb figured that Brandon was almost single-handedly righting the ship in his department.

Good to know. He liked the kid, although he wished he knew more about him. Another casualty of being gone so much. Ian was the other issue Caleb was going to talk to Roger about when he returned. Unless, of course, Ian ended up in prison.

A new message from Brandon popped into his email. Caleb smiled. One in the morning, and he was still working. Gotta love it. The kid would go far. Caleb clicked open the message.

Caleb;

Got resolution on the bio-ethics issue from the EU folks. That's one big hurdle out of the way.

How's it going in Toto-land? I asked Roger what the cops were doing here yesterday and he filled me in. That really sucks. Let me know if I can help. Dr. Jordan sounds like a great guy.

We're under control here, even without Ian...or maybe that's why? Just joking. Call if you need me.

-B

Caleb rolled his shoulders. He wondered how much Roger had shared with Brandon. Not that he had anything against the kid, but who would he tell? Could he accidentally tip somebody off?

Deciding to call it a night, Caleb logged off his computer as his cell phone buzzed on the night stand. He chuckled as Meg's number displayed on his caller ID and wondered if anyone at BioTech kept regular hours.

He knew better than to ignore her call. She'd just call again.

"Hey. Any break in the case?" Meg was never big on salutations.

Caleb's eyes widened. "It's one in the morning, Meg. I figured Rome was on fire. Literally. You're calling me about the case?" He paused. "And how'd you find out? Does *everyone* at BioTech know?"

"Get real. Cops were here. Roger pulled senior staff in for a briefing. So no, not everyone knows."

Caleb rolled his eyes. "I'm sure it's only a matter of time. Anyway, no breaks yet. I'm sure Roger told you about Lacey and Mona. They're going nuts with worry."

"Ian a suspect?"

Tensing, Caleb debated how to answer. Or if he even wanted to. Finally, he growled into the phone. "I don't know. They're looking at him, but so far they've got nothing." Pausing again, his anger rose. "I wish I was there. I'd get him to fucking talk."

Meg surprised him by laughing into the phone. "Well, at least you'll get your wish."

"What's that mean?"

"You're going to love this. Roger announced today that his wife has decided that we need to throw a company celebration for the expansion and sales growth this year."

Caleb could hear the hint of disgust in her voice. If it didn't have to do with getting work done, Meg could do without it.

She continued. "Your presence is required since you're giving the presentation about the expansion. The event is black-tie. And it's on the twenty-first."

"Of November?" Caleb choked. "That's ridiculous. I wasn't even supposed to be back from vacation yet."

"I know, but Mrs. Cantwell didn't want to conflict with the holiday rush and Roger knew you wouldn't miss it. He said since you were still in the area, it would be quick and easy to catch flights back and forth." Her voice turned brusque. "Just do me a favor and see what miracles you can work between now and then to help me keep this launch on track."

141

Caleb hung up the phone and scowled into the dark room, his gaze fixed on the shadowed ceiling above his bed. Should he go to Chicago? And how was he going to get Lacey to go with him? He'd figure out a way. Because despite the events of the day, and maybe because of them, he wasn't leaving without her. Not even for a day.

Chapter 20

"It still feels right," Sam said as she walked in the back door.

Lacey poked her head out the office. The younger girl looked relieved. And happy. Lacey couldn't keep the grin off her face. "Yeah?"

"Yeah."

"Okay." Lacey nodded. "We'll start our research tonight." She stood in the doorway thinking. "If you're up for it, we can stay here and order sandwiches or something."

"Are you sure? I feel like I'm wasting your time, especially with everything you're dealing with."

Lacey stiffened her resolve as she saw pity reflected in the younger girl's eyes. So what if she looked like she'd tossed and turned most of the night? It didn't matter that she couldn't remember the last time she'd slept more than a couple hours straight. She wasn't looking for anyone's pity.

"I'm sure. I have to stay busy or I'll go crazy. And I'm doing nothing but going in circles. Believe me, you're helping me as much as I'm helping you." Sam was watching her closely so she forced a smile, determined to focus on the day ahead. Linking her arm in Sam's, Lacey pulled her out of the office. "Seriously, I'm glad to help. I'm looking forward to it."

Flipping through the thick stack of orders, Lacey handed them off to Sam. "Looks like you'll be in the workroom most of the day. I'll take care of things out here."

The steady stream of customers kept Lacey from drowning in her problems, except for the occasional well-meaning patrons who inquired about her father. But in quiet moments, she found herself wishing yesterday hadn't happened, wishing Caleb hadn't deceived her. Again.

Better to find out now. True. But why did he do it? Did she have some big flashing sign on her chest that said "Lie to me"? She sighed. Given her history, she wouldn't doubt it.

***

Lacey locked the door behind the delivery guy and headed back to the office. Sam was already at the desk setting out the subs and chips on paper towels.

"Guess we should've thought of plates," she said, wiping her fingers.

Grabbing a couple of sodas out of the refrigerator, Lacey sat down behind the computer. "No problem here. Feels just like college. Most of the time, we chose not to eat on plates. Of course, back then, it was so we didn't have to do the dishes."

Sam was silent for a moment. "Maybe someday I'll have a story about my college life," she said with a touch of wistfulness. "I don't know. Gary always told me I wasn't smart enough to go to school."

Lacey's head swiveled. "Has he been to college?"

"No. He went to work at the feed mill after high school."

"Then how would he know? Your future's an open door," she encouraged. "Don't let the 'Garys' of the world tell you what you're capable of, okay?"

Sam smiled past the glistening tears in her eyes. "I won't. I promise."

Lacey returned to the computer screen. "Now, let's see what we can do about the present." She printed out several pages from the state website and slapped them down on the desk. "Looks like we have our work cut out for us. There are three or four agencies that look interesting. Let's check out their websites and see if we can get a feel for them."

She turned the computer over to Sam then glanced at her phone on the corner of the desk. She'd succeeded in not communicating with Caleb all day, but part of her felt bad for ignoring his calls. At this point, she was certain she'd say things that were better left unsaid.

Settling on a text, she picked up the phone and keyed in the message.

Working late with Sam. Don't wait up.

She and Sam jotted down additional questions as they plotted their game plan to contact the agencies by phone the next day.

Lacey stood and stretched the aches from her lower back. She was shocked to see that it was after nine-thirty. "Wow, time really does fly. If I'm this tired, you must be exhausted."

Sam smiled. "I should be," she admitted. "But I think I'm too excited to sleep." She gathered up the papers on the desk and stuffed them in her bag. "I finally feel like I'm starting to control my own life. And, not having to worry about Gary makes everything easier." She shrugged into her jacket then hugged Lacey. "See you tomorrow."

Lacey followed Sam to the back door, making sure she got safely to her truck. As she turned the lock in the door, Sam's words echoed in her mind and tears blurred her vision. Brushing them away with an angry swipe, she wondered if she'd ever feel in control of her life again.

The red light winked from her phone, drawing her attention to the waiting text message from Caleb.

Called Abrams. No news today. Spent some time with Spencer. How's it going with Sam?

Lacey sank back down into the chair. Taking several deep breaths, she attempted to ward off the despair that threatened to overwhelm her. She could barely remember when her biggest concern was trying to land an account, or deciding what class to take at the gym. Oh, what she'd give to have her normal, boring life back.

In the silence of the empty shop, one tear fell. She buried her face in her hands. "I don't know what else to do, God! Please, bring Dad home. I don't know what to do." A broken sob escaped her lips.

Lacey cried until her ribs hurt. Then she cried some more.

***

By the next day, Lacey wished she could blame her red, puffy eyes on allergies. She thought the crying would've worn her out, but no chance. She still slept like hell. Shaking it off, she sat down with Sam between customers and trimmed their list of potential adoption agencies to one, a local organization called Abundance Ministries. They scheduled an appointment for the following evening and drove after work to meet with Karen Russell, one of the founders and placement specialists.

As they approached the restored Victorian that housed the adoption agency, Lacey pondered the past several days. There was little progress in the investigation, but the process of helping Sam with her problems had given Lacey somewhere to focus, and the perfect excuse to avoid Caleb's company. She was grateful for both.

But now, as they mounted the steps to the front porch, Lacey's apprehension rose. Feeling like a mother hen, she leaned into Sam. "If she says or does anything that makes you uncomfortable, we have other options, okay?" She didn't even let Sam answer. "We don't have to make any decisions tonight, and we don't have to stay local."

Sam nodded her understanding. She clutched Lacey's hand and knocked on the wood framed screen door. "I think I'm going to like this place, but if you catch any vibes that I don't, please jump in." Her eyes mirrored Lacey's apprehension. "I don't want to make a mistake."

Their fears were completely unfounded. Karen met them at the door, a serene middle-aged woman who showed them to a beautifully appointed sitting area. The upholstered sofas were surprisingly comfortable and a basket of fresh scones scented the air. Surrounded by a cozy fire, they sipped hot tea as Karen shared several case stories with them along with a history of the organization. Lacey took notes then listened to Sam explain her story and her hopes for the baby.

By the time they left, Sam had in hand three profile scrapbooks of prospective adoptive parents. Karen had told her to look through them and see if she felt a connection with any of the three.

***

The following day, Lacey and Sam studied the books together during slow times at the shop. Each book contained a letter to the birth mother along with photos of the family members, their home and their community.

"What about Mike and Tina Morris?"

146

Lacey'd been leaning toward them, but she wasn't about to speak up until Sam had made her decision. "They seem like a sweet couple. Good extended family in the area too. What do you think?"

Sam's fingers tapped a staccato against the open page of the book. Then she flipped the pages back and forth. Reading and re-reading. She read the other two profiles again before coming back to the Morris family.

"I can see my baby with them," she whispered.

Lacey sat on the stool next to Sam, silent and waiting.

Sam raised her eyes from the page and nodded firmly. "Definitely them."

Lacey's throat constricted as she considered the enormity of the moment and how, with a word, a decision, two strangers' lives were getting ready to change. She thought about how her own life had changed, how at any given moment someone could be brought into the world. Or taken away. She nodded and gave Sam a wobbly smile. "Perfect."

"I need to check something in the cooler. Be right back." Lacey hopped off her stool before she lost it in front of Sam. She leaned against the door, the cold metal cooling her flushed skin.

She tormented herself daily with thoughts of where her dad might be, and what might've happened to him. But sitting there with Sam, she considered the passage of time and that there might come a day when an hour would pass, or a whole day might pass, without thinking about him at all.

The thought devastated her. If he weren't found, how would she go on? She'd been so young when her mother had passed away, and her dad had been there then to help pick up the pieces. Despair threatened again as memories tumbled through her mind. She wasn't ready to lose her dad, too. Couldn't envision a time without his happy smile, his dry sense of humor.

Taking a deep breath, Lacey straightened her apron, forcing her fears out of mind. *You're the only one who controls your thoughts. Focus on what you can control.*

Tonight, she'd make another list of things she hadn't done. People she hadn't personally talked to. Maybe Stan Jacobson's wife could help her. Hadn't Abrams said she'd been cooperative?

Lacey returned to the counter, calmer since she had a plan, as Sam finished up with a customer. "Did you get in touch with Karen?"

Sam nodded.

"Okay. Now what happens?"

Sam looked at her page of notes. "Karen said she'd set up a mediated conference call between me and the Morrises. Based on how that goes, we might meet face-to-face prior to the birth, or the meeting may wait until the baby's born."

Lacey searched Sam's features. Despite Sam's excitement, Lacey knew this was all coming at her fast. "You're okay with everything?"

Sam paused. "I think so. It's just so weird to realize that it's actually happening." She took Lacey's hand. "Thank you. For being here for me. This would be so scary otherwise."

Lacey pulled the younger girl into a hug. "Change is always scary. I'm glad I'm here, too." As the words slid past her lips, a twinge of fulfillment whispered through her. She glanced up at one of Mona's patchwork quilts on the wall and realized she'd played a small part in blending a patchwork of lives. The thought caused an unexpected smile.

***

Lacey's sliver of peace was shattered as she rounded the street corner and her house came into view. The red and blue lights from two police cars strobed across her yard.

She jumped out of her car and ran to the house. "Oh my God! Caleb!"

Lacey threw open the front door. Caleb caught her around the waist as she crossed the threshold. She pulled out of his grasp and searched his harsh features. "What's going on? What happened?"

"I was just getting ready to call you. You had company tonight, Ms. Jordan." Detective Abrams came around the half wall from the kitchen.

She whirled around to face him. "What? What do you mean?"

Caleb spoke from behind her. "Apparently, I was a surprise to the guy."

Looking from one to the other, her frustration mounted. They weren't making any sense.

Abrams took her elbow. "Come with me."

He led Lacey to the back door. Glass littered the floor and the door had been knocked off its hinges. A wave of nausea washed over her as he warned her to stay back. She clutched her middle and slumped against the wall as Abrams continued.

"The guy broke in while Caleb was in the shower."

She turned shocked eyes to Caleb and noticed a slight purpling under his right eye. "Oh my God, you were hit? Are you okay?" She started to reach up to touch his face then pulled back.

"I'm fine," Caleb grunted, his eyes following her hand. "He got in one good punch."

Lacey looked again at the broken glass, suppressing a shiver.

Caleb grabbed her shoulders, his eyes boring into her. Fear and adrenaline coursed through him as he thought about what would've happened if she'd been here alone. "To say that he was surprised I wasn't you would be an understatement. He was waiting for you to get out of the shower." Caleb paused, knowing his next words would haunt her. "He was here to take you."

Lacey stared at him, her eyes huge in her pale face. "Tell me what happened," she whispered.

What he wouldn't give to take away the raw fear on her face. Taking a deep breath, he dug deep for control. "Like I said, he got in one good punch. He was waiting outside the bathroom. As soon as he realized I wasn't you, he sucker punched me in the face and tried to run." Coiled anger sharpened his words. "We struggled but he got away. I couldn't exactly chase him down the street in a bath towel."

Abrams spoke up behind him. "At least we got some DNA potential and hopefully a few good fingerprints."

"DNA? From what?" Lacey asked.

Abrams nodded toward Caleb's right hand where bruises had formed on his swollen knuckles. "We've already cleaned him up but we have what we hope are some decent blood samples."

Lacey wrenched out of Caleb's grasp and walked to the hallway. Bitter fear trickled down her throat as she stared at the roll of gray duct tape on the floor. Oh God, it was real. Deep breaths were out of the question so she took quick shallow ones. She *would not* pass out.

Abrams approached and stood next to her. Rooted in place, she couldn't look at him. "What do I do?"

"We need you and Mr. Mansfield out of here so we can finish processing the scene," he said. "Pack a few things and head over to the Ramada for the night."

She nodded absently as she stood mesmerized by the roll of tape. Had her dad been treated the same way? Had he been bound? Brutalized? Murdered?

Pulling back her rampaging thoughts took extreme effort. She finally looked at Abrams. "Yes, of course," she nodded again.

"I had Lopez call over and make sure they have space available."

"We'll only need one room," Caleb said from the kitchen doorway.

Lacey turned on him, her cheeks hot. He was as convenient a target as any for the dark emotions swirling inside her. How dare he? "I'd prefer my own room," she said through clenched teeth.

Caleb stared hard at her. "Too bad," he snapped. "Someone broke in here tonight to take you against your will. I'm not letting you out of my sight."

Abrams spoke up after watching the exchange, obviously anxious to break the tension. "Lopez reserved a suite, if that'll work. We want to make sure you're both protected and this allows us to have just one officer posted."

Lacey turned her attention to the detective, embarrassed by their childish behavior. "Of course. Thank you. A suite will be perfect."

***

Lacey tiptoed out of the bathroom, her flannel pajamas covering her from neck to ankles. She hoped the extra fifteen minutes she'd waited would ensure that Caleb was already asleep. She needed time to think, needed to be alone. So many thoughts and questions tumbled through her mind.

What if she'd been at home tonight instead of Caleb? She shivered again at the possibility. Caleb had been right. Whoever took her father had also come for her. But what now? What did it mean? A flicker of hope emerged. She had to assume that this meant her dad was still alive. But would the kidnapper's failure cause her father's captor to retaliate against him? Or would they come after Mona next?

She wanted to pound her head into the wall. Every day there were more questions and precious few answers. She pushed the thoughts away as she walked through the common area to switch off the single lamp casting quiet shadows around the furniture. The thin remaining ray of light from the bathroom directed her steps, but she moved cautiously in the unfamiliar space.

Her mind refused to be silenced, though, as a vision of Caleb swam into focus. He'd been put in harm's way tonight. Because of her. No matter how badly he'd deceived her, the thought of him being hurt made her blood run cold. It also brought home the reality that she hadn't succeeded in completely steeling her heart against him. It was time for him to go.

"I wondered how long you were going to hide in there."

She was almost to her doorway when she whirled around, jumping at the low rumble of Caleb's voice in the dark. Her eyes, adjusted to the dim light, came to rest on his shadowed form as he lounged against his bedroom door frame. Even from across the room, she could make out his arms folded across his dark chest.

"I wasn't hiding," she lied. "And you were supposed to be sleeping."

He didn't speak, but he might have shrugged. She couldn't be sure. He was probably over-tired and sore, too. A fresh wave of guilt washed over her.

She turned away and opened her door. "It's been a long day. Goodnight, Caleb."

"Goodnight, Lacey." Caleb stood in his doorway, tempted to follow. Instead, he turned on his heel and closed his bedroom door with a quiet click.

By the third recitation of the speech he was preparing for the company meeting, his eyes burned, but he was no closer to sleep than he'd been an hour before. Maybe a little sports network would do the trick.

Thoughts of the sports ticker vanished, though, as he spied the light shining underneath Lacey's bedroom door. More than anything, he wanted to kiss away the haunted shadows he'd seen in her eyes. Tilting his head back, he rubbed his hands over his face in frustration. He needed to understand why she'd shut him out.

Crossing the small living area, he listened through the thin door. From the sounds of movement on the other side, she was no closer to going to sleep than he was.

He tapped lightly on the door and, cracking it open, peeked around the corner. "Have a second?"

Lacey turned away from the window, the sadness in her eyes quickly masked by a frown. "It's two in the morning, Caleb."

"And you can't sleep, either." He stepped into the room, his eyes trained on her. His frustration boiled over. "Don't you think it's time you tell me what the hell's going on?"

She tightened the belt of her robe. "What are you talking about?"

Caleb pinned her with his gaze. "You know exactly what I mean. You. Me. It's different now and I want to know why."

Lacey was silent for a minute but when she spoke, her words were quiet and sure. "There is no you and me, Caleb. There can't be." She turned toward the window.

That wasn't an answer, damn it. He released a deep, exasperated breath. He had to know what was going on in her head. Getting her to open up was his only option.

As he walked up behind her, she stiffened. Something like fear gnawed at him. How had they gotten here? "Talk to me." He paused. "Please."

In the dim light of the lamp, he thought she swayed slightly toward him, but her words rang with defiance and an edge of sadness. "It's late, Caleb," she said. "And I can't do this tonight."

Chapter 21

A brusque knock jolted Lacey awake, but by the time she entered the living area, Caleb was already at the door greeting Detective Abrams. The colors of dawn tinged the morning sky.

"Got some information I think you'll want to hear," Abrams announced as Caleb ushered him into the room.

Lacey cringed at his haggard appearance. "Have you even slept?"

"What do you have for us?" Caleb asked at the same time.

Abrams ignored Lacey's question. "Quite a bit, actually," he answered with a weary smile. He glanced at Lacey. "Seems your gentleman caller was working a side job. And the way I hear it, his boss isn't too happy with him."

Wide awake, Lacey sat down on the edge of the chair. "How'd you find him?"

"We got lucky last night. There's been some trouble brewing lately between a couple of players here in town. So we keep a few undercover guys on the street to get some advance warning if the heat starts picking up between them."

"Go on," Caleb said.

"Your guy, Patrick Littlejohn, went into one of the bars owned by his employer, who also happens to own a couple of area casinos. Thanks to Caleb here, he was looking pretty rough."

Lacey shook her head. "I'm not making the connection."

"Let me put it this way. Littlejohn's boss got word that somebody roughed him up. He assumed it was somebody in the enemy camp so he put the word out that he'd be retaliating. Littlejohn's one of his better enforcers. Apparently player number two was all for escalating the tension, but he made sure that Littlejohn's boss knew they weren't in on this."

"So my guy's at the bar when Littlejohn's stuttering and stammering all over himself about what happened. They finally get the story out of him and he goes for a little ride with his boss."

"How do we find out who he was working for?"

"Well, first we wait for him to wake up. He's in ICU at Mercy right now."

"Oh, my God. Is he going to be okay?"

Caleb scowled at her and rolled his eyes. "Please try to remember that this guy was prepared to kidnap you and take you to God knows where."

She glared back at him. "I realize that. But this guy could be the key to finding Dad."

Abrams stifled the budding feud. "They think he'll be okay. We'll be working on getting him to talk, but here's a little bit of info that's just too much of a coincidence in my book. This guy is an enforcer for people who get in a little too deep out at the casinos, okay? That's his full-time gig."

He flipped open his notepad. "I got word yesterday afternoon that Stan Jacobson paid off a seventy-five thousand dollar gambling debt two weeks ago. Guess who he owed the money to?"

Lacey and Caleb exchanged glances.

"Littlejohn's boss?" Caleb offered.

"Bingo. We haven't confirmed the payment source yet but we're working on it." He stifled a yawn. "I'm going to head home and get a few hours of rest. If anything else surfaces, I'll be in touch." He nodded to them both.

He turned back, his hand on the door handle. "Ms. Jordan, are you planning on being at the shop today?"

She nodded. "Do you think it'll be okay?"

"I'm sure it'll be fine. As a precaution, I'll post someone nearby but my guess is that this guy was hired by Stan because he knew him. And, odds are it'll be a day or two before Stan realizes he wasn't successful."

"That's an awful lot of speculation," Caleb grumbled. "Maybe I should hang out at the shop today, too."

"I don't think that'll be necessary. You'll need to get somebody over to the house to replace the back door though, unless you guys want to spend another night in this place."

Caleb nodded, but Lacey caught the scowl on his face. "I can take care of that."

Lacey hoped her relief wasn't obvious. She needed a reprieve from Caleb, especially when she was feeling so vulnerable. But for the moment, she wanted answers. As soon as the door closed behind the detective, she rounded on Caleb. "Tell me everything you know about Stan Jacobson."

She followed him to the sofa where they sat side by side, their legs inches apart. She turned her head, catching his gaze. "So, how much do you know about this guy? Did you know he had a gambling problem?"

Caleb shook his head, holding up his hands. "How would I have known that? He never came to work for us. I only met him briefly when we interviewed him. I couldn't even tell you what he looks like."

Lacey grunted. "How'd he get the interview? Did you guys recruit him?"

Shoving an agitated hand through his hair, Caleb stood, pacing the small room. "If I knew, I'd tell you, but I don't. In this industry, we're always looking for talent. Especially in research. So I don't know. We could've recruited him. Or he could've known somebody inside who knew there was an opening."

Lacey regarded him, the lack of information feeding her compulsion to do something. She stood quickly. "I'm going to go see his wife. Maybe Abrams overlooked something when he talked to her."

Caleb tensed, grabbing her arm. "Like hell you are! Are you kidding me? You have no idea if she's involved or not. What if you walk right into a trap?"

156

He towered over her, but she wasn't intimidated. She was sick to death of not being bold for her dad. Nothing else was working and she was losing it. She yanked her arm away and faced down his stare. "What should I do, then?" she screamed. "Sit here and keep waiting? Waiting for what, Caleb?" Her hands sliced the air. "Nothing! Vapor! That's all we've got. Nothing solid. Nothing we can act on. We don't even know where the hell Stan Jacobson is supposed to be!"

Lacey stormed to her bedroom, slamming the door. After chucking her pajamas for a pair of comfortable jeans and a K-State sweatshirt, she shoved the night clothes in her duffel bag, listening to the silence from the other room.

A quick, and thoroughly unwanted, wave of panic gripped her as she wondered if Caleb had left. Walked away. Decided it wasn't worth it.

She threw herself on the bed, anger and frustration bursting through her. Could she blame him if he had? She felt the hot tears of hopelessness drizzle down her temples into her hair. The tears weren't for him. God knew he didn't deserve them, but he didn't deserve to be in the middle of this mess either.

Caleb hadn't asked for any of this. Why wouldn't he walk away? He had everything else going for him. Her thoughts shifted to his life, his family. Was his girlfriend angry that he wasn't there for her? How could she stand for him to be away with a baby coming so soon?

She jumped at the knock on her door, her thoughts snapping back to the present.

"Lacey, we need to go."

Ignoring the pinch of relief at hearing Caleb's voice, Lacey swiped her tears and gathered her bag. As much as she hated to admit it, Caleb was probably right about meeting Stan's wife. Maybe she'd talk to Abrams and see what he thought.

In the silent drive back to the house, Lacey reaffirmed her decision from the night before. Caleb needed to go home. No way did she want to be responsible for a woman losing her husband or a child never knowing his father.

It took only minutes for Lacey to swap out her shirt and grab her keys so she could get to the shop. She was just about to walk out the front door when Caleb's words stopped her.

He approached her slowly, his eyes soft with regret. "Hey. I was a jerk at the hotel. I know I don't have any right to tell you what to do." His hands fell to his sides. "But I was scared, and I overreacted. I'm sorry."

Lacey held her ground as Caleb touched her arm, her gaze locked with his.

"I love your dad. He's the best man I know. And I want to help, but I can't get past the wall you've put up. I need to know what's going on inside your head. I really want us to be on the same page."

His apology and the sincerity in his words, and his eyes, caught Lacey off-guard. How could he talk like this? How could he betray his family? And why the hell did she care? Pulling away from his grasp, Lacey nodded, her voice thick. "I'm going to work. We'll talk tonight."

And we'll say good-bye.

***

Lacey was out of sorts all day. Nothing worked. None of the floral arrangements looked right. And, worst of all, the break she'd been praying for in the case didn't happen. She knew she was sinking but she couldn't pull herself out. Almost two weeks had passed since her dad's disappearance and the emotional roller coaster was screaming downhill.

And, by the end of the night, Caleb would be gone from her life. It's what she wanted, what had to happen. But that didn't stop her from wishing things could've been different.

She arrived home and walked right past Caleb who looked up from the dining room table that he'd turned into his temporary office.

"Mona called me today. Said she tried to reach you."

Lacey didn't glance his way as she made the trek directly to her bedroom. "I was busy. I'll call her later. Let me change clothes and I'll be out."

Caleb's brow furrowed. He'd seen Lacey angry, bewildered, and frustrated but what he'd just witnessed was a woman defeated. She'd completely isolated herself from him and, apparently, even Mona.

He didn't care if he had to tie her to a chair, he was going to get some answers out of her tonight. He was done being treated like a polite stranger, and half answers weren't going to cut it. Granted, she hadn't been around much but he was intelligent enough to know that her absence for most of the week was intentional.

Caleb had gone through the motions all day long. While he'd accomplished the back door repairs, and ironed out a few issues with Brandon, he was revved up and ready to resolve whatever the hell was going on.

"Damn it." Snapping his laptop shut, Caleb ran his hands through his hair and got up from the table. His body tight with suppressed frustration, he paced the living room as the minutes ticked by, convinced she was stalling.

Unwilling to wait any longer, Caleb marched down the hall. He raised his hand to knock, but a noise from beyond her bedroom door stopped him. When the muffled sound came again, he cracked the door open, his gut twisting. Curled in a fetal position on the bed, Lacey's entire body shook, her sobs muffled in a pillow.

Before he was even aware that he'd moved, Caleb kneeled on the bed, gathering her to him. "Baby, please, don't cry," he pleaded. He murmured loving words, stroking her back. Her anguish clawed at him, devastating him. How could he get her to share her fears, her pain?

Lacey was powerless to stop the flood of tears that drenched Caleb's shirt as he moved to the headboard and hauled her against his chest. It was wrong to take comfort from him, but she couldn't muster the strength to fight him.

Caleb didn't rush her. He simply rubbed her back, soothing her with low quiet words, letting her pent-up emotions ebb away.

Long minutes later, she exhausted her tears and simply lay against his chest, her body spasming with aftershocks. She thought about being held in

Caleb's arms and almost succumbed to another wave of tears as resentment overwhelmed her. How could something feel so right yet be so wrong? She didn't realize she'd voiced the thought aloud until Caleb answered.

"I don't know," he whispered softly.

"But it *is* wrong." Forcing herself off his chest, Lacey swung her legs over the side of the bed, her back to Caleb. She ran a shaking hand through her hair and brushed the tears from her cheeks. God, she was sick of crying.

Anger bubbled through her. Taking deep breaths, she waited until she was certain she could speak without screaming. She spoke around her clenched jaw. "You've got to go. You can't stay here."

Lacey sensed the tension filling the room. Okay by her. She'd take tension over the horrible sadness that had gripped her any day of the week.

Caleb stood, frustration evident in his clipped tone. "You've said that before and we both know my answer. What you haven't told me is why."

As much as it embarrassed her to admit she'd been duped, she needed to resolve this once and for all. Then he could leave quietly and she could make some excuse to Abrams and everyone else about him needing to get back to Chicago.

"I've been here once before. I won't do it again." She spoke to the floor, her elbows resting on her knees. No way could she turn around and look at him. She let out a deep breath as the old tentacles of guilt wormed their way into her mind. "I didn't know for the longest time. When I found out, all I could do was imagine if the roles were reversed. I vowed it would be a long time before I would allow myself to care again. And then you came along and by some sadistic twist of fate, I ended up right back there again."

The rigidity in her body told him this was a big revelation for her, but he didn't have the slightest idea what she was talking about. He didn't want to sound obtuse, so he simply stared at her back, waiting for her to continue.

She stood, folding her arms beneath her chest, defiance flashing in her eyes. "I will never be the other woman. Never again."

Lacey's bold gaze never wavered, as if she expected him to accept her statement and leave. There had to be more to the story. Caleb frowned as he continued to watch her across the bed, trying to solve the puzzle.

She threw out her hands. "Hello! Don't you get it?" she said, her voice spiking, "I know about your girlfriend and the baby."

The air whooshed out of his lungs. He felt like he had just stepped into a slightly tilted alternate universe. For a split second, he thought she was joking, but her eyes told him she was dead serious.

"My *what?*" Caleb roared. "What the hell are you talking about?"

Confusion and anger warred within him as Lacey took a step back from the bed.

Her hands shook as her voice rose. "Your girlfriend and the baby!"

He didn't give a shit that his voice boomed off the walls as he marched around to her side of the bed. "For the love of God, Lacey. Where the hell did you get the idea I had a girlfriend and a baby?"

Her eyes rounded as she once again crossed her arms over her chest. "From you, you bastard. You knew I'd started to trust you. Even like you. Then —"

He trapped her between the bed and the wall behind her, his eyes locked on hers.

She took another step back.

He filled the space until there were mere inches between them.

Caleb released a deep breath to get his shock under control. In a flash, he realized that this was the cause of her anger and detachment, and he couldn't decide if he should shake her or kiss her. He shook his head, still not quite certain he believed what he'd just heard.

"Lacey." He cupped her chin in his hand.

"Don't touch me," she ground out.

He didn't move. "Listen to me," he said, his voice low and controlled. "I don't have a girlfriend or a wife, and I sure as hell don't have a baby."

Lacey's pulled away from his grasp. "Let's not play games. Been there, done that. I don't know who she is to you, but I heard you, Caleb. Please don't try to deny it. You were on the phone Sunday morning when I came into the kitchen. I didn't mean to eavesdrop, but I couldn't help it. You were apologizing for not being able to be with her. I remember you saying you'd see her next month. And there'd be a baby. And you'd celebrate."

"I thought we'd had this incredible night, then —"

Caleb stared at the frown line between her eyebrows, his brain spinning, trying to remember. Within seconds, he let out a sudden bark of laughter that filled the room.

Lacey's eyes shot fire. "You're laughing at me?" she challenged. "I was stupid to trust you. I admit it. But you can't possibly deny the conversation."

Caleb struggled to control his laughter. "No," he acknowledged as he regained control. "I definitely had the conversation." Grabbing her hand, he pulled her along until they got to the dining room. Plucking his cell phone off the table, Caleb scrolled through his pictures. "This is the girl I was talking to." He held up the phone for her to see.

She glared at him, yanking her wrist away. "She's lovely. Thank you for sharing."

"Lacey," he said, laughter still lurking in his voice. "Do you see any resemblance at all? Same color hair? Same eyes? This is my sister, Rachel."

She whirled around, her eyes wide, incredulous.

The play of emotions on her face veered from anger to embarrassment in a matter of seconds. Her mouth opened and closed several times but no words emerged so he went on. "I'd mentioned to Rachel that Roger was making me take a few days off and that I might come through Kansas City to spend some time with the family. Obviously, I didn't do that. She was disappointed because it's been quite a while since we've been together. But she was more upset because she was afraid I was going to skip out on the family Christmas get-together that she and my other, very pregnant, sister Sarah are putting together."

Lacey's cheeks flamed red, and her eyebrows shot to the sky. "Your sister?" she squeaked.

Caleb stepped close and cupped her face in his hands. "My sister." Relieved to finally have the riddle solved, he kissed the bridge of her nose and felt something lodge in his heart. Rubbing his thumbs along her cheeks, his eyes locked on hers. "I don't know when it'll happen, but someday you're going to trust me."

Lacey looked away, her heart racing. She couldn't give what his eyes were asking. Not now. Maybe not ever.

Caleb released her, his lips barely skimming her forehead. "I'll be right back."

She lowered herself to the sofa. Why was everything so complicated? Picking at the soft pills on the sleeve of her sweater she cringed, thinking about how she'd overreacted to something that wasn't any of her business anyway. *You don't need to trust him. He'll be gone when this is all over.*

Guilt flowed through her veins. None of this would've happened if she hadn't slept with him. She'd allowed herself a diversion, an escape. And all it had done was add to her problems.

Being with Caleb had felt so good, too good. But now wasn't the time for feeling good. Closing her eyes, she sighed, unsure if that time would ever come again.

She owed him an apology though, and probably an explanation. Jumping up as Caleb came around the kitchen corner, she tried to ignore the fact that, even in a pair of sweatpants and a tee shirt, he fairly oozed masculinity. He held a bottle of wine and two glasses in his hands.

Raising an eyebrow, she crossed her arms. "What are you doing?"

He smiled, disarming her with the small dimple in his left cheek. "Relaxing."

He handed her a glass of her favorite red then sat down next to where she'd been seated. Instead of sitting next to him, she opted for the recliner. Distance would be her ally.

Caleb arched a brow, a hint of a smile tweaking his lips, but didn't comment.

Lacey sipped her wine, fortifying her courage. She glanced at him over the table, embarrassment infusing her cheeks with heat. "My dad always used to tell me that I shouldn't jump to conclusions." A sad smile touched her lips. "In this case, I probably should've taken his advice. I'm sorry about that."

His eyes held hers, but there was no anger. "Will you tell me the story?"

Could she? Lacey closed her eyes, remorse over her gullibility freezing her tongue. To Caleb's credit, he didn't push.

Lacey pulled her knees to her chin, and laid aside her pride. "His name was Jason Calloway. He came into the shop one day and he was a talker. I'm pretty good at keeping things impersonal, but he found a way around my usual barriers. To make a long story short, we started seeing each other."

She sighed, drawing further into herself. "I wasn't looking for a reason not to trust him, so the fact that we only saw each other on the weekends didn't concern me. Paige and I were busy working on the shop during the week anyway." She shuddered. "I wonder how long I'd have played the fool if fate hadn't intervened."

Caleb voice was a soft caress. "What happened?"

Lacey choked out a laugh and turned her face to his, finally meeting his gaze. "His wife came to the shop and ordered flowers to be delivered to her sweet husband. He was such a hard working, devoted husband and father, even working out of town most weekends to advance in his company. Imagine my surprise when she wrote his name on the envelope."

His eyes widened. "Holy shit."

"Exactly. Paige offered to deliver the flowers for me, and I almost let her. In the end though, I needed to let him know where I stood."

"That's my girl."

It wasn't the words as much as the protective, proud way he said them that forced a smile to Lacey's lips. She hadn't realized until now how much it mattered that he didn't judge her. So when he came to stand in front of the recliner and held out his hand, she hesitated for only a moment before putting her hand in his and allowing him to pull her into his warm embrace.

164

Chapter 22

Caleb sat with Lacey in his arms until the small hours of the morning. It took that long for him to decide not to hunt down Jason Calloway and beat the hell out of him. No damn wonder Lacey had trust issues.

He brushed his lips against her hair. "You need your sleep."

As Lacey stretched against him then rose to her feet, Caleb ignored the insistent desire pounding through his veins. By God, when she came to him again it would be with her body and her trust. With a kiss on her forehead, Caleb turned her toward her bedroom.

She wandered down the hall and into her room. Caleb wasn't certain she was even fully awake. He swirled the wine in his glass before downing it and turning out the lamp.

Lacey had started to trust him tonight, whether she realized it or not. And it was different. It wasn't about her dad, or the case. This time, it was about her. He smiled. A step in the right direction.

***

Since the shop opened at ten, Caleb let Lacey get a few extra minutes of sleep. That was probably a mistake because, Lord, was she grumpy in the morning. Twenty minutes of prodding produced a grunt of acknowledgement, but it took him almost an hour to get her fully awake.

He poured her coffee, laughing, as he listened to her muttered litany on the injustices of rising early. His laughter only darkened her scowl as he carried the steaming mug to her. He was proud of her progress, though. She'd managed to roll over and sit up against the headboard. Her eyes were closed, but the aroma of fresh coffee did the trick.

Opening one eye, she frowned up at him. "I don't know why you're laughing," she growled. "I'm in serious pain here."

Caleb smothered his chuckle. Since his goal was to get away in one piece, he silently handed her the mug and turned to leave. He was nothing if not a quick learner.

By the time Lacey finished her shower, she felt like she could face the day. While she brushed her teeth, she studied her face in the mirror. Okay. She looked like she hadn't slept in a week, but there was a little less shadow in her eyes. As much as she hated to admit it, it mattered that Caleb hadn't lied to her.

Lacey bundled up for the cold. The weatherman had predicted snow within forty-eight hours and, in western Kansas, it was a bad idea to ignore the weatherman. She wound a black cashmere scarf around her neck and was fishing for gloves in her coat pockets when Caleb's voice from the kitchen captured her attention.

She stopped digging, mentally promising to give him the benefit of the doubt if she heard anything curious. From the topic and the tone, he was obviously talking to someone at BioTech, and it wasn't a pleasant conversation.

While Caleb finished scribbling his notes, she came up behind him and touched his back.

"Everything okay?"

Caleb turned, sighing. His eyes looked tired. "Depends on who you ask. Meg Richards, our chief operating officer, would have me believe the world's coming to an end."

Lacey held her breath. It would be so much easier for him to handle things from Chicago. Twenty-four hours ago, she'd wanted nothing more than for him to leave. Today, she prayed he wouldn't say he had to.

Caleb squeezed her arm then pulled her into a light embrace. "You look ready to attack the frozen tundra," he joked, his chin resting on her head. "If we don't hear from Abrams this morning, I'm going to spend some time with Spencer today. And then I'm going to the grocery store. A guy could starve around here."

She pulled back as his words penetrated. "Spencer? Does this have anything to do with the time you spent with him on Sunday? I was dying to ask, but –" Embarrassment at her unjust conviction again warmed her cheeks as she looked away.

He nudged her chin up with his finger. "We're over that, okay?" Caleb's eyes settled on her lips, his breathing deepened.

Lacey waited, mesmerized. When he plunked a kiss on her forehead and gathered up his notes, she refused to be disappointed. Better to keep things simple.

"Anyway, I'm hoping to get to know Spencer better, see if I can help him find some direction. He admitted on Sunday that he didn't want to continue down the road he's on but he doesn't know how to get back. I'm hoping I can help. Turns out, he actually has an interest in science. I'll see what I can do to foster that."

Lacey's fingers itched. She wanted to trace the small worry lines around his eyes with her fingertips. There was no denying the physical attraction she felt, but the little twist in her heart had nothing to do with that. She considered all that he'd done and continued to do, putting his life on hold to stay here, to help.

Shaking her head, she hurried to catch up to his conversation. "Do you think Abrams will call today?"

Caleb's eyes darkened. "I don't know, and even though I think Abrams is right about Littlejohn working alone, be extra careful, okay? Keep your eyes open for anything or anybody that doesn't feel right."

***

Caleb's words rang in her ears as she drove through town. Talk about effective refocusing. She'd never get used to being considered a target. And she wasn't sure she could even tell what felt right or wrong anymore. All she knew for sure was that this morning, every crazy driver in Manhattan was on the road, adding to the surrealism of her life.

As she rounded the corner on Main, she almost ran over a man wandering in the middle of the street. What was wrong with these people?

She pulled in behind the shop and rested her head on the steering wheel. Eyes closed, she exhaled deeply, her chronic anxiety never far away.

It's not them. It's you.

Had she been less tired, tears might've flowed. Right now, she didn't even have the energy. How long until the nightmare ended? And what would the end bring? Would she ever see her dad again?

Lacey's thoughts drifted away toward memories of warm sunshine and flowers and her parents. *She was playing in the front yard. Her mother introduced her to a lady bug climbing a petunia. Squealing with excitement, she called out to her dad, excited to share the discovery. His arms came around her, lifting her high into the air.*

The rapping on her window startled Lacey awake. She jumped, smacking her elbow on the door panel. Sam's concerned face stared down at her.

"Are you okay?"

Lacey swallowed the scream that had risen to her throat and nodded. "I'm fine," she said, attempting a smile. "Short night. I'll be right in."

She waited until Sam walked away to look at her shaking hands. The adrenaline rush had kicked her fight-or-flight response into high gear. She practiced a couple of deep breaths then gathered her belongings.

Sam was already pulling centerpieces out of the cooler and stacking them on a cart when Lacey walked in. The vases of white daisies, yellow spray roses, and pink carnations were an explosion of spring, a perfect escape from the cold outside.

"Those look great, Sam. They'll be beautiful on the tables. I'll take them over this morning," Lacey said.

"You sure?" Sam looked up, surprised. "I can run them."

Nodding, Lacey opened the cooler. "If you don't mind handling the shop for awhile, I promised Marie I'd come."

Lacey looked forward to the monthly community luncheons at the nursing home. Not because of the business so much as the residents. They never failed to bring a smile to her lips. And that was one thing she could use today.

***

She'd finished her first load and was unloading the second cart of flowers when Marie arrived.

"I thought you'd be in this morning," the wisp of a woman said from the dining hall entrance. She slowly rolled up and stopped near Lacey's side.

Squatting down in front of Marie's chair, Lacey took hold of her delicate blue-veined hand. "I wouldn't miss it," Lacey smiled. "I'm sure you're in the running this month." She knew there was quite a spirit of competition for the member-of-the-month honors, especially between the ladies.

Marie puffed up in her chair a bit and her eyes twinkled. "Well, I'm not going to count my chickens before they hatch, but I'd say I'm just about due. I organized an ice cream social and crocheted an extra throw for the TV room." She winked at Lacey. "Think that'll get me in?"

"You'd have my vote," Lacey whispered. She stood as several other residents joined them.

Lacey visited longer than she should have. But surrounded by the kind-hearted men and women who longed for an attentive ear, she'd have gladly spent the whole day there. Their stories provided a wonderful escape from reality.

Duty called, however, and the remainder of the day proved to be one of the busiest Fridays Lacey could remember. But, the news she'd been praying for didn't come. Sighing, Lacey finished the deposit and sent it with Sam. She'd foolishly hoped that with the new information, the police would've located her father, or at least found Stan Jacobson. But nothing ever happens as quickly as it does in the movies.

By the time she left the shop, Lacey was physically and mentally exhausted. She cranked down her car window, and let the freezing air help her stay awake as she drove home. There wasn't any room in her fuzzy brain to focus on anything but her chattering teeth.

Caleb took one look at Lacey's face when she walked in the door. Man, she was beat. He met her in the middle of the living room and wrapped her in his arms, infusing her with his warmth. "You okay?"

She stepped back, offering him a slight smile. "I haven't slept well all week." She raised tired eyes to his. "How was your time with Spencer today?"

Caleb kissed her forehead. "It was good. I can tell you all about it over dinner." He watched her shoulders sway beneath his massaging hands. "Or, if you'd rather crash, we can talk in the morning."

After a moment, Lacey shook her head. "I'll be fine." She stifled a yawn. "Let me go change. Pour me a glass of wine and I'll be good as new."

Caleb wasn't convinced she'd emerge from her bedroom, but he stirred the alfredo sauce and finished the salad just in case. He'd pulled the garlic bread from the oven when Lacey rounded the corner, her freshly scrubbed face as pink as her sweatshirt. He was taken aback by how beautiful she was without a trace of make-up.

"Mmmm. Smells amazing," she said. "I didn't know culinary talents were part of your résumé."

Caleb raised an eyebrow, his smile hinting at his other talents, then handed her a glass of Riesling. "I don't cook much for myself, but I know my way around a kitchen. Try this." He dipped a spoon into the white sauce bubbling on the stove. After blowing to cool it, he held it to her lips.

Lacey took the spoon in her mouth then licked an errant drop of the creamy sauce from her lips. "Delicious. I thought I'd be too tired to eat tonight, but now I'm starving. What can I do to help?"

Watching her taste the sauce, Caleb's thoughts sprang to other intriguing ideas involving her mouth and tongue. He cleared his throat and almost burned his hand straining the pasta. *Focus, man.* "All done here. Take the salad bowl and your wine. I'll get the rest."

He joined her at the table and, as they ate, the topic came back around to Spencer. He'd reserved judgment about the kid, but so far, Caleb was encouraged by what he'd discovered.

Sipping his wine, Caleb shared his observations. "He's a smart kid with a lot of potential. He just needs direction. There are a lot of programs at the university that could be a good fit for him."

Lacey swallowed a bite of pasta. "He needs to find new friends. The ones he has now are going nowhere."

"Rachel used to tell my younger siblings that you become like the people you hang around most. They didn't always listen, but hopefully, Spencer will learn that truth. Fast.

"You know Zach Coughlin? He's one of your dad's researchers. I talked to him a little bit about Spencer. He seems like a sharp guy. Before I leave, I'm going to try to get Spencer hooked up with some of Zach's entry level assistants. I think being around people his age who are focused on their future will help him a lot."

Lacey's fork was midway to her mouth so she took the bite, but barely tasted it. All she heard was that he was leaving. She considered trying to continue to eat, but her appetite fled.

She toyed with her food until Caleb finished his meal. Tossing her napkin on her plate, she rose, pasting a smile on her face. "I'm stuffed. You cooked. I'll clean up."

She gathered the dishes along with the salad bowl and walked into the kitchen. Caleb followed her and refilled their glasses before Lacey shooed him away. "Go on in the living room. I'll be in there in a few." She rinsed the plates and bowls then stacked them in the dishwasher. As she wandered around the kitchen, wiping down the countertops, Caleb's words rang in her ears.

Before I leave, before I leave, before I leave...

Of course he's leaving. He has to leave. This isn't his life.

Downing her wine, Lacey rinsed the glass then switched off the kitchen light. Caleb was absorbed in whatever he was reading so she turned the television on low, a sense of melancholy stealing over her. She fought to keep her eyes open, but she knew she'd lose the battle before the first commercial break.

Lacey noticed two things immediately after she slapped the alarm clock to stop its incessant racket. She was in her own bed, which she assumed meant Caleb had put her there. And she was in her pajamas.

Refusing to ponder how she'd accomplished that feat, she stretched, reluctant to climb out from under the warm blankets. It seemed so early in the morning, but her clock told her she needed to get moving. She reached for her robe, and wandered over to the window. Drawing back the curtain, Lacey drew in a sharp breath. The weatherman had an amazing gift for understatement. The storm he'd predicted to bring an inch or so of snow had already dropped at least three inches on the ground and the enormous flakes showed no sign of letting up.

The neighbor across the street opened his front door, and a spirited puppy bounded outside. Lacey smiled as she watched the dog disappear into the thick blanket of snow. He was back at the door in less than a minute. Then a thought struck Lacey that brought another genuine smile to her lips. Paige was coming home today.

As if on cue, her phone vibrated on her bedside table. She dove for it, hoping to hear her friend's voice.

"Damn, Lacey. Talk about things changing," Paige grumbled in lieu of a greeting. "I leave two weeks ago and it's a beautiful day. I come home, and it's snowing like crazy! We just landed, so we'll be on the road to Manhattan shortly. The snow's going to slow us down, but we should be there by one or two at the latest."

"Well, hello to you, too," Lacey drawled. If the situation weren't so dire, Lacey would've laughed at her friend's distress. Things certainly had changed in the past two weeks, and she knew Paige would be anxious to get up to speed. With everything she needed to share, she didn't think it would be a good idea to meet at the shop.

"Why don't you take a few hours and get settled in. I'll get a pizza and we'll get together tonight after the shop closes. Your place or mine?" Lacey asked.

Paige didn't hesitate. "Mine. I can multi-task. I have tons of laundry to do. Oh, I've got to run. Rodney's bringing the car around and I'm freezing my ass off out here in the snow."

Lacey ignored the tightness in her chest and the first sting of tears behind her eyes. Paige was familiar. And familiar felt good. "Give your hubby a hug from me. And be careful," she choked.

Lacey got dressed in a pair of jeans and a heavy sweatshirt. To heck with business casual on a day like this. She was going for warm and comfy. By the time she came in from warming her car up, the shower was running. Should she wait for Caleb to finish? Glancing outside at the dusting of snow that had already coated her car again, she scribbled a note to him instead.

She and Sam worked like demons the entire day. Not many customers ventured out in the weather so they used their time and energy to make the place shine for Paige when she saw it again.

Paige loved the business, every aspect of it. If Lacey had any lingering doubts about whether it was her own life's passion, the past few weeks of being totally responsible for it solidified what she'd suspected. Of course, now wasn't the time to make any life altering decisions, but that time was coming.

Lacey looked out the window, anxious about the accumulating snow. "Are you going to be okay to make it home?" Lacey frowned. "I'd say there's at least another inch on the ground since you got back."

"Actually, Caleb threw a couple of sand bags in the bed of my truck the other day. That old rust bucket will probably be easier to drive than the van."

"He did?" She paused. "Okay. Make sure you call me when you get home." As she put her coat on to leave, the bond she and Sam had forged brought a smile to her lips.

Her smile froze on her face though, as the wind whipped a frigid blast of snow right at her. Man, she hated winter. She stamped through the snow and fought her way into the car. Fortunately, the engine roared to life.

"Good old girl," Lacey said through chattering teeth. As she sat in her frozen seat, waiting for the car to warm up, her thoughts wandered away from the benefits of heated seats to how she could possibly explain the past two weeks to Paige. She'd considered doing it on her own, but after reading her note from this morning, Caleb had insisted on going with her. Truth be told, she was grateful.

She inched her way home, grumbling at the snow crews that still hadn't gotten to her street. To her surprise, though, her driveway was clear.

Caleb bounded out the door. "I figured you'd be anxious to get over there. We'll take your car since it's already warmed up." He slammed the door and buckled in. "I've already ordered the pizzas. We can pick them up on our way."

"Thanks for the driveway," she said, backing out. "It's crazy out there." Lacey gripped the steering wheel, maneuvering the frozen streets in silence, a frown puckering her forehead.

Caleb's gaze kept coming back to her frown. "Roads or the meeting?"

She shrugged, keeping her eyes on what she was pretty sure was the road. "I think it's some of both. The streets stink but I'm used to that." She sighed. "I'm just not sure how to even start this conversation. How do you possibly explain what's happened the past two weeks?"

"She's your best friend."

Lacey sighed. "I know. And she's going to be supremely pissed that I didn't tell her sooner."

It would be so easy to insist that the only reason she hadn't told Paige was because she didn't want to ruin her honeymoon. But, it wasn't the whole truth. The more she talked about it, the less belief she had that she'd ever see her dad again. Her heart balked against the traitorous thought.

Two weeks. With no ransom note, and very little action. As she guided the car on the slick road, she wished that, literally and figuratively, she had markers telling her which way to go.

Chapter 23

How could it have gone wrong? The phone call letting Stan know that Patrick had failed to get his hands on Lacey came earlier in the day. Something had to change, and soon. A stalemate was not a possible outcome to their game.

Stan prowled the confines of the well-appointed apartment, restlessness gnawing at him. It had been too long, he realized. He needed to play. He needed a win. That would certainly take his mind off this mess.

Financially, his fortunes had never been better. Thanks to the proceeds from this little jaunt to Chicago, he was at ground zero. He owed no one. He was ready to start fresh and he knew he'd only go up from here.

His boss didn't understand. The smaller man shouldn't have been able to intimidate him physically, but Stan knew there lurked a madness in him that made him unpredictable. They'd already had the conversation once and it hadn't gone at all like Stan had hoped. His words still echoed in Stan's ears.

"Are you a fucking idiot? I told you no gambling until the transaction is complete." His fists had clenched then relaxed and his voice had changed to a soft, soothing murmur. "I know it's hard for you. I know all about how it feels to need something as badly as you do. We're men of strong passions. But I promise you, when this is over and you have the rest of your winnings from *this* adventure, you can master the tables from Vegas to Monte Carlo."

Stan had known he was right about the gambling, of course. The computer was too easy to track. But as he sat in front of the television, the food network droning on about the king of jambalaya recipes, the rush of anticipation for the next card overwhelmed him. He tried to curtail it, actually sat on the couch for fifteen more minutes, but today, the need was so strong. Too strong. And he had cash.

Why hadn't he thought of that before? Cash couldn't be traced. Perfect.

Now, to get his boss to agree. Oh, not to the gambling of course. Stan knew he'd never go for that. Just a night out. That's all he really needed. He rubbed his hands together in anticipation.

Stan waited another hour for his boss to return to the apartment. Any hope that Bill had agreed to the demands died the second the man walked in the door.

"How'd it go?" Stan asked. He recoiled from the hostility that blasted him. "I mean, surely he's close to unlocking the code for you, right? A guy can only go for so long –"

"He'll give me the code. If your moronic friend hadn't bungled the job, I'd have the damn thing already." The hatred in his voice sent a shudder down Stan's spine. "You'd better be working on finding another solution," he warned.

Stan watched him walk to the bar and shoot a liberal amount of bourbon into a glass. He tossed it back and then poured another before throwing himself into a chair.

He rubbed his temples, and Stan saw his opportunity. "Looks like you could use some peace and quiet," he tossed out. "Tell you what, I'll step out and go to a movie or something. Take a few hours break and I'll be back. We can formulate a new plan with clear heads."

His boss eyed him skeptically, but the smooth bourbon was already working its magic. "Fine." He waved him away with a flick of his hand. "But keep that throw-away phone handy in case there's an emergency."

Stan nodded, shrugged into his coat and headed out the door before his boss changed his mind. Maybe it would be Stan's lucky night. He stopped at a local theater to buy a movie ticket, then headed to the casino.

Standing at the entrance of the gaming room, Stan breathed deeply. The jingling slot machines and table operators called to him like a siren song as anticipation rippled through his veins.

176

It felt like mere minutes had passed, but when he glanced down at his watch between hands, more than an hour of his time was gone. Toying with his dwindling pile of chips, he considered his options. Damn. He'd be expected back in another hour, two at the most.

He'd committed to limit himself to the cash in his pocket. But he was close, so close. He could feel it. Just a little more time for fortune to turn his way.

The server came by his table, looking for drink orders. He pointed to his diet coke with a nod. He was a smart gambler, so unlike most of the idiots here who allowed their minds to be weakened by alcohol. He refused to dull his wits with the stuff.

He'd burned through his cash, but a couple hundred more is all it would take to come out ahead. No one would know. He knew without a doubt before he even got up from the table that the ATM stationed just outside the gaming area was the answer to his dilemma.

Two hours later, Stan left the casino flying high, unable to contain the euphoria coursing through him. As he walked to his car through the well-lit parking lot, he congratulated himself on his intuition. He'd known that the extra cash would put him in the black.

Taking a deep breath, he approached the apartment door. *Relax. Wouldn't want to raise suspicion.* But surely it was okay to be in a good mood. After all, tonight's show had turned out to be pretty entertaining.

Chapter 24

Pizza and beer in hand, Lacey led Caleb up the sidewalk toward Paige and Rodney's little brick bungalow. As the snow tapered off, only a thin layer covered the recently shoveled path.

Lacey balanced the pizzas in one hand and rang the doorbell, the brittle air stinging her eyes. Seconds later, Paige stood at the door and, after a surprised glance at Caleb, she took the pizzas and handed them to Rodney.

Paige grabbed Lacey in a bear hug worthy of someone twice her size. As Lacey stepped back, she could almost feel the questions that Paige wanted to fire at her. The first one would undoubtedly be about the man standing behind her.

"Well, get on in here. It's freezing out there!" Paige tugged on Lacey's arm.

As they stepped into the welcoming warmth, Lacey hastily made the introductions. "You remember Caleb Mansfield, don't you Paige?" she said, desperately trying to seem casual.

"Of course." Paige held out her hand to Caleb. "Long time, no see."

Lacey ignored the what-the-hell-is-going-on look. "You look gorgeous," she said instead. "Mexico agreed with you."

"Thank God for Rodney and his insistence on sunscreen or, with my skin, I'd have fried myself the first day we were there."

Lacey endured Paige's scrutiny, wondering what her friend was thinking. It didn't take long to find out.

Paige gave her a jaunty smile. "You look like death warmed over. Come with me and we'll put the coats in my room. I can't *wait* to catch up."

Before Lacey could respond, Paige hooked her arm and led her down the hallway. Glancing over her shoulder at Caleb, she was relieved to see Rodney hand Caleb a beer as they headed to the kitchen.

Lacey barely made it into the bedroom before Paige rounded on her. Even though Paige's auburn curls only reached Lacey's chin, she was practically immovable.

Paige's green eyes narrowed shrewdly. "Okay. What's with the heart-breaker from the past? And why the tired bags under your eyes?" She winked. "Unless those two things are related, which I could totally understand. He's still pretty freaking hot."

"It's not what you think," Lacey replied, tossing the coats on the bed. "Caleb's here helping me out with a problem I'm having. That's the biggest reason I wanted to come tonight. I need to talk to you about it."

Paige cocked her brow, hands on her hips. "What problem? Is something wrong at the shop? Is there some guy problem you didn't tell me about? Are you sick?"

Lacey needed to take control of the conversation before Paige's overactive imagination got completely out of control. She sighed and linked her arm with Paige's, steering her out of the room. "No, no, and no. Let's go in the living room and talk."

Paige stopped in her tracks, frowning. "Tell me now. Are you okay?"

Lacey looked into her friend's concerned eyes. "Not really."

"What to drink, ladies?" Rodney brought in pizza and plates.

"Just water for me," Lacey said, joining Caleb on the sofa. She waited until everyone was settled then glanced at Caleb.

Paige cleared her throat, drawing Lacey's attention. She sat on Rodney's lap, his big arm around her middle.

Lacey considered how safe and grounded Paige looked, and how with a sentence, she was going to steal Paige's peace. Just like hers had been stolen.

"I've been very patient, haven't I?" Paige leaned back to look at her husband. At his nod, she refocused on Lacey. "Spill it, sister. What happened while I was gone? I need details."

Lacey had intended to tell her all the shop stuff first. Something safe and easy. She opened her mouth but nothing came out. She reached for Caleb's hand and found warm assurance there.

Rodney filled the silence, rolling his eyes at his wife. "Paige had herself almost convinced the shop would be out of business by the time we got back."

Lacey caught the almost imperceptible tightening in Caleb's jaw from the corner of her eye.

Paige must have noticed it as well. "That's not true," she assured him. "I knew we'd still be in business. It's just that my ego won't allow me to believe it can survive for long without me." She winked at Lacey. "Caleb obviously doesn't know what a power-hungry control freak I really am."

"I'm sure he'll figure it out," Rodney teased, earning himself a punch to the knee.

"Okay. But, seriously. I'm getting a bad feeling. Start talking."

Caleb squeezed Lacey's hand, silently urging her to begin.

After a couple deep breaths, Lacey spent the next ten minutes sharing everything she knew about her dad's disappearance. Caleb interjected several comments and facts as well. With every revelation, Paige's jaw dropped a little further.

When Lacey finally finished, she looked down and realized she was squeezing Caleb's hand so hard her knuckles were white. Deafening silence filled the room.

Paige shook her head, her words coming slowly. "I want to laugh at the joke, but there's no punch line is there?"

"I wish there was," Lacey whispered.

It didn't take long for the reaction to set in. Paige jumped up off Rodney's lap and pulled Lacey into a hug. "Why didn't you call me?" Twin patches of red flagged her cheeks as she looked up at Lacey. "How can you be so calm?" Rodney joined them and Paige rounded on him, her words sharp with fear. "We have to find him!"

"I'm sure they're already doing everything they can," Rodney soothed, pulling his wife into his side.

Lacey's voice drew Paige's attention. "That's exactly why we didn't call you. There's nothing to be done that we're not already doing." She closed her eyes against the tears of frustration. "It's just a horrible waiting game."

Paige pulled out of Rodney's embrace and took Lacey's hands. "I'm sorry. I just – I don't know what I expected, but this wasn't it." Her eyes were bright with unshed tears. "What can we do?" she whispered.

Lacey wrapped Paige in a tight hug. She understood her friend's anxiety. Paige had been her dad's unofficial second daughter for a long, long time.

The phone rang from Lacey's purse on the floor. Lacey looked at Caleb. "Would you mind?"

"Not at all. Excuse me." Caleb reached into the bag, then answered the call, his back to the group. "What? When?" He turned, his eyes snapping to Lacey.

She froze in fear, waiting to hear what was next. Oh my God, was this *the* call? The one that told her they'd found her dad's body?

"Yes. Yes, I understand. Okay." His one-sided conversation ended. Before anyone could speak, Caleb shared the news. "We may've just caught a lucky break. Stan Jacobson's personal credit card was used at an ATM in a casino in Joliet, Illinois, just outside of Chicago. The police are trying to get their hands on floor surveillance so they can confirm his identity." He paused, his eyes on Lacey. "Abrams gave me the number for an FBI agent in Chicago. He said we'd be hearing from him by tomorrow. What do you want to do?"

Lacey, releasing the breath she'd held, didn't hesitate. This was the first real link to her father. "We're going to Chicago." Her wide eyes swiveled to Paige. "You asked what you could do –" She didn't even get a chance to finish her sentence.

"Go. You go." She looked at Rodney, who nodded his full support, then back at Lacey. "We'll be fine. I'll call Sam tomorrow. We'll figure it out."

Caleb and Rodney were already huddled around Rodney's laptop booking flights when Lacey returned to the living room with their coats.

Paige hugged Lacey once more before she let them leave. "How about you call me this time, okay?"

Lacey smiled and nodded, hugging her back. "I promise. Oh, I almost forgot. When you talk to Sam, there are a few things you need to know. She's pregnant and due in February. I'm helping her find an adoptive home for her baby. Oh, yeah. And her ex-boyfriend's in jail. There's a restraining order against him. He stole the shops deposit one night and knocked me out." She saw Paige fall back against Rodney's chest. "It's okay. I'm fine and we got the money back. Gotta go. Love you. I'll call you."

The door started to close, but Paige caught it with her arm. She stepped out into the cold night. "That's it," she yelled after them. "I'm never leaving again!"

Lacey blew her a kiss then hopped in and threw the car in reverse. Glancing at Caleb, his face looked harsh in the muted light from the dashboard. "Was the seven a.m. flight the earliest you could get?"

"What?" he asked, his distraction obvious. "Oh, yeah." Then almost as an afterthought, he added, "I figure we need to be on the road by two with the weather."

She nodded and silently agreed. Energy thrummed through her veins on the ride home. Now that the snow had stopped, at least the roads were visible. She wanted to talk, to theorize, but Caleb's silence discouraged her.

Within thirty minutes, she was packed and pacing the living room. Caleb glanced up from the computer screen, his bag on the floor next to him. He looked back down and resumed typing. "Pack something for a black tie event."

She stopped pacing and cocked her eyebrow at him. Surely, she'd misheard him. "What?"

"Roger's wife, Rosalee, has planned some kind of company party. I was going to try to talk you into going with me anyway because I wasn't leaving without you," he explained. "It's Friday night and I'm required to go."

How could he expect her to think about that right now? How could he even think about it? Nothing mattered except finding her dad. "I have to believe I'll be back home by then," she said. "With my dad."

Caleb neither agreed nor disagreed. "We're not in control, Lacey. Just because we show up in Chicago doesn't mean we're going to find your dad in a day. Honestly, there's nothing concrete that says he's even there, but it's the best we've got to go on. Can you bring something, just in case?"

Lacey didn't respond. But she wasn't going to comply either. Wasn't that tantamount to believing what Caleb said? Things would happen quickly now, wouldn't they? As she rechecked the items she'd thrown into her duffel bag, she centered her thoughts on being reunited with her father.

Caleb yelled from the kitchen. "Make sure your alarm's set for one-thirty. The snow's over but the roads will still be a mess."

Contrary to what he was prepared for, Caleb didn't have any trouble waking Lacey. He knocked on her door a few minutes after hearing her alarm, then cracked it open. She sat on the edge of her bed, dressed in jeans and a bulky dark blue sweater along with boots and scarf. Her short ponytail reminded him of days gone by.

Deep shadows hid her eyes and her drawn face gave her an air of vulnerability. Caleb vowed once again to make the bastards pay.

He opened the door wider and leaned into the room. "You okay?"

Startled, she looked up and nodded.

Caleb decided not to mention the lost look on her face. "Let's hit the road." He'd already loaded the car with their bags and had two steaming travel mugs of coffee waiting for them.

Standing by the door, Caleb watched Lacey walk through the house, turning out lights and unplugging appliances. He gave her the few minutes she needed to pull herself together. He didn't think she'd slept, and her emotions teetered precariously close to the surface. His thoughts screamed with the possibilities of what was to come. He could only imagine hers.

***

The two-hour trip to Kansas City took almost four. Twice, Lacey held her breath as Caleb deftly avoided near-collisions with other drivers who lost control on the snow and ice packed highway. She didn't realize how tense she was until they made it to the airport.

A stress headache gnawed at the base of her skull as they returned the rental then made their way through the security gate. Settling into a hard seat in the nearly deserted boarding area, Lacey rubbed the back of her neck and said a silent prayer of thanks that Caleb had printed their boarding passes last night. She didn't think she had the mental capacity to do anything other than zone out as they waited for the plane.

Caleb didn't look much better than she felt. She doubted he'd slept last night either. She glanced at the flight monitors. At least the weather hadn't delayed their flight.

Her few attempts to engage Caleb during the flight were met with mumbled one word replies. She knew he was trying to catch a nap but she was too keyed up to let him sleep. At some point, she must have dozed because she came awake with a jolt as the person behind her slapped their tray table into the back of her seat. She caught Caleb watching her and wondered what he was thinking. His enigmatic eyes gave nothing away.

Their arrival into Chicago-Midway allowed them just enough time to encounter the remnants of the snowstorm that had moved through Kansas the day before. A bitter wind whipped around the airport entrance and snow spit at them as Caleb hailed a cab. He urged Lacey into the back seat and climbed in beside her, giving his address to the driver.

Lacey stared out the window, nibbling on her fingernail. She'd assumed she'd be staying with him, but he'd never offered. *Shit.* She hadn't considered making a reservation anywhere else. A few short minutes later, the cab pulled over, jolting her out of her thoughts. Caleb handed over the fare and got out, but Lacey didn't move.

Leaning down, he pinned Lacey with his tired gaze. "We're here. You want to tell me what you're doing?"

"I didn't make any reservations," she said lamely. He looked at her like she'd lost her mind. She repeated herself. "I didn't think to make any reservations. I should probably find a place near the police station."

The muscle in the side of Caleb's jaw started twitching and his voice sounded strained. "Get out of the cab, sweetheart. I don't take reservations." He reached into the cab and helped her out. "I don't know if I've mentioned this before, but until we get to the end of the line, you're with me, got it?"

Lacey, too exhausted to do much more than follow, ignored his jab. She held his arm as he guided her into the foyer, his tension evident in the bunched muscle.

Caleb strode toward the bank of elevators nodding at the doorman as they passed. "Let Joe know I'm back, if you would."

The young man nodded crisply. "Certainly, sir."

Lacey walked into Caleb's apartment, dimly aware of the understated elegance surrounding her. Caleb didn't give her much time to look around as he ushered her past the main living area down a short hallway. He nodded to his left. "The bathroom's in there. Change if you want to, then we're sleeping. Neither of us is thinking very clearly right now." He handed over her bag then left her standing in the hallway.

She should've been offended by his abruptness, but she knew he was right. They were both exhausted. For whatever would lie ahead, she'd need her wits about her. She made quick time in the bathroom and then, dressed only in the tee shirt she'd worn under her sweater and her jeans, silently padded to Caleb's bedroom.

She'd intended to just check on him and then crash on the sofa, but he disrupted her plan. Sleep had softened the rugged planes of his face, giving her a glimpse of the young man she used to know.

Squelching the voice that told her to move on, she crept into the room, admiring the quality of the dark teakwood bed. As she walked toward him, she resisted an insane urge to smooth his hair back from his forehead.

Instead, she slipped out of her jeans and allowed the luxury of the thick cotton sheets to envelop her. *To hell with the sofa.* She stretched and sighed, pulling the comforter up and snuggling into the mattress. Caleb rolled toward her and hauled her up against his side, her back pressed against his hard chest, his arm draped possessively over her middle.

Chapter 25

Lacey couldn't rationalize her sudden nervousness about meeting the FBI agent. Was it normal? Or was she going crazy? She'd expected the call, thanks to a heads up from Abrams, but she still didn't know the purpose of the meeting. Good news could be shared on the phone. Bad news rarely was.

Questions swirled as she applied mascara and a touch of lip gloss. Her appearance was the least of her worries, but she wanted to make a decent first impression. Shaking her head, she made a conscious decision not to borrow trouble. They may or may not be moving in the right direction, but at least they were moving.

About damn time.

Following the sound of slamming cupboards, Lacey wandered into the kitchen and stopped short. Caleb stood at the counter whipping something in a bowl. His broad back shifted and the muscles in his arms flexed with every motion. She had no idea how long she stood watching the hypnotic motion.

"Hungry?" He turned to face her.

Her cheeks flamed. If it weren't for the amused glint in his eyes, she could've pretended his question was an innocent one.

Avoiding his gaze, she laid out plates on the bar. "Surprisingly, yes. How do you have fresh food?"

"Ordered ahead online. One of the reasons I pay a ridiculous amount of money for this place." He turned and poured the egg mixture into the sizzling buttered skillet. Within minutes, he loaded up plates and settled in the chair next to her.

"Smells wonderful. Thank you." She forked a piece of the cheesy omelet and sighed. After a couple of bites, she looked at Caleb's profile and a profound awareness rippled through her.

She'd entered the danger zone where trust and insecurity battled for ownership of her mind. It was a David and Goliath matchup: the mistakes of her past versus sandbags and omelets and all the other things that spoke to Caleb's integrity. And the more time she spent with him, the harder it was to keep the rusty hinges on the gate of her heart closed.

Munching on her toast, she wondered how she'd devise new defenses? What would happen when this was all over? Caleb had mentioned new beginnings, but what did that mean?

Thinking about the future stopped her short, bringing her right back to the present. She didn't have any business daydreaming about what might be down the road.

The thin thread of hope that her dad was near, and that he was alive, had buoyed her spirit from the moment they'd gotten the call about Stan Jacobson. But was she just fooling herself? She didn't feel her dad's presence here. Not that she was one of those people who thought they could, but she'd hoped to at least have a sense that he was close. But there were no tingling sensations, no sixth senses to encourage her. She swallowed the toast around the lump in her throat and pulled her napkin off her lap.

With a touch on her hand, Caleb leaned toward her, rousing her from her fatalistic thoughts.

Staring into his compassion-filled eyes, words failed.

Caleb laid his fork down and stood, opening his arms. "Come here, babe. Talk to me."

Grief seeped through her. She crumpled into his arms, taking comfort as he pulled her close. Cocooned in his embrace, she released the words she'd held for too long. "I'm so afraid, it's hard to breathe sometimes. And if I admit it, I feel like the biggest coward in the world. What if we don't find him here?" Her voice rose. "And what if we do, Caleb? What if we find him and it's too late? What then?"

Caleb's arms tightened around her, his voice low and deep. "We're not too late. I don't believe that. But, no matter what happens, we're in this together." He nudged her chin up. "Listen to me. You. Are. Not. Alone."

Lacey couldn't escape the conviction in his eyes. Nor did she want to. She needed to lean on his hope. Breathing deeply, she snuggled into his chest. He rocked her in his arms until she allowed his words to penetrate her fear. "Thank you for believing. I don't think I realized how badly I needed to hear that."

Caleb's pulled her face to his, warm lips whispering against hers. Her arms stole around his neck, her fingers winding into his hair, holding his mouth more firmly to hers.

Breaking the kiss, Caleb pulled her tightly against him once more. His rapid heartbeat matched hers as he kissed the top of her head. "We better finish eating and be on our way," he said with only a hint of regret. "I'm anxious to meet Agent Stepanek and find out what he knows."

***

Caleb leaned down, his breath a frosty mist as they left the apartment building. "Want to walk? Or would you rather take a cab?"

Lacey pulled her hood up. "Which gets us there faster?"

"With traffic, it's probably a wash."

Lacey glanced at the cars as they fought each other for position. "It's only a few blocks, right? Would you mind if we walked?" The last thing she wanted was to take a chance on being late.

Caleb took her arm and headed left. "Not at all."

The snow had dissipated over the past several hours and the sidewalks were mostly clear, so they arrived at the coffee shop a few minutes early. The welcoming heat surrounded them as Caleb guided her through the door.

Lacey glanced at his windblown hair. Without a thought, she took off her mitten and smoothed it, dusting the few snowflakes that had gathered. Caleb caught her hand, pressing a quick kiss on her palm.

She turned her attention to the other customers brave enough to venture out into the elements, hoping Agent Stepanek hadn't arrived ahead of them. But the only people in the shop were two middle-aged women chatting by the gas-lit fireplace in the back corner, and the young man behind the counter.

Lacey read the menu and wandered toward him. "I'll take a grande white mocha, please."

He tossed his head to the side, shifting the curtain of black hair that covered his face. "Anything else?"

Caleb pulled out his wallet and handed him a ten. "Tall, Americano. Keep the change."

The kid tossed his hair again then dumped the change into the tip jar. "Be right up."

Lacey followed Caleb to a small grouping of leather chairs surrounding a low table, the inlaid checkerboard waiting for old men with nothing but time on their hands. She'd just enjoyed the soothing warmth of her first sip of coffee when Agent Hank Stepanek walked in. It was impossible not to recognize him even though they'd never met.

He reminded Lacey of a bulldog. His lower lip jutted out with a serious under-bite, his military buzz cut more gray than black.

"Ms. Jordan?" he asked, striding toward her.

He was probably mid-fifties, she guessed. She and Caleb stood and shook his hand as introductions were made. Agent Stepanek removed his heavy trench coat and Lacey fought a surprising urge to laugh at how stereotypical he seemed. She'd seen way too many spy movies. But, his sharp eyes and no-nonsense attitude somehow comforted her and calmed her anxiety.

"I've read what's in the file," he began, his voice carrying an east coast edge, "but I want you both to recap the past couple of weeks from the beginning." In a jerky scrawl, he jotted notes as Caleb and Lacey recounted all that had happened.

189

When they'd shared everything they could think of, Agent Stepanek leaned forward, elbows on his knees. "We now know for certain that Stan Jacobson used his own card at the casino in Joliet."

A nervous flutter rippled through Lacey as she glanced at Caleb.

"We're hoping he makes another appearance so we can track him. We believe he'll surface again, based on his history of compulsive gambling. There are a dozen or so major casinos in the area and we've assigned round-the-clock teams to each of them."

Lacey was encouraged by the news. "What can we do to help?"

Stepanek's dark eyes reflected his sympathy. "I know what you'd like to hear, and I wish I could give it to you, but the most important thing you can do is lay low. People in and around your father's industry are aware of his abduction. You guys showing up here is going to raise questions. Work out your story. But here's the deal. When you talk to anyone, and I mean anyone, other than each other, you don't discuss the case. No particulars at all, no leads, no nothing, got it?"

Lacey nodded.

"We watch and wait," he said. "That's all we can do right now. If that changes, I'll be in touch."

***

"What's up?" Caleb's shoulder squeezed the phone to his ear as he jostled his key into the lock. His hand froze. "That's bullshit, Brandon. They're full of it."

Lacey stepped in front of Caleb and finished unlocking the door.

Caleb followed her into the apartment and made a beeline for his laptop. "I'll send an email now to schedule a conference call. That wasn't part of the deal and they know it."

Tension radiated through the room. Lacey waited as Caleb booted up his laptop.

"No, we're here. Just got in today."

Lacey's eyes flew to Caleb. *Shit.* They hadn't even had a chance to figure out their story and Caleb was already telling people they were here.

She'd leave it up to him to figure out what to say. It was too late for her to jump in now, anyway. He could fill her in when he got off the phone.

Lacey took the opportunity to study her surroundings. Definitely a bachelor's home, she noted, pleased by the thought. Every piece of furniture was sleek, minimalist. Floor-to-ceiling windows lined one wall, which she was sure normally offered a stunning view of Lake Michigan. Tonight though, even the city lights were subdued with the combination of early winter dusk and the thick looming mist left from the earlier snowstorm.

Lacey shivered and turned from the window, touching a control on the wall that swooshed the vertical blinds closed. She wandered down the hallway and found her way into Caleb's office. The simplicity of the room mirrored the rest of the apartment, but the austerity made her vaguely sad. Fingering the few framed photos on his desk, she studied the faces of his siblings and wondered if Rachel had sent the pictures. Did he have a sense of connection to them? Or did he consider himself just a provider?

In their time together, there'd been so little opportunity for her to learn more about him. She thought back to the driven young man he'd been years ago. Even though she'd only known him for a summer, there'd always been an edge of reserve. He'd rarely talked about his past, and never about his parents. She'd tried once to get him to tell her about his family, but his eyes had turned hard and he'd walked away from her. She never tried again.

Lacey turned to the bookshelf lining the wall, tilting her head to peruse the titles. She felt rather than heard Caleb's approach.

His arms circled her waist, pulling her tight against his chest. He leaned down to her ear. "See anything interesting?"

She turned in his arms and looked into his eyes, still wondering about his past. "I do."

A smile played at the corners of his mouth. A quick jolt of pleasure caught him by surprise when he'd walked into his office and saw her standing there. It felt like she belonged here. With him. The simple words she'd just spoken sparked a vision of her in a white dress, with his ring on her finger.

191

Don't think about the future. Hell, he couldn't even begin to predict when or how this would end. But as he watched her lips quirk up in an answering smile, he decided that, no matter what else happened, he'd take this temporary gift of her being here.

"So what's on the agenda this evening?" she asked.

You. That's what he wanted to say. Instead, Caleb sighed. "I need to meet with Brandon. One of our EU distributors is trying to dick with us. Trying to get us to modify a product for them to edge their competitor." He ran a hand through his hair. "Not happening."

"Are you going to the office?"

Caleb shook his head. "No. I told him I would, but he's cool with coming here. Practically insisted."

Not even close to how he'd wanted to spend the evening. He rubbed his hands down Lacey's arms, wishing he could explore whatever was happening between them. She was opening up to him. And every real smile, every real revelation, was like a drug. He wanted more.

She nodded and squeezed his hands. "At least let me put something together for dinner. I'd say it's about time for me to return that favor."

***

Brandon Thomas wasn't at all what Lacey had expected.

As Caleb took his coat, she accepted the hand Brandon offered. He was about her height, with intelligent eyes. At a glance, she'd call him attractive, in a soft, metro kind of way.

"Caleb mentioned you'd joined him. I'm terribly sorry about your dad."

His eyes made an almost imperceptible trip down then back up. Lacey chose to ignore it, focusing on his words instead.

"Thank you," she replied. "We're still hopeful." Stepping back, she glanced at Caleb's inscrutable features, wondering if he'd noticed Brandon's perusal.

Maybe she was just being oversensitive. She pasted a smile on her face. "Caleb tells me you've been a huge help with the expansion."

Brandon stepped closer, a smile tweaking the corner of his mouth. "With Ian dropping the ball, I had to step in. But don't get me wrong. I love it. Gives me a chance to show what I'm capable of."

Could the guy be any more full of himself?

Lacey took a step toward the kitchen. "Sounds like they're lucky to have you, Brandon." She glanced at Caleb. "I've set the bar for two, and dinner's ready if you'd like to eat before you guys get started."

Caleb shook his head. "Thanks, babe. We won't be long and we can eat after, if that'll work."

Brandon's gaze swiveled to her. "Won't you be eating with us?"

"Unfortunately, no. I've got a few phone calls to make."

He flashed another smile. "Join us, please. I insist. We'll try to avoid boring you with shop talk. Right, Caleb?"

Lacey suppressed a shiver as Brandon touched her arm. His familiarity unnerved her. The move seemed innocent enough, but Lacey had no doubt that it was a move. This time she didn't have to wonder if Caleb had noticed.

He scowled and stepped between them, ushering Brandon to his office. "We've got work to do."

Lacey called down the hall after them. "Dinner's on the stove. Help yourselves when you're done."

An hour and a half later, Lacey glanced up from the television as Caleb entered the bedroom. "Is he gone?" Rude, but to the point. She didn't like Brandon Thomas.

Caleb rolled his neck and shoulders then flopped down next to her on the bed. "Finally. He hung around after we ate. Thanks for dinner, by the way. I think he was hoping you'd join us."

Lacey rolled her eyes. "Seriously?"

"Yeah," Caleb grumbled. "He seemed more interested in you than Europe."

What a creeper. Anxious to put him out of her mind, Lacey hit the TV remote to shut off the TV and nudged Caleb. "Roll over."

He raised an eyebrow, but obliged. "What did you have in mind?"

Straddling his back, Lacey rubbed his knotted shoulders.

"Mmmm…feels good." Caleb sighed, closing his eyes.

Lacey worked the strong planes in his back and shoulders. "Did you get your problem straightened out?"

Caleb took his time answering. "I think so. We'll know for sure in the next couple of days. Brandon was distracted. He forgot some of the information he was supposed to bring for our conference call."

Lacey pulled his shirt over his head then renewed her exploration, fascinated by the lines and contours her fingers traced. Her heart raced as the minutes ticked by. *Step away.* The words were as clear as a soft wind chime on a cloudless spring day, but the heat from his skin through her fingertips fueled her desire and numbed her fear. She leaned down and placed a soft kiss on his shoulder blade then found a sensitive spot behind his ear.

Caleb growled low in his throat. "A man can only take so much torture. My turn." In a split second, he had her on her back, towering over her.

She expected him to dominate her, knowing she was playing with fire. But instead he tenderly teased her senses, his lips and fingers touching everywhere and nowhere in particular. Lacey drifted on a sea of pleasure, undone, willing to admit that Caleb was much better at this game than she. She willed her body to slow down, tried to stave off her pleasure, but he knew her too well. He made sweet love to her, bringing her to the edge of satisfaction before tumbling over with her in perfect time.

Lacey took the scenic route back to reality. When she could finally form a thought, she looked at the handsome man above her. "How do you do that?" she sighed.

Caleb shifted to her side so he wasn't crushing her. With one hand, he pushed his hair off his forehead, his breathing still not quite steady. Lacey propped herself up on one arm, enjoying his profile.

As he opened his eyes and caught her staring, a slow lazy smile formed on his lips. The look in his eyes heated her blood. She almost laughed when she recognized her own body's reaction. The man could turn her on with those eyes from across a crowded room.

"Well?" she whispered.

"Well, what?" His husky voice demanded. She did smile then. He had no idea what her question had been.

"How do you do it?" she repeated.

"Do what?" His gaze strayed to her breasts where his finger drew lazy circles around her nipples.

She put her hand over his. He was threatening to break her concentration. His eyes met hers again. "Get better every time."

"I could ask you the same question." His face turned from teasing to serious as his eyes searched hers. "God, I –" She kissed him to stop whatever words were next, but as he gathered her into his arms, Lacey had a horrible suspicion he was going to say that he loved her.

And that would've been perfectly awful.

Chapter 26

Lacey stretched and pulled her gaze from the brilliant morning sunlight peeking around the blinds. Feeling more refreshed than she had in days, she pushed her hair out of her eyes and leaned up on her elbow. A moment of unreality seized her. She was in Caleb's bed, in Caleb's apartment, in Caleb's city.

And, hopefully, closer to finding her father.

She scurried out of bed, anxious to get started on the day. But started with what? She heard the shower running, so she wandered into the kitchen and put on a pot of coffee.

Now that she was here, she wondered if coming to Chicago had been a mistake. What could she do here? If she were home, she'd at least have the shop to keep her busy. Stirring in a liberal amount of creamer, she shook her head. It didn't matter. It was the best lead they had, and she'd stay unless or until something better came along.

Lacey's phone jingled from the bedroom. She raced to grab it then listened as Mona's sweet but worried voice asked about any new developments. "I didn't get your message last night until after choir practice and then Spencer and I were up late talking. I had no idea until almost midnight that you were in Chicago." She paused, as if realizing she was rambling. "Have you learned anything new?"

"No, not really. It's pretty much like my message said yesterday. We're just waiting for Stan Jacobson to make another move. The FBI seems confident that he will." They visited a few more minutes as Lacey spread preserves on a toasted muffin and poured a mug of strong black coffee for

Caleb. Just before Mona hung up, she asked Lacey if she'd have Caleb call Spencer.

Still smiling over that request, she marveled at the impact Caleb had made in Spencer's life in such a short period of time. Of course, he'd made a pretty big impact in hers as well.

"Breakfast and a smile…and it's not even nine o'clock? I must be hallucinating." The soft timbre of Caleb's deep voice, still husky from sleep, did funny things to Lacey's insides.

"Look who thinks he's a comedian this morning."

He advanced toward her, a predatory gleam in his eyes. Deciding to follow the insane urge to run, she bolted to her left, but he was too quick. His arm snaked out and grabbed her wrist, pulling her toward him. She laughed at the spontaneous play, the sound foreign to her ears. When was the last time she'd laughed without a care?

Caleb hauled her up against him. His deep, solemn eyes connected with hers and Lacey's laughter died in her throat. He rubbed his knuckles against her cheek. "What am I going to do with you?" he asked, almost to himself.

Visions of last night's almost-declaration flashed through Lacey's mind. She knew she needed to step away, but instead she stood in his embrace until she couldn't stand the intensity of his gaze any longer. Thinking to bring them back to neutral ground, she blurted, "You could always hire me as domestic help. I make a mean toasted English muffin."

"Hmmm…Give me a little time. I'm sure I could come up with something better than that." He grinned then released her. "How's the coffee?"

She handed a mug to him and raised her own to her lips. "Not bad, if I do say so myself."

He took a long swallow. "I've got to sit in on some meetings today at the office. You're welcome to come with me, which will most likely be pathetically boring. Or, you can hang out here and drown yourself in daytime TV."

She grimaced. She didn't relish the prospect of running into Brandon Thomas again, but sitting around Caleb's apartment sounded like pure torture. "I think I'll take my chances with pathetic boredom if it's all the same to you."

He chuckled, but he couldn't hide the flash of relief in his eyes. After a quick peck on her cheek, he checked his watch. "I need to meet with Meg at ten. Can you be ready to go in thirty minutes?"

Lacey jogged down the hall to the shower. "I'll make it twenty if you find me a decent breakfast place between here and there."

***

Lacey pulled her attention away from the huge metallic bean-shaped sculpture that dominated the park across the street from Caleb's office. "That's interesting. Do you get much tourist traffic here?"

"Definitely. Animal bioscience research is all the rage on the guided tours."

Lacey caught his wink as he led her into the atrium. Thin tree trunks reached toward the glass ceiling and the trickling fountain made her think of fairy tales and castles.

She smiled. "That's not exactly what I meant. I was talking about the giant bean. I've never seen anything like it."

Caleb put his arm around her and, pulling her close, whispered in her ear.

Lacey's eyes crinkled, and heat rushed to her cheeks. "Stop," she warned, trying to pull away. The man was impossible. Before he let her go, Caleb brushed a quick kiss on her neck.

As they approached the reception area, Lacey's steps slowed. Both women seated there stared at them, brows raised. Lacey elbowed Caleb. Great. Her first impression on his coworkers and they were gawking like she had a second head.

"Good morning, Mr. Mansfield," the one in glasses said around a smile. "Glad you're back."

He smiled at both women. "Good morning." he said. "Gretchen, Susie, let me introduce a friend of mine. This is Lacey Jordan. Her father and Roger have been friends for years. She's in Chicago to spend some time with us."

Lacey reached out to Gretchen and shook her hand. "Nice to meet you."

"You, too," Gretchen replied with a sincere smile.

Lacey turned to Susie and once again reached out her hand, surprised by the animosity she sensed. "Hello," Lacey said uneasily. She didn't recoil from the hard pressure the other woman put into the handshake, but she came close.

Susie dismissed her with a disdainful sniff and turned her attention back to Caleb.

"Lacey will be working with us here for the next few days," Caleb said, apparently oblivious to the exchange. "She'll be in my office if anyone asks." He took Lacey's arm and steered her away.

"I can only imagine the kind of work she'll be doing in his office," Susie muttered under her breath. "What on earth does a skinny little thing like her have to offer that I don't?"

Gretchen wisely turned her back on that comment. After listening to ten minutes of additional commentary, she sighed and finally spoke up. "I told you weeks ago to put any notions of dating Mr. Mansfield out of your head. But did you listen? No. Don't think I haven't seen the emails you've been sending him. Completely inappropriate." She opened a new Word document and began typing. "Personally, I'm glad she's here. It was good to see him really smile."

Susie rolled her eyes. "Why wouldn't you be happy she's here?" she sneered. "You're married."

***

Lacey crossed the threshold into Caleb's office. "Wow. I think Susie has the hots for a certain BioTech executive," she said dryly.

A frown puckered Caleb's brow. "She's a little over the top."

Lacey rubbed her hand. "I got the distinct impression from the way she looked at you that she'd like you to be her exclusive property." She crossed the room to a small table in the corner and set her purse and day planner on the table.

She didn't hear him come up behind her.

"Jealous?" he whispered near her ear.

She cringed, but tried to turn the tables. "No more than you were last night."

Without warning, she found herself in his arms, his mouth on her neck. "Good," he murmured. "Then we're even." Her thoughts scattered as he nipped the sensitive spot just below her ear. "Just for the record, she's not my type."

"Oh. Good to know," Lacey whispered as his lips journeyed along her cheek causing a tremor to pass through her. She turned her head, forcing his lips to meet hers.

Caleb squeezed her shoulders and gently put her away from him. "If I don't stop now, I'm going to find a new and thoroughly satisfying use for my desk."

Lacey opened her dazed eyes and comprehension quickly followed. She smiled and watched him stride to the other side of his desk. He removed his jacket and had his laptop booted up within minutes. As he rifled through the paperwork on his desk, his ability to switch gears and refocus impressed her. Her mind was still muddled from his sensual assault.

Today, she intended to detail as much as she could about the events of her dad's disappearance. Any thought, no matter how insignificant, could potentially be helpful. She took out her day planner and settled herself at the little table.

Minutes later, a perfunctory knock at the door interrupted her musings. A stout gentleman walked in and headed to Caleb's desk.

"Where is she?" He asked without preamble. "I can't wait to see her after all these years."

Caleb smiled. "Good morning, Roger." He came around the desk and motioned toward the corner. "I'm assuming this is the 'she' you're referring to?"

Lacey rose from her chair as Roger pivoted toward her and felt the years fall away. "Hello, Uncle Roger," she said quietly. "You haven't changed a bit." A knot of emotion rose in her throat as Roger wrapped her in a bear hug.

Roger finally pulled back and clasped both her hands in his. "I certainly can't say the same about you," he exclaimed. "I think the last time I saw you, you were chasing animals around the farm with your pigtails flying out behind you."

Lacey grimaced. "That must've been a sight."

Roger shook his head. "Seems like last week," he sighed. "Hard to believe how fast time passes." He switched gears in a heartbeat. "Caleb and I have been staying in touch the past couple of weeks. We've got feelers out all over the industry trying to dig up anything that might be related to your dad's disappearance."

Lacey looked over at Caleb. She trusted Roger, but she also remembered Agent Stepanek's instructions. Caleb nodded to her, indicating his trust as well. "Do you know why I'm here?" she asked.

Roger didn't miss a beat. "As dedicated as Caleb is to the company, I seriously doubt it's because he couldn't stay away. So, if I had to guess, I'd say it's about the investigation, isn't it?"

Nodding, Lacey continued. "We're focusing in on Stan Jacobson."

Roger looked sharply at Caleb. "The guy we almost hired? That you had me check on?"

"He's just popped up on the radar here in the Chicago area," Caleb confirmed. "It's a direct contradiction to the story he gave his wife. We're hoping he can lead us in the right direction."

Roger nodded, a scowl crossing his face. "I didn't much care for him then either."

***

Lacey sat lost in thought, the page in front of her devoid of any major revelations. Stretching, she wandered over to Caleb's empty desk and noticed the dead plant on the corner. Curious, she read the card.

Thanks for the hard work. Glad you're back. Maybe it's time for you to put down some roots of your own. Roger.

Tapping the card against her hand, Lacey pondered the words. Putting down roots, huh? Was that something that Caleb wanted in his life? Or was that Roger's goal for him?

Her phone vibrated, startling her out of her thoughts. She dashed to the table, catching it just before it went to voicemail.

As soon as she answered, Sam breathlessly launched into conversation. "Lacey, Karen just called. She's scheduled a conference call with Mike and Tina Morris for one o'clock today," she squeaked. "What am I going to do?"

Lacey could almost see her pacing around the counter at the shop. "Well first, you're going to take a deep breath and relax."

"Okay." A pause. "Okay, I'm better. I'm just nervous. I didn't expect it to happen this fast."

"It'll be wonderful," Lacey predicted. "And since it's a conference call, I'm sure Karen wouldn't object to me linking in from here if you want."

Sam released a breath. "Would you? Oh, Lacey, I know you're in the middle of everything with your dad but if you could be on that call, I would feel a million times better."

Caleb returned to the office from his meeting and was immediately struck by the excitement on Lacey's face. His first thought was that she'd received news about the kidnapping, until he caught her side of the conversation.

"I'll call Karen now to get the conference call number and I'll talk to you at one. Just remember…be yourself and be confident." She hung up the phone and beamed at Caleb. "The coordinator set up a conference call for us to meet the adoptive parents at one today."

Caleb smiled at the joy in her eyes and the frustration of the last hour receded. It wasn't just that Sam's adoption process made her happy. It also served to take her mind off things she couldn't control, and for that, he was grateful.

"I don't want to impose on you in your office. Is there a conference room I can use to make the call?"

"There's no need." He checked his watch. "I've got another meeting at noon which will probably take a couple of hours. Make yourself at home." The glow in her eyes mesmerized him. "You're pretty excited about this, aren't you?"

Lacey squeezed his hand. "Oh, Caleb. It feels so surreal just being a little part of this. If it goes like I'm hoping it does, it's going to be such a win-win. Sam will have peace knowing that her baby will be in a happy home and this wonderful couple will have a sweet little baby to love."

Caleb's hands glided over her cheeks, then anchored her head as his mouth lowered to meet hers. "You have an amazing heart," he whispered, a breath away from her lips.

The buzz of the intercom interrupted. "Mr. Mansfield?" Gretchen's efficient voice broke the silence.

Caleb sighed then brushed Lacey's lips before walking to his desk. "Yes?"

"Mr. Cantwell suggested that we cater in lunch today because of the meeting schedule. We have boxed lunches up at the front desk for you and Miss Jordan if you're interested."

"Thank you, Gretchen," Caleb said. "We're starving." He winked at Lacey, who rolled her eyes at his innuendo. He flicked the button to end communication then glanced down at his laptop and noticed a new email message from Meg. He glanced at Lacey. "I'll just be a second."

"You do what you need to. I'll go grab the lunches." Lacey was back within moments. "Ham or turkey?"

Caleb glanced up from his computer. "That was fast. You pick. I've got to head upstairs." She handed him a box as he headed toward the door. "I'm surprised Gretchen let you get away that quick."

"She wasn't there. Just your groupie," Lacey muttered. "It's probably a good thing she didn't know which box was mine."

"How'd your meeting go?" Lacey asked when Caleb entered his office, surprised to realize it was already close to four.

He ran his hand through his hair. "It was okay. Sorry it took so long. I didn't mean to leave you stranded in here. Brandon was out today which slowed us down a little bit, but I think we have most of the product stuff back on an even keel."

Caleb closed down the laptop and loaded his briefcase. Lacey thought he looked tired, but as he glanced at her, she felt the warmth in his gaze. She liked being in his space, liked hearing about his day.

"Let's get out of here. You can tell me all about your conference call over a bottle of wine and the best Chicago style pizza you've ever eaten."

Lacey leaned back against the red vinyl booth as the voices of the other patrons blended with the soft music to create a pleasant buzz. Added with the glow of the soft yellow light from the lamp above their table, the mellow atmosphere encouraged conversation.

"So, what happens now?" Caleb caught the rich red pizza sauce dripping down his chin, barely saving his white shirt.

Lacey was pleased, but not surprised, that Caleb seemed genuinely interested in Sam's future. She picked up her glass of merlot and swirled the dark red liquid, still basking in the afterglow of the call. "It was awesome. Karen was there to moderate but, there wasn't much for her to do. The potential adoptive parents, Mike and Tina Morris, were wonderful. And Sam did such a great job. You should've heard her. By the end of the conversation, they were all chatting like old friends. Sam and I both loved Mike and Tina." Lacey tried to slow down, but the words tumbled out.

"Afterward, Karen said she was very encouraged. She's putting all the necessary paperwork together. I'm so excited for Sam. She's not going to have to worry about her ability to handle things financially. It sounds like Mike and Tina will take care of the rest of her prenatal care. They're also going to make sure the starter on Sam's truck gets fixed so she can make it to her doctor appointments safely."

Lacey couldn't stop grinning. She tried to explain the feeling of "rightness" that permeated the call but she knew she was failing miserably. It didn't matter. From the look on Caleb's face, he knew she was flying high.

"There are so many more options involved than I ever even thought of. Did you know that the birth mother gets to decide if she wants an open adoption?"

Caleb shook his head. "Open adoption? What's that mean?" he asked, finishing off his slice of pizza.

Lacey wiped sauce from her fingers, finally giving up on the massive slice of cheesy pizza and digging in with her fork. "The birth mother gets to decide to what extent she wants to be involved in the baby's life after the birth. If the adoption is closed, the birth mother isn't involved in any way. If it's an open adoption though, the level of involvement can be anything from an occasional photo as the child grows all the way up to open disclosure and periodic visits from the birth mother."

Caleb's eyebrows lifted in surprise. "Really? I guess I never really thought about it. I just assumed that the mother gave up the baby and that was the end of it."

"I'm willing to bet that most people make those same assumptions. I certainly did," she said. "Birth mothers actually have a lot of control and a lot of choices."

Lacey paused, the words she'd thought about all afternoon poised to leave her lips. "You're going to think this is crazy." She sat silently looking down at her plate. "I think this is crazy." She knew from the tension that had filled the space between them that she had his attention. Long moments passed as trepidation and excitement twisted her insides.

Caleb reached over the table and hooked his finger under her chin, his eyes searching hers. "What?"

"I think this is what I'm supposed to do with my life," she whispered, her lips hinting at a smile. With shaking hands, she picked up her glass again and downed the rest of her wine. "I've never felt so exhilarated by anything I've ever been involved with. I think I'm supposed to help young mothers find adoptive parents and help them through the process." She released an excited sigh. "How insane is that?"

Caleb smiled as he raised his glass in a toast, his eyes filled with encouragement. "Here's to insanity."

Chapter 27

Ian strode toward the elevator that would take him to R&D, pushing the button for the second floor. He didn't want to be here. None of this mattered anymore. But he couldn't get that bitch Meg off his back. He pushed the button again. Damn elevator. How the hell could it take this long to get here?

"Excuse me. Dr. Cox?"

He half-turned toward the reception desk. "Yes?" he snapped.

"Ms. Richards left something for you." Susie stood at the reception desk, her clinging yellow dress providing an ample view of her chest. When he realized she wasn't going to bring the file over to him, he scowled and headed toward her.

"Give me just a second," she said as she fumbled through the stack of papers on her desk. "It's a manilla envelope."

Ian listened to his elevator door open, then close. What was she prattling on about? Just hand over the damn envelope already. "What's it for?" he queried, trying for patience. If she took any longer, he'd come around the desk and find it himself.

Gretchen found the envelope and handed it to him. "I believe Ms. Richards said something about updated projections she and Mr. Mansfield wanted you to have before the meeting today."

"Mansfield. Is he here? I thought he was on vacation."

Susie rolled her eyes. "He brought his vacation back with him," she said snidely.

"Susie," Gretchen admonished.

Susie swiveled on her chair. "What? I can't help it," she whined. "It's just not fair. If I'd known he was the knight-in-shining-armor type, I could've made up some story about my daddy gone missing, too."

Ian had turned to walk away but swiveled back around at her words.

Gretchen's voice was a tight whisper. "Except this isn't some made up story. My God, Susie, would it kill you to show a little sympathy for the poor girl?" She shook her head and turned away.

"Are you talking about Bill Jordan's daughter? Is she here?"

Gretchen nodded. "Do you know her?"

Ian sighed. "I'm afraid not, but I'd love to meet her. Her dad and I used to be friends."

Susie's lips twisted into an ugly sneer. "Great," she mumbled. "I'll add you to the fan club."

Ian tore open the envelope as he walked away. "You do that."

***

Caleb locked the door to his office and guided Lacey down the hall. This had been one of those days that made him long to be back in the lab, by himself. Things were much simpler there and he didn't have to deal with people. Today's endless carousel of meetings, some productive, but most mind numbing, was surely the cause for the pressure he felt just behind his eyes.

He checked his watch and felt Lacey stiffen.

Ian stepped in front of them, effectively blocking their path. He didn't speak as his quizzical gaze focused on Lacey. Since Ian's stubbornness had been a major source of today's challenges, Caleb wasn't in the mood for idle chit-chat. "Lacey, this is Ian Cox. Ian, Lacey Jordan," he said curtly. "We were just leaving."

Lacey extended her hand and uttered the usual pleasantries. Ian didn't move. He continued to stare at Lacey. Finally, he took her hand. "I heard a rumor you were here," he said. "It's so nice to finally meet you. My God, you look just like your mother. She was beautiful."

Lacey tugged her hand away. "Thank you."

Caleb interceded. "As I said, we were just leaving. If you'll excuse us."

Ian turned and walked with them, matching Lacey's quick stride. "This is certainly a surprise. The police talked to me about your dad, but I don't know why. I certainly had no reason to hurt him. We used to be friends, you know. A long time ago. Do the police have any leads? Is that why you're here?"

Caleb stopped and whipped around. "Lacey is here because, for obvious reasons, she didn't feel safe by herself. And, since I needed to get back to make sure things happen," he paused pointedly, "we decided it made sense for Lacey to come back to Chicago with me." He grabbed Lacey's arm, giving Ian a nod of dismissal.

As they reached the building entrance, Ian yelled after them. "Hopefully we'll have the opportunity to visit more Friday evening. You will be attending the big to-do with Caleb, right?"

Lacey started to respond to him, but Caleb's vice-like grip forced her out the door. Caleb didn't turn around as he answered. "We'll be there." He shuffled Lacey through the door and hailed a cab.

"He seems kind of sad. Lost, you know?" Lacey said as she climbed into the back seat of the taxi. "I thought he was out on leave or something."

Caleb held tight to his frustration, his teeth clenched. He wouldn't call Ian sad or lost, but something was definitely going on. He could feel it. The police hadn't come up with anything else on him, but Caleb wasn't satisfied. He needed a way to search Ian's apartment, see what he could find.

He rolled his shoulders and turned to look at her. "We had a meeting today that Roger called Ian in on. I really need to talk to Roger. He's coddling Ian and I just don't get it. Ian wasn't himself. And all he did was throw up roadblocks the whole time."

"I'm sure Roger has a plan," Lacey soothed. "Maybe he's just waiting until after the party."

***

By Thursday afternoon, Lacey was at her wits end. At least at home, she had things to keep her busy. She could almost hear the clock ticking, reminding her that time was wasting away. How much longer did she have? Or was she already out of time?

She ended her check-in calls with Mona and Paige and wandered aimlessly around Caleb's office. Her fingers traced the edge of his desk, touched the writing pad where she briefly skimmed his bold scrawl. She gazed out the window at the huge metal sculpture across the street, getting lost in the reflective patterns. It surprised her that people were outside milling around, although for Chicago in winter, the sunny mid-fifties afternoon was probably considered a heat-wave. The tourists appeared to understand and appreciate just how fickle mid-western weather could be, and had decided to take advantage of the temperature upswing.

The door to Caleb's office opened with a whoosh. Meg stopped abruptly, a perplexed look on her face. "Where's Caleb?"

"He went to a meeting." Lacey looked at her watch. "I could've sworn he said it started at one, but I could be wrong."

"One? Is it one already?" Meg checked her own watch. "Shit. Shit. Shit. I'm supposed to be in there." She whirled around on the balls of her feet. "Gotta go. See you tomorrow night," she yelled from somewhere down the hall.

Lacey groaned. The big party. She slumped into Caleb's chair. She knew Caleb wanted her there, but how could she? How could she pretend, and smile, and socialize, when her dad was God knows where?

She slammed her palm flat on Caleb's desk, anger burning in her chest. Where the hell was Stan Jacobson? Her entire life was on hold until the bastard surfaced again. *Come on, you asshole. Show your face.*

Lacey shoved away from the desk, and with deep breaths, willed herself to calm down. Agent Stepanek's reminders about playing along and not raising anyone's suspicions echoed through her head.

Fine. She'd go to the damned party. Maybe she could mingle with some of the other employees. What if she got solid information from someone there? Okay, odds weren't good, but it couldn't hurt to try.

Lacey raised her face to the sun shining through the window, cursing herself for not packing anything to wear. She'd have to go shopping.

Resigned to her fate, she took one last look at the people across the street, envious of their carefree laughter.

Gretchen sat alone at the reception desk. Breathing a sigh of relief, Lacey sauntered up to her, her mind on the task ahead. "Gretchen, can I ask for your help?"

Pulling a couple sheets of paper off the printer, Gretchen stapled them then smiled up at Lacey. "Of course. What can I do for you?"

Lacey tugged her purse strap up onto her shoulder. "I forgot to pack anything for tomorrow night's event. Is there anywhere close I could get something appropriate?"

Gretchen laughed out loud, her eyes twinkling. "Lacey, you're on Michigan Avenue. In downtown Chicago. I think you'll be able to find something that will work. Let me see what I can do." Her fingers flew across the keyboard. Within minutes, Gretchen handed her a printed list of the stores in the area.

Lacey read down the list of possibilities as Gretchen filled her in on their proximity to BioTech, their average prices, and who usually had the best sales, until she finally raised her hands in mock surrender. "Okay, okay," she laughed as she folded the list into her purse. "If Caleb comes looking for me, will you let him know where I went?"

"Sure thing," she replied and waved Lacey out the door. "I'm cutting out for the day for a doctor's appointment, but I'll leave a note for Susie. Have fun!"

Outside the doors, Lacey was thrust into the bustling activity that seemed to be ever present on Michigan Avenue. She turned left and headed toward the Magnificent Mile. It felt so strange to be doing something as normal as shopping when her world was completely upside down, but the sunshine on her face and the breeze that ruffled her hair combined to lift her spirits. Her mood improved with every step until a soft smile was tugging at the corners of her mouth. It just felt good to be outside and alive.

She made her trek through one store then the next, surprised that she was actually enjoying her light-hearted afternoon. In the third store, she found exactly what she was looking for. Then, not quite ready to surrender the peace of the day, she headed toward the Navy Pier. Lacey ordered a latté and small bag of caramel and cheese popcorn and sat at one of the many outdoor tables.

At the noisy insistence of several birds, she shared her snack before resuming her stroll. Her eye caught a little girl, holding her dad's hand as they headed toward the enormous Ferris wheel at the center of the pier.

"Will I be scared, Daddy?" the little girl said in a loud whisper.

Lacey's heart smiled as the little girl's father leaned down and scooped her up in his arms. "I'll be right there with you, Baby. You'll be just fine."

A wave of melancholy swept over her and she watched the little girl cling to her daddy's neck. Lacey stiffened her spine and strengthened her resolve. *We'll find you, Dad. I promise.*

***

"Who does she think I am? Her personal secretary? She doesn't even work here." Venom dripped from every muttered syllable. Susie crumpled up the note Gretchen had left and threw it toward the wastebasket under the desk. It bounced off the side and landed on the floor. Susie kicked the plastic bin and sat down roughly in her chair.

"Is there a problem?"

His sudden appearance startled her. "Oh! I didn't see you there." She murmured. "No problem really. Nothing the Wizard couldn't help me with anyway. You wouldn't happen to have any ruby slippers, would you?" She snorted at her own jest. "I'd love to send little Miss Dorothy back to Kansas."

He clucked sympathetically, nodding. "You know, I've watched Caleb and how he looks at you."

Susie's eyes narrowed. "What are you talking about?"

"I've caught him several times looking at you. He wants you. I can tell. Of course, he hides it whenever *she's* around."

Susie banged her pen down on the desk. "Ha! I knew it! I've seen it, too. Gretchen kept telling me I was wrong but I wasn't." She stood abruptly. "I think she's secretly afraid I'll end up married to him and then I'll be telling *her* what to do."

Susie paced, surprised but pleased that he continued to listen to her. It was so refreshing that somebody besides her knew what was really going on. She had to talk to Caleb alone. Let him know that she was aware of how he really felt.

The man stood silently, waiting for the perfect moment to speak. "You know," he said, "if you're willing to help me, I may just be able to help you."

***

Lacey polished off her latté and glanced at her watch. The encroaching dusk cast long shadows and the air turned chilly. She buttoned up her jacket and made her way quickly back to Caleb's office.

She'd just taken the gorgeous little black dress out of her bag when she heard the door to Caleb's office open. "Oh good, you're here. I went shopping for tomorrow night's party." She started to hold up the dress then broke off, embarrassed, when she realized it was Roger who'd walked in. "I'm sorry. I thought you were Caleb."

Roger's eyes darted around the room. "Caleb? I thought he was with you." He shrugged. "Hmm. Must've heard wrong. I'm a pretty poor substitute, but I'd love to see your dress," he smiled.

Through her awkward embarrassment, she held up the dress, the black silk rustling. Roger whistled appreciatively and Lacey could feel the heat on her cheeks. "Do you think it'll be okay?"

"Trust me," Roger laughed. "It's perfect."

The door flew open and Caleb stormed into the room. He stopped in his tracks as his gaze swiveled toward Lacey.

Roger slapped him on the shoulder. "Lacey was just showing me her dress for tomorrow night. Very nice."

Caleb's eyes didn't waver from her face. "Where the hell have you been?" His voice lashed out at her.

Lacey bristled. With efficient moves, she quickly hung the dress back in the bag with its wrap. She straightened her shoulders and turned back around to face Caleb. She noticed Roger had made a quick getaway. Coward, she thought. "What do you mean where have I been?"

His face was set in taut, angry lines. "I've been searching the whole building for you. No one seemed to know where you'd disappeared to."

Taking a deep breath, Lacey tamped down the retort that sprang to her lips. He was obviously worried. She'd had her moment of reprieve but he was still in the midst of the battle. Not just the battle to keep BioTech moving forward on schedule, but the deeper, more emotional battle of finding her father.

She laid her hands on his forearms, the tight muscles like steel. Leaning up, she kissed him softly on the cheek. "I'm okay. I just went shopping for a little while." She nodded toward her bags. "Want to see what I bought?"

Her arms wound around his neck, and she nudged him down to meet her lips. "You don't have to be worried about me," she whispered. "We're in Chicago now. Very few people from home know I'm here and the ones that do are trustworthy."

Chapter 28

Caleb's heart had finally slowed to a normal rhythm by the time they grabbed takeout and returned to the apartment. He'd been keyed up anyway, and coming back to an empty office had scared the hell out of him.

Lacey scooped out the paper cartons and loaded up plates. He felt her gaze as he returned from changing clothes.

"Were you supposed to meet with Roger this afternoon?"

Caleb's breath lodged in his throat. *Did he look guilty?* "No, why?"

She frowned. "I don't know. He seemed surprised that you weren't with me." She was silent for another minute, but her eyes never left him. "So, you know all about my afternoon. What did you do?"

Shit. He was hoping she wouldn't ask. He could've dodged anything other than a direct question. He'd stood still so long that Lacey put down the plates and came to stand directly in front of him.

She crossed her arms, her eyes probing. "Why do I get the feeling I'm not going to like the answer?"

"It's better if you don't know."

Her hand touched his arm. "Uh-uh. No secrets, remember? You told me once that we're on the same team." Her eyes penetrated. "We are, aren't we?"

He'd be damned if he wanted to break the trust they'd begun to build. But to tell her could do her more harm than good. He pulled her into his arms, her light citrus scent surrounding him. "I broke into Ian's apartment today."

She pulled back, her eyes huge. "You what? How?"

Caleb could hardly believe he'd pulled it off, but sharing the information with her helped him, calmed him. He drew her to the sofa then pulled her close. "Technically, I didn't break in. I borrowed his keys from his desk while he was meeting with Brandon."

"And? Did you find anything?"

Caleb frowned. "It was weird. I didn't find anything that said he's involved with your dad's disappearance, but his table was piled full of stuff from college. His yearbooks were sitting out and he had pictures of him and Roger and your dad circled. And a blond woman with a beautiful smile." His eyes studied her face. "He was right about one thing. You do look a lot like your mom."

Her brow furrowed. "But, what do you think it means?"

A deep sigh escaped Caleb's lips. "I don't know. His place is a pig sty. There are dirty dishes and laundry everywhere." He shook his head. "It doesn't make any sense. That's not Ian at all, unless he's a completely different person at work. He's always been very organized."

Lacey's eyes held his for several seconds then she shook her head and walked away from him. Tension vibrated from her as he came up behind her and clasped her shoulders.

"Lacey, I –"

She rounded on him, fear and anger sharpening her words. "How could you take such a huge risk? What if you'd been caught?" Lacey tried to shrug out of his grasp, but he refused to let her go. He pulled her into his embrace, rubbing slow circles on her back until she finally relaxed into him with a heavy sigh. "I know you did it for me, but don't ever do something like that again."

They talked late into the evening about her dad and Ian and the whole nightmare until there was nothing more to say. Caleb's fingers stroked her hair as she lay on the couch, her head resting on his thigh.

Clicking the universal remote to switch the sound over to the MP3 system, he scrolled through the play list on the screen. "Any preference?" he asked.

"Hmmm…not at all," she murmured.

She wondered what he'd choose, realizing she didn't even know his taste in music. Of course, there hadn't exactly been time or opportunity to talk about such ordinary things.

As she appreciated the mellow blues beat that filled the room, her mind filtered through all the other things she didn't know about him. Starting with his family. Would he open up to her about them if she asked now? A reminder of the last time she'd tried trickled through her mind, but she gave a mental shrug. There was only one way to find out.

Her words were quiet so he could pretend not to hear if he chose. "Do you always spend the holidays with your siblings?"

Caleb's hand stilled on her hair. He thought she was sleeping. "I try," he said, hoping the short answer would discourage further conversation. It didn't.

"Are your parents still living?"

He pondered the question. And the questioner. What had prompted her to ask? Would she find his answer strange, especially in light of how close she was to her family?

Avoiding the issue was his standard mode of operation. The slick, practiced words stood at the ready. But, as he stared at the opposite wall, with only the music breaking the silence, avoiding his past didn't seem as important anymore. Lacey had begun to trust him. Maybe it was time for him to do the same.

He expelled a deep breath. "My dad isn't. I don't know for sure about my mom."

Lacey shifted onto her back and looked up at him, but stayed silent, linking her fingers through his. She was giving him an out. Making the decision, to share his past or not, his alone. He didn't look at her, couldn't stand to see what her expressive eyes would reveal.

Finally, he spoke again, his voice strained. "My mom left when I was twelve. I never saw her again." A pause. "And, for reasons I never completely understood, while my father was alive, me being around caused him a lot of anger and resentment. By the time I graduated from high school, I went from being his son to some kind of competition."

Lacey squeezed his hand, urging him to go on.

"He was an abusive alcoholic, Lacey. Very angry and bitter that his life didn't turn out like he'd planned." The words tasted dirty. Shrugging, he brought himself back to the present. "He stopped working, went on disability, and basically drank himself to death. Taking care of the kids fell to me and Rachel. When he died, Rachel was a junior in high school and I was twenty, in my second year of college."

"There are six of you altogether, right?"

He listened for pity, but didn't hear anything but curiosity in her tone, so he continued. "Yes. Sarah's after Rachel. She's twenty-five. The boys are twenty-two. Kyle and Kevin. Then there's Seth who just graduated from high school last spring. He's nineteen now."

Lacey sighed, her smile lighting her face. "I would've loved to have had siblings. Did you all get along well?"

Caleb thought about that one for awhile. "It was a different kind of childhood. Rachel and I have talked about it some. Since it was all we ever knew, we didn't realize it at the time, but it definitely wasn't what you'd call typical. So, yeah, we got along but there was way more fear than joy in our house. I can't remember ever being a care-free kid."

Lacey sat up on the couch and snuggled into his side. "Are they all doing okay now, though?"

Caleb's nod bumped Lacey's head. "Rachel did an amazing job taking care of them."

"And you made sure they had the resources so she could. Do you see them often?"

Caleb shrugged. "Sometimes on the holidays. But other than that, not much. First it was work and school but for the past several years, I've been

218

traveling as often as not, so it's just become the norm. They're used to me not being around much."

When the old familiar anxiety that had always accompanied thoughts about his past didn't come, he leaned his head against the back of the couch and relaxed.

"So what happened with Seth?"

He'd forgotten he'd mentioned his littlest brother to Mona. His lips quirked into a smile. "Ah, Seth. I did end up jumping in last year with him. He's a brilliant kid. Thrill-seeker. School was a total bore to him. He was close to getting out of control. Just needed a little male influence." *And a whole lot of military influence.*

"Are you looking forward to seeing them again?"

"Yeah, I am." He pulled Lacey tighter against him. *You'd like them. And they'd like you.*

As the evening wound down, Caleb shared stories about growing up. Some funny, some poignant. Lacey asked questions and probed deeper than he'd allowed anyone before. But there was none of the pain he'd expected from the memories.

Lacey turned to face Caleb, her dark eyes looking deeply into his. "Thank you," she murmured.

Truth was, though, that he should've been thanking her. Lacey's sweet persistence had opened a conversation about possibilities that he'd long since thought closed off forever. He had a family he was missing out on. He promised himself that when Bill was found, he'd work harder to build real relationships with them.

Sleep escaped Caleb as he laid in bed hours later, Lacey tucked in his arms. He wanted a future. A future with his siblings, and a future with Lacey. Pulling her closer, he listened to her quiet even breathing as deep anxiety consumed him. He needed to get to the bottom of Bill's abduction, needed to protect Lacey. If the bastards had tried for her once, they'd do it again.

Damn it. He'd been so damn sure he'd find something in Ian's apartment to incriminate him. But, he'd found nothing. That left only two possible scenarios. Either Ian was involved and was a crafty son of a bitch. Or, he wasn't involved at all.

Caleb felt like banging his head into the wall as the question with no answer pinged around his brain.

If not Ian, then who?

Chapter 29

The cell phone on the bedside table jangled. Stepanek jerked awake and fumbled for it, hoping the insistent racket didn't wake his wife.

"I knew you were probably sleeping, but I didn't want to wait until morning. Figured you could use a little good news."

Stepanek recognized the agent's voice immediately. Sitting up, he rubbed his eyes. "What do you have for me?"

"Dumb ass used his credit card again." The agent laughed. "Different casino, but same drill. Looking at surveillance, he got there around seven. Used cash. Played up for a little while then around nine, he started losing. Bad. Couldn't buy a hand."

Stepanek could hear the agent rustling through his notes.

"He used the ATM at the casino around nine thirty. He finally ran out of money about eleven. Not a great night overall."

"Not for him, maybe, but just what we needed. Nice work. You got a tail on him?"

"Yes, sir."

"Let me know when he lands." He disconnected the call and got out of bed. He threw on a pair of pants and his robe. He patted his wife's shoulder as she mumbled. "Everything's fine, sweetheart. Go back to sleep."

He put on a pot of coffee then grabbed his notes and sank into his favorite recliner. He allowed his mind to run free with the details of the case. He'd been doing this a long time and this was the best way he'd found to try to connect seemingly random dots.

The old familiar feeling of the tumblers in a lock starting to click into place stole over him. He didn't know much yet, but the next day or two would be critical. He grabbed a cup of coffee and waited for an update. It was the hardest part of the whole damn job.

***

Stepanek was up and dressed when the call came in. "The eagle has landed. Nice digs too. You want us to go in?"

The quick staccato of the agent following Stan was music to Stepanek's ears. He shoved into his overcoat and grabbed his keys. "Why don't you hang tight? I'll be there in thirty minutes."

He hadn't gone back to sleep since the earlier call, but driving over to the Lakeshore area gave him time to clear his head. He circled the building a couple of times before finding a parking space. As he climbed out of the car and headed over to meet his contacts, he craned his neck all the way back to check out the recently renovated thirty-floor high-rise.

Polished steel and glass gleamed as far as the eye could see. The entry, surrounded by festive holiday greenery, was manned by a liveried doorman. Nice, very nice, Stepanek thought. Wonder how our boy is paying for the place?

He walked up next to the unmarked car and rapped on the passenger-side window. He heard the snap of the lock and quickly slid into the back seat. He looked from one agent to the other as they turned to greet him. "What do you know? Any activity since he went in?"

The driver kept his eye on the entry after a quick glance at Stepanek. "It's been quiet since he got back." He cranked the car heater down a notch. "Standard procedure?"

"Yep. Let's do things by the book. I'll go have a little visit with operations and security and see what our guy is up to." He grabbed the handle and shouldered the door open. "Give me a call if he happens to split."

It took Stepanek four hours to overcome the countless stonewalling attempts before he finally got the information he needed. Damn if people weren't overly sensitive about their privacy. Only after threat of subpoena did the ridiculous ex-para-military excuse for a security manager allow him access to the camera records and tenant data.

But it was enough. Stepanek whistled as he stepped out into the sunshine and gave instructions to his surveillance team. "I need you to keep your eye out for this guy." He shoved a printout of a security video freeze frame image into their hands. "Looks like he's Stan's Chicago connection. I've got a call in to downtown to get more info on him."

"Do you want us to pay a call to our guy in there, sir?"

"Nah. Don't want to raise any flags yet. I'll continue to see what we can dig up. Call me if they move." Stepanek walked slowly back to his car, his wheels turning. With any luck they might have enough connections for a search warrant.

He was stalling, but he didn't mind. This thing needed to go down nice and tight. He already knew who the asshole was, knew a little bit about him. Stepanek wasn't a fan of coincidences and this was a big one. Now for the fun part, putting all the pieces together.

Smiling, he slid into the driver's seat. *Click, click, click,* went the tumblers.

Chapter 30

Caleb looked up, the crystal snifter he'd poured arrested halfway to his mouth.

Lacey's skin grew warm under his intense gaze. She'd taken time with her make-up and hair, the honey-blond curls falling just past her shoulders. But as he continued to stare, she nervously ran her hand down the black sheath, afraid it was clinging to her.

The liquid heat in his eyes mesmerized her. "Say something," she breathed.

He lowered the glass then crossed the room until he stood inches away. His strong hands enveloped her bare upper arms then slowly skimmed down their length until his fingers held hers. He leaned into her and whispered in her ear. "Let's stay here."

She shivered, her quiet sigh filling the space between them. "I think someone might notice if you didn't show up tonight."

He stepped back, his eyes traveling her length in a long, thorough journey. "I've got news for you," he murmured. "When I walk in there with you, looking like that, no one's going to remember if I was there or not."

"If you keep looking at me that way, we'll never know for sure." Pulling her fingers out of his grip, she distanced herself from the energy simmering between them. "We'll barely make it on time now if we hurry."

Caleb stood still a moment longer, obviously torn, before reaching for Lacey's silver silk wrap. "You're going to freeze to death in this," he admonished softly, nuzzling her neck as he placed it around her shoulders.

"I know," she said, reaching for her black clutch. "But it was either this or my winter coat. Somehow, I didn't think it would quite go. Besides," she added as she turned to him, "I'll have you to keep me warm."

He growled and pulled her to him. "You can count on it." He kissed her deeply then pulled abruptly away. "The driver is downstairs waiting for us. We better go before I convince you to change your mind."

She looked up at him, her eyes wide. "You got a cab already?"

"Didn't need to. Roger sent over a limo." He smiled at her, a wicked gleam in his eye. "Roger's no dummy. My guess is he knew what my reaction would be when I saw you in that dress."

***

Handing her wrap to the petite girl behind the counter, Lacey gazed around the festive atrium. Twinkling lights blinked from the high tree boughs. Several of Caleb's coworkers, a few of whom she recognized from the past week, gathered around the champagne fountain obviously already enjoying the evening.

In another reality, this might've been any of the countless holiday parties she'd attended to promote the business. But this was so inevitably different, so wrong. The celebration made a mockery of her nightmare.

She touched Caleb's arm as her chest tightened, unable to swallow around the ball of anguish in her throat. If she hadn't just handed off her wrap, she might've bolted for the door.

Caleb turned her into his arms, his eyes searching hers. "Babe," Caleb whispered, "If this is too much, we don't have to stay. I'll tell Roger —"

Looking into his worried gaze, Lacey worked to contain her runaway emotions. *You have to get a grip.* Freaking out every time life confronted her wasn't going to work. This was her new normal. This middle-ground between living and not moving on. She had to figure out a way to deal with it.

She placed her hand on his arm. Tonight was his night to shine. She'd overheard enough over the course of the week to realize that Roger's pride in Caleb's accomplishments was the biggest reason for the gathering.

"Sorry. Just a little overwhelmed." He didn't look convinced. "I'm fine," she whispered, nudging him farther into the room. "It'll be okay."

Straightening her shoulders, Lacey remembered her goal for the evening. Somebody here might have information about her dad's disappearance. Glancing around at the laughing faces, she vowed to find out what she could. Hopefully, the flowing alcohol would loosen a tongue or two.

"Caleb. Lacey. So glad you're here." Roger's exuberant voice interrupted her thoughts.

Lacey turned to see Roger striding toward them, a diminutive Hispanic woman in an empress-waist emerald gown in tow.

Roger gave Lacey a quick hug and kiss. He whispered in her ear. "I was right about the dress. He can't take his eyes off you." He winked at her and straightened. "I've been looking forward all week to introducing you to my wife, Rosalee."

Lacey was captivated by the smile that crinkled the older woman's eyes. Her lightly accented voice lilted musically. "Roger has been bursting at the seams this week, waiting for tonight. He has spent the week regaling me with stories about him and your father." As soon as the words came out of her mouth, her expressive eyes darkened and she grabbed Lacey's hand. "I'm so sorry. How unbelievably insensitive of me."

Lacey squeezed her hand. "It's okay." She glanced at Caleb. "We think the investigation is making progress. We're trying to stay positive." Lacey found herself wrapped in a fierce hug.

"Our prayers are with you, my dear." Rosalee released her then turned her attention to Caleb. "It's good to have you back home, Caleb," she said, hugging him. She nodded toward Lacey before turning her keen dark eyes back on Caleb. "It does my heart good to know you have something else to come home to now instead of just business, business, business."

Lacey stiffened, wondering how Caleb would respond, but before he had the chance, the caterer appeared at Rosalee's side.

"Mrs. Cantwell, we have a bit of confusion regarding the timeline of events this evening. Can you spare a moment?"

"Of course. Excuse me, Darling," she said to Roger. She hugged Lacey and Caleb one more time. "I hope you enjoy yourselves tonight. I will be praying for your father, Lacey." She left in a flurry of green chiffon.

Roger's gaze lovingly followed his wife. "She sure keeps life interesting," he said, smiling. "But she's not going to rest until this night goes off without a hitch, which means I better get my notes together. She has me slated to speak for twenty minutes during dinner." Roger pulled cards from his breast pocket, tapping the stack with a finger. "Off to practice. I know I'm not going to be the one to mess up her schedule. I'm sure we're seated together at dinner, so see you then."

Caleb ushered Lacey to their table. She fished her phone out of her bag and checked it for what seemed like the hundredth time since Agent Stepanek had called earlier in the day.

"Anything?" he asked.

She frowned and shook her head. "I just keep expecting him to call again with an update."

"I know. I'm sure he will as soon as he's got something." Caleb scowled as his attention was drawn to the place card with Ian's name on it adjacent to his own. He rolled his shoulders. "I'll get us a drink. Are you okay?"

Lacey found her seat and relaxed into it. She looked up at Caleb and smiled. "Much better now."

She glanced around the room. No sense in wasting the opportunity to talk to people in her dad's industry. Her thoughts swiveled to Brandon. She'd avoided him throughout the week, but maybe that had been a mistake. So what if he was a narcissist, it couldn't hurt to talk him up a little bit, and this was the perfect environment to do it.

Craning her neck, she continued to scan the crowd. She'd just have to keep her eyes open for him. Taking a deep breath of the holiday scent that filled the air, Lacey checked her phone once more then tucked it into her purse as something hit the back of her chair.

Someone, actually. She swiveled as Susie Blakely grabbed the back of Caleb's empty seat and fell into it. "Don't think I don't know what this is all about," she hissed, her eyes glittering.

Lacey's eyes widened as the stench of too much alcohol threatened to overwhelm her. She scooted her chair out of range of Susie's drink, surprised it was mostly still contained in the glass. "I'm sorry?"

Susie's face contorted with anger, her heavy make-up garish in the low light. "He told me Caleb was using you to make me jealous. I'm the woman for him and I will have him." She suddenly stood and teetered on her four-inch heels. Lacey watched in stunned silence as Susie marched away from the table.

"What was that all about, or do I want to know?" Caleb asked quietly. Lacey jumped as he came around the table and placed a glass of champagne in front of her.

She shook off the hatred she'd seen in Susie's eyes. "Told you she was a groupie. Looks like I've been warned off you." She reached out for her glass and was frustrated to see that her hand trembled.

Caleb looked around, his eyes landing on Susie. "Stay here," he ordered.

Lacey quickly stood and grabbed his arm, holding him there as subtly as possible. "Caleb," she whispered urgently, "now is not the time." He pried her fingers off his jacket sleeve as he went to move around her. "Please," she continued. "Let's not ruin this for Roger and Rosalee. She didn't do any harm. She probably won't even remember saying anything to me tomorrow." When he didn't pull away, she pressed her advantage. "Surely this conversation can wait until Monday, don't you think?"

Caleb looked at her, his eyes still hot with anger. He allowed Lacey to nudge him toward the table then sighed hard enough to ruffle her hair as he held out her chair before taking his own seat. "On Monday, she will no longer be employed by BioTech."

Lacey smiled and finally began to relax as dinner was served. Ian never showed, which seemed to elevate Caleb's mood. She checked her phone once more to no avail then turned the ringer to silent in anticipation of the speakers. Meg and Rosalee turned their chairs toward the small stage as Roger began his speech.

Toying with the filet and steamed asparagus, she listened to Roger share the story of the company. His eyes glowed with pride as he spoke of the growth of the organization under Caleb's tenure. Caleb shifted slightly in the seat next to her. His chiseled features cloaked the discomfort she was sure he felt at Roger's high praise. He glanced over at her briefly and smiled.

"And in conclusion, I'd like to thank you all for your loyalty and service through the years. As we all know, nothing stays the same forever. We'll have a major announcement in the coming weeks that will continue to move BioTech to the forefront of the industry. Stay tuned." With that, Roger stepped down from the stage and came back to the table.

As the clapping ended, the din of quiet speculation spread through the room. Caleb looked up as Roger seated himself. "Nice speech. Can I assume that your coming announcement has to do with a shake-up in the R&D department?" he said under his breath.

Roger took a long drink of ice water. He winked at Lacey. "You could, but you know what they say about assuming." Roger chuckled as Caleb's eyes narrowed slightly. He clapped Caleb on the back and murmured, "Don't worry, my friend. All will be well. Trust me." He turned to Rosalee and kissed her cheek. "I'm running a little ragged. Do you think we might be able to get out of here a little early?"

Rosalee covered his hand with hers. "Of course. Let me check with the caterers and the deejay to make sure they're set up for the rest of the evening. Then we can go." She rose from her seat and hurried off behind the festive partition at the side of the room.

Lacey felt the sudden tension as Caleb searched Roger's face. Concern marked his words. "You sure you're feeling okay?"

Roger smiled, but fatigue shadowed his eyes. "I'm feeling fine. Don't worry about me. But if I don't get Rosalee out of here soon, she'll make it her mission to stay until the last candle is extinguished. Call me selfish, but I intend to have her to myself tonight."

Caleb still didn't look convinced, but he let it go. "Well, don't let my speech keep you here. The details on what our EU operation means to the folks here is certainly nothing you haven't heard before."

Meg got up and started to go back stage. "You better be ready in five. After I introduce you, I've got a conference call with the director of the California facility."

Roger laughed as he and Lacey stood. "Meg, you're a treasure," he said sincerely. "If I have any genius at all, it's surrounding myself with people who are way better than me." Roger turned to Lacey and enveloped her in another of his bear hugs. "If there's anything you need, you let me know."

She nodded and felt the moisture in her eyes. "It's no wonder my dad loves you so much. You are a very good man."

As Roger walked away from the table, Caleb touched Lacey's arm. "My speech should only take a few minutes. I'll make it quick then we can be on our way, too."

Lacey took a tissue from her purse and dabbed her eyes. Trying to recover from the unexpected emotional exchange with Roger, she did her best to lighten the mood. "Are you trying to get out of here quickly to have me all to yourself tonight?"

Caleb stood back and made a slow, thoroughly hot perusal from her head to her toes. He smiled that casual sexy smile that made her toes curl. "How'd you guess?" He gave her a quick kiss and then disappeared behind the stage.

Lacey returned to her seat and stuffed the tissue back into her purse. The red blinking light on her phone caught her attention. *Crap. Who had she missed?*

One new voicemail message. She didn't recognize the number but she grabbed her purse and moved down the hall toward the executive offices so she could hear the message. The muted wall sconces provided the only lighting as she walked away from the noise and revelry.

Stopping at the end of the hall, she pressed the button to retrieve her message. Listening intently, all she could make out on the line was street sounds and rustling. *Great. Someone drunk dialed me.* She listened again, hoping that there really was some kind of message there intended for her.

One ear to the phone, and her hand covering the other to block the sounds of the party, Lacey barely registered the soft whoosh of the emergency exit door. Grabbed from behind, Lacey gasped as a powerful hand pressed a cloth over her mouth and nose.

Twisting violently, she tried to scream, but she couldn't get away from the odor filling her nostrils. She wasn't more than thirty feet from the party

230

and she tried to run, but her legs felt like putty. She needed the self defense moves she'd learned. *What were they?* Her brain shrieked at her, but she couldn't remember. And why was she fighting, anyway? She was tired. All she wanted to do was go to sleep.

Within seconds, the sounds of laughter and conversation faded to silence.

Chapter 31

He hated making speeches. The way the champagne was flowing, Caleb doubted if anyone would remember it anyway. Resigned to making the best of it, he listened to Meg's introduction then quickly walked to the makeshift podium. He looked up, the glare of the lights facing the stage making it virtually impossible to see into the crowd. Leave it to Rosalee to make it a professional production.

He spent the next ten minutes talking about the expansion and the value they would collectively bring to the market. Contrary to his preconceptions, the party-goers paid attention, and seemed genuinely excited about the expansion. Not only would the company's reputation become even greater, they apparently understood that their own personal stock options would be worth substantially more in the months and years to come. Caleb hooked them from the word go.

When he finished, the crowd was fired up. His obvious belief in the company and their direction drew them like flies to honey. It took another few minutes for him to get even close to his table. He finally plowed his way over, inordinately curious to find out Lacey's opinion.

The smile froze on his face and his blood ran cold when he realized she wasn't at the table. *Cool it, Caleb. She's probably in the restroom.* Still, he couldn't shake the nagging feeling that had plagued him all evening.

He tried to rein it in. Give her a minute. She'll be right back. His eyes scanned the room. What the hell was she thinking? She knew he didn't want her going anywhere without him. Uneasiness rippled through his veins. He didn't even pretend to listen to the people around him as he headed out of the atrium.

He stalked to the coat check. The two young girls standing with their backs to the counter, engrossed in conversation, visibly jumped when he slapped his hand on the counter. They whirled around in unison, their eyes wide at his rapid-fire words. "The woman I came in with, dark blond hair, black dress, tall. Did she get her wrap in the last fifteen minutes?" The girls looked at each other and then back at him. As one started to open her mouth, he pulled the tag out of his pocket and thrust it toward them. "This is her ticket. Did she get her wrap?" He enunciated the last sentence slowly, controlled.

The girls both looked at the ticket and then promptly started shaking their heads, reminding him of bobble head dolls on the dashboard of an off-road vehicle. The shorter of the two finally spoke up. "No sir," she stammered. "No one has come to get their coat in the last fifteen minutes. The party's just getting going…"

Caleb didn't wait around. His gut was churning. If she hadn't left, maybe she was in the restroom. He strode quickly to the executive hallway and went to the women's restroom door. He jerked it open and called out her name when something caught his peripheral vision. In the corner toward the back of the hallway, he spotted a small black bag that he immediately recognized as Lacey's. Fear lanced through him.

He bolted toward the bag and as he knelt to grab it, he spied her phone as well. The back panel and her battery were splayed out next to the unit. He quickly put the pieces back together while he pulled out his own phone and dialed nine-one-one.

He relayed as much information as he could to the operator then hung up as soon as he knew they were on their way. His next call was to Agent Stepanek.

"They got her. They took her." Caleb's voice rose. "BioTech offices. Hurry."

"I'll be there in ten minutes." Stepanek's calm rational tone did nothing to allay the savage anger coursing through Caleb's body.

Damn it. Ten minutes was too long. What had possessed her to come back here alone? He paced the hall, checking the empty offices then opening the exit door. Wandering the darkened alley behind the building, Caleb looked for anything out of place, but found nothing.

He closed the door and heard the lock click into place. *Where the hell was she?* Checking Lacey's phone again, he noticed a new voice mail message. His fingers shook as he tried to access the message but he realized immediately he didn't have her password. Looking at the call history, he redialed the last number listed. The phone rang as he paced.

"Hello?" the slurred feminine voice answered.

"Who is this?" he demanded.

The woman's voice rose. "Who is this?"

"Caleb Mansfield. This phone –"

"Oh," the voice crowed. "It's about time you called me. I've been waiting weeks for you."

Caleb gripped the phone even more tightly. "Susie? Susie Blakely?"

"Oh, yes. I knew you'd be calling. I've seen the way you look at me when your little goody-two-shoes girlfriend isn't around. I knew it was only a matter of time before you realized we were s'posed to be together. I'm looking forward to –"

Caleb saw red. "Are you here?" Stalking back into the atrium, he scanned the crowd until he saw her at a table in the corner, an empty glass in front of her.

He stormed to her table through the gathering crowd of curious onlookers and slammed the phone down. "Why the hell did you call her? What did you say? Where is she?" It was all he could do to restrain himself from physically trying to shake the answers out of her.

The crowd parted as two uniformed police officers followed Agent Stepanek to the corner. Stepanek came to stand between Caleb and Susie.

Caleb cast him a quick glance. About damn time he got here. "This bitch dialed Lacey's phone about thirty minutes ago." He turned back to Susie who seemed to shrink before his eyes. "I'm going to ask you one more time, Susie. Why the hell did you call her? And how did you even get her number?"

Susie shook her head. "No, no, this isn't right," she mumbled. Tears began flowing down her cheeks, her mascara creating twin rivers of black. Caleb and Stepanek leaned closer, barely able to make out her words. "He told me he'd get her out of my way so I could have you," she whispered, her voice reed thin. "I wasn't even supposed to say anything on the message."

"What the hell are you talking about?" Caleb's words were ice. "Who? Who told you to make the call?"

Stepanek moved fully in front of Caleb. "Susie, is it?" He squatted down at the table and tried to grab her attention, but her eyes were glued to the table. "Susie." She jerked and stared at him blankly. "I'm Agent Stepanek and I need your help. Did you make a phone call to Lacey Jordan?"

Susie's eyes welled up again as she nodded. Caleb shifted his weight, his patience long since gone. He started to speak, but Stepanek reached back and punched him in the calf.

Stepanek continued in stride, his voice a soothing murmur. "Susie, who told you to make that call?"

Susie dry heaved. "I'm sorry. I'm so sorry. I'm going to be sick." After leaning into the trash can someone hustled over, she came up for air, her napkin covering her face.

Her color was off, but when her eyes met Caleb's, he knew she'd been a pawn in someone else's game. He leaned over the table. "Susie. There isn't much time. Please. Tell us who told you to make the call."

"The phone call." She hiccupped and a fresh wave of tears began. "Brandon got me the number and told me that's all I had to do and he'd take care of the rest."

The air whooshed out of Caleb's lungs. "Brandon? Brandon Thomas? Son of a bitch." Caleb hissed. *What a fool I've been.*

Stepanek rose and barked instructions to the two uniforms standing by. "Get this place closed down. Send these people home. Get her down to the station," he nodded toward Susie who wretched again into the container. "I'll deal with her later."

Caleb grabbed Stepanek's arm. Panic laced his words. "How do we find the bastard?"

"We've got people watching his place."

Caleb stopped abruptly. "Brandon's? Why? Since when?"

235

Stepanek reached for his phone, glancing at Caleb as he dialed. "Since a couple of hours ago when we figured out that's where Stan's been staying." He turned slightly and barked into his phone. "Get in there. Now. I'll be there in fifteen minutes."

Caleb matched the agent's quick stride. "I'm going with you."

Stepanek looked like he was about to argue until he saw Caleb's eyes. He must've known Caleb would go on his own. "Then you're going to stay out of the way and let us do our job, got it?"

Chapter 32

Lacey's stomach protested as dull awareness crept into her foggy brain. She tried to raise her hands, but her wrists were bound behind her back. Slow, deep breaths through her nose kept her from getting sick. As she opened her eyes and got her bearings, the nausea receded, replaced by a sick sense of dread.

She was in a car. A song with a heavy bass beat blasted through the speakers, keeping time to the throbbing in her skull. Using the seat for leverage, she got half-way to a sitting position before she recognized the back of the driver's head. Stunned, she met Brandon's gaze in the rear-view mirror.

"Oh, good. You're awake." He turned down the music. "I've been patiently waiting. Did you sleep well?"

The conversation was all the more perverse for its normalcy. Icy tendrils gripped Lacey's spine. Her tongue felt like it was fighting through saw dust. "Where are you taking me?" she whispered.

Brandon smirked into the mirror, before his face turned hard. "Family reunion," he said. "I know you've been missing your daddy. He sure has missed you."

The evil in his eyes made her cold. Lacey couldn't keep the fear out of her voice. "My father? Is he okay? What have you done to him?"

Lacey's mind swirled with visions of the torture he might've endured at this monster's hands. She shook her head to clear it, struggling against the bindings at her wrists and ankles.

"You bastard," she hissed. "If you've done anything to him –" her voice broke as Brandon slammed on the brakes. She flew forward in the seat, a hard plastic trash holder hooked over the passenger seat lacerating her cheek. Her body crumpled to the floorboard.

Brandon threw the car in park and yanked her up by her hair. Biting back a cry of pain, Lacey stared into his wild eyes. "What I've done to him isn't shit compared to what I'm going to do to you if you don't shut the fuck up. You got it?"

Her dad was alive. And Brandon was taking her to him. She had to stay focused and keep him calm. She took a deep breath. "Please," she said quietly. "Please. I need to see my dad."

He glared at her for another minute, before pulling the car back on the highway. "Don't worry, princess. I wouldn't have it any other way."

Lacey watched out the window, her anxiety stretched to the breaking point. She tried to get her bearings but all she could tell from the brief snatches of highway lights was that they were heading toward a part of town she'd never venture to during the day, let alone at night. Graffiti marked several buildings as they exited the highway. As they slowed and turned onto a poorly lit side street, she might've considered yelling to someone for help, but there wasn't a single person anywhere. Lacey had a feeling that this was the kind of place where it was smarter for people to look the other way.

Brandon turned, his eyes narrowing. "I'm going to open your door and snip the ties at your ankles. You're going to walk in front of me. Fight me in any way and your dad's a dead man, got it?"

She nodded slowly.

They made their way up the broken sidewalk to the cement slab porch. Brandon unlocked the door and shoved Lacey inside. His grip on her arm bruised her as he bolted the door. The smile he gave her made her skin crawl.

"Bill," he crooned, "Guess what I've got. I've found the key." He steered Lacey down a short dark hallway until they came to a closed door.

Lacey couldn't hear anything on the other side, but the hair on the back of her neck rose. Brandon reached into his pocket and pulled out a single key on a paperclip. He released her arm to work the lock then turned the handle.

Lacey craned her neck but couldn't make out anything in the dark room until Brandon switched on a small lamp. Then her eyes took in everything at once. The room was grimy, from the nasty carpet to the stained walls, but her gaze immediately flew to the only piece of furniture in the room – the bed where her dad was lying face down, his hands bound behind him.

Fear raked over her as she cried out and ran to him. Oh God, was he sleeping or drugged? Or dead? "Dad! Dad! Wake up. Dad! Answer me!" she shrieked.

His cuffed hands twitched, sending ragged relief rushing through her. Powerless to help him, Lacey squatted by the bed, the stench of dried urine and feces gagging her. Her dad's eyes squinted open, disoriented.

He frowned and blinked several times. "Lacey?" he croaked.

"Dad," she cried. "I'm here." She strained against the ties at her wrists, needing to touch him, to convince herself that she was really here with him. His gaunt face frightened her. How much weight had he lost?

Her father licked his cracked lips. His voice came out a little clearer. "How did you find me?"

Brandon cackled from behind Lacey, a tight brittle sound. "How do you think she got here? She's my key. Your incentive. When the goon we sent to get her failed, I honestly thought I was fucked." He reached down, grabbing a fistful of Lacey's hair. "Imagine my surprise when I found out she'd come to me. I'd call that a sign."

He tightened his grip before releasing her then caressed her face. "I didn't expect her to be so pretty though." He reached lower, cupping her breast, pinching her nipple. "Might have to help myself to some of that when we're done here."

Lacey swallowed the bile that rose in her throat, her gaze flitting around the room for a means of escape, but the only window in the room was boarded up. Tears of frustration stung her eyes as they settled on her dad. But, even in the midst of their nightmare, his eyes, now clearer and more focused, tried to assure her they'd make it through this.

His hope had been reborn, but hers was fading. Her dad looked so fragile. Could he walk, or even stand?

Surely Caleb knew by now that she was missing, but no one knew where they were. No one suspected Brandon. She wanted to scream. Instead, she prayed like she'd never prayed before. For her dad. For herself. For a future past this night.

Brandon's mood shifted again, raw anger radiating from him. He pulled a silver blade from his pocket and pricked her neck with the tip, forcing Lacey to stand. Spittle flew from his mouth as he glared at Bill. "Now, you'll tell me what I need to know."

"Yes," Bill nodded, his eyes wide. "Free my hands. I'll disable my encryption."

Brandon dropped Lacey to the floor, his eyes gleaming in the weak light. "Now, that's more like it." He opened Bill's personal laptop and plugged it into the wall outlet by the bed. Lacey's breath caught in her throat as Brandon used his knife to cut the duct tape from her dad's wrists. He unlocked the handcuffs and glanced at Lacey. The disgust on her face must've been obvious.

"Oh, I know what you're thinking," he said as he sheathed the knife. "Duct tape seems so inhumane, doesn't it?" He laughed. "It's your dad's fault, really. I'd have been okay with handcuffs until the mother fucker hauled off and hit me."

Lacey scooted closer to her father as Brandon moved around the bed. The volatility of his moods was more frightening than the pure anger. His instability made him unpredictable. Still, he wasn't that big. If she could just get him to lower his guard, maybe she and her dad would be able to overpower him.

Lacey watched her dad sit up, slowly working his fingers and his arms, pain etched on his face. All thoughts of getting Brandon to relax flew out of her head. Seeing her dad's agony and the dried blood on his wrists, Lacey cried out. "Oh my God! How long were you bound?"

Her dad shook his head, fear in his eyes, but she ignored him, rage boiling up inside her. She struggled to her feet and faced Brandon. "You're a monster," she spat, heedless of the madness in his eyes.

240

Pain radiated through her jaw as Brandon's fist connected with her face. Lacey lost her balance and fell back on the bed next to her dad. He tried to stand but collapsed on the mattress.

Brandon snarled at his puny attempt to defend her. "Don't even think about it old man, or I'll make her sorry." He handed the laptop over. "Unlock the fucking code. Now."

Tasting blood in her mouth, Lacey sat up and leaned into her dad, letting him know she was okay. She hid the rage that burned through her as the smell accosted her again. My God, had they not even let him shower or use the restroom? Brandon deserved a fate worse than hell for what her dad had been through.

She marveled at the inner strength of her father as he turned toward the keyboard, with Brandon watching every keystroke. Lacey wasn't sure she'd have survived the torture he had.

Brandon squirmed as the data started flowing on the screen. "Fascinating," he mused. He could've almost been reviewing results in a lab with his peers. Excitement dripped from his words. "This will be worth millions."

Lacey couldn't quite hide the disdain in her voice. "Is that what this is all about? The money?"

Brandon refocused his attention on her. A ghost of a smile crossed his face but didn't reach his eyes. He nodded, as if dealing with a slow-witted child. "You'd think that would be enough, wouldn't you? When I first started hearing some rumblings in the community, I have to admit that my initial thoughts were about the money. So, I found a way to get someone close to you." He looked down at Bill. "It was actually quite simple. A few well placed phone calls and of course, the perfect candidate." He sneered. "Addiction and a family man. What a combination. Opens a man up for all kinds of enticement."

Lacey's fingers itched to scratch his eyes out. She strained against the ties on her wrists, slick now with blood from her efforts.

"But it's not just the money. The person who brings this to market will have fame. And not in some shit-hole bio-feed industry. This is the fucking cure for cancer!" His voice turned shrill. "The whole world's going to know who I am."

Lacey stood again, fury blazing through her. "You're out of your mind! Everyone will know this is my dad's research. You could only wish you were half as smart, half as brilliant as him. You're nothing but a lazy fraud hack!"

Brandon advanced on her, his face bright red, his voice tightly controlled. "And you're a fucking dead woman."

"No!" Bill shrieked, his voice shaking. "Here's the research, all of it. You'll be a wealthy man. You get everything you've ever wanted." His voice broke. "Please," he said, his hand grasping toward Brandon. "Let her go."

"Dad, no," Lacey cried.

Brandon slapped Bill's hand away and sneered. "Do I really look that stupid?" He took the computer. "Now, stay put. You two can take a minute and say your good-byes."

He paused next to Lacey, the heat from his breath in her ear as he rubbed his crotch against her thigh. "I wish I had time to give you a going away present. I'd keep that smart ass mouth of yours occupied."

He walked out of the room, laughing, and returned moments later with a can of gasoline. He doused the pile of hardware in the corner then poured the remaining gas on the carpet and splashed it up on the drapes.

Lacey's paralyzed mind flew into overdrive. This couldn't be happening! She was no closer to freeing the ties at her wrists, but she had to find a way to get her hands free. How else could she fight him?

Time stopped. She watched in horror as Brandon struck a match. Holding it between his fingers, he gave them one last glance before he dropped the burning match on the carpet.

"See you in hell."

Hungry flames licked the drapes and the walls. Brandon closed the door and locked it. Lacey swore she heard his crazed laughter above the sounds of the growling blaze.

Chapter 33

Caleb called Roger on the way to the apartment. Talking it through helped keep him from crawling out of his skin. *They had to get to Lacey in time. Anything else was unthinkable.*

Following Stepanek and his badge into Brandon's apartment, Caleb's fury was palpable. Stan better have some answers. His eyes went straight to the table where the son of a bitch sat across from two agents.

"It was never supposed to be like this." Stan's voice mirrored his rising panic, his bulging eyes tracking from one agent to the other.

Caleb stalked toward him, but strong fingers on his arm stopped him.

"I see the look in your eyes." Stepanek growled low, out of earshot. "You want this guy to walk? You do one fucking thing to him. Say one word. And our entire case could get thrown out. You gotta let me do my job now."

Turning his back on Caleb, Stepanek got briefed by the other agents before addressing Stan. "I'm Lead Agent Hank Stepanek. We're in trouble here, Stan. We're out of time. Where'd Brandon take Lacey Jordan?"

Stan's voice rose even higher. "Wait. This is all a mistake. He told me from the beginning that no one would get hurt. We were just supposed to get the data. It's gotten completely out of control." His eyes darted to the front door of the apartment.

Caleb moved to the door. *Let the bastard try to run.*

Stepanek's slow and steady style grated on Caleb's nerves. They needed answers and they needed them now.

After getting a couple more evasions, Stepanek slammed his palms flat on the table, his face inches from Stan's. "I'm only going to ask you one more time. Where the hell is she?" Apparently that was enough motivation to start talking.

"Th- There's a house, southside, it's all boarded up, like all the others. I bet every house on the block has some bad shit happening inside."

Caleb advanced and stood at the table as Stepanek nodded. "An address. Give me the address."

Stan's eyes grew wide. "Wait a minute. What do I get? I want immunity. I'm not going down for this. I've got a wife and twin babies to take care of."

Caleb's hand burned with the need to punch the son of a bitch in the face. Stan should've thought of them a long time ago.

Stepanek stepped between the men and looked at Stan. "Understand me, Jacobson. You're not in a good position here. You give me an address right now and your cooperation will go in my report. That's the best option you got."

Sweat broke out on Stan's brow. "I don't know the exact address," he said. "I've only been there a couple times."

Stepanek leaned down in Stan's face. "Can you get us there?"

Stan glanced at Caleb again, swallowed, then nodded. "Yeah, I think so."

The call to alert the S.W.A.T. team went out. Stepanek walked out of the apartment with Caleb after instructing his agents to take Stan in their vehicle and lead the way. The door closed and Stepanek stepped in front of Caleb, his face somewhere between a glare and a grin. "That's not exactly what I call staying out of the way."

Caleb stared at him and shrugged his shoulders. "Arrest me."

Stepanek rolled his eyes. "Come on, cowboy. Let's go. This time, you're a spectator or you're outta here."

They barreled down the highway, but as Stepanek shot orders to the other agents, Caleb's control slipped. He glanced at his watch, willing time to stand still. Every minute that went by lowered their odds. *Brandon*

Thomas. He still couldn't believe it. He'd had the bastard in his house. *No freaking wonder he'd been so interested in Lacey. Mother fucker.*

Their car finally hopped off the highway then turned onto a short street. Stepanek cut the lights. A voice crackled through the radio. "This is it. Third house on the right."

Did anyone really live here? Caleb stared at the dilapidated row housing. Most of the windows he could see were busted-out, leaving gaping holes that reminded him of rotted teeth. Some had haphazard slats of wood or cardboard nailed to the outside walls.

Every house was identical. Single-story slabs so small they resembled trailer houses. Mere inches separated them. Busted out street lights stood on the corners like scarecrows. He doubted the city came by often to replace them.

Stepanek's car stopped at the end of the block and parked behind the S.W.A.T. van. "What do we do now?" Caleb asked.

"What do we do now? *We* don't do anything now." He nodded. "That's the team commander. Stewart's his name. Good man."

Caleb frowned. "I thought this was your case. Aren't you in charge out here?"

Stepanek grinned. "Hell, no. I'm the case agent but out here, he's in charge." He nodded to Stewart again. "I'd only be in the way. Think of it like I'm the one holding the leash and I just let that bad ass pack of dogs off the tether."

Nodding, Caleb looked in his side mirror and noticed two ambulances and a fire truck waiting in the darkness behind them. Trying not to think about them, or why they might be needed, he turned his attention back to the agents and watched as they approached an empty structure a few doors down from the unit Stan had identified. "What are they doing?" he whispered.

"Checking the structure's layout," Stepanek replied. "They want to know as much as possible about what they're walking into."

The team emerged and Caleb listened to their communications over the radio. "No back exit, one hallway to the back of the house. We need the imagers to get a fix on the perp."

Within minutes, thermal and acoustic imagers were in place. "We've got three in the back room." The chatter over the radio continued as Caleb listened intently. "Looks like the perp may have two captives, not just one."

"Could there be two perps?" the commander asked.

"Could be, but I'm betting against it."

"What the hell?" Caleb's anxiety clawed at him. "It's got to be Bill and Lacey in there with that bastard."

Stepanek waited until the chatter finished. "Agreed. He's just reading the acoustic imagers. There's usually a disparity between the heart rates of the perp and the victim. Victim's heart rates are usually pretty elevated. The perps generally feel in control so their rates are more in the normal range. My guess is he's basing his assumptions off that."

"What are they doing in there? Can they tell?" Stepanek opened his mouth to answer, but Caleb cut him off. "Why haven't they gone in to get them yet? It's only one punk ass guy they're after."

Stepanek released the quiet sigh of a man who'd been on many raids in his day. "Look, I know you're scared but these guys know what they're doing. They're not going to go in there half-cocked if they can avoid it."

Caleb rubbed his face and blew out a breath. "Christ, waiting sucks."

Stepanek nodded. "Yep. But it's better this way. The only thing that'll collapse their timeline is –"

The voice on the radio interrupted his thought. "Sir, we have an event. Fire in the back room."

Caleb bolted upright and grabbed for the door handle.

"Go, go, go!" the commander yelled.

Within seconds, the heavily armed team was inside the house. Caleb heard several pops that sounded like gunfire accompanied by bright flashes. As he ran toward the house, he was tackled from behind by Stepanek.

"What the hell are you thinking? You're not going anywhere fucking near that door," he screamed.

Everything happened in a moment. Before Caleb even had a chance to throw Stepanek off his shoulder, the S.W.A.T. team tackled Brandon to the ground as he tried to run. Within seconds, his hands were cuffed behind him and Caleb heard them reading Brandon his rights as they hauled him toward a waiting cruiser.

Savage rage ripped through him. *That bastard had no rights.* He'd rip his head off to get to Lacey. His face must've revealed his intent because before he moved, he heard Stepanek's voice, low and controlled, from somewhere behind him.

"You take one step toward him and you'll be on the ground with a rifle on you."

Caleb sucked in a breath. "That mother fucker —"

"Let them do their jobs. Besides, you have better things to do," he said as he motioned toward the door.

Caleb caught his breath, fear lancing through him. Controlled chaos reigned as fire fighters headed into the structure, but he barely noticed. His eyes landed on Lacey's crumpled body in the arms of one of the police officers.

"Lacey!" His voice carried over the din. Panicked, he raced to her side as she lifted her head. "Oh, my God, Lacey. Talk to me baby. Are you okay?"

"Caleb?" Her voice was so thick and raspy, he could barely hear her.

He grasped her hand as she was laid on the gurney. "I'm here, babe. Everything's going to be okay."

Her head snapped toward him and she struggled to sit up, her bloodshot eyes wide. "My dad!" Racking coughs shook her body. "Caleb. My dad! He's in there. Caleb, get him! Please!"

The desperation in her voice fueled Caleb. As he turned to alert somebody, relief flooded him for the second time in as many minutes. Bill was out of the house and on a gurney being wheeled into the second ambulance. He pulled Lacey close, his hand soothing her hair as paramedics placed the oxygen mask over her dad's face. "He's right behind you. He's here. He's okay."

Lacey nodded and, with a ghost of a smile, laid her head back on the gurney and closed her eyes. Caleb watched over the paramedics as they loaded her into the waiting ambulance. His hands shook with adrenaline. Holy Christ, it was over.

Chapter 34

Her nostrils burned from the smoke, but she couldn't get out. Couldn't leave until she found her father. Lacey screamed, and lunged awake, gasping for breath. Her eyes landed on a middle-aged woman in purple scrubs.

"Relax, darlin'," the woman's sweet southern voice crooned. "You're okay now." She laid her hand on Lacey's forehead, gently forcing her back against the stiff white sheets.

As memories bombarded her, she ripped the blanket off her legs. Where was her dad?

"Oh, sugar. You can't get up just yet." She patted Lacey's arm and rearranged the covers.

Lacey grabbed the woman's hand. "My father. Where is he? Is he okay?" Even to her own ears, her voice sounded strained and hoarse.

The aide smiled. "He's fine, honey. I'm sure he's resting. The young man who was sitting in here worrying over you left a few minutes ago to check on him. He's been wearing out the elevator back and forth between the two of you since you all got here."

The room spun. *Her dad was alive. He was here.* Her breath sharpened and she bit her lip to keep the tears away. Lacey half-listened to the small talk while the aide adjusted the blood pressure cuff and took her temperature before rolling her cart toward the door.

"Wait." Lacey's voice shook. "When can I see him?"

The aide turned, her eyes full of understanding. "It won't be long. You're going to be released in a little while. When the nurse comes, check with her."

Lacey let her head fall back against the pillow, her mind working overtime to absorb and process everything that had happened. She still couldn't quite believe she was lying in a hospital bed, and her dad was safe.

They'd made it.

With trembling fingers, she tested the swollen skin under her eye. It was sore, but she was sure it looked worse than it felt. How had her dad survived the torture he'd endured? She groaned as images of him in that stinking room under those god-awful conditions haunted her. That nurse couldn't come fast enough.

The door to her room swung open and Agent Stepanek poked his head in. "You sure do clean up well," he said by way of greeting.

She shelved her disappointment. Motioning him in, she smiled, knowing full well she looked like hell. "Thank you," she said. "Have you had a chance to talk to my dad yet?"

Stepanek nodded. "Just left him. What a sense of humor. Not too many people could endure what he did and smile so soon afterward."

"So he's feeling okay?"

"Seems to be. Of course, I'm not a doctor. He's worn out, but they're pumping fluids to rehydrate him. Overall, he looks to be in pretty good shape, considering." Stepanek walked directly over to the side of the bed. "You up to telling me what happened?"

Lacey closed her eyes, letting her memories surface. "I only met Brandon once before last night. I thought he was a little full of himself, but I'd have never dreamed he was capable of something like this." She shuddered as she recounted Brandon's delusional rants. "He's insane. There's just no other explanation."

She finished recounting as much as she could remember then paused for a moment, thinking. "So, Stan Jacobson was working with Brandon?"

"Yes," Stepanek confirmed. "And he's singing big time. He's doing his best to extricate himself from the worst of the situation, but there's no getting around the fact that he kidnapped your dad and took him across state lines. No matter how you slice it, he's in a world of trouble."

"What about his family? Were they involved?"

"We don't think so. From what we can gather, his wife isn't guilty of anything except being too gullible and trusting."

Lacey nodded, a spark of empathy igniting for the woman. She knew exactly how that felt.

Stepanek finished up a few more questions then squeezed her hand. "Just do this old guy a favor. Why don't you and Caleb try to stay out of trouble from now on?"

Her heart stuttered at the mention of Caleb's name, but she laughed and crossed her heart. "I'll do my best."

The agent left and Lacey got up from the bed, determined to see her dad. She located her clothes inside the little plastic hospital storage bag, and pulled out the evening gown with two fingers. The reek of smoke and gasoline nearly gagged her. There'd be no salvaging that one.

Stepping into the hall, she signaled an aide. In no time, the resourceful woman handed Lacey a pair of scrubs and a small toiletries kit. Lacey could've kissed her. After donning the clean scrubs, the faint stench of smoke lingered on her skin, but she could live with that.

Glancing in the mirror, she assessed the damage. Other than her eyes still being a little bloodshot from the smoke and the small gash on her puffy cheek, she didn't look much the worse for wear.

Her mind shifted to Caleb. She was anxious to see him. How he'd come to be at the house she had no idea, but there was no doubt he led the cops to her. He'd been there for her through the whole ordeal.

A sobering thought struck her. *This was the end of their time together.*

Questions filled her mind. Questions that she hadn't considered before and couldn't possibly answer. *What if they'd met again under different circumstances? Could there have been a future for them?*

She shook her head because it didn't really matter. What they'd shared was a fantasy caught in a nightmare.

And now it was time to go home.

She squared her shoulders and clamped down on a twinge of regret. Today was a day for joy. There wasn't room for anything except that.

The simple tasks of brushing her teeth and hair kept her occupied, but by the time she felt almost human again, the urge to get upstairs was overwhelming. Five more minutes. If the nurse wasn't there by then, she'd go find him herself.

"Sounds like you have a date with a gentleman on the sixth floor," the nurse drawled as she knocked on the door and entered the room.

Lacey's peeked around the bathroom wall, unable to contain a mile-wide smile. Finally. "Yes, ma'am. I'm ready." She sat in the chair and pulled on a pair of slipper socks, listening to the nurse read through the discharge instructions.

"Dr. Powers explained to you earlier when you came in that you had some smoke inhalation but I'm not sure you remember. He also cleaned up the cut on your face. It wasn't deep enough to require stitches, so your primary job is to get plenty of rest." She handed Lacey the printed instructions. "Any questions for me?"

"What about my dad? Is he going to be released also?"

"I'm not sure. You'll want to check with his doctors when you get up there."

"Thank you," Lacey said. "Do you know what room he's in?"

"I do."

Lacey's head snapped toward the door at the sound of an achingly familiar masculine voice. Caleb stood in the doorway, still in his evening attire. His jacket and tie were gone, his shirt cuffs rolled up. Lacey itched to smooth his disheveled hair, to touch the contours of his face. Despite the tired lines around his eyes, he'd never looked more handsome.

She didn't have time to sort out the mess of emotions that stormed through her. Her feet were already moving toward his open arms. "Caleb!"

He squeezed her to him, his face buried in her hair. "You scared the hell out of me, you know." He whispered. "If I never see you and an ambulance in the same vicinity again, it'll be too soon for me. You're okay, right?"

Lacey nodded into his neck. "Yes, thanks to you." Finally, she pulled back from his grasp. "How did you know where to find us?"

His eyes turned a deep cobalt blue as he reached into his back pocket and pulled out her cell phone, handing it to her. "Long story, but bottom line is if it hadn't been for you, I might not have." His face darkened. "I don't know what the hell I'd have done if I hadn't found your phone."

"But you *did* find it, and we're all okay. That's what matters." She twirled out of his arms, unable to contain the laugh that escaped her lips. "My God, Caleb. My dad's alive. He's here."

Caleb's lips turned up in an answering smile. "And he's very anxious to see his daughter. I'd say we've kept him waiting long enough. You ready?"

As the elevator doors swooshed closed, Lacey stepped away from the light pressure of Caleb's hand on the small of her back. There was no denying the current of energy they shared, and when he touched her, she wanted to forget she was leaving him.

She had to strengthen her resolve. She was right about this. Yes, they'd made love and shared secrets. But that was yesterday, when they were in the throes of a nightmare. Today, everything was different.

Lacey glanced at him and caught him watching her, a slight frown marring his brow. Did he sense the change too?

Offering a brief smile, she ventured into neutral territory. "So. How is he?"

If Caleb realized things had changed, his tone didn't reveal it. "I'd say pretty good. He's dehydrated and weak. Throw the smoke inhalation on top of that and he's definitely here for at least a day or two. But the good news is, if his oxygen levels continue to get better, and he's feeling well enough, they should let him go within the next couple of days."

She nodded, letting an awkward silence reign. Without the drama, was there anything else to say?

To her vast relief, the elevator dinged. Caleb took her hand, and as she followed his long strides down the hallway to a closed door, her heart lodged in her throat. Crossing the threshold, the release from the fears and uncertainties that had defined the last month almost brought Lacey to her knees.

"Dad!" she cried. On rubbery legs, she rushed to the bedside and flung her arms around him. "I've never been so scared in my entire life. Oh, my God, I've missed you so much. When I saw you in that disgusting place –"

Her dad's arms came around her, comforting in their very existence. She finally pulled back, looking into his familiar face. He was thin, so much thinner than she'd ever seen him, and his bruised cheeks and cracked lips devastated her. "Oh, Dad, can you talk about it? Can you tell me what happened?"

She sat up and perched her hip on the side of the bed, squeezing his hand. Her dad looked over at Caleb standing near the entrance and smiled. "You up for this story again or do you want to make a fast getaway?"

Caleb walked over and put his hand on Bill's shoulder. "I think I'll let this reunion be among family. I'll go get cleaned up and gather Lacey's things from the apartment."

Her dad grasped Caleb's hand. "I owe you a debt of gratitude for taking care of Lacey like you have." His watery eyes focused on Lacey. "Sounds like you two made a heck of a team, huh?"

Lacey couldn't find her voice as the reminder of everything they'd shared flooded her memory. *Damn it.* She swallowed hard.

"That we did." Caleb brushed Lacey's cheek with a kiss, his eyes searching hers. "We'll talk later, okay?"

Captured by his crystal blue gaze, she nodded.

***

Bill's throat ached with the effort it would take to tell the whole story, but the look on Lacey's face moved him. Hell, the fact that he was looking at her face at all spoke to the miracle of his rescue. He scooted over on the small mattress and patted the spot beside him.

Lacey crawled up next to him and snuggled. He waited until the tears in his throat subsided from the simple joy of having his daughter next to him.

He moistened his throat with the jug of water on the side table and began. "Stan had called to say that he needed to see me that Friday afternoon. I agreed to have him over to the house because I'd hoped he was tendering his resignation and I didn't want to start any rumors on campus. For several weeks, Stan had acted oddly and I had a nagging feeling of uncertainty about him.

"I was such a fool. So many little things just weren't right. And then, he showed up at the house in a rental car. Said his was in the shop for repairs. I invited him into the kitchen and started a fresh pot of coffee. When I turned around, he had a gun pointed at my chest." Bill swallowed. "He was nervous. I could tell. The gun was shaking but I was still convinced that he was capable of using it. I tried to talk to him, to rationalize with him, but the more I talked, the more agitated he got."

Lacey's fingers tightened on his, almost to the point of pain. "When did he show up? How long after you called me that morning?"

Bill shrugged. "I don't remember exactly. It was afternoon. It wouldn't have mattered though," Bill assured her. "He wasn't there long. It was obvious he'd thought through his plan."

He paused, reliving the night in his mind before he spoke again. "Anyway, he bound my wrists and ankles then injected me with something. I'm not sure what happened after that." He shook his head. "The next thing I know, I'm in that little shack and I hear voices in the next room. Brandon had apparently coerced Stan into acting as his accomplice. It's almost beyond imagination."

Lacey lightly touched the bandages at his wrists. "What was their connection? Does anyone know?"

Bill opened his mouth to speak, but a racking cough escaped instead. Lacey's worried gaze followed his face. After several deep breaths and another tug on the straw of his water cup, he continued. "The FBI agent, Stepanek?"Lacey nodded. "He said they were looking into Brandon's own gambling history. They're also pretty sure he had a potential buyer for my formula."A flash of sadness crossed his face. "How horrible to think that something designed to save lives would motivate someone to kill."

"I know. Your work is going to change lives. Caleb told me some of the details." She ducked her head. "I'm sorry I didn't know more about it."

Bill pulled her in close. "There will be plenty of time to learn if you want to. And because of you and Caleb, I'll be around to make sure it comes to market the right way. But whatever else happens with the formula, there's not much doubt that both Stan and Brandon will be put away for a long time."

Lacey smiled and patted his hand. "I'm assuming you talked to Mona already?"

Bill's heart swelled. "She was my first phone call." He paused, unable to contain his smile. "It took me five minutes to convince her it was really me then once she believed me, she couldn't stop crying. She wanted to hop on the next flight, but I told her we're coming to her. God, I love that woman." Bill reached up and touched Lacey's cheek with a shaking hand. His smile died on his lips. "I love you, too. My God, when he brought you in the room, I wanted to die. I'm so sorry, Lacey. If I'd given him the information he wanted before, you'd have never gone through that."

A tear trickled down Lacey's cheek as she shook her head. "He'd have killed you."

She was right, and Bill was too tired to try to convince her differently. Wiping away Lacey's tear, he smiled. "Let's get a few hours rest. I think we're both exhausted."

Lacey laid her hand over his and squeezed softly. "I'm right behind you," she promised. "I'll just make a quick phone call to Paige."

She climbed off the bed then tucked the blankets around him. He listened, eyes closed, as she recounted the story from the blue recliner she pulled next to the bed. The joy in her voice sent a wave of gratitude and relief through him.

The nightmare was really over. He knew he'd sleep peacefully for the first time in a month. When he didn't hear Lacey's voice, he glanced over at the chair. She'd shoved a blanket under her head and she was out.

His thoughts turned to the chemistry he'd witnessed earlier between her and Caleb. He drummed his fingers on his sheets, a smile lifting the corners of his mouth. A man could always hope, couldn't he?

Chapter 35

Caleb couldn't remember ever being this nervous. His steps slowed as he headed to Bill's room, Lacey's bag slung over his shoulder. So many words jockeyed for position in his head, it would be a miracle if any of them came out right.

Now might not be the best time, but it didn't matter. He needed Lacey to know the truth. Caleb took a deep breath then cautiously opened the door to Bill's room and peeked around the edge. It was close to noon, so he was surprised to find the drapes drawn and only a single fluorescent light on above Bill's bed.

Bill looked up and set aside the magazine he was reading. "Come in, come in," he motioned.

Caleb set his bags down near the side table. "Why is it so dark? Were you resting?"

Bill shook his head and pointed to Lacey's prone form sprawled out on the recliner. "Actually, I just had lunch. I'm glad you're here. I was hoping for some time to talk privately."

Caleb jolted, his mind on Lacey. Did Bill already know his intentions? "Sure." He lowered himself into a chair, relieved when Bill began talking about his captivity. Not only because Lacey wasn't the topic of conversation, but the fact that he could talk about what he went through was a sign that he'd heal emotionally.

"Were you surprised that Brandon was behind the crime? Do you know him very well?"

"Not well enough, obviously. To tell you how bad a judge of character I am, I was almost certain Ian Cox was involved."

Bill shifted toward him. "Really? He wasn't, was he?"

Caleb shook his head. "No. But Roger said he'd changed a lot over the last several months. Personality and behavior. Made me suspicious. And he seemed to be focused on you and your college years together. Even emailed you about how unfair it was that your lives had turned out so differently."

Bill frowned. "That *is* odd. A few things came between our friendship back in the day, but I never had any ill will toward him."

Nodding, Caleb folded his hands in his lap, elbows on his knees. "I finally got answers this morning. Roger found out a week ago and got permission from Ian to tell me." He glanced at Bill but the words were tough to say. "He's been diagnosed with early-onset Alzheimer's. He's going to retire from the company at the end of the year and Roger's going to make sure he has people to take care of him."

Bill was quiet for a moment. "How sad. Life is so precious." Caleb absorbed the intensity of Bill's gaze. "Every single day is a blessing. I thought I understood that before, but I'll never take it for granted again."

Caleb glanced at Lacey to make sure she was still sleeping then leaned in. "I know." He rubbed his palms on his jeans and blew out a breath. "We need to talk about that. And what I'm going to say might not make sense to you right now, but it makes perfect sense to me." He stood and began pacing. "I'm not even sure where to start."

Bill chuckled. "Well, the way I see it, you can either begin six years ago or a month ago."

Caleb stood silently for a moment, matching Bill's steady gaze as he spoke. "I'm in love with your daughter." He waited, not sure what to expect. When Bill didn't respond, he started again in earnest. "I was a fool once. And I don't want to make the same mistake twice. I'm not sure exactly when it happened. Or how. All I know is that I'm staying here in Chicago and she's going home and it's killing me. She's supposed to be with me. I'm certain of it."

"I'm glad you figured that out. Hindsight's twenty-twenty. I know we did what we thought was best all those years ago, but I'd always hoped you two would find your way back to each other." A brief smile. "I could've probably come up with a much simpler scenario, but…"

Caleb choked out a laugh, releasing the breath he hadn't realized he'd been holding. "Yeah, no kidding. Now, I just need to convince Lacey. I stole her choice last time. This time it's got to be her call."

Bill sobered. "I don't envy you that task. She's pretty jaded when it comes to love."

"I know. She told me about her last relationship."

Surprise lit Bill's features. "She did? That's encouraging."

"You think so?" He paused. "We've managed to build some trust over the past few weeks. I'm hoping it's enough."

Caleb returned to his seat and reached for the Nordstrom's bag on the floor. "I have a couple of other things for you. First, Rosalee sent me with these." At Bill's questioning frown Caleb smiled. "She said you weren't going home in hospital clothes."

Bill laughed out loud. "What a sweetheart. Thank her for me, will you?"

Caleb nodded. "Of course. They're planning on coming tomorrow." He pulled out a FedEx envelope. "Then there's this. I owe you an apology."

Bill glanced at the envelope and blinked. "An apology?"

"You sent this to me before…," he paused, guilt choking him. "I never got back to you on it. For weeks now, I've wondered if it was some kind of message or warning…"

Bill took the envelope and grabbed Caleb's wrist, surprising him with his strength. "Son, I've been accused of being a lot of things in my lifetime, but psychic isn't one of them. I sent the data to you so you could get your eyes on it. That was all." He paused for a second. "Who knows, though, maybe subconsciously I had a feeling all wasn't well."

Relief coursed through Caleb as he searched Bill's face and saw nothing but the truth.

Bill smiled. "I was hoping you had the copy. I'm not certain the laptop made it out of the house." He cleared his throat and began to cough vigorously. Caleb grabbed the water glass and handed it to him.

"So," Caleb ventured when Bill's cough subsided, "any word on when they're going to let you out of here?"

"They're talking about tomorrow, and I'm doing my best to be a model patient. That means you don't have much time with Lacey, so I'll make sure she gives you a call when she wakes up. Maybe a nice dinner?" He winked. "I'll do my best to encourage her from my end, but you're going to have to do the heavy lifting."

***

Lacey frowned at the voices disturbing her dreams, but they persisted. She stretched her legs and almost fell out of the chair. Realizing where she was, she wrestled herself to a sitting position, shoving the hair out of her face.

She ran her tongue over her teeth and grimaced. "Sorry I crashed so hard. You should've gotten me up. What time is it?"

A nurse hovered over her dad, taking his vitals. He spoke around the thermometer. "Close to three. You missed the doctor. He said my numbers look good and I should be out of here tomorrow. Oh, and Caleb came by a while ago and dropped off your bag."

Her eyes slid to the black duffel in the corner. It was probably better that she hadn't been awake. There was no point in making things more awkward than they already were.

She got up slowly, stretching out all the places that didn't appreciate sleeping in a chair, and looped the bag over her shoulder. "Good," she said. "Just being back in my own clothes will be a step toward normal."

After a very short and thoroughly unsatisfying shower, Lacey shoved her legs into a pair of old comfortable jeans. She was relieved they'd be going home tomorrow. The sooner she got back to real life, the better. Already, the past month felt like so long ago, almost a dream. Normal was exactly what she needed now. Normal work. Normal family. Normal life.

Her dad's voice drifted in from the other room. "Lacey, honey? Why don't you call Caleb and let him know about the discharge time? Maybe you could get tickets for tomorrow afternoon and make sure that works in his schedule."

After she agreed, Lacey cringed. It was unrealistic to think they'd leave Chicago without seeing Caleb again, but she still didn't know how she'd handle saying goodbye.

It was a proven fact that people imagined all kinds of deeper levels of commitment and love when they were faced with extraordinary circumstances. And the past month clearly qualified. Using the tiny bathroom mirror, Lacey ran a comb through her hair. Leaning in close, she stared at her reflection. "You are *not* in love with him. Been there and done that," she muttered. "Whatever this was, it's over."

She ignored the shadow of doubt and sadness in her eyes, and went in search of her phone. After booking their flights, she rang Caleb's cell.

"Hey, babe. Sorry I missed you earlier."

The slow easy timbre of his voice turned her insides to mush. She cleared her throat, hoping for a casual friendly tone. "That's okay. Hey, it looks like my dad's going to be released tomorrow around eleven. I've booked the two-fifty flight. Would you mind giving us a ride to the airport?"

"Of course not." He paused then his voice lowered. "We still need to talk, though. Have dinner with me?"

Lacey's shoulders tightened. "Dinner?" Maybe he was looking for closure, too. She glanced at her dad, hesitant to leave him. "I was thinking I should stay here. Dad might need me."

Her dad smiled from the bed. "Don't worry about me, Sweetie. It'd probably do you good to get out of here for a little while anyway."

She quirked a brow at him. Was it her imagination or was there a twinkle in his eye? *Crap.* Okay. Maybe this was for the best. She sighed into the phone. "Is there somewhere casual nearby?"

***

Caleb helped her into the black Range Rover. "Hope you're hungry. For your last night in the city, we're going to one of my favorite places. Anteprima. Best Italian in Chicago."

Lacey smiled, but she could hardly swallow around the lump in her throat. He was acting like they were on a date, like they were a couple, like nothing had changed.

But everything had changed. Didn't he realize it?

On the drive, Lacey absorbed the city lights and sounds. It seemed like a good metaphor for the words she needed to say to Caleb. By the time dessert was served, the small talk had dwindled and she knew it was time.

She dipped a fork into her tiramisu. "I was thinking on the way over how interesting perspective can be."

Caleb cocked a brow as he took a sip of wine. "How so?"

She took a deep breath, gathering her courage. "I've been in Chicago for a week, but tonight was the first time I really saw the city. Because my perspective changed. It's not clouded anymore with everything else going on. My mind's free to see it."

"And?"

And there's nothing binding us together.

His warm gaze distracted her. "And," she muscled on, nodding, "I wanted to let you know that I've gained perspective on what happened over the last month. Between us. I don't want either of us to have false impressions." Her words began to run together, but she needed to get them all out before her courage deserted her. "We were thrown into a situation that was beyond our control. Things happened that I don't regret, but they're things that probably wouldn't have happened under normal circumstances, and I think its best —"

"I'm in love with you, Lacey."

She stared at him across the table. There was a time that she'd have given almost anything to hear him say those words, but that was a lifetime ago. Now, they didn't feel right. "No, you aren't. See that right there? That's what I mean." She crossed her arms. "You can't love me. You don't even know me. And I don't know you. Not really."

He touched her cheek, his eyes holding hers. "I know that I love you." He tugged at her hand and placed it over his heart. "I know it here."

Panic gripped her. What did a real relationship look like? She had no idea. Her voice rose. "In our entire lives, we've spent a sum total of four months together. I don't know your favorite foods, or movies. I don't know your pet peeves. I don't even know your family."

She was getting on a roll when Caleb stood and slid into her side of the booth. He pulled her body into his, wrapping his arm around her. He nodded into her hair and placed a light kiss against her temple. "Okay." His hand rubbed her upper arm. "You're right."

Lacey stiffened. Really? Was it that easy to talk him out of loving her? She avoided his gaze, afraid he'd see her uncertainty.

"All I'm asking is that you leave the door open to explore the possibility. I probably won't be able to leave Chicago for the next week or two, and you need to go back to Manhattan. But that doesn't mean we can't talk. It doesn't mean we can't get to know each other better." He nudged her. "What do you say?"

Lacey chewed her lower lip, her mind spinning. He believed what he was saying, but she knew what would happen. He'd realize soon enough, as he settled back into his life, that she was right about everything. She was only hurting herself by prolonging the inevitable, but a tiny piece of her heart wasn't quite ready to let him go.

"We're both going to be busy," she hedged.

Caleb turned in the seat and whispered a tender kiss against her lips. "Then we'll have to get creative."

Pulling back, Lacey recognized the challenging gleam in his eyes. *Oh boy, was she in trouble.*

Chapter 36

Lacey clicked the app on her phone. Their flight was right on time.

In the back seat of Caleb's SUV, she listened as he and her dad discussed the cancer formula and BioTech's future. She tuned out the words, allowing them to float through her mind as she studied Caleb's profile.

Despite all that he'd said the night before, she wondered if today would be the last time she'd see him. She toyed with the strap on her bag, coming to grips with that very real possibility.

Caleb caught her eyes in the rearview mirror and winked. She shook her head, trying not to smile. Hopefully, her dad hadn't noticed. He'd ask too many questions. And she didn't have any answers.

Forcing her gaze out the window, Lacey watched the city buzz by. By the time they arrived at the gate, she was ready to go. Her old life was waiting, not to mention how much she was looking forward to delving into adoption research.

Caleb hugged her dad then whispered something to him that Lacey couldn't quite catch.

Her dad chuckled. "I'm looking forward to it." He turned to Lacey. "I'm going to head to the gate."

Lacey watched like a hawk as her dad managed his way through security.

"He's going to be just fine," Caleb murmured.

Lacey sighed. "I know. It's still hard to let him out of my sight."

She allowed Caleb to gently pull her away from the security line. It was time for her to say good-bye to him. Her stomach knotted. *Was she making a mistake?*

Digging in his pocket, Caleb's hand emerged holding a robin-egg blue box with a white ribbon. Lacey's wide eyes darted to his and she began to back away.

He tugged her back to him. "Relax," he said. Placing the box in her hand, he urged her to open it.

With shaking fingers, she lifted the lid, revealing a stunning diamond tennis bracelet.

Caleb lifted it out of the box. "May I?"

Dazed, Lacey eyed the glittering piece. "Caleb, I can't. It's too much."

"You said you didn't know enough about me, so I decided to start working on the list." At her raised brow, he shrugged. "I like to play tennis." His lazy smile teased her senses. He slipped the piece around her wrist before his lips connected with hers in a kiss that left her breathless. Too soon, he lifted his head, his eyes searching hers. "I already miss you."

Heavy pressure weighed on her chest. "You're not going to make this easy, are you?" she whispered.

"Not on your life." He feathered kisses on her eyelids and the tip of her nose before once more claiming her mouth.

"Now boarding Flight 718, non-stop to Kansas City."

Lacey jumped at the booming impersonal voice, startling her out of Caleb's arms. She cleared her throat. "That's my flight." She hoped her eyes looked less unsettled than her heart.

Taking her bag from Caleb, she felt the last brush of his hand against hers. She tried for a smile, but she wasn't sure she made it. "Good-bye, Caleb."

She hurried through security to meet her dad and board. It wasn't until she was in her seat and the plane taxied away from the gate that she realized Caleb hadn't said good-bye.

***

"Lacey, we're home."

She mumbled, turning her head away from the source of the noise. Seconds later, her mind recognized her dad's voice and her eyes flew open. Reality returned in a flash. Sitting next to him on the airplane as it arrived in Kansas City, she absorbed the wave of relief that rolled over her.

She squeezed his hand and pulled it to her cheek, staring into his loving brown eyes. "It's really over, isn't it?" she breathed.

He put his other hand on her cheek and spoke over the flight attendant's arrival announcement. "Yes, baby. It's really over."

As they exited the plane and walked down the gangway, Lacey leaned into her dad. "I feel a little bit like Alice climbing back out of the rabbit hole."

"I know exactly what you mean." He started to say something else, but as his eyes scanned the faces waiting at the terminal, he broke off. "Mona," he cried.

Lacey watched the reunion with tears in her eyes. Mona's sobs drowned out whatever her dad was saying to her as they rocked and hugged each other. Swallowing several times, Lacey tried to dislodge the lump that had settled in her throat.

Mona finally pulled back, but she never let go, even as she turned to Spencer. She grabbed her son's hand and nudged him forward.

Spencer looked very young as he held out his hand. "Welcome home, Dr. Jordan," he said humbly as he looked over at his mother. "I'm sure glad you made it back safely. My mom's been beside herself worrying." He jammed his hands in his pockets. "And I'm really sorry for the trouble that I caused between you two. You won't see that again."

Lacey hid her smile as her dad looked past Spencer's bowed head to Mona. He pulled Spencer into a hug. "I'm glad to hear it, Spencer," he said. "Because I'm pretty crazy about your mom and I'd really like for us to be friends."

Spencer nodded and stepped back. "I'd like that, too."

Her dad touched her arm. "What do you say we get out of here and head home?"

Lacey slung her bag back over her shoulder. "Let's do it."

***

By the time Lacey got home after helping her dad get settled at the farm and dealing with the local press who were all once again anxious to run her father's story, she was exhausted. Dumping her bag, she plopped onto the sofa. It seemed like a million years ago that she and Caleb had high-tailed it out of town. She glanced around, letting the quiet familiarity soothe her.

Was it odd that she half-expected him to walk out of the kitchen? Or hear the shower running? Her thoughts drifted as she closed her eyes, wondering if Caleb would be in touch tomorrow.

The peal of the doorbell startled her. She looked at her watch and jumped off the couch. Who'd come calling at nine-thirty? For a split second, she froze in fear before she remembered that her dad was home safe and sound.

Lacey peeked through the hole, a surprised laugh bubbling up from her throat. Throwing open the door, she pulled Paige into an awkward hug around an enormous bouquet of red roses. "What are you doing here? I was going to call you, but I thought it might be too late."

Paige handed over the flowers, a mock frown furrowing her forehead. "Yeah, yeah. Well, I hope you know that I don't deliver after hours for just anybody. But this customer was really insistent. Out-of-towner." She screwed up her nose then broke out in laughter. "Oh, Lacey. I don't know what you did to him, but the poor guy's got it bad."

Despite the unexpected surprise, Lacey rolled her eyes over Paige's declaration. "I didn't do anything." She shook her head. "He's confused. He thinks he's in love with me."

"Really. I hadn't noticed. You should read the card," Paige drawled, heading to the fridge. "What do you have to drink?"

Lacey followed her to the kitchen. "Some wine I think. Did you hear what I said? He's got everything mixed up in his mind."

"Yes. Which is why I asked. Sounds like we have some girl time to catch up on."

267

Lacey was torn. She wanted to spend time and catch up with Paige, but she was dying to be alone with her thoughts. If she could just figure out a way to quiet the world, maybe she could hear her own heart.

Her friend whipped out a couple of wine glasses and poured. "I already told Rodney I was sleeping over."

The quiet would have to wait. What else could she do but laugh? Taking her glass, Lacey tapped it to Paige's. "Here's to being home."

She couldn't remember the last time they'd pulled an all-nighter, sitting around talking and getting a little bit drunk together. Probably college. By the wee hours of the morning, they'd sprawled out across Lacey's bed.

Lacey poured the remaining contents of bottle number two into their glasses and looked over at her friend. She hadn't intended to share all the sordid details about Caleb, but Paige had always been good at getting her to talk. "So now do you understand why I needed some distance?"

Paige shook her head. "Not really. I think you're overcomplicating things. He's obviously crazy about you. I don't even think that's up for debate. So, what are you so afraid of?"

Being challenged didn't set well with Lacey. "Don't try to put me on the defensive. You have no idea what it's like to trust somebody and watch them stomp on your heart."

Paige shrugged and finished off her drink. "Maybe not, but I do know what it's like to be in love and have that loved returned. And I want that for you." She scooted next to Lacey, and threw her arm around her shoulder. "Know what I think? You say I'm the control freak, but I think you ran away because you're in love with him and it scares the hell out of you."

Lacey closed her eyes and let her head fall back against the headboard. "Only a fool makes the same mistake twice."

Chapter 37

Lacey stared at her phone. This was pathetic. It had barely been twenty-four hours since she'd spoken to Caleb and, if she was honest, she wanted to hear his voice. How was she supposed to break the habit if she couldn't get through a single day?

She should've been exhausted after the day's chaos, but she was keyed up. Her afternoon with Karen Russell couldn't have gone better if she'd written a script. The woman was open and kind, willing to give Lacey insight into her twenty plus years of experience as an adoption coordinator. More than ever, Lacey knew she was heading in the right direction, at least with her career choice.

She wished she was as certain about her personal life.

She took a deep breath and punched in Caleb's number, wondering how he'd spent his day. Before she hit send, she plunked the phone on the kitchen table and walked away. *If he wants to talk, he'll call.*

By ten, after straightening and cleaning the house then indulging in a relaxing bubble bath, Lacey was ready to crash. As much as she could, she avoided thinking about Caleb. She needed to reestablish her life without him in it. How else would she know what she really wanted?

She should've been proud of her mental victory, but as she climbed into bed alone, it rang hollow. After plugging in her phone to charge, she switched off the lamp casting the room into darkness. On her back, with her hands stacked behind her head, Lacey stared at the shadowed ceiling. She'd missed him today. There was no way to deny it. But he hadn't called. Was he giving her space, or had he already gotten too busy?

Moments later, the phone lit up and vibrated. Sitting straight up, she fumbled for it with shaking fingers.

"Hello?" Did he hear the breathlessness in her voice?

"Hey, Babe. I was hoping you'd answer. Did I wake you?"

For less than a second, Lacey tried to pretend that it didn't matter that he'd called. But it did. "Uh, no. Actually, I'd just gone to bed."

Caleb groaned. "You're killing me," he muttered. "You know that, right?"

Lacey's mind shifted to the nights they'd made love in her bed and she tried, without success, to tamp down the stab of desire the memories evoked. She cleared her throat, grasping for something generic to clear her thoughts. "So, how was your day?" She wanted to slap her forehead. *Was that the best she could come up with?*

If he thought the question inane, he didn't let on. "Long. But good. I'd have called sooner but I just got home."

He chatted for several minutes, sharing details of his day. The low timbre of his voice resonated through the phone line, lulling her into a comfortable place. She could almost pretend he was here with her.

She forgot her exhaustion as their conversation continued. She told him about her day with Karen and the things she'd learned, and answered as many of his questions as she could. They talked for another thirty minutes before Lacey yawned. "I need some sleep. Talk tomorrow?"

"I can't wait." The desire in his voice sent an unexpected dart of heat to her middle.

"Good night, Caleb." She pressed the end key and squeezed the phone to her chest. Within seconds, it vibrated again. A new text message arrived. She clicked on the message and felt her defenses crumbling.

There are 10,000 unwed mothers in the Chicago area waiting for you. I'm waiting for you too. I love you.

*** * ***

The noise reached her as soon as she opened the back door. Talking and laughter mingled with the aromas of roasted turkey and homemade rolls.

Bill and Mona had invited Rodney and Paige along with Sam to the Thanksgiving festivities. As Lacey walked in, everyone was clustered around the island or at the table.

"Oh good," Mona grinned. "Lacey's here."

Paige thrust a glass of white wine in Lacey's hand. "Good timing. Mona and I were just talking about the shop. She's agreed to come on part-time through Christmas to help out. What do you think?"

Lacey hoped the relief didn't show on her face. "Really? I think that's a great idea." Maybe Mona would consider becoming a partner. It was probably too early to talk about it, but Lacey decided to plant the seed. She winked at Mona. "Didn't I tell you weeks ago that you'd be a perfect fit?"

Bill pulled a pan of rolls out of the oven. "No surprise. She's a perfect fit for me, too." Grinning, he laid the pan on a trivet and grabbed the electric knife to carve the turkey, adding to the noise.

Lacey blinked away the moisture in her eyes as she watched him. He looked so carefree and happy. She waited until he finished carving then placed a kiss on his cheek. "How are you feeling?"

"Like I've been given a second chance at life." Popping a piece of turkey in his mouth, he studied her. "How about you?"

Lacey nodded, ignoring the question behind her dad's eyes. "Good. Better every day."

"You better hurry with that turkey. I'm starving," Spencer joked from the hallway. He and Rodney lugged a long table into the living room. Sam pulled out a tablecloth to cover it and placed a centerpiece of colorful mums.

Her dad chuckled. "I'm coming, I'm coming."

Lacey stepped back, thankful for the interruption. She patted her dad's shoulder. "Looks like you're going to have a mutiny on your hands if you don't feed this bunch pretty soon."

She gave Mona a quick squeeze and a peck on the cheek then scooped up the bowl of mashed potatoes and the cranberries and put them on the dining room table.

After everyone settled at the table, Bill stood. "Before we get started, I've got something to say." He cleared his throat and reached into his pocket. "Spencer and I had a little talk earlier today," he said, nodding toward the younger man. "I felt like it was the right thing to do under the circumstances."

Lacey and the others started smiling. Mona stared at Bill, wide-eyed. He braced his hand on the table and knelt down in front of her chair.

"Mona, there's something about going through a life and death situation that makes you take an inventory of what's important. And one of the thoughts that got me through some of the toughest times was thinking about how much I love you and how thankful I am for you." He opened the lid on the small box. "Will you marry me?"

Tears spilled down Mona's face. "Oh, Bill," she cried. "Yes, yes!"

Bill slipped the simple solitaire on her finger and returned to his seat, holding her hand in his. He smiled over at Lacey. "I'm the luckiest guy in the world."

Lacey nodded and grabbed his other hand. "You sure are," she acknowledged as she blinked away the tears for the second time in fifteen minutes. "I'm so happy for you." She looked over at Mona. "For both of you."

The table erupted in applause and Mona's cheeks flamed. Flustered, she swiped again at the tears that were still coming. She sniffed. "Well, then," she said briskly, "how about we dig in?"

Throughout the meal, Lacey let the conversations flow around her. She listened as Sam updated them on the baby's progress. She chimed in when Paige and Mona talked about the needs of the shop during the holiday season. She even pretended to pay attention as Spencer and Rodney talked about what football teams they believed were shoe-ins for the playoffs. But her mind constantly strayed to Caleb, wondering if he was alone today. It wasn't until she heard his name in conversation that her attention snapped back to her surroundings.

"– Caleb said that if I do well in the spring semester, he might be able to get me an internship up in Chicago for the summer." Spencer slathered on the butter and bit into his roll. "I'm going to give it my best shot."

She took a sip from her wine glass. "I hope you get the chance to do that. You'll like Chicago," she said.

Lacey glanced around the room as a realization dawned on her. Spencer was moving on. So were her dad and Mona. Everyone was moving on, settling back into their routines and creating new ones. It bothered her more than she wanted to admit that she wasn't settled. Was it really as simple as just saying yes to Caleb? Was she ready to trust him with her heart?

She caught Mona's worried glance before the older woman rose. "Anyone up for dessert? We've got pumpkin and pecan pie."

Sam stood with an offer to help serve the dessert.

"I'm going to skip the pie," Lacey said. "I think a nice walk's what I need right now."

Paige looked over at her, something akin to sympathy in her eyes. "You want some company?"

"No, no. Stay here and enjoy." She pushed in her chair. "I won't be long. I just need some fresh air."

The weather cooperated, providing bright sunshine over a chilly breeze. She grabbed her jacket and was out the back door before she had to make any more excuses.

She'd planned to walk to the creek at the back of the property, but the barn beckoned her. Running her hand across the cracked leather of an old saddle, she breathed in the faint smell of hay and horses. The crunch of footsteps alerted her to her dad's presence before he rounded the corner. He stopped inside the door.

"Hey. Mona was a little worried. I told her I'd come check on you." He lowered himself to the bench in front of the tack room and propped his elbows on his knees. His voice carried a hint of nostalgia. "Remember when we used to work out here for hours and talk about everything under the sun?"

She could still feel the horse flesh under her hands. "Yeah."

Minutes passed before he spoke again. "There's not much work to do out here anymore, but I'm here if you want to talk."

Lacey sighed and plopped down on the bench next to him, laying her head on his shoulder. Why not? She sure wasn't making much progress on her own. Without preamble, her greatest fear came out in a whisper. "I don't want to make a mistake."

His arm came around her shoulder and squeezed. "I don't think you will."

She shrugged. "My track record's pretty lousy. How can I trust my own judgment?"

"Because our bad experiences don't define us." He nudged her to meet his gaze. "You were made to see and believe in the good in people. That's part of who you are, but sometimes our greatest strength is also our greatest weakness. Believing in others, trusting others, can open you up for heartache."

Lacey bit her lip. She knew that well.

"But it's also the gateway to genuine happiness." Her dad stood abruptly, shoving his hands into his pockets. "Caleb and I talked about that summer, and I know we both contributed to your heartache." His back was to her but Lacey heard the thickness of his words. "Neither one of us wanted to hurt you. I could see what was happening between you and Caleb, but you were so young and it happened so fast, *I* didn't trust that you knew your own heart." He turned to look at her, his eyes misty.

Lacey wrapped her arms around him. "It was a long time ago, Dad." She paused, her voice quiet. "Do you believe I know my own heart now?"

He pulled back and looked into her eyes. "Well, let me ask you this. Do you miss him?"

She'd been so busy all week, but there was no denying the truth. She looked into his eyes and nodded. "I do. Every day when we talk, I ask if we'll talk tomorrow and he says 'I can't wait'. He makes me want to believe him."

Her dad's eyes crinkled. "Okay. Then my answer is yes."

Lacey watched her dad retreat to the house before she trekked to the creek, his words echoing in her head.

She sat down on an old tree stump and felt the bite of the brisk wind as it rustled the dried leaves. For several minutes, she simply watched and listened. The bare branches creaked and the water still babbled on.

As the peace of this place settled over her, she remembered why she'd spent so much time here after her mother died. She picked up several smooth stones and tossed them into the creek.

It was decision time. Closing her eyes, she shut out the noise and got alone with her heart, accepting what it told her. Her new life was waiting for her. She stood wiping the dirt from her hands. Time to take action.

Chapter 38

"Let's have dinner." Roger caught up with Caleb as he climbed the stairs to the second floor. "You must've spent all day here yesterday, even though it was a holiday. There's so much going on, we could use a little time away from the office to get caught up."

It was true. Caleb had spent the entire week, including Thanksgiving Day, working like a mad man. Even though Brandon's departure on top of Ian's diagnosis, didn't create the wave of mass chaos he'd anticipated, there was no shortage of things that had to be done.

Caleb was tempted to refuse Roger's invitation. Not because he didn't enjoy the company, but because he had plans. The biggest reason he'd busted his ass all week had nothing to do with the business. It was so he could get out of town. He'd given Lacey a week and his flight to Kansas was booked for six tomorrow morning.

Roger must have sensed his hesitation. He stopped, forcing Caleb to either stop or run over him. He smiled smugly. "Rosalee's cooking."

Caleb's mouth watered at the words, and all thoughts of refusing fled. There wasn't a more authentic Mexican meal in all of Chicago. He grinned. "You got me. What time should I arrive?"

***

Caleb handed his jacket to the fresh-faced young girl who answered the door and sniffed appreciably. His stomach rumbled in response. No doubt about it, Rosalee knew how to cook.

Dressed in a black velour jogging suit, Rosalee hurried into the foyer and accepted Caleb's hug and the bottle of merlot he handed her. "You look tired," she said as she laid her hand on his cheek. "Come into the great room and relax with Roger. I'll have dinner ready in no time."

Caleb joined Roger at the bar and perused the half dozen salsas and dips spread out before them.

"What can I get you to drink?"

Caleb rolled his shoulders and looked at Roger's glass. "That sangria looks good."

Roger grabbed the pitcher and poured the fruity liquid. "Looks like things have settled nicely."

Caleb grabbed a chip and buried it deep in the homemade guacamole. "Yep," he said around the big bite. "I've got a call in to Zach Coughlin in Manhattan. We're going to need new blood in R&D. I think he'd be a good addition to the team."

They bantered back and forth about the business and worked their way through the mountain of appetizers. Everything they discussed was important, but Caleb couldn't shake the feeling that something else was going on.

He forced himself to be patient. His thoughts drifted to Lacey, as they had all week, and a grin tugged at the corner of his mouth.

Roger leaned forward, smiling. "So how's Lacey doing?"

Was he that transparent? He sighed. "I don't know. I'll find out tomorrow."

"You haven't spoken to her?" Rosalee entered the room and came around to glare at him. With Caleb seated on the barstool, she was able to look him right in the eye. "Caleb, I'm ashamed of you. That darling girl is in love with you. I felt it the night of the party. You are being unkind by making her wait for you."

"Rosalee," he laughed, raising his hands in mock surrender. "You've got it all backwards. I'm in love with her. And I hope you're right. But right now, she's back in Kansas trying to convince herself that she's not in love with me."

Rosalee patted his arm then smiled. "Oh, good. She'll figure it out. I'm certain." She turned to her husband with an expectant look. "Is it time yet to talk to him about the future?"

Caleb cocked his head, his shoulders tightening. Finally he'd find out what was on their minds. Before he had time to speculate, Roger blew his mind.

Roger pulled Rosalee into his side. "Yes, darling. It's time." He paused then turned serious eyes to Caleb. "We want to offer you the company."

Caleb stared at Roger, then Rosalee who nodded silently. "You want to offer me the company," he repeated, sure he'd misunderstood. Roger smiled and Caleb's brow furrowed. "Are you ill? Has something happened?"

"Nothing's wrong," Roger assured him. "I'm as healthy as can be. It's just time. The company is poised to explode, thanks in large part to you. The kids have all pursued different career paths and have let us know they don't want to run it."

Caleb chuckled, trying to get his brain around the conversation. His world had tilted yet again. He'd lost count how many times that had happened in the past month. Roger's speech flashed back to him. "So this was the change you had in mind at the party, huh?"

Roger clapped him on the shoulder. "Sure was. So, tell me Caleb. Are you interested?"

The restlessness that had dogged Caleb during his time in Europe evaporated, instantly replaced with a new energy. He couldn't wait to share the news with Lacey, but he'd wait until he could do it in person. Holding out his hand, he smiled at Roger, excitement coursing through him. "Absolutely."

Roger beamed. He took Caleb's hand and wrapped him in a bear hug while Rosalee put her arms around them both. "We'll talk details over dinner. Rosalee has a feast prepared for us. She's been waiting for this night for a long, long time."

***

Lacey gathered her bag, anxious to get to the airport. There was so much she wanted to say to Caleb, but it needed to be said face-to-face.

Stepping out into the bright mid-morning sun, Lacey did a double take. A black rental pulled in behind her old muscle car. Time warped as Lacey once again stood slack-jawed, watching Caleb exit his car.

"You're up and around awful early, aren't you?"

He sounded so calm, like his being here was perfectly normal. She, on the other hand, was certain he could hear the ferocious pounding of her heart. She had so much to say, but the words weren't quite in order yet. "I, uh, had somewhere important to be."

Caleb strode toward her, not stopping until their chests were almost touching. With bridled energy, he tucked his sunglasses into his coat pocket and leveled his blue gaze at her, stealing her breath with his words. "I've given you a week."

If there had been any lingering uncertainty in Lacey's mind, it faded away as she glimpsed the vulnerability lurking behind the boldness in his eyes. *Oh, how she loved this man.*

One corner of her mouth rose. "Technically, it's only been four days," she teased. Reaching into her bag, she pulled out her boarding pass and handed it to him. "But I've fallen in love with you twice in four months, so getting it all figured out in four days doesn't seem all that unreasonable. I love you, Caleb."

Caleb's face split into a grin as he glanced at the page then tossed it aside and pulled Lacey into his arms. Holding tight, his lips found hers. "I love you, Babe," he whispered. He stepped back and for the second time in a week, he produced a jewelry box. But this time, he didn't wait for her to open it. He took out the princess-cut diamond and slid it onto her finger. "Marry me, Lacey. Let me spend the rest of my life loving you."

Lacey tumbled back into his arms, joy bursting through her as she repeated the words he'd said to her every night on the phone. "I can't wait."

Epilogue

Lacey held Caleb's hand as the joyful sound of a group of carolers headed off into the night. "Do you think they'll mind that I came with you?"

"They're going to love you," Caleb assured her as he rang the bell. He squeezed her into his side and planted a quick kiss on her lips.

Music and revelry spilled out onto the porch as the beautiful girl from Caleb's picture threw open the door. She took in the scene and her eyes lit with excitement "Caleb's here," she yelled back into the room. "And he brought a friend!"

Caleb rolled his eyes and Lacey laughed out loud. Before she knew it, Rachel pulled them into the middle of the living room as Caleb's family gathered around waiting for an introduction. Finally, the chaos receded.

Caleb looked at Lacey, then at each of his siblings. "This is Lacey Jordan. And you're right, Rachel," he nodded. "She is my friend. She'll also soon be my wife."

After a few seconds of stunned silence, the room broke into a chorus of congratulations and hugs.

Lacey spent the evening fascinated, learning even more about her future husband from the family who loved him. They took turns regaling her with stories and memories of their oldest brother. She came to realize that in many ways, he was their rock. Just like he'd been hers.

Her eyes misted as she closed a photo album Sarah had shared with her. She joined Caleb as he returned from the kitchen with his younger brothers. He looked into her eyes. "You okay?" he asked.

She nodded and wrapped her arms around him. "More than okay."

Caleb pulled her over to the mistletoe hanging in the dining room archway then kissed her soundly. She got her breath back in time to see Rachel sauntering toward them.

"So you made a liar out of me after all, huh?" She punched her brother in the arm, her quick grin so much like his.

"Did I? How's that?"

She leaned over to Lacey. "I asked him if he'd be bringing anyone home with him. He, of course, said no. So I, as always, had to be the bearer of the bad news to the rest of the family."

Caleb cocked a brow. "You know, I'm not the only one who never brings anyone to meet the family."

Rachel rolled her eyes. "Touché. But seriously, I'm really glad you changed your mind."

Caleb pulled Lacey close, his grin wide. "Yeah. Me, too."

THE END

Acknowledgements

Thank you to my critique partners, Darlene Deluca and Janice Richards who know just exactly what my stories are missing. Their varied and complementary talents have helped me immeasurably.

Thank you to my beta readers, Becky, Susan, Chris, Genita, Elyse, and Jill. You all gave me belief and hope that this story that I believed in might actually have merit and value in the real world. Your encouragement means more to me than I could ever express in words.

Thank you to my brother-in-law, Mike, and my friend, Tom Smith, for their knowledge and expertise in the field of law enforcement. Thank you also to Ashley Allen, for teaching me so much about the adoption process and Don Puchalla for the crash course in EMS training.

Thank you to my husband and kids. I love that you are not only watching me pursue my dreams, you are right there with me, challenging me to reach even higher. God has blessed me in more ways than I can possibly count, but in no way greater than the family He's given me. I truly am the luckiest human being I know.

Last, but certainly not least, thank you to my readers. I write because I absolutely love it. I said from the beginning of this journey that I would write even if no one ever read my stories. And while that is still true, I am genuinely humbled and honored when someone enjoys my work. It is my sincere hope that I've brought you a few chuckles, a few sighs, and a smile or two along the way.

Turn the page for a sneak peek of

UNSPOKEN BONDS

Coming in 2013

Chapter 1

Caller ID was a blessing and a curse. Rachel Mansfield rubbed the burn from her eyes and plucked her cell phone off the table.

She shouldn't have fallen asleep in the first place. There were still a few things to get ready for tomorrow, and she wanted everything to be perfect for her brother's first weekend pass from the Marines.

But she couldn't, in good conscience, ignore the call from the hospital's number. Sighing, she hit the talk button. "This is Rachel."

"Hey, Rachel. Corinne Ross, Child Protective Services. Sorry to call so late. Do you have a moment?"

Rachel's tired mind flashed to a time when a call from CPS might've involved her younger brother. But that time had long since passed. She released a breath and checked her watch. Must be important. "Sure. How can I help you?"

"We have a situation that requires your expertise."

Rachel sat up straighter, rolling her neck in a vain attempt to recover from her impromptu nap in the chair. "Emergency room?"

"Yes, there's a little girl here who's hearing impaired."

"I'm assuming the parents are deaf, too?" Rachel stood and stretched.

"Ah, well. That's the thing. We don't know. She's alone. We're going off the note pinned to her shirt."

Pressing the phone closer to her ear, Rachel was certain she'd misunderstood. "Excuse me? Did you say a note pinned to her?"

The disgust in Corinne's voice was clear. "Yes. It says, 'My name is Lily. I am deaf. Please take care of me.' That's all we've got to go on."

Incredulous, Rachel shook her head. She'd worked several cases over the years with Protective Services, but this was a first. "Any idea on age? Is she hurt? What else do you know?" Jogging to her bedroom, Rachel pulled a clean pair of jeans off the hanger and shimmied into them, the phone wedged on her shoulder.

"If I had to guess, I'd say she's probably four or five. I got here just a few minutes ago. From what I understand, the emergency room was hot tonight. There was a four-car accident out on Lake Road, total train wreck, so it was all hands on deck. It wasn't until everything calmed back down that a janitor straightening the waiting room found her asleep in a chair."

"She's not a patient, then?"

"Not yet, but they want to examine her to be sure. Problem is, she's agitated and no one can calm her down. Can you come? Now?"

"I'm on my way." Within ten minutes, Rachel whipped into the parking lot of the Olathe Medical Center and hurried through the sliding double doors, her eyes landing on Corinne. "Where is she?"

Corinne waved her toward the examination rooms. Anxious moans reached Rachel's ears before she was halfway down the hall. Breaking into a run, she followed the sound and pulled back the curtain.

A waif of a girl with a pile of wayward strawberry-blond curls cowered in the corner of the bed, her frightened eyes darting around the room. Squeezing between two male nurses, Rachel stepped to the bed, her hands extended and open, speaking aloud as she signed. "Hi there, sweetheart. My name is Rachel. You don't need to be afraid. We just want to help you."

Beautiful green eyes followed her movements then scanned Rachel's face, but the little girl didn't respond. Rachel tried again, finger-spelling her name. "Lily?"

If anything, the girl shrunk farther back against the bed, a low guttural sound escaping from her lips. Rachel glanced around, her heart aching for the girl. There were six other adults in the room, all focused on Lily. Not exactly calming. "Hey guys, give me a few minutes here. Corinne, Doctor, stay if you would, please. Everybody else, we'll call if we need you."

Rachel shuffled them out and pulled the doctor and Corinne toward the exit. "Hang out over here for a minute. I think she's overwhelmed." Rachel walked back over to the bed, but Lily had dropped from the mattress and was wedged behind it, eyes closed, her small body rocking to a private rhythm. Careful not to touch her, Rachel sat down on the floor.

Minutes later, the rocking stopped and Lily opened her eyes. Rachel smiled and slowly lifted her hand, smoothing Lily's curls, pleased when she didn't pull away.

Taking a chance, Rachel rose from the floor and held out her hand, waiting to see what Lily would do. She smiled again, silently encouraging. Patience was something Rachel had gotten pretty good at and she could wait all night if she had to. The decision had to be Lily's.

She was rewarded as Lily slowly emerged from her hiding place and slipped her small hand into Rachel's. Her big eyes were still wary as she scanned the room, but Lily wasn't in panic mode anymore. Rachel shot a quick smile to Corinne.

Now, to figure out how to communicate and determine what Lily knew. Obviously, her grasp on American Sign Language was very limited. That was okay, though. Rachel welcomed the surge of energy that came with the challenge.

She brought her fingers to her mouth. "Are you hungry?" Lily's eyes followed her hand, and she hesitantly repeated the movement and nodded. "She's hungry. Can you get me something?" Rachel signed the words she spoke to Corinne, staying connected to Lily's gaze. The distrust she saw broke her heart. How many people had let this little girl down already in her young life?

She tried a few more signs as she waited for Corinne to return, but didn't have any luck. Doctor Gibson tapped her shoulder. "We'd like to examine her, make sure she's okay."

Rachel nodded, "I think that's a good idea." She patted the bed and tilted her head toward it. Lily shook her head. She must've known the direction of Rachel's discussion with the doctor because the fear was back in her eyes. Not that it had ever left, but it was front and center now.

Lily's anxiety had to come back down before it got out of control again. Climbing onto the mattress, Rachel motioned toward Lily, holding out her arms and after several long seconds, Lily joined her. Sheltering Lily in a gentle embrace, Rachel nodded to the doctor who made quick work of his initial exam. Fingers clenched around Rachel's wrists, Lily squeezed herself tight against Rachel, crying out when the nurse drew a vial of blood.

Rachel soothed the little girl and by the time the doctor returned with the results, Lily had finished a package of animal crackers and drained a juice box.

"She's a bit undernourished but, overall, in pretty good shape. Whoever brought her in seems to have done a fair job taking care of her. I can't see a reason to admit her as a patient."

Lily's weight sagged against Rachel's side. Poor little girl had run out of steam. "What do we do now?"

Corinne snapped her phone closed. "Hopefully we'll get a hit on her tomorrow through the endangered child registry, but for now we have someone lined up. We can take her as soon as she's released."

Rachel's heart tripped as she looked at the crust and dirt smudges on Lily's face. She'd met her only hours earlier, but something about Lily's beguiling eyes and tarnished innocence pulled at her. Shaking her head, she ignored the feeling. Protective Services was simply doing its job.

Shifting, she roused Lily awake. There was no slow, easy awakening though. In a heartbeat, the little girl was wide-eyed and fearful. Rachel touched her arm, drawing her attention. Questions bombarded Rachel again. What on earth had Lily been through? And how had she survived?

Corinne moved forward and Rachel scooted off the bed, but Lily scooted right along with her, scrambling behind her back and forcing Rachel to act as a barrier between them. Lily's fingers dug into Rachel's hip. With gentle hands, Rachel pried herself loose and squatted down next to Lily.

The little girl's eyes filled with tears as cries broke from her throat. An answering sting of tears pricked Rachel's eyes. The plans for reunion weekend with her siblings tumbled through her mind, but there was always room for one more. And they would love Lily.

4

"Corinne, Lily is obviously traumatized. I have background clearance through the hospital to work with children. Under the circumstances, is there any reason she couldn't stay with me until her family is located?"

Corinne frowned. "You sure you want that responsibility?" At Rachel's nod, she pulled out her phone. "Let me make a call." She left the room, and Rachel wiped Lily's nose then rocked her in silence as they waited. Lily's ramrod posture stiffened further when the agent returned. "Good news. My supervisor's giving us some latitude." Smiling, she laid out paperwork on the counter. "They've given us permission to allow Lily to go with you. Record your contact information here, then I'll need your signature in a couple of places."

Rachel felt Lily's eyes on her and simply signed "yes" and nodded. Lily's shy answering smile was all the validation Rachel needed that she'd made the right decision. After endorsing the documents, Rachel jotted down her home and cell phone numbers, and her email address for good measure. She touched Corinne's hand and was met with another smiling face. "Thank you for making this happen."

"My pleasure. Thank *you*. I'm glad you were on call tonight."

The first pink fingers of sunrise tinged the eastern sky as Rachel hoisted Lily from the back seat and climbed the stairs. Her third floor apartment had been an intentional choice to augment her regular cardio workouts, but right now, her back wasn't buying it. Of course, she wasn't used to hauling forty-three pounds of sleeping girl, either, but Lily had been through enough for one night and Rachel didn't have the heart to wake her again.

She dropped her purse in the entry hall then gently laid Lily's sleeping form on the sofa. Exhaustion might've triggered the extra tug at her heart, but Rachel couldn't deny that it felt good to be needed again. As she tucked a throw around the slender girl and wondered again about her circumstances, the momma-bear instincts she'd honed over the years slipped back into place like well-worn gloves.

No matter what else happened, she'd do everything in her power to make sure Lily was never abandoned again.

Stay in touch for new stories,
release dates, and more
from Michelle Grey

https://www.facebook.com/michellegreyauthor

https://twitter.com/MichelleGrey13

Sign up for email updates at
www.threewritersofromance.com

CPSIA information can be obtained
at www.ICGtesting.com
Printed in the USA
LVHW080712020519
616347LV00037B/825/P

9 781480 189263